They had been household na[...] set out to the stars—specifically, to explore exoplanets discovered during the early 21st century probes launched into the Alpha Centauri and Proxima Centauri systems. Six heroes who stepped on board humanity's first starship, purely on faith. The world had waved them goodbye with tears of pride and had held its collective breath as the rendezvous rocket took what the media had branded the Six to the Stars up into the shipyard in Earth orbit where their craft waited for them—the Parada, new-built, shining with promise, with dreams, with hope.

Captain Hanford Millgar, First Officer Jerry Hillerman, Navigator Rob Hillerman, Engineer Bogdan Dimitrov, Ship's Medic Alaya McGinty, Science Officer and Astronomer Lily Mae Washington.

Their faces were on every screen, in every home. Children were taken out of school to watch the launch of the rendezvous rocket, and then again when the cameras in orbit showed the Parada slowly easing out of dock, hanging there as though posing for her close-up against the backdrop of space glittering with stars, and then turning away from the home planet, nose pointed into the dark. The people of Earth watched her begin moving away, getting smaller and smaller until she vanished from sight.

For a little while, the media kept up with the ship, passing on such telemetry data as was received back. There were even occasional messages from the Six to the Stars sent while the ship still tiptoed her way through the Solar System, passing Mars, sending images of Saturn that became as iconic as that first photograph of Earth hanging in the black skies of the Moon had been back in the days of the Moon shots, because those were literally the first images of a distant planet which had been taken by living human hands while living human eyes rested on it. But then the star drive kicked in, news from the ship became scarcer, and then other things took over the headlines, as other things do. The next time the Parada returned to the news was when word came that contact with the ship was completely lost.

And then a hundred more years went by.

A Mystique Press Production - Mystique Press is an imprint of Crossroad Press.

Copyright © 2020 by Alma Alexander
ISBN 978-1-951510-39-8
For information address Crossroad Press at 141 Brayden Dr., Hertford, NC 27944
www.crossroadpress.com

First edition

THE SECOND STAR

Alma Alexander

To Mike,
with thanks for so many things.

"Once I believed that space could have no power over faith, just as I believed that the Heavens declared the glory of God's handiwork. Now I have seen that handiwork, and my faith is sorely troubled."

– Arthur C. Clarke, "The Star"

1.

The grim-faced man at the head of the conference table wore a uniform unfamiliar to Stella Froud; somehow that simple fact made him strangely threatening. As if to underline that impression, he swept an intense gaze around the table, catching and holding the eyes of each of the six people seated there for one long, powerful moment.

"This meeting is classified," he said. "You have all already signed documents which state that you will not speak of anything you see or hear in this room to anyone who is not presently in it. The penalties for failing to do so are severe and they will be enforced. Is that absolutely clear to everybody?"

There were wordless nods. The uniformed man frowned.

"I need verbal agreement. Do you understand?"

He went around the table again. Everyone murmured their assent. They had been interested, before. Now some of them were alarmed. Stella, who had trained to observe the tiniest nuance of human reaction, could feel that wariness building behind the carefully schooled expressions of the five people sitting around the table with her. There were no grimaces or scowls—but their eyes had changed. Dr. Vivien Collins's pupils had dilated in shock. She was the only pure academic in the room and probably not used to this kind of military atmosphere.

"I am General Aristide Niarchos," the man in uniform said. "You are all here because our history has just collided with our future, and we hope that you—you in this room—will be able to find a path forward for us. Dr. Collins, would you please start us off with what is known about the *Parada*?"

Vivien Collins took a deep breath. Stella could see her hands clutching at the table in front of her in a white-knuckled grip.

"There are lots of things I could tell you about that ship," she said. "We have the specs right there—" She flicked a wrist at the screen wall, and it displayed a dense schematic of the guts of a starship, completely meaningless to most of the rest of the people in that room. A further wrist flick started the screen shifting into close-ups of individual parts of the schematic, or scrolling tables full of incomprehensible numbers. Vivien glanced up at the screen with an almost distracted air, and then back at the rest of the group, and with a third flick of the wrist produced an image of a stocky ship floating against space in the orbital shipyard and froze the screen there. "But that's the *Parada*," she said simply.

"We've all seen pictures," muttered John Lumumba, the engineer. "I'd know that ship..."

Another woman at the table, sitting on the far end, as far from the screen wall as was possible in that room, sat forward, peering at the screen with a squint.

"Wait," she said, hesitating, "that's not right. The Gamma Wing of the shipyard wasn't even built when the *Parada* was made. Is that a composite?"

Vivien swallowed. "No, you're right. It wasn't. Not when the original *Parada* was in the shipyard. But that... is the *Parada*. Up there. Right now."

The reaction ran down the table like a shiver.

"It's been almost a century since the last time anyone heard from that ship!" Alicia Hernandez, the woman who had observed the incongruous Gamma Wing, said. "It's been nearly two hundred years since it was launched! What do you mean, that's the *Parada*? The ship? The actual ship? The real ship? How...?"

"Where did you find it?" John Lumumba interjected.

There was a small awkward pause and then the medic in the room, Dr. Ichiro Amari, cleared his throat. "The crew?" he asked softly.

He was most likely thinking about their physical wellbeing, the state they might have been in when they were found—or their extinction.

But Stella Froud suddenly knew why she was here. It had been something she had been puzzling over ever since she had got the summons and met the rest of the people in this room—all of them might have something to do with the physical mystery of the ghost ship that was the *Parada*, drifting home from the deep past. But only she, Stella Froud, pioneering Psychometric Counselor, dealt in the mind.

The crew was alive. Somehow, impossibly, the crew was still alive.

And apparently insane enough to require Stella's ministrations.

Individual pieces of the *Parada*'s story were laid out in the boardroom as the day unraveled into evening. Stella understood very little of the math—which *was* presented in detail and which at least two of the people in that room knew enough about to literally gasp as the implications were revealed to them by the numbers—but the number that stopped her in her tracks and sent her deep down the rabbit hole of its potential implications was staggering. She broke the rules and sat up and demanded that the General repeat the last thing he had just said.

"In the two hundred years that the *Parada* has been out there, its crew has aged by less than three," General Niarchos said. "Yes, you heard that right. Its drive was calibrated to run at 90 percent of light speed. For reasons unknown to us, it suddenly and somehow went much faster. It ran at closer to 99.99 percent. The tau factor increases by ten in the speed it hit, and the time dilation effects increase exponentially."

"I don't understand that," Stella said impatiently. "It's technobabble to me. Tell me in real terms."

"In real terms, at the specifications which the *Parada* was built for, in the time frame we are talking about, the crew would have aged just over twenty eight years for the two centuries that have passed for us back here. Which in itself feels hard enough to believe. But because their drive impossibly kicked into a higher gear, without their sanction or their knowledge, when we found them the crew had aged by less than three years. 2.8 years exactly, to be precise."

"So have we found the fountain of youth?" asked John Lumumba with heavy-handed levity.

Stella favored him with a quick scowl, and then turned back to the General. "I can see why they might think I could be of use here," she said. "That kind of Grand Canyon can be difficult to grasp or to adjust to. Some psychometric issues might well have arisen. But why do I get the feeling that there's more to this than just a handful of disoriented star-farers trying to come to terms with their two lost centuries?"

"Because there *is* more to it than that," the General said. "The *Parada* had a crew of six. If we are to believe the evidence we have before us, well, six people went out. More than seventy returned."

Stella sat up. "What?"

"Extreme stress seems to have fractured..."

She finally got it, in a rush. "They have multiple personalities?" She paused. "All of them?"

The General gave a small, almost unwilling nod. "Some more than others. And then it gets complicated. Rob and Jerry Hillerman are twins. They *share* a couple of the personalities."

"That's... not possible," Stella said, frowning.

Alicia Hernandez snorted inelegantly. "You're buying that they aged less than three years in two centuries but you don't accept that weird shit happened to their minds in the process?"

"I have some idea of what the human mind can do when it's broken," Stella said. "But..."

"And then you put that human mind into a thin metal shell and hurl it at the stars," Alicia said, interrupting. "I think you can throw out the usual equations. I think we're in uncharted territory. Here there be dragons. And some of them may be itching to eat us."

"How do they... the multiple personalities... manifest?" Stella persisted.

The General scowled again, and spoke in a low voice into the communicator on his wrist. Moments later, two people in uniform stepped smartly into the room and stood waiting just inside the door. The General tossed his head in their direction.

"Lieutenant Marsh and Lieutenant Colonel—and Doctor—Peck," he said to Stella. "I think you'd better go with them, I don't think you're even going to hear anything else that's said in this room after this, and, well, given your own specialty, you probably have no need to."

Ichiro Amari rose and gave a small bow in the General's direction. "With your leave, this is more my area of expertise, as well," he said. "I assume I am here to provide some sort of a medical opinion of the crew members. I may as well begin now."

"And I'd better go with her, too" said another voice, one which had not spoken before, and a man dressed in black, whose presence had been so unobtrusive that some of the people in the room only just realized that he had been there all the time, stood up. He was wearing a priest's cassock, and his identity was immediately obvious. "Doctor Froud, I am Father Philip Carter. And I think that the reason I am here is the same as the reason you are. The engineers have the problem of the ship's malfunction. You and I and Doctor Amari, we are here to take care of the people."

The general nodded and the two military people led the way out of the conference room. Before the door had fully closed behind Philip Carter, Stella had already slipped into place beside the clean-shaven, dark-haired man who had been identified as Dr. Peck.

"Sir—Doctor—what do I call you?" she said, with a tinge of exasperation. Military hobbles in communication were never her thing.

"Outside of the General's presence, Martin will do," Martin Peck said. "My fellow officer is Lydia Marsh. And what we can tell you is very little, really, and most of that is difficult to believe."

"That's probably why I am here," Stella said grimly. "You'd be surprised at what I would believe."

"What do you know about them?" Martin asked.

"What everyone does. They're historical figures, they've been extensively written about—I've read that stuff. In the data banks. Online. If you're asking if I was fan enough to read the biographies and the books and all the accumulated piles of stuff which it is increasingly tough to figure out whether it's actually true or not, no, I haven't. I know their names. I could probably tell you one or two things about them. But anything more than that..." Stella shrugged. "Frankly, I'm still trying to wrap my mind around the simple fact that I'm going to be face to face with them in a moment. I haven't really gone beyond that yet."

"You'll know more about them than you ever wanted," Martin said. "We have entire data banks on them. On what they were. On... on what they have become. Before you get to face them I suspect you'll want to sit down and do some reading."

Ichiro stepped up to Martin's other flank and fell into step. "Excuse me," he said, "but is there information in those folders on their actual physical wellbeing? I mean, were they examined..."

"Doctor," Martin said, "they were put through the wringer when we got them back. First they were kept under wraps up in the *Parada*, you know, just in case they came back carrying some extraterrestrial plague. For at least ten days. They passed their physicals just fine. In fact, they were healthier than we had any right to expect them to be. They read like they'd just stepped off the farm, having eaten healthy food straight from the good earth rather than all that synthetic junk they had to live on while they were out there."

"But there were indications of a problem, up at the ship. We saw the first manifestations of the splintering up there, as the first medical tests were done. But we chalked it up to the situation—given what they had lived through, they were certainly permitted to be a little stir crazy. So we brought them down here, to see if being back on the actual dirtball of the home world would help," Lydia Marsh chimed in from behind. "We said nothing to the public, not yet, but their numbers were so good—at least their physical numbers—that we had every intention of releasing them out into the world, straight after their three weeks' mandatory quarantine period had ended, and we thought we could deal with their... quirks... as necessary. We had no idea that anything was actually *really* wrong. And then... they began to manifest... or at the very least they began to let us see that there were more of them than we thought..." She grimaced.

"You'd better get that from the transcripts," Martin said, interrupting. "We don't want to influence your own reading of the matter."

"But do I at least get to see them?" Stella persisted. "I mean, before I get taken off to the library to do my homework?"

"Sure," Martin said. "We have surveillance at all times in their habitat. CCTV, and more sophisticated 3D options if necessary. Them, and the other lot."

"Habitat?" Stella echoed, frowning. It had a distressing echo of a zoo.

"The other lot?" Ichiro asked, rousing.

Martin glanced at him. "The *Juno* crew. The ones who found them, who brought them back. After *this* lot went nuts, we thought we'd better hang onto the other three for a little while, just in case."

"You have *two* ships' crews in lockup?" Philip Carter said incredulously. "What have you told their families?"

"Well, the good news is that the *Parada* crew don't have any to speak of," Martin said. "They themselves had no children—they all left before permanent relationships on Earth anchored them with progeny. Their parents and grandparents and great grandparents have come and gone. The Hillerman twins did us the favor of taking each other's only sibling along for the ride—so that line ends right there. Two of the others had left siblings behind, and those have gone on to have descendants—but I don't think they're losing any sleep over the fate of their great great great uncles and aunts, not this long after they'd been presumed dead and gone."

"What about the other crew?" Philip asked.

"As for the *Juno* crew," Martin went on smoothly, "one of the guys had a wife, and a small daughter. Well, *he* basically more or less released that woman from the relationship when he boarded the craft. The other two were unmarried, with a couple of living parents in the mix. We just haven't told those people their kinsmen have returned yet, and won't until we're certain that we can."

"That's cold," Philip murmured.

"Wait, have the second ship's crew also... splintered?" Stella interrupted.

"Not as yet," Martin said. "They're under observation." He grimaced, giving her a side-eyed look. "You'll have folders on them, too."

"I will want to examine them," Ichiro said, softly but insistently.

"Of course," Martin said. "That, after all, is why you are here. Our doctors have called in a second opinion."

Stella had thought she knew exactly where the meeting had been held—in the headquarters of World Government, the glass-and steel tower overlooking the Strait of Bosphorus, wider these days, from the sea rise, than it had been in the day when it had received that name, on the European side of the channel. But after they descended by a secure elevator down to a subterranean level, and passed beyond a set of solid doors on the strength of several levels of sophisticated facial recognition ID, Stella realized that she was in no place that she had ever known existed. Corridors were chopped into short passages each divided from the next by sealed security gates requiring biometric clearance before they would provide grudging admittance; by the time they had passed three of those, and zigged and zagged their way in the bowels of this secret edifice, Stella was hopelessly lost.

Martin caught her glancing backward at one of the gates closing inexorably behind the small group, and managed a small smile.

"You have clearance," he said. "It isn't a prison. You'll have to lodge a scan and a set of prints but you have access, both ways. I mean, within reason."

"It isn't a prison for *me*," Stella murmured.

"Nor for them. God knows we don't want to lock them away like animals in a menagerie. That's why you're here, Doctor. To try and free them."

"I have a feeling none of us are all that free to come and go either," Philip remarked. "After all yon General upstairs has impressed upon us all that we are not to speak of any of this to anybody anywhere ever at all—so where would we be allowed to go, exactly...?"

"Let us first see what there is to see, without jumping to any conclusions," Ichiro said, lifting his hands in a gesture of peacemaking. "Just where *do* you have these poor people buried, though?"

"Right here," Martin said, taking an abrupt turn and opening yet another door with a thumb pressed into a scan reader. "This would be your first stop. This is the Surveillance Room."

He walked into the room, followed by Stella, Philip and Ichiro in single file, with Lydia bringing up the rear. Three of the four walls of the room were covered with multiple screens showing various rooms and common areas. The three team members instinctively sought the time travelers, the crew which had so improbably returned from the deep past, but Martin steered them first towards the left-hand wall. The operator sitting at a computer workstation before the screen wall obligingly moved aside as the group approached.

"The simplest first," Martin said. "These are the *Juno* people. The man in the first set of screens, top row, that's the captain—Hugh de Mornay. Next row down, First Officer Tyrone Kidman. Third row, Second Officer and Ship's Medical Officer Joseph White Elk. As you can see, they're perfectly nice normal people."

"For now," Lydia muttered.

Stella shot her a look but forbore to comment. She and Ichiro both leaned forward for a closer look, scanning the screens. Each row had three separate screens covering three separate areas—a sleeping cubicle, with a private workstation, and an angle of the shared central common atrium into which individual private quarters gave out, with the relevant camera in each row covering as much of the common area as possible in its range while including the doorway into each man's private quarters. There were six of those leading off the common area, but only three were occupied here; currently, Tyrone Kidman appeared to be asleep on his bunk. Hugh de Mornay and Joseph White Elk sat opposite one another in the common atrium looking equally bored while sitting hunched over a game of backgammon, a striking contrast of a Viking-blond muscular man and a slight, almost effeminate, bronze-skinned Native American with a long black braid lying on his narrow back.

"You spy on them in their private quarters?" Stella said, taken aback, staring at Tyrone's sleeping form. "Isn't that... I don't know... in violation of something? It feels intrusive—they aren't lab rats..."

"When there may be a danger of them doing harm to themselves, privacy isn't an option," Lydia Marsh said.

Stella whipped her head around, her eyes wide. "Somebody tried to commit *suicide*? Which one?"

"Not those three," Martin said. "However, it's only Joe—that's Joe White Elk—who doesn't seem to care where he is. The other *Juno* two are getting antsy. They haven't been here all that long, yet, and they've been assured they aren't prisoners—but they're well past believing that."

"Didn't you tell them *why* you're holding them?" Stella said, more astonished by the minute.

"Well... in the beginning they accepted the quarantine," Martin said. "Then we had our hands full with the other lot. And after a little while going back to the *Juno* crew and telling them that they're under observation to find out if they're going to go nuts or not... seemed like it would push them into going nuts, if you see what I mean."

Stella straightened, and looked Martin straight in the eye. "Well, for one, we're going to start telling everyone the truth," she snapped. "I can understand that you don't want word of this spreading prematurely into the general populace but for Heaven's sake these people are directly involved. I can't be lying to people I am trying to help. If these need any help. They are apparently behaving exactly as any normal human beings should. Just how long have you had them in there?"

"Just over two weeks, now," Martin said. "We thought we could stretch the quarantine story for at least a month."

"That ends," Stella said sharply.

"I'd read their files first," Lydia said, all military in the moment. "I mean, we have no idea when, exactly, the others... went crazy... or how long that took. We just know when *we* noticed it. What if we let these three go and they implode out there where anyone can see it? They're going to be public figures when they emerge—the world knows their names—they can't just go into quiet anonymity. If they go crazy they do that in the full glare of the world media. That isn't going to be very good for any..."

"Would you please stop saying 'crazy'?" Stella said. "We aren't in the Middle Ages, burning people for being witches if they say they hear voices. DPD has been known for quite a long time now, and..."

"DPD?" Philip asked, frowning.

"Dissociative Personality Disorder," Stella said. "I could give you guys folders to read on *that*, if you are interested. Its history and its symptoms and its cures, or lack thereof. Still, it isn't 'crazy'. Not in the way you are implying."

"Yeah?" Lydia said, goaded out of her stiff military persona just for a moment, and responding with some heat. "So this lot look perfectly normal, and they have been, so far. Now take a look at some of the other screens."

They stepped over to the middle wall, with a similar arrangement of screens in three rows. It was Ichiro who identified the people covered by each row.

"That's Rob and Jerry Hillerman," he said softly, "and if I am not mistaken, Captain Han Millgar."

"The entities who used to answer to those names, anyway," Martin said. He peered into the screens. "Actually, the twins are themselves right now, I think. Han...what is he *doing*? Is he Raff again?"

"Raff?" Stella said, leaning in to pay closer attention to Captain Han Millgar's screen row. In the last of the three screens, in the common area, the captain was engaged in building an elaborate construction of emery sticks and playing cards. His hands moved very delicately, as though he was operating a completely different body than the one she could see on the screen; Stella found herself fascinated by his movements which, even though she had never seen the "real" Captain Millgar, she instinctively knew had never belonged to that man as he used to be.

"Again, it's all in the files," Martin said. "That's why I wanted you to read those first. Raff is one of Captain Millgar's splinter personalities—one of ten that we know of right now, but we don't know if these people are through splitting off yet or if it's an ongoing process. They didn't all manifest to us at once, after all; we picked up individual fragments one at a time, really. That one—Raff—maintains he's thirteen, and has never let a thought stand between him and something he wants to do. He fancies himself as something of a budding scientist and we had to take an inventory of anything in that area which he could use to 'do experiments' with. We can barely allow him toothpaste."

The house of cards trembled at a careless movement, and as they watched the whole thing collapsed in a heap. Captain Millgar's face twisted, and Stella could clearly see a change in his features, in his eyes, in the angle at which his wrists suddenly held his hands, as he looked up for a moment and gave the camera a direct and venomous stare.

Martin noticed her noticing, and nodded. "Yup. That's Cap. Han's 'evil twin'."

"He has a twin too?" Ichiro inquired softly.

"No. Not a physical one, not like the Hillermans. Cap... is the 'bad' part of himself."

"Martin called the Cap personality Han's Devil's advocate," Lydia said.

Martin shrugged. "Or perhaps his Devil. I am not sure. It's hard to be sure of anything when it comes to these people."

"You said the twins were 'being themselves'—what did you mean?" Stella asked, transferring her attention to the other two screen rows and the two apparently identical men they showed, both, at this moment, reading quietly inside their own quarters, sitting on their beds in cross-legged positions that mirrored one another exactly.

"They like to read," Martin said. "They always did, according to their profiles. That said, though, they are going through books at an astonishing rate. We are supplying them with real physical books, which they seem to prefer, as well as eBooks on their digital readers—and I can tell you, both have had their problems—paper books are bulky and sometimes unavailable, and as for the digital ones, it's been *two hundred* years since they've last played around with that kind of thing. The formats have changed, and so has the hardware—we supplied the current tech but they prefer the stuff they're familiar with... if we can provide compatible material for it. They're plowing through what we do give them at an uncanny speed. Anything—they'll read a work of fiction, and it doesn't matter if it's recent or something from back in their time, and something on all the history they missed out on in the past two centuries, and a textbook on the latest developments in quantum physics, and they won't bat an eyelid about any of it. They're sucking it all in, as though they're trying to catch up with two hundred years of the world in a handful of weeks. And what's more, the way they retain what they read is weird—different personalities seem to remember different books. It can be most disconcerting."

"And you've been dealing with this... yourself?"

"Myself and a small medical team," Martin said. "Including a psychiatrist. But he's been a little out of his depth."

"And all sworn to secrecy. Nobody able to ask questions of anyone outside this building. No expert help?"

"Well, it all looked manageable, initially, until it blew up in our faces," Martin said defensively. "And anyway, we called in the cavalry. That's why *you're* here."

Stella's teeth clicked together. "And the rest of them?"

The third and final wall showed three more of the *Parada* crew, and again it was Ichiro who named them.

"Alaya McGinty... Lily Mae Washington... Bogdan Dimitrov," he said.

"Correct, but not accurate," Martin said, peering at the screens. He pointed to the rows in turn. "Hard to tell from out here, precisely, but I think Alaya might currently be Joan—that's the personality, with her, that gravitates towards research, and look at her, concentrating over that reader—there's a set to those shoulders that we've learned isn't strictly Alaya's—and Lily Mae, from the way she's slitting her eyes, might be channeling Diana, which is why Boz is looking very much like he's being Boris, and if I'm right we're probably going to have to send an orderly in there to stop them from getting physical with each other."

Philip was getting lost in the names. "Boz?" he asked plaintively. "And Boris is...?"

"Boz is what Bogdan is known as, by the rest of the crew. It's a sort of shorthand nickname. He answers to that, still. And Boris—that's one of the fragments. He's the backstreet thuglet, and apparently always spoiling for a fight," Martin said. "Unfortunately, when Lily Mae goes full 'street', which is what Diana is, that brings out Boris real fast. And it got bloody at least once."

"But why don't you separate them?" Ichiro asked, appalled.

"Because, Doctor, when they *aren't* being Boris and Diana they are actually rather attached to each other. We tried separating them. One of Boz's personalities threatened suicide."

"Personalities? Or the individual...?"

"Good question—but either way, the act would harm the physical body they share, so it's moot. We didn't want to have these people survive a trip out to the stars and then end up drinking bleach back here on Earth."

"It wouldn't be a good look for you, no," Philip murmured, his eyes downcast.

Martin drew his eyebrows together into a frown, but Stella wasn't even paying attention to the last exchange. She seemed unable to tear her eyes from the screens where, indeed, a pair of orderlies had just stepped inside and separated the crew members who used to go by the name of Bogdan Dimitrov and Lily Mae Washington, herding each into their own private area to cool off by themselves. Lily Mae's personality... Diana?... wasn't taking it quietly. Stella saw the orderly grimace as he was kicked in the shin. A third orderly had slipped into the common area, keeping an eye on Han, who was still wearing the expression of Cap the Evil Twin but who was watching the separation of the two combatants without attempting to interfere.

"I think you're right," Stella said faintly. "I think I need to sit down and swot up on this before I wade in there with hob nailed boots."

"This way," Martin said. "We have a library."

"When can I interview the crews—both the crews?" Stella asked as they stepped back into the corridor and Martin led the way to the library. "I mean, once I've had a chance to catch up with everything you've found out so far..."

"I, too, would like that opportunity," Philip said quietly

"When you come to a point where you have decided how you

want to set up these interviews, we will make the necessary schedules," Martin said. "I suspect it will take you at least a little time. Give yourself a couple of days." He grimaced. "At *least.*"

Stella touched the purse she carried cross-body style, the bag lying just above her left hip. "My phone," she said. "I haven't been able to access service since I've been in this building—and I need to make arrangements..."

"Your luggage has already been transferred to your quarters from your hotel," Martin said. "Close proximity to your subjects for the duration of your research seemed to be indicated. The same applies to you, Dr. Amari, Father Carter."

"My practice..." began Ichiro, frowning a little.

"Your employers and your patients have been informed that you have been seconded to Government service," Martin said.

"We're in quarantine, too?" Philip asked, with a small smile that showed rather a lot of teeth. "I mean, I know you made us sign NDAs but this feels rather more substantial than that..."

"But... I have a cat," Stella said stupidly. "I only made arrangements to come here for a couple of days. I don't *have* that much luggage, I just packed for a week. And I have a cat. I need to..."

"We are aware," Martin said quietly. "All the arrangements are in place." He pulled out a clear device and tapped on it; the transparent screen morphed into several windows of rapidly updating data streams and studied it for a moment as he walked. "We have all the details on file," he said. "Down to your cat's favorite canned food. All the commitments of your personal and professional lives will be taken care of while you are here, and there is going to be someone available 24/7 to cover your needs while you are here."

Stella looked a little spooked at being told that Smokey the cat's preferences in the realm of cat food were on file in a government dossier, but Philip, passing over the cat issue, nodded at the phone in Martin's hand.

"Your device works," Philip commented.

"There is a protected network," Martin murmured. "I am afraid that for now your own outside communication is going to be limited—it's all in the NDAs. Copies of those will be in the comm units you'll be getting. In here," he added, indicating a door to his left. "The library."

They entered a utilitarian room, bright white, with stark black metal shelving holding a number of books and folders against the far wall and four computer work-stations arranged at individual desks, with individual adjustable glows set above them. Bright overhead lights recessed in the drop ceiling flooded the rest of the place with almost painful glare; one of them had the faintest of flickers, twitching at the corner of Stella's eye, and she knew that she would have a splitting headache if she had to stay in here for too long. She grimaced up at the offending light.

"That..." she said, glowering at it for a moment.

Martin made a note into his tablet. "Maintenance will replace the light immediately," he said, making Stella give him a sharp glance. The pendulum swing between 'virtually incommunicado and held here at our pleasure' and 'we will take immediate action to correct a barely voiced complaint' was dizzying. "Let me just give you the quick rundown of the facilities. The hard copy materials on the shelves over there may not seem too plentiful, but those are possibly the most relevant records in physical form—at least some of us, and I plead guilty to that, are still enough of an anachronism to find that actually seeing something in hard copy does help in understanding it. The rest is on the servers, there." He nodded at the computers. "You may use both or either at your will. There are just a few formalities that need to be done—the computers are voice activated—would you please wake a monitor, and just say your name?"

Philip was the first to move, taking the few steps towards the nearest station and sitting down in front of it. The thin, transparent, rectangular screen that served as a monitor irised into a light blue background with a red eye on it.

"Identification required," it said, in a melodious female voice. "Voice print initiated."

"Philip Carter," Philip said steadily.

The eye blinked, rotated, and the screen turned green. The smooth gray plastic surface of the desk directly in front of Philip transformed into a keyboard and a set of lighted touch-sensitive controls.

"Voice print accepted," the computer said. "Welcome, Philip Carter."

"The controls on the side will give you privacy or soundproofing of your workspace if you need it. Individual databases can be accessed directly. Please feel free to familiarize yourself with the station. In the meantime—Dr. Amari, Dr. Froud, would you do the like?" Martin asked, indicating unoccupied stations. "And while we're about this, we might as well get the rest over with. Father Carter, would you look this way please? Look straight ahead and don't blink for a moment, if you don't mind..."

He held the phone in Philip's line of sight, and a pale green light scrolled across Philip's eye.

"That's the scan on record. Would you please press your thumb on the screen...?" When Philip obliged, Martin tapped a few characters on the screen, and then repeated the procedure with the other two after they had finished their voice print procedures. "That should get you anywhere you need to go that you have clearance to enter," Martin said. "That includes the crew quarters for the subjects, when the time comes. All right..."

"*Subjects* makes them sound like guinea pigs," Stella said faintly.

"I beg your pardon?"

"You're a doctor. They're people. You might call them patients, except that even that isn't right..."

"One has to call them something, as a group," Martin said. "I know. But this isn't your average waiting room. Their backgrounds, their charts, everything we know so far—that's all either in those folders on the shelves, or on those computers. The computers are data banks; they are not connected to the Net or in any way equipped for outside communications. You may search the data banks for any information contained there, or you may make a request for any information that you require. That request will be received and processed, and the requested material will be made available to you but you will not be able to directly access any other data banks from here. This is a self-contained unit—and yes, in a way, it's all under quarantine. Until such time as we can make a decision on what—or if it comes to that, who—will be released into the world, and the media. For now, it all stays in this building."

"For how long?" Ichiro asked quietly. "Does that pertain to us as well? Our own lives..."

"You are all here to help us investigate the *Parada*'s return," Martin said.

"How long is that going to take?" Philip asked, leaning his chin on the arm he had draped across the back of his chair.

"As long as it takes," Martin said. "It isn't just you. All of us in here are in lockdown together with that crew, until we can figure out what happened. I don't need to tell you that humanity's future out there in the galaxy depends on what we find out. On whether the *Parada* was an aberration, on whether the *Juno* crew fall apart too, on whether we can do anything at all to put the pieces back together or if we're faced with something that there's no coming back from."

"DPD has only really been diagnosed—as a syndrome—very late in the 20th century," Stella said. "Before that, it was just sectionable insanity, and nothing for it but asylums or questionable medical procedures which probably did nothing at all for the syndrome and only physically crippled the patients. But even in the years since it's been identified, and studied, we only know more about what it actually *is*, how it works—not much about how to cure it. And that's just talking about the classic syndrome, the kind that rears up in the wake of a personal childhood trauma of some sort which initiates the splintering off of personalities which exist to deal with a specific issue. This... I have never heard of anything like this. If you're hoping for an actual cure, I don't know if you're going to be very happy with the outcome of anything that I or somebody like me can bring to the situation. And if you're waiting for a cure to happen, none of us might ever leave this building."

"I have done some research into the matter," Martin said grimly, "and I am aware that there is no magic bullet. But there have been reintegration studies. There has been some success in particular cases..."

"It's not a body of evidence," Stella said. "It's case by case, and here you have six, and maybe possibly nine, fairly severe cases, from what I've learned so far. The first question I have to ask is, do you have any idea what actually triggered any of this?"

"Some of the personalities have given us theories," Martin said. "You be the judge of how much weight we can put on any of that. If you feel the need to discuss issues directly with people who have interacted with the crew so far that can be arranged. Starting with myself—you will find a list of relevant people in the data bank—but video, holos, and transcripts of every conversation we have had with every single one of the subjects..."

Stella winced, and Martin grimaced, but went on. "All that material is available to you directly. All any of us will be able to tell you is second-hand data seen through our own very human filters and possible prejudices. Like me calling them subjects."

It was somewhat black humor, but Stella gave him a ghost of a smile. Wisely, Martin didn't pursue the matter.

"Can I start now?" Stella asked, turning to glance at the waiting monitor.

"Certainly," Martin said, "if you would like. If you need anything—just tell the computer. Someone is always on duty."

"You spoke of quarters being assigned," Philip said quietly. "If I may, I would prefer to retreat to mine, for now. I have no direct research I feel I need to follow up on immediately but I would very much appreciate an opportunity to reflect on the matter in a quiet place. My answers might lie elsewhere entirely."

"Of course. I will escort you there myself." Martin turned to the other two. "It is getting rather late," he said, "if you would prefer to sleep on it before starting fresh tomorrow? There will be a communication device—a replacement phone if you like—for each of you in your quarters, with relevant information already programmed in—I might just add that breakfast opens at oh-seven-hundred, and is served for three hours, but there is hot food available at the cafeteria at any time. Information on how to find the Caf is going to be on your comm units."

"I'll stay here," Stella said. "I couldn't sleep anyway."

"Dr. Amari?"

"Myself also," Ichiro said. "I feel likewise very awake right now."

Martin nodded. "When you are ready, call," he said, "Father, if you will follow me..."

Philip said nothing more to the other two, rising from his chair and following Martin out of the room.

Stella and Ichiro met each other's eyes and sat for a long moment in absolute silence. Then Stella sighed, looking away towards the computer monitor.

"I feel a little kidnapped," she said softly.

"Assuredly," Ichiro murmured. "Particularly since they seem to have competent medical personnel already in place, at least when it comes to physical health. I am not sure what precisely my role here is."

"You are probably needed as someone who will look at impossible data and verify that it is in fact true, if not precisely easily explained," Stella said with a small smile. "You're here because you are non-military—a civilian authority. Someone they can point to when awkward questions are asked that they may not want to answer themselves."

"A possible scapegoat?" Ichiro asked, raising an eyebrow.

"Anything goes," Stella said, feeling a wild urge to giggle. "There's only one thing I know, going forward—and that is that I know nothing. Yet, anyway. Will you excuse me? I think I'll go rummage around in the data banks they seem so proud of and see what I can come up with..."

Ichiro gave her a small bow. "I will look at the medical records," he said. "It is a place to start."

They had been household names, the crew of the *Parada*, when the ship set out to the stars—specifically, to explore exoplanets discovered during the early 21st century probes launched into the Alpha Centauri and Proxima Centauri systems. Six heroes who stepped on board humanity's first starship, purely on faith. The world had waved them goodbye with tears of pride and had held its collective breath as the rendezvous rocket took what the media had branded the Six to the Stars up into the shipyard in Earth orbit where their craft waited for them—the *Parada*, new-built, shining with promise, with dreams, with hope.

Captain Hanford Millgar, First Officer Jerry Hillerman, Navigator Rob Hillerman, Engineer Bogdan Dimitrov, Ship's Medic Alaya McGinty, Science Officer and Astronomer Lily Mae Washington.

Their faces were on every screen, in every home. Children were taken out of school to watch the launch of the rendezvous rocket, and then again when the cameras in orbit showed the *Parada* slowly easing out of dock, hanging there as though posing for her close-up against the backdrop of space glittering with stars, and then turning away from the home planet, nose pointed into the dark. The people of Earth watched her begin moving away, getting smaller and smaller until she vanished from sight.

For a little while, the media kept up with the ship, passing on such telemetry data as was received back. There were even occasional messages from the Six to the Stars sent while the ship still tiptoed her way through the Solar System, passing Mars, sending images of Saturn that became as iconic as that first photograph of Earth hanging in the black skies of the Moon had been back in the days of the Moon shots, because those were literally the first images of a distant planet which had been taken by living human hands while living human eyes rested on it. But then the star drive kicked in, news from the ship became scarcer, and then other things took over the headlines, as other things do. The next time the *Parada* returned to the news was when word came that contact with the ship was completely lost.

And then a hundred more years went by.

The Six to the Stars were recognizable, vivid, remembered faces, because they had been who they had been. They were written into history. Generations of children had learned their names in classes; millions had mourned them when they were presumed lost. But they were gone from living memory—no human on Earth in the present day had been alive when the *Parada* had left the planet. Seeing those historic faces on actual flesh-and-blood people under surveillance by way of CCTV cameras, changed so little from the images remembered from historical documents of what for her had been two centuries ago, in a room only a few corridors away from the one in which she was sitting, had shaken Stella Froud more than she knew.

She fought down her feelings, quashed thoughts of resurrection and immortality.

But she still felt uncanny as she accessed her computer terminal, and asked for material dating from the time of *Parada*'s launch. She would start there. At the beginning.

The data banks were thorough. All the official documents were there, but Stella discarded them for the time being—they would always be there, if she needed minutiae like height, weight, age, eye color and shoe size, education. She might need a cheat sheet for those at some point, but those facts would be easily enough accessed when she required them, and she knew where to look—she had always been fond of a saying, whose origins she might have known once but had long since mislaid, that 90 percent of research lay in simply knowing where to find the facts you needed at the time that they were needed.

But she let instinct override the scrupulous scientist ethos here and turned instead to less stringent but perhaps more revealing material. The six crewmembers had been quite the media stars before their departure, and there was a lot of interview material available—text only and video, individually and in groups that ranged from two at a time (the twins were particularly popular as an item) to the full six in a panel format. Putting aside the purely biographical data, it was this that Stella dove into.

She didn't know what she was looking for, other than she would recognize it when she saw it—so she deliberately scrambled the chronology, accessing things at random rather than in order, assimilating the material she was presented with as she observed it. Some of this stuff she already knew—it was widely known and public knowledge. Some she knew, some she had once known and forgotten, and some of it was a revelation.

Rob and Jerry Hillerman were a bottomless source of entertainment. They could range from the ridiculous to the profound, sometimes pivoting disconcertingly from one to the other in the space of a single interview giving little warning. There was an entire subject of study right there, for those so inclined.

Stella pushed the button invoking the privacy zone, soundproofing her console from anyone else working in the area. She watched several video interviews with the pair, falling into the same fascination that they held for audiences of two centuries before.

"Are you happy that you are going out there together?" a once very famous anchor of a morning chat show on TV asked brightly, flashing a smile too full of perfect teeth and wearing hair that looked like it had been sprayed on.

The twins, lounging on a red couch in poses that were so identical that a viewer's eyes watered at the prospect of simply seeing double, chose to answer this one seriously. At first, anyway.

"Well, we thought about it," Rob said. "Quite a lot, actually. We knew that there had been at least two instances, back in the days of the early space station crews, when they sent out one of a pair of twins, and kept the other one back on Earth, to compare with afterwards."

"A control experiment," Jerry said. "As in, would outer space change one human and leave his planet-bound twin untouched? Or would there be no changes at all? Or would the magic of twins kick in and the planet-bound twin would suddenly sprout the same pointed ears and cat-pupilled alien eyes that the guy up there somehow got?"

Jerry was always the snarkier of the two. When they did do the 'twin act', it was usually Jerry who began it. But he wasn't trying to derail the subject here. He just couldn't help being who he was.

"And you didn't want to be a lab rat?" the anchor said sweetly.

Rob actually smiled. Tightly, but he managed to smile. "Look," he said, "when it came to those early instances, the space-faring twin really was just up there in orbit, might stay there for a month or a year or whatever but still—Earth was just *there*. If necessary, there was the illusion that all he needed to do to get home would be to just strap on a parachute and jump."

"It wasn't like—you know—a permanent split. A terminal goodbye," Jerry said, and he wasn't, for once, smiling at all. "We understood on a deep level that if we were chosen for this mission it would be unlikely that we would see each other again in this lifetime. And if we by some miracle did—things would be very different."

"Time dilation is too complicated, perhaps, to get into here," Rob said. "But if one of us went and the other stayed behind, the one who returned—if he returned—would return as still relatively young. If he found the other—the one who stayed behind—still alive to greet him, the one who had waited would be an old, old man. Having lived a sundered life. You don't understand—you can't—the bond between twins, unless you are one. We both knew that we wanted the stars—but with us, it was a double or nothing deal, all the way. Both of us went, or neither. We didn't want to think about the consequences of anything else."

"But you wanted the stars?" the anchor prodded.

Rob looked up and there was something in his eyes that made Stella hold her breath, even all these years later.

"Always," he said, and his voice had softened, to the point that the mike he was wearing on the set almost struggled to catch the words. "We would both stand out in our back yard and count them, what we could see of them—we lived too close to a big city, and London lights did their best to drown out the stars. We grew up with a washed-out sky."

"But our uncle took us fishing, in the summers," Jerry said. "And out there in the country, the stars were different. Closer. More real."

"And then we'd go home," Rob said, "and they'd disappear again. But once we had seen them, we could not forget they were there somewhere, lost in the haze. And the less we saw of them the more we wanted them. So we decided to become spacemen any way we could."

"We devoured education," Jerry said. "We skipped at least a quarter of your average kid's school-going years, because we kept on jumping grades. We were doing college courses at the same time as we were sitting our O levels—that's graduating high school, sorta, for you Yanks; by the time we'd finished our A levels we had also accumulated nearly two years' worth of college credits. We made short work of the rest. We both graduated college before we were twenty, and had advanced degrees by the time we were twenty five."

"And then you joined the World Space Agency?"

"It was the European Space Agency still—for about a year after we joined. And then the mergers happened, and everyone finally pooled resources and knowledge, and that was the reason we could accomplish the *Parada*," Jerry said. "Before that ship, yes, we joined the space agency—and we did so with the full knowledge that we might well end up being one of those twin experiments that they seemed to be so fond of. Like I said—we knew that, coming in. It was an acceptable level of risk. Even with those straight-up miles of air and space that would separate us if they split us, we would still be essentially connected by the same world. But then they came to us about the starship."

"They approached us separately," Rob said, with the same tight smile he had worn before. "We'd been given no chance to talk to one another about it. But we gave them the same answer, individually, even without the opportunity of discussing it. That far... was too far. We both said we would stand ready to go out there, if chosen for the mission. But only together. Or not at all. They agreed."

"So what is it that draws you there, in the end?"

Rob got that faraway look again, the one that made Stella's hackles rise. "It's the stars," he said, and his voice had dropped again. It was as though he couldn't speak about this except in hushed tones, as though it was almost too big a miracle to utter out loud at all.

"I wanted to look at the stars, up close—to look the stars in the eye," he said. "We are all star stuff, you know that, don't you? The molecules inside you and me were all forged in the heart of a star once. The stars are our brothers. I *always* knew they were there, waiting for me—and when this chance was offered to me it wasn't the WSA that I heard calling me. It was their voices, the high sweet voices of those stars. Where I was always meant to be."

"Yes," Jerry said. Only that.

It was remarkably easy to hold that depth in a corner of her attention when Stella watched a different show, a late-night chat show which was clearly more entertainment than informational, and the twins responded accordingly.

"So what do you plan on doing up there?" the host asked, grinning broadly.

"The same thing we do down here," said Jerry.

"Finish..."

"...each other's sentences. Drive..."

"...everyone mad. Be..."

"...the thing that keeps everyone sane up there. Make..."

"...everyone laugh. There's going to be a need..."

"...for finding things to laugh about, when things go wrong."

"As they inevitably will."

"As they always do."

The host lifted both hands in surrender, laughing. "I almost wish I was going with you," he said, and sounded almost sincere about it.

"Probably not," Jerry said.

"And that's okay," Rob said.

"Not everyone..."

"...is cut out for this stuff."

Everyone else was laughing. The two of them weren't. Not quite. They were smiling, but there was always a part of them that knew exactly where they were and what they were doing and how they were doing it—and they were a tag team in whatever they did.

Drive everyone mad. And here they now were, and the world called them mad instead.

Was the presence of twins a factor in what had happened? Could it have been? Could this rapid disintegration of personality have occurred because there was *already* a 'split personality' up there as a model—these two men who were obviously capable of thinking as a single mind if necessary? Or should it have made them immune to the splittage—already carrying, as it were, parts of each other's personality? Stella tapped out a note to herself on her phone. The Hillermans might hold at least part of the key to the mystery of what had happened to the crew of the *Parada*.

Surprised by a bone-cracking yawn some time later, Stella straightened at her workstation. She cast her eyes around the library, finding herself alone—so absorbed had she been in what she was watching that she had completely failed to register it when Ichiro had left. Glancing at her watch, she noted with faint surprise that it was just past three o'clock ... *in the morning*. She was suddenly and very sharply aware that she needed to grab a few hours' sleep, and only vaguely remembered talk of her "quarters" from before she had dived into the data banks, without the first idea about where these would be or how she would go about finding them. She recalled Martin saying that she should call if she needed anything; rising from the workstation, she eased a stiff body and stretched until she heard her joints pop with it. Then she studied her workstation, looking for the correct controls, wondering if there was anybody in fact on duty at the other end at this hour, and experimentally touched a likely icon on the screen.

To her surprise, the response was instant. A woman with brown hair scraped back into a tight knot at the back of her head looked up and straight into Stella's eyes, giving a small nod of acknowledgment.

"Yes, Dr. Froud?"

"Yes. Um, I find myself in need of somewhere to take a nap. I was wondering if I could..."

"Yes, ma'am. Someone will be with you at once to escort you to your quarters."

The contact was terminated. Almost immediately she heard the door open behind her and turned to see a young ensign, in a uniform so crisp and freshly pressed that it might have been taken out of a replicator five minutes before she donned it. The thing seemed a little over the top for three in the morning, but Stella allowed for being exhausted and cranky and decided that she was just being petty and cross.

"Ma'am," the ensign said politely, and waited.

Stella yawned again. "Bed," she said, partly to the ensign and partly to herself. "I think."

"If you'll follow me."

Stella was simply too tired, her mind too blown, to keep track of where she was led. She simply meekly thanked the crisp ensign when she was delivered to a blankly featureless rectangle of a door which, she did register, had her name on a sign beside it. She stared at the door owlishly for a moment.

"Just say your name," the ensign said helpfully.

She did and the door soundlessly slid open and she stumbled inside, murmuring a mushy response to the ensign's "Good night, ma'am." She dropped her bag where she stood, crossed to the bed, and fell on it fully dressed, already asleep before her head touched the pillow.

When her eyes fluttered open again, she lifted her head and focused blearily on a dimmed digital clock on a touchscreen built into the wall above the head of the bed. It read 7:45. To the best of her recollection she had collapsed on this bed somewhere close to 3:30 AM. She was still tired, but as she came more awake she also became aware that she was hungry, and also that she could barely remember coming into this room. Grimacing as she sat up and smoothed down her slept-in clothes, she looked around.

The room was spacious enough not to be claustrophobic, but there were no windows or any other openings other than the door she had entered through. The bed she sat on was smoothly molded into the wall, with the screen that presently displayed the clock sitting just above the head of the bed; Stella noticed a row of symbols arrayed vertically along the side of the screen and surmised the touch screen would yield other useful functions if those were put to use, but put them aside to investigate in more detail later. On the floor by the foot of the bed was the suitcase she had packed for this trip and last seen on the luggage rack in her hotel room. Her coat hung in a closet area revealed by an opening in one of the sleeping section's walls, obviously left open in order to permit her to see the purpose of the enclosure although she could see that it could be closed so that it presented a smooth seamless wall when not in use. Beyond that was another door that led into a compact bathroom area, in which she could glimpse the necessary facilities—a sink, a toilet, a small square shower. She could see a bath towel draped over a towel bar. The archway to her right opened into a sitting area with a small two-seater couch, shorter and narrower than the bed but otherwise very like it, built in as part of the wall, and a free-standing chair; she couldn't see it from where she was sitting on the bed but her brain obligingly presented her with a picture of a desk tucked into an alcove on the sitting room side of the wall at the foot of her bed, with a chair tucked into place and a screen that might have been a computer monitor or a video screen hanging on the wall above it. The lights were pleasant, and unobtrusive. It was a disconnect; the room they had described as a library was almost a throwback to early 21st century office utilitarianism, practically an anachronism if you didn't count the state-of-the-art computers, but this place—Stella almost felt as though she was herself on some sleek new-built starship hurtling into the unknown.

She wasn't, but there were people waiting who had been exactly there. Stella winced, and slipped off the bed, stepping into the bathroom to splash cold water on her face.

"You've looked better," she informed her reflection in a mirrored wall above the sink, inspecting dark circles under her eyes and an expression she couldn't quite name settling her features into a mask of what she could only describe as the beginnings of a deer-in-the-headlights look. She made another half-hearted attempt to straighten her clothes but she knew that it would take more than that to make herself presentable; a stray thought did swim across her mind about whether these quarters, too, were subject to the same kind of surveillance as the two crews' quarters—but she frowned at herself in the mirror, shaking her head. No, she wasn't going to let herself get paranoid about things.

On her way to ascertain if they had brought all her belongings in the suitcase that waited for her, she glanced into the closet again and saw that the coat wasn't the only thing in it—the closet also contained a couple of what she could only describe as a uniform-lite—it wasn't the crisp military garb as worn by last night's ensign but more of a matching set of pants and tunic in a neutral blue shade. A rectangular patch on the right front panel looked like some sort of flexible hi-tech screen woven into the material. Stella reached out to touch it experimentally, and under her fingertips it blinked and resolved itself into an ID badge, with her image and her name coming into quick focus.

She gave in. The clothes were obviously there for a purpose, and she would have to investigate laundry facilities later for the things she was taking off. The provided clothing fit her perfectly and Stella retrieved her bag from where she had dropped it before the door when she had been delivered to this place, drew out a small hairbrush with her left hand in almost the same motion that she tossed the bag onto the bed with her right, and stepped back into the bathroom to drag the brush through her hair. She supposed there would be a toothbrush in there somewhere if she just took a moment to look, but first she needed to find out how—and if—she could actually get out of this comfortable confinement.

When she stepped into the sitting area she saw a transparent rectangle of a tablet, similar to the one she had seen Martin use, lying on a charging mat on the desk. She picked it up and swept a finger across the screen; the thing came to life, offering her a number of icons to choose from. One at least was immediately obvious—a crossed knife and fork—and Stella realized that she was in fact ravenous, something that her stomach punctuated immediately by giving a confirmatory growl. She tapped the icon; it resolved into directions to the cafeteria and a menu of available offerings.

"Breakfast sounds good," she muttered to herself, mostly just to hear herself speak out loud, and tucked the tablet into a long pocket in the side of her tunic that appeared to have been made to house it.

She turned to the door.

It seemed to be an intelligence test because at first she could see no way to open it directly.

The ensign had said something about saying her name.

"Stella Froud," Stella said experimentally, staring at the door. And then, just because something more seemed necessary, "Open."

The door obligingly whooshed open for her.

She stepped into a featureless corridor. The door closed behind her with a vaguely threatening finality.

Stella drew a deep breath and hauled the tablet back out, calling up a map. Probably anything would look better after a good strong cup of coffee.

The first person Stella saw in the cafeteria was Father Philip Carter, sitting with the Lieutenant whom Stella could vaguely remember having been their escort the day before but whose name she could not immediately fish out of her back brain and another man, also in military uniform, whom she did not recognize. She hesitated, and while she did Philip looked up and noticed her. He gave her a smile, waving her over to the table where he was sitting; she mimed coffee, and he nodded. Stella took her time gathering up a cup of coffee and a plateful of breakfast (a pancake that looked passable, two fried eggs, and a piece of toast on the side) and carried her tray over to the table where Philip and the others waited.

"Did you get some sleep?" Philip asked, rising to his feet to pull a chair out for her.

"You might say I passed out, finally," Stella said, grimacing. "Still trying to process all this."

Philip nodded. "We all are. By the way, this is Lieutenant Barriéres. Louis. Lydia you will remember from yesterday."

The two people he named nodded at Stella, and she acknowledged the nods over the rim of her coffee cup. "Stella Froud," she said, for Louis's benefit. "Will you guys excuse me while I eat?"

"Of course," Philip said. "Does anyone else want any more coffee?"

"I could use a cup. I'll get it," Louis Barriéres said, pushing his chair back.

Philip, who was dressed in the same kind of outfit that Stella wore except for an obstinate addition of a shiny black pectoral cross made from something that looked like obsidian, indicated the clothing with a wave of his hand. "They sure seemed ready for us, weren't they?"

"They're always ready for anything," Lydia said. "The ID badge is programmable. The rest—it's a matter of replicating the uniforms in the correct size which is trivial."

"So these are actual uniforms?" Stella said, through a mouthful of toast.

"It's what we wear when off duty," Lydia said. "Congratulations, you've joined the military. I'm sure you'll get an honorable discharge when your tour is up..."

"What about the other lot? Philip asked. "I mean, we get the wetware, so to speak, I understand that—between us, Ichiro Amari and Stella and I are supposed to cover the bases—body and mind and, I suppose, when it comes to me, soul. But the ones we left upstairs— the hardware crowd and the IT contingent—are they somewhere here or is it just the three of us who got conscripted?"

"At least you're still on terra firma," Lydia said. "As far as I know, everyone other than the historian, that professor—what's her name, Vivien Collins?...— everyone else was bundled up and packed off upstairs, to the *Parada*." She indicated the ceiling with a thumb. "Up *there*. Floating above the clouds and looking down on us all, trying to dig around that ship's innards and find out just what the *fuck* went wrong there. They've got a crew fine-tooth-combing the *Juno*, too. I mean, that ship didn't exactly get the bit between her teeth and go careening off into the galaxy. So that *worked*. But we lived for two hundred years under the *Parada*'s loss and the martyrdom of the Six for the Stars. They finally tossed another crew out there and they *seem* to have come back okay but that first lot... they don't know what happened. And until they figure that out they are completely stalled out. Nothing can ever be done again until something concrete is learned from the situation."

"The problem," said Louis, returning with the coffee and catching the tail end of that conversation, "is that we have precisely two data points, and they are a hundred and eighty degrees apart. Either we have a working star drive, or we don't. Either we can send humanity out there, or we can't. And until we find out which is the right answer— and they don't really want to send another ship and crew out there just to weigh the scales one way or another—they simply don't know if this is actually something we have accomplished, or something that has come down on us like a hammer of God warning us away from the stars altogether."

"God," Philip said equably, "would seem to be my department."

Stella swallowed another piece of her toast. "It took them two hundred years to get over the *Parada* and try again," she said.

"Exactly," Louis said. "They don't want to wait another two hundred until *Juno* is given a clean bill of health and they can start thinking interstellar again. I mean, it's all very well playing around in our back yard and all—but we've bitten into the interstellar travel now and had a good taste of it and that doesn't just disappear."

"Even if the taste was pretty bitter?" Philip asked. "I mean, look what happened when we tried..."

"It's a craving now, one we are going to have to feed," Louis said. "If there's something to be discovered up in the bowels of those ships, they'll try and find it. But even though my brain would fry if anyone asked me to attempt such a thing, I think they have the easy part. I mean, inanimate things are supposed to work a certain way, *non?* That is how they are made—how we made them. We know how they were made, know what they were supposed to accomplish, know what we did. If something unexpected happened we know that it was unexpected, and why. They literally have blueprints to follow, and lines of code to debug. It's going to take time but it's drudge work. You have to have a certain kind of knowledge to be able to do the drudgery but it's just that—a slog."

"And in some ways, it's easier to enforce the gag orders," Lydia said. "I mean, even if they ran out and started blabbing about things they shouldn't to anyone they met I suspect people's eyes would just glaze over in short order. They could talk forever but nobody would be listening any more. But the crews..."

"For the record, they probably won't be very happy today," Louis said. "Your Dr. Amari has put in a request for new bloodwork, and for a new set of all scans. He says he wishes to start fresh with the work ups, to start using data he can know the chain of custody of, and the timeline of, and can trust. The *Juno* crew are first up, and they are going to be marched off for more poking and prodding today. I talked to an orderly who works in that compound, and he says he heard Tyrone Kidman say he was starting to feel like a colander, he'd had so many holes poked in him by needles. And it's starting over today. There could be riots."

"And that's just the bodies," Lydia said, glancing at Stella, who was keeping her head down and mopping up her eggs with the last of the toast. "The rest..."

"Yeah," Stella said, not lifting her eyes from her plate, but her voice edged with sarcasm. "Here comes a new headshrinker to tell them they're all incurably insane, right?"

"We haven't told them that," Lydia said. "Leastways, we may have said this or that to some fragment who may or may not remember a full conversation. You haven't seen them yet, up close. You have no idea."

"They aren't insane!" Stella said, more sharply than she intended, flashing a glance of pure rebellion.

"At least you've got something clinical to go on," Philip murmured. "Sane or not, I suspect I am here to find out whether they're still human... and if they are, then just how damned they are."

2.

Stella dove into the data banks and let them close over her head—over the next three days she spent every waking hour either hunched over a terminal in the library or over the personal one in her quarters, or haunting the Surveillance Room watching the two crews wait for some sort of deliverance from their captivity.

Fascinated as she was by the *Parada* six, she watched their monitor screens endlessly, and quickly began to pick up different personalities and the changeover moments. It was a dizzying and ever-changing array and although she kept on trying to take notes things were constantly running away with her as she got caught up in different interactions and forgot to keep track of what she was trying to annotate. She was still wading through copious amounts of material on them, and didn't feel nearly ready to face them directly. Despite both a personal curiosity and a professional interest, some part of her kept recoiling from the idea, perfectly certain that she would be indulging in some sort of time travel if she tried to talk to these people from the past.

The *Juno* crew, however, kept on being refreshingly normal.

Ichiro's new round of tests and scans revealed absolutely nothing out of the ordinary. Whatever had infected the *Parada* people didn't appear to be contagious, or even an obvious inevitable artefact of near-light-speed travel. Given access to all the necessary facilities that he wanted, Ichiro put the three men through a medical wringer and—when all the results came back as unremarkable—pronounced the crew to be, as far as he was concerned, in perfect bodily health. He moved on to the more complicated matters involving the *Parada* crew, bowing out of the *Juno* situation, having done all he could do there. That left *Juno* in Stella's lap. And at the very least the three crewmembers were not—to her—two hundred years old.

She decided she could handle these interviews. And that she needed to put some distance between her and the *Parada* six while some things sedimented out in her mind. So she put in a schedule for one-on-one interviews with the *Juno* three, starting with the captain.

Captain Hugh de Mornay awaited her in an interview room that distressingly resembled an interrogation cell. He was sitting on a straight-backed chair at a centrally-placed table in the small room, but actually rose to his feet in a gesture that was a courtesy when Stella opened the door and slipped into the room. She actually did a double take; she knew, from the surveillance footage that she had seen on the CCTV screens, that he was a large man, but seeing him in person was a different matter altogether. He was big and blond and really did look like he would have been quite at home in Viking clothes; the top of Stella's head was literally level with his collar bone, and she had to tilt her head up to meet his eyes.

"Captain," she said cautiously. "I'm... Stella Froud. Doctor Froud. Um, I'm here to... won't you sit? I'm sorry about the accommodations but I'll get a stiff neck if I have to hold my head at this angle for much longer."

"Doctor," he said, obliging her and subsiding back into his chair. There was the faintest curl of a smile at the corner of his lip, but he didn't allow it to make further inroads in his expression. His eyes weren't exactly friendly—and Stella was hardly surprised, given that she must have been just another in a depressingly endless stream of people who seemed bound and determined to keep him immured in his comfortable prison forever more.

"Stella," she said. "Please."

"More than some would permit," he said, his tone not exactly confrontational but certainly edged with sharpness. Stella didn't blame him.

She had demanded from Martin the authorization to finally spill the full beans to these men, but now that she was faced with the opportunity she suddenly wasn't sure she entirely relished the thought of being alone in the room with this man when he learned the whole story behind his 'quarantine' in this place. She cast about for a place to begin, and he wasn't helping—he sat there, his big hands folded on the table in front of him, and just watched her in silence, his face set into a bland mask, giving no real hint of what he was thinking.

"What, exactly, happened out there?" Stella said at last, into the silence.

That wasn't what she had meant to say, and clearly she had taken him by surprise, too. His fingers flexed, relaxed again. A spark of wary interest had kindled in his eyes.

"Ma'am?"

"*Stella*. Look, I'm going to tell you quite a story in a minute. But first... tell me. Because I have read reams on everything. And there's a heap of stuff I just don't get at all. How on earth did you find the *Parada* at all out there? I mean, it's a big, um, universe out there. I would have thought that the odds of tripping over a ship lost two centuries ago would have been so unlikely as to be described as impossible. Were you looking for them? How did you know where to look?"

"We weren't sent out as a search party, if that's what you mean," Hugh de Mornay said. "The *Juno* had a modified drive, not the same as the *Parada*. Ours... bunny hopped, if you like. Not sure if that was an improvement or not, but the thinking was that taking short bursts and then coming out of it might give a better chance of catching something that might have gone out of kilter before it really screwed things up and you ended up doing something from which you couldn't recover. They figured something like that might have happened to the *Parada*. They thought that if we came out of a burst and found that we needed to turn tail and run for home it would be easier to do it if we weren't already halfway across the galaxy."

"So you bunny hopped right on top of the *Parada*?" Stella asked, frowning.

"Not exactly," the captain said. "The *Parada* was equipped with a transponder signal, a signature, if you like. Of course, that was programmed into our ship's computer—I mean, the only other starship there ever was? Of course they would write its call sign into our data banks. If nothing else, then as a memorial. We didn't expect to hear it coming at us from space, though, when we came out of one of our hops. And once we heard it, we could not ignore it. You can understand that, can't you?"

"Of course," Stella said.

"We could hardly believe it," Hugh said, "but once we all agreed that it was out there to be homed in on, there was no question but that we had to do it. *I* had to do it. Even if I had absolutely no idea what I would find, if anything, or what I would do with it when I did find it. We were called, and we went. And we found her, drifting. Not under drive. The life support systems were functioning but their ability to do anything else or go anywhere at all... that had just spent itself. I had absolutely no expectations. When I tried establishing a com link, on several possible frequencies, I didn't expect to hear anything but silence echoing back at me. And then... I heard Captain Millgar talking to me. *Hanford Millgar.* I learned about the man in school. I thought he was long dead. And yet—there he was, finally, on the *Parada.* My medical officer didn't exactly suggest a mass hallucination, but I figured he was halfway to thinking it. We were seeing it, but we weren't believing it. I don't know that any of us could really come to grips with the idea that we might actually get to meet Han Millgar and the rest of them. Shake their hands."

"But how did you bring them back?"

"That was Ty. You should ask him that. He's the engineer. But he more or less thought about nothing else at all from the moment that we sighted that other ship. He would have sooner had us all die out there than even consider the idea that we three could somehow return to Earth and leave the *Parada* behind, out there. There were just so many things we did not know—but we knew one thing. We were *all* going home."

"Did you have any idea what you might be bringing back to Earth?" Stella said quietly.

"It occurred to me," Hugh de Mornay said carefully. "At some point halfway between here and there. I had nightmares of bringing back...

not the lost *Parada* crew... but some sort of doppelgangers... that I could be loosing all kinds of insanity on the world. But that wasn't something that I could share then, not with Ty who was so fiercely focused on accomplishing this thing and completing the miracle we had fallen into the middle of, not with Joe who... well, Joe has his own issues. Joe is one of those people who knows when he is going to die, and so anything that happens to him in the interim is almost completely inconsequential. He wouldn't have understood."

Stella let a moment pass before she spoke again. "Do you have any idea why you three are still here?"

He flung his hands into the air in a gesture that was pure helplessness. "They keep on using the word 'quarantine' as though it was a magic spell," he said. "I'm not sure what they would be quarantining for. They are aware—they *have* to realize by now, God alone knows we've been subjected to every possible test you can imagine—that we aren't carrying anything that they *know* about. And if they're waiting for the unknown to pop up—I'm not sure any more how long they intend to wait."

"I want to talk to your crew," Stella said. "And then I'll talk to all of you, together. There are... things you should know, that you should have been told long ago. But first, just humor me. Answer a few simple questions. And don't ask why I'm asking them."

Hugh frowned a little, and then consciously cleared his brow. The sigh that came out of him was deep and fully resigned. "Of course."

He denied ever having 'lost time', or having had no memory of having done, said, or acquired something that he later found difficult to remember or recognize. He denied ever hearing or listening to 'voices' in his head, but he looked like he was thinking that another member of his crew might not answer that so easily. He denied having been accused of lying when he knew that to the best of his ability he was telling the truth. He denied having trouble distinguishing between real memories and things that might have only have happened in a dream, and he even looked genuinely bewildered when asked if he had ever had trouble recognizing himself in a mirror. He took a number of questions that sounded like they came from Alice from beyond the looking glass, and gamely tried to give the sanest answers that he could.

"All right," Stella said at last, having got all that she could get out of him, "I'm sorry, I know I must sound like all this has all crossed into a whole different kind of crazy. But please trust me. I can straighten at least some of it out, I think, but I'd rather I had to explain the guts of it once, and to all three of the *Juno*'s crew rather than one at a time. You've waited for a long time for answers—can you wait for a little longer? And send Tyrone Kidman in to me?"

Hugh hesitated. And then pushed his chair back and stood up. "Okay," he said slowly, "but there was one other question that the others asked that you haven't."

"What?" Stella asked, genuinely startled at this unsolicited offer.

"One of the military brass who did the initial interviews asked me if I regretted bringing the *Parada* back. And I'll tell you what I told him. At the time that it was happening, there was no space for such thoughts in my head. I did the only thing I believed I could do, I took the only course of action I saw as being open to me—and as the captain of the *Juno* it was my word that was the final one although I don't believe any of my crew would have opposed that decision, or indeed did at the time. But looking back... I have had nothing but time to think about this, for the duration of being cooped up in here while someone else did their own thinking. I did the only thing I could do and I would do it again—but I have had the luxury, if you want to call it that, of wondering if the best of intentions haven't resulted in some kind of enormous mistake. And it's *that*, that error, whatever the error might have been, that has caused all this trouble. Like I said, my final decision, my word, although I believe completely that my crew was a hundred percent behind it—but if anyone is being brought to any sort of justice for this, if there is any blame to be passed, I don't want Tyrone or Joe saddled with any of it. If it comes to paying a price... I am prepared to pay it." He paused, dropped his eyes briefly, and then looked back up and met Stella's steadily and perfectly calmly. "I just wanted to have that on the record. Thank you, ma'am. Stella. I'll send in Tyrone to see you now."

He actually gave Stella a snappy salute, made a smart turn, and marched out of the room without looking back.

Tyrone Kidman, the First Officer and Chief Engineer of the *Juno*, was not nearly as physically imposing a man as his captain—if Hugh de Mornay was a lion, Tyrone was a fox, his face pinched and pointed and full of sharp angles and a flop of ginger hair falling over his forehead. His eyes were small and dark green, like moss under water, and they shone with a bright intelligence, and, because he was not Hugh de Mornay and dignity was not something that came easily to him, with frustration and impatience. Tyrone had been the crew member Martin Peck had mentioned as having been married, with a child. He had not strictly speaking severed that relationship legally when he had departed in the *Juno*, but the passage of enough time had ensured that he could never really pick it up where he had left it off, either. He knew that, and he knew that the child he had left behind was already turning into a young woman, one with only scattered memories of her father from her early childhood.

He knew all that, and yet he was the one who chafed the most at his immurement in the so-called 'quarantine'—all the years he had given willingly were as dust in the face of every day that he was here, back on Earth, and kept from at least going back to see if the woman and child he had left behind had survived his leaving, if they were safe and happy. He resented every moment that he was locked up and away from them, every poke and prod and scan that he had to endure, resented them all the more, perhaps, because he realized that they were functioning as a sort of safety net for him. Here, in the comfortable captivity of his return to Earth, he still had a Schrödinger's family— they might have still existed, or they might not, he would not know until he actually looked, and as long as he was kept away from them he could not look.

But that was on the return journey. While he was still out on the mission, in a very real way, Tyrone Kidman was responsible for the miracle, almost single handedly.

The last word might have been the captain's, but the necessary technical expertise had been Tyrone's. Without his obsessive need to return to Earth with the *Parada* or not at all, both ships might have been lost.

He was clearly tired of telling the story over and over, but perhaps the captain had said something to him and he bit down on his impatience and, at Stella's asking, told it again.

"The captain said something about a transponder signal," Stella said.

"Yes, it was in our data banks," Tyrone said. "Not because we were sent out to look for them, you understand, but simply because... they were the *Parada*, and they were the first, and we carried their memory out there with us. When we first became aware that we were receiving the signal from *out there* rather than just triggering our own memory banks, I think I may have lost my mind for a moment. And then... then I did what I always do. I have a bad habit of reducing every miracle to its nuts and bolts. It may have still obstinately stayed a miracle, but it became my business to make sure that miracle survived. I just stopped thinking about everything except that. Except them. Except what had to be done to make sure we did not have to end up turning our backs and leaving them there."

Tyrone gave Stella a burning look. "I... don't think I could have faced returning, if that had ended up being our only choice," he said. "I could not face this world having committed that sin. I could not have looked anyone on Earth in the eye. I would probably never have made it back at all, I would have found a way to die. It's easy enough to die out there if you make a mistake. I don't make those mistakes—but I know how to make one if I need to."

"I understand," Stella said, and she did. Her heart clenched painfully at the thought of being faced with this impossible situation in a place where everything came to rest on whether or not one man could accomplish things that nobody else had even considered as possibilities.

"Do you?" Tyrone challenged. "Do you have any idea what it felt like to hear *Captain Millgar* answer a hail you never expected to hear a response to? I think Captain de Mornay pretty much reached out and closed my mouth with his hand. Before I could speak again. We were all... we were... I cannot even begin to tell you. And the worst part of it is that in those first moments, as we spoke—as we impossibly *spoke* to them—the only thing I could think of is that it was not possible that we had found them, and that it may have been even less possible for us... for me... to do anything at all about it, now that we had accomplished that. Do you have any idea what it feels like to have your mind fill with a hundred schemes, each worse and less practical than the last, with all the knowledge you'd ever accumulated about anything at all that might have been relevant pouring into your brain all at once and competing for attention?"

Tyrone's was not the kind of madness they were afraid of, in this place, but a part of Stella watched the man's pure intensity and the flame of bright passion that burned inside him and had to wonder if he would ever be completely sane in a real sense, ever again. Even if going out on only the second starship humanity had ever built hadn't been enough to trigger this, the meeting with the *Parada* and what it had pushed Tyrone Kidman into doing, into becoming, had changed the core of the man. He might have been shining, before, Stella had not known him and could not say—all she could tell was that now, in the aftermath, he was incandescent. And those fires would end up burning him into cinders from the inside. Stella looked at Tyrone Kidman and knew with a sick certainty that he would not live to see a ripe old age. Whatever he had been before, he was a comet now, a comet burning itself out.

"So what did you do?" she asked gently.

"We could only talk to them," Tyrone said. "There was no video link; we could not see them. We had no idea what the journey had done to them, what the tau factor had done to them, none of that. But we could speak to them as we both hung there in the night, And I spoke to Boz—Bogdan Dimitrov, the engineer on the *Parada*—and I'll tell you, it was astonishing just how much, between the two of us, we did not know. The two engineers on Earth's two starships, talking across empty space at one another, trying to figure out how to save everybody. And whatever we came up with, there was a reason it would not work. We did not have compatible hatches, so we couldn't even form an airlock and get them off that crippled bird and into ours and maybe limp home together that way. We had a smaller craft that could detach from *Juno* and then dock back—but, again, the shuttle couldn't attach to the *Parada* in any meaningful way. We *could* attach, like a limpet, we had magnetic clamps in addition to the physical docking clamps we were equipped with, and we had a grapple arm, but that... had been something of a weird afterthought on the ship and its possibilities were not all that well thought out, as it happened. I'm not entirely sure what they expected us to latch onto and bring home with that grapple..."

"Certainly not the *Parada*," Stella murmured.

Tyrone glared at her, and then gave a short sharp laugh. "Certainly not the *Parada*," he agreed.

"So... you just clamped on and hoped for the best?" Stella said, blinking. It seemed like the most unlikely of schemes to her, but then she was no expert—except that Tyrone, who *was*, inasmuch as anyone could be, seemed to agree with her. He bared his teeth in what was only nominally a smile.

"If you want the exact specs," he said, "I flipped the *Juno* and then we clamped onto the *Parada*, belly to belly. And then I had to figure on the added mass, and find out if the drive would even work with the other ship attached, never mind do anything coherent or necessary or, well, non-lethal—Boz had already tried to tell me that their own drive had somehow gone nova on them and then fried itself..."

"It *exploded*?" Stella interrupted, startled.

"Not literally. Metaphorically. Things just went faster than they anticipated or should even be possible and that screwed up the..."

"I get the general idea, I don't think I could follow a detailed explanation."

"Even if there was someone who could give you one," Tyrone said, still with that feral grin. "So we tried the first bunny hop back towards home and I swear, I just closed my eyes and hit the right buttons and had no idea if we would come out at the other end of the jump with the *Parada* still attached... or having lost it somewhere in transit and this time permanently and with no hope of finding it ever again...

or if we'd somehow bring them through and get lost ourselves... or if neither of us would ever see anything sane in real space ever again." He closed his eyes, briefly, as the remembered adrenaline surged through him. Stella could see him try to suppress the shudder that wanted to shake his entire body. But all he did was ball his hands into fists and dig his fingernails into his palms, until he mastered the moment.

When he looked at her again, he was almost calm. "We both made it. It took three hops. I nearly lost it at every single one of them, but the *Parada* hung on. When we crossed back into our system I bawled like a baby. And then I slept for fifteen hours. I was barely awake when they transferred us off the *Juno* and down into this place. I was hoping that I could at least see if the *Parada* crew had made it, to speak to Boz, to shake his hand. But..."

"They made it," Stella said carefully. "Thanks to you."

"So they tell me," Tyrone said, "But that's all they tell me."

"I'll tell you the rest," Stella said. "All of it. But like I said to your captain... I'll do that with all three of you, after I've spoken to everyone first individually."

She didn't ask him any of the questions she had asked of his captain. Tyrone Kidman had gone through the crucible. If he had had any predilection to disassociate he would have done so. He might have been held together by passion and sheer intensity, but those were enough—he was one of the most solid, coherent personalities that Stella had ever met. Tyrone might live the rest of his life being tortured by memories he could not put aside—but that was all they would be. Memories. He would not get lost in them and create a new personality every time he came back to that crossroads in the hope that a new soul might take him to a new destination when he trudged the same difficult road.

"Thank you for telling me what happened," Stella said as she ended the interview. "Could you please arrange for Joseph White Elk to come in, as you leave?"

If Tyrone Kidman had been pure fire, when Joseph White Elk walked into the interview room Stella felt as though she was in the presence of cool deep water. He met her eyes squarely, calmly, without any hint of disturbance at all. They were a light golden brown, unusual, like a wolf's.

Stella actually took a moment to give herself a stern word of warning. Lion, then fox, now wolf, she was reverse-anthropomorphizing the *Juno*'s crew, retro-fitting them into a fable. She was supposed to assess their sanity, not lapse into oddness and whimsy herself.

"You wished to speak to me," Joe said after a moment, a polite breaking of the silence.

Stella mentally shook herself. "Yes," she said. And then, without planning, asked the first thing that came to mind. "Tell me about yourself?"

Joe lifted his hands in a small gesture that seemed to indicate several things—assent, resignation, polite confusion. "I am three quarters Cheyenne," he said, "but I was raised by the grandparents who came from the only part of my family who was not—my white mother committed the ultimate sin of marrying an Indian, and her parents didn't speak to her for years. I was seven when my parents were both killed in a car accident, and my white grandparents swooped in and took me—and tried very hard to make me forget anything in me that wasn't part of their world. But I was seven. It was too late. They might have erased some memories but the roots had sunk in and they were deep enough."

He paused. "My grandparents gave me a good education, and even sent me to medical school, but by the time I turned eighteen I was already pulling away from them and when I graduated from med school, I claimed my Cheyenne blood. My grandparents did the same thing they had done to my mother. They practically disowned me. The rest is administrative history. I found a job, then another, then applied for the space program without any great hopes of getting in, but I did. And then came *Juno*."

He paused again. "I was not the first to volunteer to be considered for the mission—and they only took on volunteers for this, nobody was going to be appointed to this crew—I may quite possibly have been the last person to put my name into the hat, as it were. I thought long and hard about this, about whether I was capable of doing it at all, if I could bear being torn from this world, from the dust and waters of which I was made. But then I walked out into the wilderness one day, to ask my questions of the wind, to see if the spirits of my ancestors who still haunt the land had any answers for me. When I returned to my home, I had a handful of soil in a box, and a canteen full of water I had gathered from a creek. I made a thing, myself, that would hold these for me—half of it the dirt gathered from my world, half of it in a glass vial the living waters that run on her—and the next day I volunteered for *Juno*, knowing that I would be on her when she left, knowing I would return."

"Your captain said you were one of those people who knew when you were going to die," Stella murmured, hardly aware that she was speaking out loud.

Joe inclined his head, and smiled. "He may be right. I knew that my death didn't wait out there. I would have to come home to meet it."

It was pointless asking this man if he had ever heard voices inside his own head, voices other than his own. Clearly, he did, and he listened to what they said. But it wasn't remotely the disassociation that plagued the *Parada* people. Joseph White Elk knew how to hold multitudes, and that was just part of what he was. But they weren't splinters, poking out at all angles. They were all part of a greater whole, making him stronger, like a sequoia.

"You still have it? Your talisman?"

"Of course," Joe said. He patted his chest, where something hidden underneath his clothes rested on his skin. "It never leaves me. And I never leave it. So long as I hold it, I am always here, I am always home. Wherever I am. Whatever the exile. I carry my world inside me."

Stella found tears prickling at the corners of her eyes. "I think I understand."

"I think you may," he said, giving her both courtesy and a high compliment.

She didn't really need to ask any more questions, but she was interested from a purely personal vantage point as to his take on the *Parada* rescue. So she sat back in her chair, her legs straight out in front of her, crossed at the ankles.

"What do you remember, about finding the other ship?"

"The Captain had his hands full with command," Joe said quietly. "Tyrone had his own full of logistics. Both their minds were full of noise, and they could not hear anything outside of that. But... I listened. Out there in the great emptiness that lies between things, you would think there is only silence—but that isn't true, not quite. The stars have their own songs, and if your mind is still enough, you can hear them. But what I heard when we came to the *Parada* was... chaos. There were... too many voices inside that ship."

Stella had thought she had asked all the questions she needed to, but now she sat up sharply. "What was that?"

Joe just *looked* at her, out of those improbable golden eyes.

"I haven't said anything to the others, because if we weren't being told everything there was probably a reason for it—I may not have stayed silent forever, but for now the better part of wisdom seemed to be to hold my peace. But for what that is worth—when we found that other ship... there were children on it."

"Children?"

"Children's voices. At first I tried to understand in terms of the possibility that the ship had been lost for so long that there were actually children who had been born on it—but that could not have happened. The *Parada* was not built for that. If things had come to that point they would all be dead already, the children and the crew members whose progeny they might have been. There was simply no logical way there could be children on that ship—when we finally contacted the *Parada* we spoke with the people whom we knew had been on board when the ship left, and there was no background noise that would have indicated anything other than those same six people who left with her were still with her now."

He looked pointedly at Stella but she said nothing. "And yet, I could sense children on that ship. As though they were physically present there. Every time I stilled my mind enough to listen, I could catch an echo of them. They were so young, and they were so wise. In my own mind, I called it the Children's Collective. I almost had the feeling that those children were the circle of sanity that remained in that ship, that they were the ones who decided what was possible. It... even made sense to me. Out there, everything that makes us feel big, competent, grown-up—all you have to do is look at those many indifferent stars and it all shrivels away—we are *all* children, out there, facing all those other things so immeasurably older and greater than ourselves."

Joe paused and studied Stella's face for a moment. "You look as though you are seeing ghosts. Just like I was hearing them, back there."

Stella fought the urge to laugh at the bone-headed and paranoia-fed idiocy that had decreed that someone like Joe White Elk was to be kept behind a wall of ignorance, when he was already more than half aware of it all anyway, and already arguably knew—through instinct, through whatever wisdom (natural or supernatural) was his through blood and heritage—more about the secret than the people who thought they were guarding knowledge of it from him. He wasn't Stella's patient—or 'subject' as Martin Peck might have called him—as much as her potential colleague.

"Thank you for sharing this with me," she said, feeling a real warm kinship with this man, despite the vast differences between them. "I need to have a quick consult with the people in charge of this whole thing—but I don't think that should take long. I'll call you, the *Juno* crew, back, when I'm ready. It's past time you were brought up to speed on what is going on. And perhaps it's more than past time you were all allowed to just... go home."

"That will be a good thing," said Joe tranquilly, brushing one hand, perhaps even without having been aware that he was doing so, against the talisman he wore. Whatever its powers were, whatever the powers it had been imbued with by Joe himself and the powers that it held over him, the thing had traveled too far, had been stretched too thin. Stella suspected there were limits, and that Joe, if he reached those limits and was forced past them, might end up quite a different kind of crazy than the authorities were afraid of.

He stood now, and gave her a small bow of respect as he did so, and turned to make his way to the interview room's exit. At the door, he hesitated, and turned back to face her again.

"Are they all right?" he asked, very softly.

"I don't know," Stella said, finding the strength in his own dignity and courage to offer him no more than the truth. "But I do intend to find out, and if they are not, to do what I can to fix it."

"That is fair," he said. "That is everything. I will tell the others to be ready for your return. I look forward to hearing what it is that you have to tell us."

The room seemed far emptier than it should have been after Joe White Elk stepped out of it. And in the silence he left behind, Stella listened to her own heartbeat, to the blood rushing through her body, and took a guilty, illicit moment to herself in which she wondered what exactly a star sounded like when it was singing.

Martin Peck might have been the designated liaison between Stella and the military and government juggernaut which appeared to be in control of the whole matter of the starships' return home, and the officer nominally in charge of the quarantine area and its inhabitants, but he was not the ultimate authority. He had his superiors, and Stella's crusade to have at least the *Juno* crew released from their captivity had to be sold to those. Before she could have the talk she had promised with the three *Juno* crewmen, Stella herself sat on the other side of an interview table, in a conference room that looked very much like the one in which she had seen her first presentation before diving into this situation in what seemed such an unconscionably short time ago, before a committee of high-ranking officers and functionaries who didn't look too happy to be there or to be put in a position of making the necessary decisions.

Martin himself, in full dress uniform, sat on the far end of the table; he looked uncomfortable, as though he was very aware that he didn't quite belong there. One of the other men wearing a military uniform, General Aristide Niarchos, was someone whose path Stella had already crossed once—he was the one who had chaired the original presentation, at the beginning of her adventure here. But there were three other people behind that table whom she had not personally met before the day that she was summoned to make her case before them—a man in a uniform not too different from General Niarchos's, and two civilians, a woman in elegant clothes who managed to look every bit as stern as the hatchet-faced military personnel surrounding her, and an elder statesman with silver hair at his temples and the kind of cleft chin that would have looked good on a leading man in old-fashioned action movies.

She knew their names and faces, of course—the civilians were Dag Nyland, the Minister of Information, and Premier Katarina Vasilieva, head of the World Council; the second staff officer was General Jose Camacho, who had (rather disconcertingly under the circumstances) acquired the nickname 'Diablo' somewhere in his checkered military past. It did Stella's frame of mind absolutely no good at all to be reminded every time she looked at General Camacho's face, which bore an almost theatrically appropriate scar, thin but impossible to ignore, from the corner of his eye to the edge of his sharp jaw, that she was literally here to make a case before the Devil himself.

Stella was outnumbered and outgunned. On her side, she had only Ichiro Amari, here to present his own findings on the *Juno* crew, and Father Philip Carter, who had conducted his own interviews with the three. She could only hope that they would be able to add sufficient weight to the proposal that the crew of the *Juno* be declared sane before God and man and be released back into the world.

Martin Peck might or might not speak up for her on the judgment panel. She knew she'd have to talk a very good game to get past an already half-raised wall. So far as she could tell, they didn't exactly have an endgame plan—but not knowing exactly how they wanted everything to play out didn't mean that they didn't have an excellent idea about how they didn't want it to go. The two Generals, in particular, looked as though they had been sucking on sour lemons.

The return of not one but both the starships to their home planet should have been a public relations coup of the first order, something that could have been extremely useful in firing up the populace, whipping up enthusiasm and goodwill, and there would have been plenty of credit that they could have claimed for it all, had everything not gone so potentially catastrophically awry. As it was, things had unraveled quickly and were still in the process of coming unwound. As far as Stella could tell, from things that Martin Peck had let slip, those who had the power to influence events seemed to be of the unilateral opinion that things could only get worse from here. The potentially disastrous possibility that any attempt at straightening the twisted story could dig a deeper hole for them, at this point, was a very real danger.

One of the few cards that Stella had in her hand was that they had *asked* for outside input, that they had hustled people like Ichiro and herself, and all the engineering and technical experts they had hauled in to look into the hardware problems, and brought them in—and now presumably they would have to listen to their opinions.

The flip side of that was that she had already taken stands she probably wasn't supposed to have been allowed to take, voiced opinions she wasn't supposed to have, and made promises she had no way of living up to on her own authority. All this, and she hadn't even started on the real problem, the *Parada...* insanity, although she bristled when anyone else used the term. This hearing was only the barest tip of the iceberg, dealing only with the *Juno* crew.

They had asked Martin Peck to provide his own report, first, and he had been giving that for the last ten minutes or so. Stella's mind was so full of her own thoughts and stratagems that she kept having to remind herself to stop and listen. Of all the people on that panel, he was the only one who could potentially take her side, after all.

When she zoned in on his voice again, what he was saying was encouraging.

"...in all conscience, and in possession of both data collected by my own team and then redone almost from scratch by Doctor Ichiro Amari of the research experts team you have gathered, I can only state that there is no further medical reason to hold the crew of the *Juno* in anything that can be called a quarantine any more. They have been kept strictly separated from the *Parada* people and no direct interaction has taken place between the two crews at all. There is no real way of knowing, of course, the exact timeline of how long it might have taken for the *Parada* crew to have reached the stage we currently find them in—but we cannot, legally and ethically, imprison the crew of the second starship for what would for all practical purposes be the rest of their natural lives waiting to see if anything untoward did happen to them in the aftermath of their own journey out into the reaches of our galaxy. I have in my possession copies of Dr. Amari's reports, which you all also have in your folders, and also a copy of Dr. Froud's report. She has suggested that keeping these three people—whom we should have welcomed home as heroes—in both physical lock-up and a prison of ignorance and disinformation could be the very thing that precipitates, if not the responses we were initially afraid of, then something just as bad. And that would be something that we ourselves would be responsible for, not anything that might have happened to them on a mission on which after all they undertook on our behalf. Perhaps..."

Stella stood up, the scrape of her chair on the floor suddenly extremely loud in that room, silent other than for Martin's voice. Martin, interrupted, looked over at her, and then nodded sharply, closing a folder that had been open in front of him.

"Perhaps Dr. Froud can give her own report in person, at that," he said, and Stella could read what seemed to be a measure of relief as he abdicated further responsibility.

"Well?" said the Premier, her voice a deep dark alto.

"I wrote it up and you have it and you know what I think," Stella said, having to clear her throat twice before she found a strong enough voice to speak. She leaned on the table in front of her, hard, both for support and to literally stop her hands from shaking. "But if you need me to stand here and tell you again, in plain language, I can do that. Yes, when I was first brought in and I first learned about the whole situation my very first instinct was that the two crews were not and would never be equivalent, which was the first mistake that was made here. They were separated immediately, and they were kept apart—there would be no 'cross contamination' of any sort, you decided, even though the *Juno* crew wanted, needed, to see the people they had rescued at such cost, to meet them, to speak to them. Initially at least you had no reason—from what I could gather—to ensure that this did not happen, but you made the decision to keep the two crews apart. And completely ignorant of what had happened to the other ship's people. The *Juno* crew, at least, thought about that a lot. It has affected them."

"They've been under study for some time," General Camacho snapped. "You've had, what, days? And you can come to sweeping conclusions already?"

"You brought me here as someone who could," Stella snapped back. "Your extended period of observation—and with all due respect, General, that wasn't as extended as all that in any event—was initially done by people who did not have the training or the experience you needed. You had a basic medical and psychological team, to be sure, and no specialists—but these people have been telling you for a while that, to the best of their ability to judge, the *Juno* crew were clean. But because you never told the *Juno* crew the truth—about anything—their 'quarantine' became a convenient excuse for you to hold on to them—because you didn't know what else to do with them. You have to realize that the moment the fact of the *Juno*'s crew's actual return percolates to the public you will have an uproar on your hands—they will want these people, they will want to own them, to celebrate them, to reach out and touch in whatever way they can the people who have gone out to the distant stars and have come back to tell the tale. Your problem right now is that you have lied to them, about a lot, and now you have to make it a condition of their release that they have to lie for you—or at the very least be prevented from speaking out at all for a very long time and perhaps forever about the thing that they have done, and the miracle they have accomplished. Because I haven't even begun to work on the *Parada* situation—there may be a lifetime of work in that, but you cannot justify sentencing the crewmen of the *Juno* to a life sentence of solitary confinement, simply because they are who they are, they were where they were, and they did what they did. They did their duty, ma'am, gentlemen, as they saw it, to the fullest extent that they were able. And now you owe them their freedom, and as much of the truth as you can provide. You owe them that much."

She took a deep breath and then hurried on, afraid she would be interrupted, cut down. "You said I had a very short time to make my decisions and diagnoses here—and yes, under ordinary circumstances I would have had a much longer, much deeper, much more intense relationship with any patient under my care. But I cannot justify taking a year to slowly and painfully make my mind up that yes, you can let them go. I am standing on my training, my knowledge, my experience, and my instinct here—I have spoken to each of these men, and it is my professional opinion that there is literally nothing wrong with them, nothing that you can use to justify keeping them locked away any further, and nothing that a dose of truth and freedom will not cure. There may have to be conditions for such freedom, that is for you to decide, not me. But the day you brought me here I took a stand for that truth, and I still believe that they deserve that. And that's why I promised I would go and speak to the Juno crew, all of them, in the aftermath of this commission's meeting. I strongly suspect that an existence that is too much longer endured under the present circumstances would break these men faster than any extraterrestrial shenanigans you are still afraid of."

"But the *Parada* situation..." General Niarchos began, and Stella lifted a hand to stop him.

"Leave the *Parada* problem out of this for now," she said. "We're talking about releasing Hugh de Mornay, Tyrone Kidman and Joseph White Elk to continue their existences as free men, and as heroes of Earth, no matter how much of the true story ever gets out there. I mean, they aren't the only people who know that the *Parada* has returned, are they? There are already more of us than that—the team you assembled, myself, my colleagues in this room, the others whom you sent to investigate the ship itself, the team that already dealt with the crews before any of us came on board, even people who were in the shipyards up there where even now the *Parada* still sits as far as I know or someone who happened to be on duty when the first communications from *Juno* filtered through when the ships returned to our system. All the people you can find who know about the fact that this happened... you can keep it a secret for a little while. But sooner or later some story will come tumbling out. Are you seriously considering holding the *Juno* crew captive until such time as an unpreventable leak from somewhere else trickles out from some hole you forgot to stopper?" She paused, looking at each of them in turn.

"All of us signed NDAs—but did absolutely everybody? Did you catch everyone in your net? Every comm operator? Every mechanic? Every engineer? Every janitor? Every pilot? Every orderly? And think about that—right now there are medical orderlies out there who know more than the *Juno* crew actually does. How do you justify that? You trust the orderlies more than you trust three men you yourselves hand-picked to take humanity into the stars?"

Stella was breathless and shaking when she collapsed back into her chair. She literally had to clench her jaw to stop her teeth from chattering. She had never in her entire life faced down even one such august personage, never mind four who now sat staring at her impassively. And if it had been about herself, alone, she probably could have never done it at all. But now, here, she spoke for those three men to whom she had spoken so briefly and yet each of whom had touched her in a profound way. It was a simple as that—they were owed a debt, those three, and if she was the one who was in a position to call it in then that was the way it had to be.

"You were magnificent," Philip Carter said in a low voice as he leaned to whisper into her ear. "Remind me never to get you mad at me."

Stella uttered a sound that might have been a whimper.

Philip touched her shoulder gently, and then rose to his feet.

"I can't weigh in on any scientific evidence," he said, facing the panel. "Perhaps one of you knows why I was added to this team at all—perhaps one of you is a person of sufficient faith to take the opportunity to ensure that the spiritual aspect of the situation was covered. And yes, I do realize that our time with all of the people we are supposed to assess and investigate as part of the task you have appointed us to has been limited so far. But I think you will find that we have all used what time we have had to the limit. I haven't had much sleep in the last week; I know that my two colleagues here haven't either. We don't take any of this lightly, and we certainly have no wish to make a difficult situation even harder. But what I can tell you about the *Juno* men, with whom I have also talked, is that while none of them are persons whose faith precisely matches up to my own I have found all these men to be, if you will permit me to use the word in this context, very special souls. All three of them have that sliver of pure nobility of spirit that could easily make a man eligible for sainthood, in a manner of speaking—but I do have to remind you that some saints got there through martyrdom. And you may not want to have your names become known, in the fullness of time, as the people who visited martyrdom on the crew of the *Juno*. History will have its say, in the end."

As he sat down, Stella surged to her feet again.

"Yes," she said, "think of history, if you won't think of the people. Everything that you have done so far has *already* changed the history books—because we aren't releasing the *Parada* six, or allowing information on their return to get out, if and when that does come out it's already a very different story from what really happened. And all that is irreversible—we're hip-deep in *that* big muddy, what is done is done, and we can't turn back the clock and make different decisions. But you have already layered so much secrecy on this that every tiny inconsistency in the story is going to have the conspiracy theorists working overtime to get to 'the truth'. And the truth will come out, eventually."

She saw one of the Generals stirring, and rushed on before anyone could interrupt her. "And it isn't like it's the first time that this has happened—we have plenty of precedent. We may all be dead by then, and people might look like they've forgotten all about it, but it took us a hundred and eighty years to find out who really shot President Kennedy, it took us almost as long to get to the bottom of the dirty bomb that took out Denver, we still don't know which of any number of theories about the death of the last Dalai Lama is anywhere near the truth, and after two hundred years people are still wondering about the *Parada* and what really happened to her. You're just feeding that particular beast with too heavy-handed a secrecy fiat. Tell what story you will about the *Parada*, to give us time to properly figure out what is to be done with her crew. But the *Juno* people have done nothing wrong, they deserve to know the truth even if you then tell them that they may never speak of it again or reference in public the astonishing thing that they have done, and they deserve to be released. We all know—and they probably do too—that the 'quarantine' may have been a necessary thing in the beginning but has been changing steadily into just a euphemism for something quite different."

She drew a deep breath, and actually delivered an ultimatum to power. "We are here to do what you asked us to do," she said. "We are doing what we can to get that done. But if you aren't prepared to listen to our recommendations when we reach an opinion, you may as well end all of this right now. Unless you are going to hold all of us in an open-ended 'quarantine' situation for the rest of our lives because you are afraid of what we now know, let us do our work or send us home. I, for one, miss my cat."

"Just exactly what do you propose we do?" General Niarchos asked. "I mean, we can all see that they're holding it together right now, in here, but this is a strictly controlled environment—can you guarantee that they are *not* going to fall apart as soon as they leave here?"

"Of course not!" Stella said, rousing. "How am I supposed to prove a negative? How can I make a categorical statement—at a first encounter, a brief association or even after years of therapy—that any given person won't develop some more or less marginal psychological aberration the moment they leave my presence? How could I possibly be certain enough that any one of you won't suddenly acquire a strange obsession with butterflies in the next five years, or an aversion to eating pasta, or a phobia about going out when the moon is full? The future isn't ours to guarantee. All I can tell you is what I think, based on instinct and experience and actual study of the situation we find ourselves in."

"But that situation is still our responsibility," the General said. "You have to realize that revealing what happened to the *Parada* is simply going to throw gasoline on a fire and we will never get a chance to figure out anything because we won't be allowed to."

"Yes, and while you're juggling all of that, the people you're trying to help fall through the cracks," Stella responded. "But, General, we aren't talking about the *Parada*. Not here, not now, not yet. We're talking about *Juno*. The *Juno*'s crew is being punished for a heroic deed, all while people sit back and figure out how to get a political advantage out of this. I understand there are probably going to be conditions—but you have to tell these people the truth. You *have* to. You cannot condemn them to permanent isolation from the rest of the human race simply because they are in possession of a piece of information you think might be dangerous. Perhaps, mostly, to the people in charge, at that, who might get held responsible for it all. With all due respect." She drew another ragged breath. "I said when I first came here that we needed to tell the truth—at the very least, to Hugh de Mornay, Tyrone Kidman, and Joseph White Elk. And I stand ready to do that. In fact, I promised them I would do that."

"You had no standing to make such a promise," General Camacho growled.

"You gave me standing," Stella said. "You hauled me in here, as an authority on the subject. I am telling you what needs to be done. I will do it. But these are three brave men who have lost their freedom for doing the only thing they thought they could possibly do under the circumstances. You cannot possibly blame them for any of what happened after, for things they could have had no knowledge of. The Captain told me that if anyone is to be called upon to pay any kind of price for the decision that he thought it necessary to make, it should be himself, and not the other two men. That is not the act of somebody who is feeling guilty, and it is not in any way an 'alternate personality'—you knew who he was before you sent him out there, and that you would expect him to make this kind of decision if one became called for. He is still a leader, and he is even willing to sacrifice himself so that the others can go free. You shouldn't make him do that, it just isn't fair, and it's an ill way to reward someone who has brought honor to humanity. These men understood completely the need for a period of isolation after returning from the unknown. But now it is time to end that. Past time. I understand that much is still unknown but they aren't in a position to help you learn any of it. Tell them the truth. Let them go."

"You're going to tell them anyway, aren't you?" the Premier questioned, the faintest hint of a smile curling her lip upwards.

Stella lifted her chin. "I made a promise to three brave and very sane men—still sane, for now. If at all able, yes, I intend to keep it."

"You do realize that there may be steps we could easily take to prevent that, if we thought it inadvisable?" The Premier said, and while the smile remained hovering around her mouth her eyes were very serious.

Stella actually had to swallow hard before she could respond.

"I am aware of that," she said, her voice sounding very thin to her own ear.

"And you are taking the responsibility for that stand?"

"Yes, Ma'am," Stella said. She hoped she sounded more emphatic than she felt.

Dag Nyland leaned in to say something to the Premier in a low voice, and she turned and glanced at the General on her other side; they conferred in low voices while Stella, whose face was flushed with heat and whose hands had gone so icy that she could barely feel the table beneath her fingertips, found herself holding her breath.

When the whispered colloquy came to an end, the four having reached some kind of conclusion, they all settled back into their seats, the Premier sitting straight-backed in hers like she was perched on a throne.

"We agree," she said, and even though she meant the entire committee it almost came out sounding as regal as her position in her chair already seemed to indicate. "And it probably should—at this point—best come from you. You will provide a detailed overview of the topics you intend to cover in this interview, and provide it to us; we reserve the right to amend the agenda, but we will not do so unreasonably. When an approved agenda is returned to you, you may schedule your meeting. It will be recorded, and archived. It will also be the last time that you will have contact with the *Juno* crew, or have any further input on their circumstances, barring any specific actions we, as the responsible authorities, might require of you. You will make *no* further attempt to communicate with that crew, or influence any future events concerning them. From here on, your only duty will be to concentrate on the six from the *Parada*, and to provide us with a full report on what must, should, or even can be done in that situation. Is that understood?"

"Yes, Ma'am," Stella said faintly. And then, because her blood was still up and she could not let this go without at least an assurance, "And you'll let them go?"

"We will consult on ways in which that can best be accomplished," the Premier said. "They *will* have to make... certain promises. But yes, we will make every effort to release the crew of the *Juno* to the rewards that all of their accomplishments so richly entitle them. Lieutenant Colonel Martin Peck will supervise and liaise, as usual. We will await your interview proposal."

Philip took Stella's elbow as she pushed back her chair and shakily walked out of the conference room, with Ichiro, after giving the panel a formal bow, bringing up the rear. When the door closed behind the three of them, Stella collapsed against the wall.

"You won," Philip said. "Hey, you *won*."

"A battle," Ichiro said. "Perhaps an important battle. But the war is still ahead and remains to be fought."

"Let her have the moment, can't you?" Philip said. He was smiling, but he was also very serious.

The door of the conference room opened again, and Martin Peck stepped out, all but running them down.

"I have to say," he said, after taking a moment to give Stella a long and not easily interpreted look that was equal parts annoyance, astonishment, and respect, "that I never saw this coming from you when I first met you, Dr. Froud. I misjudged you."

"She was strong right from the start," Philip said. "In that first stop in the Surveillance Room. I remember. I was there."

"Yes, but that was a quiet little roar," Martin said. "I'm not sure *I* could have faced that lot down the way you did in there, though."

Stella pushed herself off the wall, the hectic flush fading from her cheeks.

"Thanks," she said, "I think. If you'll excuse me, I have some work to do. You'll have what they asked for, as quickly as I can put it together."

Martin gave her a salute. "Ma'am," he said, and it wasn't a mockery, despite the smile that accompanied it. "I'll be waiting."

The demand to oversee Stella's 'agenda' proved to be a gesture, largely a way to pass on the torch of responsibility. She received the approval note in less than forty eight hours, which startled her considerably. The text from Martin Peck came through on her official comm unit, which bleated at her while she was hard at work at her computer terminal in the library, trying to keep busy with something relevant while she waited for a response.

You're a go, Martin's message said. *Amended doc attached. Make the arrangements. Let me know.*

Stella had paused only long enough to retrieve the 'doc attached' and scan it for anything she absolutely couldn't accept as being changed or deleted. All the important stuff was in there, however, and that was fine... except that there was also a message from the committee. A set of conditions for the *Juno* crew's release, something that she was to ensure they were informed about; she was also to make it perfectly clear that a full acceptance of these conditions was a prerequisite for the lifting of their 'quarantine'. This would be done—but it would be done under their rules, in their way. Stella had to catch her breath a couple of times as she read the carefully worded document, which never issued a direct threat but managed to make perfectly clear the prospect of looming consequences—ones that would be implemented without hesitation or regret if they were judged to be necessary. Ichiro had been right; she had won an important battle, but this document was not the endpoint. It was the next move in the war.

But all she could do at this point was speak the truth.

She swiped aside the document, opened a new contact, and sent a message to the officer in charge of the *Juno* group (copying Martin) to set up the necessary meeting as soon as that could be arranged.

They all waited for her behind the table in the interview room this time, *Juno*'s captain in the center and Tyrone and Joe flanking him.

They all looked professionally calm. But the atmosphere in the room was charged, and Stella felt the weight of all three pairs of eyes as she crossed the room and sat down in her chair.

"When we last spoke, Joe," she said, without preamble, "you asked me if the others were 'all right'. The short answer to that is no, they are not. And the reason they are not is the reason you three are still here. They were already... affected... by the time you brought them back here, as best we can make out. You have been watched, day and night, for as long as you've been held here, waiting to see if you would start to react the same way. Hoping that you would not. That is partly why they brought me here in the first place. To make that diagnosis. As far as that goes, it *was* quarantine—but not for anything that you thought they were holding you for."

"What happened?" Hugh said, calmly enough. "I assume, since you are here and you are telling us this now, that someone higher up finally decided that we had a right to know?"

"I said I was going to tell you the truth," Stella said, "I can tell you *what* happened, to the best of my knowledge, but not *why* it happened. Although I am certain enough, from what I have learned about them and about you, that you three aren't likely to have caught this by any kind of direct 'contagion', if you like—the reason they were afraid is that you two crews did share a similar experience and they simply can't trust that you won't go the same way. I think you won't. They told you I was a doctor, and I am, but not just a physician. I am a Psychometric Counselor."

"They went crazy?" Tyrone said. "The *Parada* crew?"

"That is not a word I use lightly," Stella said. "Have you ever heard of Dissociative Personality Disorder?"

"Like, multiple personalities?"

"Multiple souls," Joe said quietly. "Or maybe a single soul, broken into pieces."

"There are different theories," Stella said. "Both of those things. Maybe even some combination of them. Perhaps when a single mind, or soul if you like, shatters ... each piece grows a whole new self, as it were, while regenerating. And sometimes those pieces don't regenerate into blind copies of the original, but create versions of themselves which... address certain needs."

"Starfish," Joe said, with a slight nod. "Like starfish. Regenerating from a single ripped limb. If you ripped all the limbs off you might get that number of new starfish—but they'd be new starfish, different starfish, not identical to the one that had been ripped apart to create them."

"A soul is like a starfish?" Hugh asked, sounding a little perplexed. "So—the *Parada* people—they—"

"Something shredded those people," Stella said. "Could you tell anything was amiss when you first crossed paths with them out there? Because the people working with them think that it must have started back then, back in the ship. They became... different people. Collections of different people. Some of them more than seven or eight different people. Some of them more than that. It is stable, on the one hand, in that the personalities they now carry are fixed and they can be interacted with directly while the personality in question responds in predictable ways and can directly remember specific things. It is also very much not stable at all, because the personalities can get triggered by unexpected things and manifest without any kind of control by the... by... the original starfish, if you like." She grimaced. "Let me give it to you in more clinical terms," she said. "The six crew members of the *Parada* returned to Earth... in pieces. Or in multiples. Each of them carries a number of strongly defined individual personalities, some of which it may be possible to trace back to issues or events in a particular person's life or past, some of which appear to be without any known root—and both kinds are equally strong and present. Individual sub personalities respond as fully human people, consistently, and in a chronologically accurate manner. So far, so known, about the syndrome—but there are aspects to this that are unprecedented. The fact that all six individuals were affected at the same time and presumably through a common trigger, but as full adults, and not, as usual in such cases, rooted in some trauma from their childhoods. The fact that all the shared personalities appear to be fully aware of one another. The fact that there doesn't seem to be any 'lost time', which is something that has often been a big, not to say defining, factor in such cases." She shook her head helplessly. "There is just so much I don't know yet. The personalities that have manifested have been at least partially mapped and documented, but their origins—the exact moment of their manifestation—the reason they exist at all—we don't have answers to any of those questions. There is something out there—something that affected all six people in some significant and reproducible way because every single crew member is affected in the same manner. The personalities we have met so far range from entities chronologically equivalent to their own physical self's age, to those older than they currently chronologically are, to those younger than they are."

She paused, and looked straight at Joe. "Every single one of them appears to have a personality who claims to be between five and eight years old. And more often than not when one of those manifests it somehow triggers all the others. It's as though it is necessary for all of them to be out, present, and communicating at the same time. The splinters—personalities—fragments—sub-identities—appear to have means of internal communication inside each given physical host, if you like. They're aware of one another. When they switch, they... retain a certain amount of memory, or they are able to access another personality's memory if they need to. I'm not sure yet how this works. In cases I've seen up until now, a personality which is in control of the body is in charge of that body while it's 'out' and other personalities can 'lose time' over it—they are blacked out, unaware, not conscious, a personality can wake up in a strange place and have no idea how they got there because that personality wasn't in charge when the body arrived there. But that doesn't happen with this crew. It's like they're reinventing the syndrome from within. Not only that, they also have established pathways of interacting with individual chosen personalities in other hosts. There is a complex social organization there which we have only begun to unravel."

"That sounds intense." Hugh said. "The ones who are in charge of this whole circus... they thought this crew would... splinter... too?"

"Some of them are still not entirely convinced that you won't,"

Stella said carefully. "Having observed the *Parada* crew... they are understandably uneasy about what would happen if you succumbed to this... out there... after they let you go back into the world. Where they couldn't control it."

"But you...? You don't think...?"

"We have no idea, as I said, just how and why and how long ago the point of fracture was for any the others, or how long it might take to manifest," Stella said. "So far as I can tell, you three aren't showing any signs of such fragmentation. I can't tell you that you never will. But to the best of my knowledge and experience, I don't think that it's something that just randomly happens, say, in a starship, and that anyone who sets foot anywhere near a star drive is going to end up being fifteen different versions of themselves. That is certainly one possibility that might be put forward to explain what happened to the *Parada* crew. Another is something they found out there before you found them—something that might have affected their drive to, as best as I understand it, malfunction in the first place or made it cut out which you say it had done by the time you arrived on the scene. They're checking that out with the hardware—I daresay every inch of that ship is going to get a thorough examination—but there are a lot of things we can't answer right now. Some of those answers might take years to figure out. If we ever do. I told them that it is ethically indefensible to keep you imprisoned here any longer. And they agree with me, up to a point. They are ready to let you go. But there are conditions."

"I think I know them," Hugh de Mornay said. "But go on."

"Silence," she said. "The price is silence. If you step out of this place, you forget that you ever saw the *Parada*. And they mean *forget*. There is a way to block the memory, if necessary. They might actually prefer that. But one way or another... if you go out there and you are asked anything about your mission—where you went, why you returned, what happened while you were out there—you may not speak one word about the most important thing of all. Where you are involved, the name of the *Parada* doesn't exist outside these halls, and that ship's crew must remain dead as far as the world is concerned. You can never say anything about your part in bringing the *Parada* home."

"They want to take part of my mind," Tyrone said, barely getting the words past clenched teeth.

"Not take it. Not erase it. There are ways... but tampering with memories in that kind of permanent way is always potentially messy. I would not condone that, or perform that on you."

"They would probably be able to find someone who would," Tyrone said.

"Probably," Stella said steadily. "But it won't be me. There is another way. Not...take a part of your mind. Just put it behind a wall—keep it more yours, if anything. I can sequester it. I can do a hypnotic block. You are simply not going to be able to communicate anything about the blocked subject—not directly—not verbally, or in writing, or in any other form. The most heroic thing you have ever done, you can never tell anyone about."

She wove her fingers together, where her hands rested on the table before her, and stared down at them for a long moment before looking up again and meeting each pair of eyes in turn.

"They record these sessions, as you have to be aware that they do, and what I say now I say knowing that I am on the record," she said. "*I will not do harm.* I can put a block in place. I will do no more than that."

"I can give you my sworn word that I will not speak of it," Hugh de Mornay said. "But that isn't going to be enough, is it? Not for the people holding the keys."

"I would accept that, from you," Stella said. "I know I can take that from Joe, because I have a feeling that he already keeps his secrets close and this would not be a hardship. But you, Tyrone..." She turned to look at the engineer, flushed under his shock of red hair, and there was sympathy in that look, even pity. "I don't doubt that you would give your word. But you are too full of this thing. You're brimming with this memory. You might swear that you will never utter a word about it—but you could never have a conversation about this subject with anyone else, ever. Maybe you could cling to the silence in a formal situation like a media interview—but the moment you let that guard down, it would probably come spilling out in some form. It isn't that I don't trust you. It's just that... it would be more than you could hold on to."

Tyrone's eyes were actually full of tears. "But I don't have to forget it? If... if you..."

"I would never take that away from you." She hesitated. "Father Philip Carter—you met him, I know he came to speak with you all—I don't know if he told you this. He should have done, but you may have had other things to talk about. But he's also been reading up on the *Parada* people, and there are interviews on file with all of them—and Tyrone—Bogdan Dimitrov asked after you. Repeatedly. In several interviews. Not just him, the man who used to be fully and completely him, but at least two of his splinter personas, too. *They all remember you.* They all know what you did. It isn't going to disappear."

"I would still like to have been able to speak with him," Tyrone said. "Shake the man's hand and have a drink with him and talk about things..."

"Things that nobody else but you and him would even understand," Joe said. "I would like to do the same. But even in the silence, out there—we keep the memory, no? We may not speak of it, but we can carry it and hold it close and let its presence in our own spirit shape the course of our lives from here on?"

"Can we... at least see them?" Hugh de Mornay asked. "Before we have to bury them behind walls?"

Stella tapped her tablet screen, and pushed it across the table. "I have this."

The three men bowed their heads over the tablet and watched the fragment of a video that Stella had transferred there from copious quantities of material stored in the *Parada* data banks. It was very short, maybe a minute and a half, and it showed the six crew members of the *Parada* sitting around a table sharing a meal. Bogdan, the engineer, seemed strangely solitary, concentrating on his food, paying close attention to his plate—but Han Millgar was actually laughing at something with Alaya McGinty, who sat next to him, and across the table from them Lily Mae was fielding what looked like a double-pronged conversation with the Hillerman twins who flanked her on either side.

"Are they all... themselves... here?"

"That's one of the early videos they recorded, straight after they were brought here," Stella said. "They might have been. That might be the real people there. They didn't know about all the personalities yet—then—so it's hard to tell. With the Hillermans it's always difficult, anyway. But from what I learned of some of the fragments Lily Mae does look a little like Mamie there. Mamie is one of her 'people'. At least, that's what she calls herself. She's the one who keeps telling them things are going wrong, but is never believed until it's too late—the twins insist on calling her Cassandra."

"Is there any hope...?" Tyrone said, looking up, the expression on his face almost stricken.

"I don't know," Stella said carefully. "We have no means of knowing whether they've stopped fragmenting yet. I don't know how far that can go, without a complete dissolution of personality. But I've seen case studies where patients carried hundreds of fragments, and we might only be seeing the beginning of this right now. My guess, and it is no more than a guess at this point, is that it won't get that far. But any hope of them walking out of here as the same six people who first walked onto the *Parada*?" She shook her head slightly. "I think we're past that. They may never each coalesce into a single entity again; if they do, they may not integrate the way they fit together before. When something like this changes, it leaves permanent traces."

"Do what you must," Hugh de Mornay said calmly, looking up and pushing the tablet back at her. "I will not betray them, or speak of this to people who cannot possibly be expected to understand. But I won't promise to erase the *Parada*. She belongs in our legends. She and her crew. I will remember them. Alone, if I must."

Communication with the outside world from within the bunker that housed the *Parada* secret may have been strictly monitored, but Stella, Philip and Ichiro were permitted to watch live when the *Juno* crew was permitted to step back out into the world. Stella felt something constrict her throat as the door of a large white building opened. Huge crowds waited in anticipation, and a thundering roar of human voices rose to greet the first man who stepped through—Captain Hugh de Mornay of the *Juno*, freshly barbered, wearing his dress uniform, his eyes squinting a little in the sunshine but forswearing sunglasses which would have hidden his face. The roar increased, if that was possible, when Tyrone Kidman and then Joe White Elk followed him outside. Stella saw Joe touch his chest, and knew why he did it—he had brought his talisman home, or permitted it to bring *him* home, and the power that resided there, so thin, so nearly worn out, was starting to recharge now that Joe stood with his own two feet on the soil of his home world. He closed his eyes, briefly, as though he was saying a prayer, before he opened them again and gazed out at the crowds, his features relaxed into an expression of calm serenity. Tyrone, the only one of the three who did choose to wear dark sunglasses, was also the only one of the three to look tense, his shoulders hunched a little as though he was folding his body protectively over something very precious.

The men waved to the crowd—Stella could see the first ranks, as the media camera drones panned and swooped around, and people were screaming, crying, laughing, hugging their neighbors at random, children carried on their fathers' shoulders so they could have a better view, a forest of phones and tablets and cameras rising out of the throng to take any kind of photo that they could. There was an open walkway from the bottom of the steps where the men stood, cutting a swathe through the crowd, set apart from that space with barriers, like the channel that Moses supposedly once made in the sea; the crew of the *Juno*, the Captain a step ahead and the other two falling in abreast behind him, descended the steps and started down that path. Stella could barely make out anything coherent out of the roar and thunder of the crowd, but some things drifted through, when a drone camera swooped in closer and caught fragments of what was being shouted at the three who walked steadily down through the people.

Welcome home! Thank you! Wow! You're back! You returned to us!
Welcome home!

They were the world's now, those three. They would always be.
Their faces would be remembered and recognized from here on.

There was a press conference for a globe-spanning, dizzying
array of media representatives, after. The questions—some serious,
some deeply silly—came thick and fast, and the air was electric with
flashes.

"Are you glad to be home?"

"Profoundly," Hugh de Mornay said. "It is lonely out there. We
dreamed of blue skies while we were so far from them."

"What's next for you?"

"Give us a moment," Tyrone said. "I'd just like to get used to real
gravity again."

That was obviously a rehearsed remark done for effect—the man
had been in 'real gravity' for some time—but if Stella knew it was fake
nobody else did. That one was quotable, and would be quoted.

"Would you go back out there if they called you?"

"I would do whatever my world asks of me, if able," Joe said. "Even
go back into the dark. But going out again... you know what you can
expect, this time. And that makes it both easier and that much harder
to do."

"What would you say was the greatest thing you accomplished out
there?"

Stella held her breath for a moment, knowing that the true answer
to that question was forbidden for them to offer, and wondering
which of them would take on the burden of the big lie.

She saw Joe and Hugh exchange a long look, with Tyrone keeping
his own gaze on the folded hands that lay on the table before them.
Then Joe gave the faintest of nods, and it was the Captain who turned
to face the news throng.

"We survived," Hugh said, and that answer wasn't gung
ho or grand, it was a piece of simple truth, served up without
embellishment. He waited for it to sink in, and gather just a little

bit of silence as a reaction. And then, drawing a deep breath, he went on. "We learned that it was possible to survive the uncanny, the unexpected, the unspeakable. You have to understand that there is a price for that lesson, and that the price may not, indeed, cannot, be the same for any two people. Some of us pay more than others. But what we pay... is not something that is easily shared. Someday, maybe. Not today. There is a promise between us and the stars, and we may not break it."

He had skated as close as he could to implying that there was more, of which he could not speak, but even the harshest reading that could be put on those words by some General or a watching politician could not possibly be misinterpreted into his having broken the compact, or his conditioning. Hugh de Mornay had told the truth as best as he could without actually lying. Stella could see, from an almost imperceptible change in his stance, a slight relaxation of a stiffness he had carried in his shoulders, that he had chosen his words carefully, had said what he could say, and was now free of that. He could talk circles around this subject in the years to come—but with these words, in answer to the first direct question that addressed the thing of which he could not speak, he had actually defied every command of prohibition that had been laid upon him without ever having directly breached the conditions of his freedom. He was an honorable man, and his honor cut both ways. Obeying the orders of higher authorities and his own personal principles he had buried a seed of that unspoken truth into the ground of the rest of the narrative. The rest would take care of itself.

There was more, of course—so much more. The world celebrated for days. There were actual fireworks. The *Juno* crew seemed to have no respite at all from the full glare of public attention. Stella kept an eye on it all, particularly in the evenings, when she retired to her quarters and reviewed the day's unadulterated adoration of the 'star-men', as they quickly became known.

"There's a part of me that wishes I was out there," she said to Philip over breakfast on the fourth day after the *Juno* crew left the compound. "You know, sharing the party."

"You started the party," Philip said. "A good part of the reason that *they* are out there at the party is because you unlocked the doors. And remember, it wasn't a free ride. They had to pay quite a price for it."

"So did I," Stella said quietly. "And I don't think any of us are done paying it yet."

3.

Stella didn't really believe in coincidences. There were times, of course, when everything in the world seemed to conspire to make something turn out a certain way—but if she was honest with herself few of those occasions occurred in a manner where she couldn't trace at least a faint line of causality, even if she had to do so after events had played out. It was the way she saw the world, the way she saw a human mind function, the way she saw the human mind take the lazy way of explaining things it didn't want to dwell on too much.

Perhaps it was coincidence that she happened to be in the Surveillance Room when something odd happened on the screens, something that caught her eye and her immediate attention. It was the day after the *Juno* crew was released into the world's adoring gaze, but the *Parada* crew had not been supplied with any kind of real-time link to the outside world—it had been decided that they needed a more gradual introduction to a world two centuries older than the one they had left behind and the only one they remembered—and they would have had no way of knowing of the events concerning the other crew or that those three men were no longer on the same premises as themselves. And yet something drew Stella's eye—a reaction—both intriguing by itself and something that forcibly reminded Stella of Joe White Elk's words: *I heard children.*

As Stella watched from the Surveillance Room the *Parada* six were gathered together into a tight little knot in the middle of the common area. They sat on the floor, in a circle, their heads bowed so that they were close together, and they held hands—not in a way an adult would hold hands with another adult, but in the almost awkward way a small child would do so. In fact their entire body language had changed completely, and even the six-foot-nine frame of Hanford Millgar had somehow managed to fold itself up into the space that might have been occupied by a child.

A six-year-old child.

She snatched up her tablet and called up the *Parada* profiles which listed the known personalities which had been observed in each crew member. She found the captain, and scrolled down his list with a finger until she halted abruptly when she found what she sought.

Glory, presenting as a six-year-old girl self-describing as red-haired.

They all had them, the child personality. Every single one of them.

Half-watching the screen, waiting for the group to do something she could observe more closely, Stella looked up the other crewmembers.

Alaya: *Momo, presenting as seven years old, gender indeterminate.*

Bogdan (or, as even she had already started to think of him, Boz): *Jiminy, presenting as an eight-year-old self-described blond little boy.*

Lily Mae: *Coco, presenting as a seven-year-old girl.*

Jerry: *Gadfly, presenting as a seven-year-old boy.*

Rob: *Gem, presenting as a wheaten-haired seven-year-old girl.*

The children. All the children. All of them out, all of them together. What did Joe call them? 'The Children's Collective'.

"Well," Stella murmured to herself, tucking her tablet into the side pocket of her tunic and straightening, "Children. It *had* to be children."

Stella had always been a little ill at ease around children, particularly very young ones, although she had always been able to conceal that fairly well from anyone who wasn't really paying close attention—to the point that she had a reputation, in her practice, of being 'good' with children. But being 'good' with them merely meant that she had evolved a strategy to interact with them so that she could help a young patient through a difficult time. It did not mean that she liked them, or even wholly trusted them. Children were... difficult. It was just the crowning glory of this entire tough, unique, unprecedented *Parada* situation that it involved personalities that were this young.

She turned sharply before she could talk herself into changing her mind and marched out of the Surveillance Room, heading straight to the holding area where the six crewmembers were held.

The surveillance operator must have overheard her, drawn the right conclusions, and alerted the proper authorities—because Martin Peck met her in the corridor just outside the crew quarters.

"What are you doing?" he asked, standing firmly in her path.

"I have to meet them sometime," Stella said.

"Now?" Martin still questioned, not moving.

"You have a better time?" Stella riposted. "Look. I need to speak to these people. I freely admit that doing that freaks me out on some level because it... it doesn't feel real to be talking to people who should realistically have been dead long before I was born. I have come to terms with that, to the point that 'I need to speak to these people' has become something I need to do... soon. And right now, in there, I have an opportunity I may not get again soon, or be around to see it if it does happen. I don't relish this, or even particularly look forward to it, but something is happening in there that I do need to investigate. That's the Children's Collective in there."

"The what?"

Stella sighed. "I will come straight to you, and explain," she said. "After. Joe White Elk spoke of this in the interview I had with him— I'm sure you have that on the record somewhere, you can go find that particular section. But he only gave me hints, and here I have a chance to observe the real thing in real time. Please let me through. Before I lose this." Her grip on her temper slipped just a little—she didn't have all the answers and perhaps she never would but she was trying to learn, and having to beat her forehead against a brick wall or having to keep vigil outside a locked gate until the paperwork came through wasn't the way she would accomplish that. "Don't you understand? This may be the best way in I have got. And over and above that, I have reason to believe that these child personas might have been the first to fracture off. There is a lot I could be learning in there, *right now*—even if I could just stand around and eavesdrop! Would you please just start trusting..."

"You should make a plan," Martin said, stubborn and digging in just a little against the perceived attitude he was getting. "A schedule."

"This won't work according to a schedule," Stella said, still patiently enough, but biting the words off nonetheless. "Those people in there don't subscribe to your schedules. You're trying to impose order on a kind of chaos that I don't even know the fullest extent of. But this might be a beginning." She softened her tone. "Please, Martin. Now. Let me go."

He hesitated, but then she saw his jaw clench as his teeth clicked together. "I am responsible," he said. "For... for safety."

"Whose?"

"Everyone's. Yours."

"There are no actual guarantees," Stella said. "But if I am to make a connection this is a place to start, an opportunity that might not come my way again."

Martin's right hand balled into a fist, and then relaxed, in a gesture of resignation. He stepped to one side. "I'll be watching," he said. "From Surveillance."

"You do that," Stella said, slipping past him and on to the door into the crew quarters.

There was a permanent guard on duty outside those doors. The one standing there now stared at Stella as she defiantly flashed her ID at him.

"I have access," she said, irritated. She saw his eyes flick over to Martin, glanced over just in time to see him give a small sharp nod and resented both him and the guard for disregarding her rights here and colluding over her head on whether or not she was allowed entrance. The guard nodded and stepped away from the door—and Stella wasted no further thought or energy on him. She simply ignored him, reached past him, and slipped into the room which she had watched so often since she had been brought here but inside of which she had never been... and into the presence of six people she was fascinated by, frightened by, bewildered by, six people whose physical presence in this room with her she could barely believe in even when she was less than six feet away from them. She caught herself holding her breath.

The black woman lifted her head out of the circle to look up at her. Instinct—and all professional experience—would have had Stella address her by her real name, the name borne by the physical body she still inhabited. But this was not Lily Mae Washington. The eyes that met Stella's were wary, wide, and very young.

"Coco?" Stella asked softly.

The child simply gazed back at her solemnly.

"My name is Stella. Will you introduce me to your friends?"

"Okay," Coco said. She started by nodding her chin to her right, where she held hands with the hunched-over nearly seven-foot figure of the captain and said, "This is Glory. She's only six. She's the youngest of us. And that's Momo, and Gem, and Gadfly, we're all the same age. And that's Jiminy. He's the oldest. He's nearly eight. And he's always last. Always late."

Stella wasn't quite sure what that meant—late to what? To this gathering?—but she let that go, filing it away for further consideration later, and concentrated on what was happening in the moment. The bodies of the adult crew members sat cross-legged in a circle on the floor of the common room, holding hands. The eyes that rose to meet Stella's at every introduction were the physical eyes that graced the adult bodies. But in every single pair of them Stella could read only the children who had been introduced to her by these names. There was nothing else there, no trace of an adult mind at all, the only expression in those eyes an innocence, a childlike wonder, a wary but not frightened serenity, and a kind of wisdom and knowledge that had always been beyond an adult mind which made Stella's hair stand on end.

"Hello," Stella said. "It's nice to meet you. What are you all doing?"

"They're gone, aren't they?" Jiminy said, and Stella's heart did a backflip.

"Who's gone?"

"The others. Those others. Who were out there when we were there. Who helped bring us back here. They're gone."

"Yes," Stella said carefully, "they're gone. How do you know about them?"

Jiminy tilted his head a little. "They're just... far away now," he said. "When they first talked to us, they were close to us. And then they were in a different place, but still very near. But now... they're gone. We can't hear them anymore."

Stella took a few steps forward and sat down on the floor beside them, just behind the linked hands of Jiminy and Coco. To her surprise, they released one another's hands and on either side of her a hand sought one of her own. She was admitted into the circle, which widened to include her, and six pairs of childlike eyes rested expectantly on her.

"Where did they go?" Momo asked. "How come they left?"

"Can we go with them?" Gadfly asked seriously.

"Maybe. One day. But first there are people out there now who really want to talk to you about things. There is so much you can tell them."

"We can," Glory said, and even though it was still mostly Hanford Millgar's voice there was a sufficient difference in tone and timbre that Stella actually did a double take on the voice alone before she focused on the words that he had spoken.

"You can?" she asked gently. "Then will you start by telling me?"

"We don't know you," Jiminy said. But the hand in hers was not withdrawn. It was a statement, not a declaration of hostilities.

"Yes, we do," Glory said unexpectedly. "She's been out there. She helped the others. They knew her. She's a friend."

"Who said?" Gem said, lower lip thrust out in a pout. "They could have just done something bad and got punished. What about when we do something that we... IllogonIllogonIllogonIllogon..."

The gibberish word snapped the circle. Hands were snatched away, individuals shivered and re-formed. Lily Mae ripped her hand away from Stella's and swore at her in language that would have terrified the seven-year-old self of a moment ago. Gadfly and Gem—or the bodies that used to be them—uncoiled from the floor and, still uncoordinated in the new configuration their brain was telling them their bodies now wore, stumbled and nearly fell as they tried to gain their feet and retreat from the circle. Hanford

Milgar stretched out and groaned.

The last to leave, Jiminy, stared across the broken circle at Stella and said, "Not time yet."

And then Jiminy was gone, and Boz's face took a moment to rearrange, and a whole different person appeared to be looking at Stella out of his eyes. "You can't ask children to give you all your answers," this new person said, from an imperious height.

"Do *you* know the answers?" Stella said, regrouping quickly.

"Fucker thinks he knows everything," Lily Mae growled. Stella thought she'd seen this one before—Diana, was it? The wild-child from the streets, the feral foul-mouthed adolescent... who had some sort of special relationship to Boz...?"Fucker thinks he's a god or something. Calls himself Pearoon, or some weird shit like that. You know what? If gods are pretty much full of themselves and fucking wrong about everything most of the fucking time, then I guess he be one. But he'd better keep his fucking mouth shut about things he thinks he knows everything about."

"Another time, Diana," Stella murmured, getting to her feet in time to wave off an orderly who had come into the room and stood waiting warily just inside the door. Stella looked away to where one of the twins—she still couldn't tell them apart at just a quick glance— was just disappearing inside his own private quarters, with the door shutting rather emphatically behind him. But the other one had paused beside his own door, looking back. Looking back almost expectantly.

Well, she had to start somewhere. She'd take that as an invitation.

Diana spluttered something else laden with expletives at Stella's back, but Stella had already started to cross the room towards the waiting twin.

"So," she said as she reached him, "want a chat? Which one are you?"

He bared a set of perfect teeth. "You can call me Loki," he said.

"You can ask me anything you want," he added. "I promise I'll either tell you the truth, or I'll lie. I'll never do anything other than one of those two."

"Yes," Stella agreed dryly. "Most people do."

"Oh, clever," he said, giving her a mocking grin. "Of course, they do. But when it comes to me, all you want to know is how to distinguish between them."

"Are you going to tell me?"

"I know what you are, Doctor Fraud," Loki said, wagging a finger in Stella's face. "That's for me to know and for you to find out. Do you suppose I have a tell?"

"It's *Froud*," Stella said, "if you insist, although 'Stella' will do and I think I'd probably prefer it. As to the tell... I don't know. Do you?"

Loki smirked. "Of course. But I can fake it."

"You're his snark, aren't you?" Stella said calmly, leaning back and folding her arms across her chest. "I recognize you. From all the early interviews. Somehow or other you were always there when the cameras were on Jerry Hillerman—you were the defense mechanism..."

"Clever," he said again. "But not quite true. If you want to talk defense, you ought to go a round with Attila—we all have our warriors, and he's mine. As for the snark bit, you'll find that it's far too great a part of the man you might have seen interviewed as Jerry Hillerman, far too great a genie, to fit into only one bottle. You'd probably find a goodly dollop of it in the Fourth Wise Man—he's the book-learned one that is part of my crew. Some of it you'll find spilled into the other me. And a bunch of it probably went into Tweedle."

"The other you...? Oh, you mean your brother? What do you mean, spilled into... and anyway... who's Tweedle? How many of you are there rattling around inside that brain pan, really?"

"A hundred," Loki said without missing a beat, and then laughed— Stella had schooled her features almost instantly but he had seen her eyebrow leap and he knew he had startled her. "There," he said. "You get your first fork in the road. Am I lying, or telling the truth? Oh, and as for Tweedle... He's one of the ones we share, my brother and I. He lives in both of us. He's an arrogant little prick who thinks that he is basically the one true person that the two of us should really have been in the first place, and that he's better than both of us, by default. We try not to let him out too often. He takes over, and he annoys us."

"But you can't *share* a personality," Stella said. "I mean, did you have Tweedle around... before you guys went up there or did you pick him up with the rest of you when you all came apart?"

"You mean is it a twin thing,." Loki said. "Don't ask me. You're the Muppet master, not me. As for Tweedle... you figure it out."

Stella had to blink twice at that one, but the cultural reference was still there for her to grasp in the end, even though for her it had been a lot longer ago than it had ever been for him. Still, her surname meant that she was closer to the concept than some might have been. "Hey, Kermit," she snapped, "you're thinking Henson, not Froud. I'm more Goblin King than your average hand puppet. Keep that in mind."

He gave her a small salute. "Yes, ma'am," he said. He was still grinning though.

"How many?" Stella said, sharply, without preamble, and scored an unexpected hit.

"Twenty seven of mine the last I looked and three...*hey*." The smile slipped. "That wasn't fair."

"Was that a tell?" Stella asked innocently.

"Stop it now," said quite a different voice, and Stella blinked again. The switches were sudden, unheralded, and always took her by surprise.

"Have we met?" Stella asked quietly.

"They can be a bunch of unruly little boys, and they need sending into corners to sulk themselves straight." Jerry Hillerman lifted a hand and patted the back of his head, as though he was checking on the tidiness of a neat nape-of-the-neck chignon. "Edwina," he said, his voice a couple of shades higher than Loki's had been. "I'm den mother. I'm the adult in this room." The expression shifted, just a little. "Present company excluded, of course."

"So as the adult," Stella said, hiding a smile behind a hand she raised to rub her cheek, "what do you know about this shared persona thing?"

"Oh, Tweedle rarely listens to anybody except himself—he's usually too busy trying to prove that he is the superior breed, what the boys could have been that they had been born as two separate halves, he himself of course being the vastly better undivided whole. And that it's simply unjust that he was thus halved in potential, as it were. That the world would have been a better place if there had been only one Hillerman instead of two of them; he sees the twins as taking up *his* place in the world. The problem is that this 'whole' incarnation seems to have gathered together the worst of the two of them. He is basically quite unbearable, sitting in judgment on his own selves. As for the rest... Jehosaphat is too busy judging other people to care about himself, and when he's out nobody will talk to either of the boys— because sooner or later Jehosaphat is going to sniff at something and dismiss anything that anyone says or does as in some way unworthy or lacking in any demonstrable value. And insist on making a case for that position. He's an unpleasant man to be around for long. And then there's Murphy... the only one who can handle Murphy for long is Mamie, and that's because they commiserate."

"Who's Mamie?"

"One of the others," Edwina said. "Not my problem."

"Sounds like the universe knew what it was doing when Jerry and Rob were born as different people," Stella said. "Can you tell me more about them? The way they were before the *Parada*?"

Edwina raised both hands in a gesture that was almost helpless. "The usual twin stuff. The kind of thing that other people always found amusing or intriguing. They may not have shared headspace— literally—but they shared a girlfriend once."

"Openly? I mean—cheating and pretending to be one another, or did she know?"

"She knew," Edwina said. "I think. Most of the time anyway. They may look identical but they can be very different people. Which you can probably understand far better now than anyone ever could before."

"Why do you say that?"

"Because, sweet child, of the people who came out of them, whom you now get to meet in their own right. There are very few you can just swop in and out, if you remove the..."

"Remove the what?"

"Oh, that may be something somebody else can tell you about," Edwina said. "I'm just here as the hall monitor, stepping in and keeping the peace when things start getting rough. Go delve into Rob's gallery for a bit, why don't you, if you want more on the twin factor. I think Jerry could probably use a bit of time out, before he scatters enough to let someone like Tweedle through—and then you've lost them, Jerry and Rob both, for the duration. It's always a fight to get him to let go of the wheel when he starts steering the boat."

"I think I might like to meet Tweedle," Stella murmured.

Edwina looked down the bridge of her nose, like a librarian looking accusingly over a pair of spectacles which weren't there. "Oh, *darling*, you don't," she said. "You really don't. You probably *will* but you don't want to. I promise you he is a trial and a bore." She made shooing motions with both hands. "Go on. Go now. We need to be alone."

"I'm your doctor," Stella said, with a small smile.

"We aren't sick," Edwina retorted.

"Oh, I know," Stella murmured as Jerry Hillerman's body turned and slipped away into the sanctuary of his own private quarters and the door closed decisively behind him.

Rob hadn't given an indication that he would welcome visitors or conversation, but after Edwina's envoi Stella thought she couldn't lose anything by trying. So she took the few steps that led from Jerry's door to Rob's and hesitated for a moment trying to piece together the best way to announce her presence and request, as it were, an audience with the second twin—but even as she stood mulling it over the door opened and Rob Hillerman leaned on one side of the doorway, his arms folded across his chest.

"Uh, hello," Stella said.

"I suppose I was expecting you," Rob said.

"Expecting me? How?"

Rob jerked his chin in the direction of his brother's quarters, without speaking, and Stella tried to regroup.

"What, did Tweedle tell you...?"

Rob laughed—a short, sharp laugh, with little mirth in it. "I don't need *Tweedle* for that," he said. "Well, you'd better come in then."

Stella did, cautiously. "...Rob?" she assayed, her tone carefully neutral.

"For now," he said. "I seem to find it easier than Jerry does to hold onto the person whom I used to be. Yes, there are splinters—but I somehow... it's hard to explain... I can make them work together, if necessary. And then I'm me, the me I used to be, the me I am right now."

"Reintegration?" Stella said, her gaze sharpening. "Are you saying that you're able to reintegrate? Are any of the others..."

"I can't speak for the others," Rob said. "All I know is that Jerry's had his troubles. But in that sense we really are more different than we look. You know how you might have heard that there's always a fiery twin and a quiet twin, like a sort of fire and water thing? Well, he got the flames. I get the occasional flicker but I'm much more... quenched... than he is. And those parts of me that stepped out and sort of gained their own life... they're different."

"From what? His people?"

"Yes, but also from what I might have expected, when it comes to myself. They're... more me than me, some of them, to be sure. But some of them surprised me when they surged out and made themselves known. Some of them I would never have anticipated at all. Some of them were downright disconcerting."

"Jerry said he had twenty seven," Stella said. "Do you have any idea...?"

Rob's eyes went unfocused for a moment, as if he were doing an internal head count, and then he shrugged. "Hard to say," he said. "Some of them are fragments of fragments, just whispers in the dark. But if I were to tell you the ones I know, I can differentiate, the ones I can communicate with directly as if they were entirely separate entities... then eleven. Maybe twelve."

"Counting the three 'shared'..."

"Oh, those. No, and them. That makes twelve whole ones, and I really couldn't say how many disembodied bits of flotsam and jetsam that are my own, and the three that Jerry made it his business to burrow into from his end."

"You really sound..." Stella began, and then bit down the word she was about to say.

Rob just looked at her, a faint smile playing around his mouth. "I sound... *sane?*" he finished for her.

Stella flushed. "I was doing a lot of research," she said, aware she sounded defensive. "From what they think they know, the people who have been keeping an eye on you since your return—from what they've gathered—it's been pretty chaotic in here since the *Parada* came back. Reintegration—putting the pieces back together to recreate at least a semblance of an original self that fractured as badly as some did in this crew—is sometimes a possibility, but sometimes very much is not—and then things become... really interesting. You... you are encouraging."

Rob Hillerman looked at her in silence for a long moment. "What makes you think they—at least some—actually want to reintegrate?"

She was suddenly aware that she was on the outside, looking in, and that there were walls blocking her view everywhere she looked, even in places where she would have sworn with a certain degree of hubris that no walls existed for her. "Tell me," she said, humbly enough.

"There are things many of us carry that aren't part of the original mind, the original body," Rob said. "There are memories only some of us are ready to hold and to keep and to carry. There are memories that some of us literally don't share and have only the word of another of us that it was so—but even if we accept that word completely, and believe that other without reservation, it will still be their memory, not ours. It might well diminish it for the entity which treasures it, to have it diluted by a second-hand view of it that some other mind brings in—haven't you ever had a memory you didn't completely trust, something that you had a feeling happened a certain way, but you aren't quite sure, and so you can't find the certainty in it to call it really true, and so you eventually lose it, to that? To the feeling of 'I may have imagined this'?"

It felt familiar, when he said it, although Stella could not immediately produce a memory of hers of which it was true. But she could not help nodding. "Yes, I know what you mean."

"It's like that, except it's worse—because you are completely aware, you know what is happening," Rob said. "You know you would be losing something true, because there are reintegrating fragments which may not have never experienced it directly and so do not believe it is true, not really true. And so memory passes into dream, and is lost."

"You hold one," Stella said. "One like that. Don't you?"

"Not I, but another," Rob said, and then his eyes changed, deepened, Stella could have sworn they actually changed color and became a brown that was a shade more golden than Rob Hillerman's eyes were, flecked with stars. So did his voice, when he spoke again, a voice that was rich and strange, a voice that had recited volumes of beauty out loud. "*I carry it,*" this new entity said, and the tiny hairs on Stella's arms stood on end.

"Who are you?" she asked, almost hypnotized. She rummaged in her mind for the list of personalities they had recorded for Rob Hillerman; she knew her memory was inexact and incomplete, but even given those faults she could find no equivalent for the being who stood in front of her. And someone would have recorded him. This wasn't someone who was easy to miss. "Has anyone met you before now?"

"I might have allowed them a glimpse, but I do not think they really knew me," the new persona said.

"How could they not know?" Stella breathed. "Who are you?"

"I don't own a name. I don't need one. I'm the Poet."

"What is it that you remember? That you consider so precious?"

The Poet lifted his head and gazed with those great golden eyes somewhere beyond the four grey walls that held him. His hands lifted, like leaves caught up in a gentle wind, and his fingers curled, weaving patterns in the air.

"What we saw, no human eye had seen before," he said, and that voice was both whisper-soft and resonant like thunder. "The vast empty sea of stars lay around us, lapping at our ship, surrounding us, present right beside us and yet so far, so endlessly far away. There is a whisper of voices in languages we will never learn and never understand. There is a river of light, and an ocean of darkness, and so much life, and death, and eternity. It is not only bigger than we know, it is bigger than we can ever know, an infinity of mystery and enigma, with something always, always, just out of reach and out of our grasp. It may be unknowable, and it may be that the day we completely understand such a universe we simply cease to be ourselves and become beings made of dust and starlight and clouds of darkness, not understanding the thing that surrounds us so much as being a part of it...”

The eyes dropped again, rested on Stella, and they were brown again, only brown, only Rob Hillerman. Stella's eyes were full of tears and Rob reached out with a gentle hand to wipe away the trail of one that had escaped and rolled down her cheek.

“Do you begin to understand?” he asked quietly.

“I'm sorry,” she said, not quite knowing what she was apologizing for, and fled.

Stella had broken the barrier she had erected for herself, the wall of centuries that stood between herself and the people whom she had been called here to diagnose, to analyze, to treat, to help. Instead of avoiding them she now started every day with the *Parada* crew, sometimes even eating breakfast with them—with whichever personalities happened to be out at the time. Some of the fragments seemed to take delight in needling her and baiting her, and there were times she even lost her temper with them—but mostly she learned to adapt her own attitude to whichever persona she was talking to at the time, changing when they changed, to the point that Philip Carter asked if she was in danger of developing the split personality syndrome herself just by proxy.

“It isn't catching,” Stella snapped. “And anyway, I know what I am doing.”

“Really? You've dealt with this kind of thing before?”

“Yes! That's why they brought me in!”

“...to this extent?”

“If you're asking if I've ever been in a position of being a therapist to six people who just came back to Earth after what appears to be a mind-blowing experience out there in the cosmos, of course not,” she said. It came out more sharply than she had intended; perhaps he was right, and they *were* starting to rub off on her. She sounded rather too much like one of Jerry Hillerman's snarkier selves than she might have liked. She took a moment to wrestle down the spark of irritation, and brought herself back to a degree of equanimity in a couple of long deep breaths. "Anyway. I'm learning new things every time I talk to them. It's just a shame I'll absolutely never be able to publish this work in my lifetime. What about you? I know you've been spending some time in there yourself...?"

Philip spread his arms in a gesture that was equal parts helplessness and frustration. "I've met Hanford Millgar's Ephram, and Lily Mae's somewhat astonishing Sylvester," he said. "They're both priestly sorts, and they seem to be triggered when they see me there. I've actually had fairly high-level theological discussions with Ephram. He is, as you might expect from somebody as highly educated as his primary persona is, very erudite on things. On unexpected things, sometimes. Our good captain has called me on at least one point of doctrine which I had to make an actual effort to counter. I think Hanford Millgar started out Methodist, and then went non-conformist for a while—not identifying with any particular faith—but he officially adopted Buddhism in his late twenties, it actually says so in his professional biography. Either way, I am not somebody he might have considered suitable for his spiritual requirements at all. Sylvester..."

He inclined his head for a moment, considering. "I think Sylvester started out with Catholic trappings but then he got embroidered with all kinds of other things," he mused. "It comes through when he speaks to me. Sometimes he can spout orthodox dogma in the same breath as something that might be considered as dire heresy, and sees nothing wrong with either. It's like doing ecclesiastical mental gymnastics. But, again, not exactly somebody who might have wanted me as a spiritual counsel. As for the rest of them... the Hillermans might be lapsed Anglicans, but that shared quality of... of *Englishness*... is all that we have in common and I'm only half-English, at that. Alaya is a devout atheist. Neither she nor the twins have much to say to me at all—I mean, they are polite enough, although Jerry tries to get under my skin by being deliberately provocative sometimes..."

"Yeah," Stella said. "Jerry makes a career of that."

"But Boz," Philip said, bringing his eyebrows together in a puzzled scowl. "Boz, I cannot make out. From his vitals I know he is a bit of an outlier—he does call himself a Catholic but he's Bulgarian and that is, shall we say, an uncommon denomination there—it's a crucible of Orthodoxy, if anything at all, and the number of actual Catholics is minuscule. But there's something else there, too, some kind of overlay that goes beyond Catholicism as such—I think Boz is a rare if not a singular beast, and yet one closest to my own faith as I perceive it, at least in doctrinal terms."

He paused as if gathering his thoughts, then went on, "However, unless you count his Perun persona, which is a pagan god, he doesn't have any religious fragment that I know of—and admittedly that is something that could be taken as shaky because he is the only one in that group who appears to be actively avoiding me, to the point of being rude if I try to engage him in any kind of direct conversation. He'll get up and walk away if he can't shut me up any other way, just showing me a clean pair of heels. And yet... here's the strange thing about this. From what I have been able to glean from the data we have access to... Boz is the one who asked for a priest."

Stella looked up, startled. "I didn't know that,"

"Yes," Phillip said, "He was the only one who did. Directly. *Boz asked for a man of faith to be brought in*—and then he makes every possible effort to avoid that man or to say anything to him. It's like he wanted to make a confession but is in such despair over what he perceives as his sin that he is rendered completely incapable of even speaking it out loud, never mind asking for absolution for it."

Stella, whose own opinions on personal guilt and the absolute authority of a designated representative of an earthly church to confer absolution in the name of a celestial overlord would probably have been just as provocative to Philip as Jerry's needling, forbore to take the discussion further on that matter—but Philip did raise an interesting point, and she tapped her lower lip with the tip of her right index finger in a reflexive gesture that indicated she was pondering something weighty. Philip had seen the gesture before, and recognized it.

"What did I say?" he asked, with a small smile.

"Boz," Stella said. "He's something of an enigma. I think I may have exchanged a couple of dozen words with him, and a bunch of *those* were with Jiminy, back when I first walked into the Children's Collective. He was the one who insisted that they didn't 'know' me well enough to... I don't know... tell me a secret... and then, when they scattered, he was last to go and he said something weird... something like, 'Not time yet'. Not time for what? And you aren't the only one he avoids. He's part of that group and they protect him but he's bitterly alone, in some ways. Completely isolated. Remember when they said they couldn't split the group apart because one of them—one of the personas?—had threatened suicide... well, that was Boz. So far as I can figure it, it might have been Boris who precipitated that crisis, and Boris who might have threatened the suicide—come to think of it, I don't know if I've ever met or even seen 'Boz', the original one, the personality from whom the rest of them broke apart. He seems to take great care that I don't—he's always on his guard. Against something. Even Jiminy—even the child personality—is suspicious of someone he 'does not know'."

She shook her head. "As for the rest of them... the others, the original others... they may come out more or less often, but they come out. I've had conversations with Hanford, the original Hanford, the captain; I've talked directly to Alaya and to Lily Mae; Rob seems to be capable of holding the Rob identity together better than most of them, and can present as his own original self longer and more coherently than any of the rest. But Boz—when the split happened, *he* seems to have disappeared. There are only the fragments now. Or at least that's the only thing he shows anybody. The central core seems to have dissipated or is dissipating fast. That, or there are *walls* around it."

"Do you know they take turns with him, at night?" Philip said quietly. "One of the others stays with Boz when they all retire at night, until he falls asleep. That one is relieved by somebody else at some point during the night—sometimes there is more than one watch change a night—but it's always someone coming in and only then the one who had been on duty, as it were, leaves. They don't leave him alone at night. Ever."

"That's on the record?" Stella said, startled.

"Yes. Actually, the reason they might have mentioned it is that there seems to have been a spectacular meltdown of some sort right after they brought them down here and assigned private quarters, and Boz was left isolated. There's a report on that, on how it took two orderlies to hold him down, like he was having a fit of some sort. Apparently being on his own—being solitary—is something that he cannot bear. It was the others who came in and calmed him down in the end, after that initial incident. And it's the others who appear to be the only thing preventing a repeat of it."

"I think I remember seeing that somewhere," Stella said. "But I don't recall if they said *who* calmed him down."

"The rest of the crew, his..."

"Yes, but *who* were they when they did so? That might matter." The finger was tapping the lower lip again. "I have to go hunt that up. If that information isn't in the report—and it mightn't be, come to that, they were only just starting to get a handle on this at that point and they might not have even known to ask—maybe I can find those orderlies. Maybe they remember something that wasn't considered worthy of putting into the official record, or sounded too insane when said out loud so they never said it at all... I don't recall any other mentions of such a fit, do you?" She sighed with pure frustration. "I wish Ichiro was still here. Now I have to ask Martin Peck for information on the medical side of that."

"I don't remember seeing anything but then I wasn't really looking for it," Philip said. Whatever the situation ended up being, they don't try to stop it. It's tacitly permitted for the others to hold Boz's hand, metaphorically speaking, while he sleeps."

"There's something," Stella said. "*Something.* With the rest of them, they can switch from one persona to another, smoothly, instantaneously, sometimes between one word and another. I am starting to recognize the moment of change. But it's... I don't know how to explain this any better to you... it's *organic*. It's smooth, it's natural, it's just another soul that's put the actual body on and although it sometimes woefully doesn't match the physical aspect of that body it still feels as though there's a living connection there somehow, as though they are all independently alive even though they do have to share the same physical shell. Boz... it's just a different feeling. It's like his personalities are more like little wooden toy soldiers, self-contained, self-identifying, but completely non-organic, as though rather than being living boughs off a living tree they were whittled out of a dead stump and no longer hold a link to what the actual tree once used to be. He doesn't shift into a different personality so much as bring up the mask that he wants and then puts it on. I mean..."

She paused, for longer than Philip could bear. "What are you thinking?"

"The names," Stella said. "The names of the Boz personalities I know. They're... kind of... invented, you know. Like they were bestowed upon those fragments because Boz knew they had to have a name. So he gave them names—but only from the most familiar contexts that he could cull them from. I mean, Perun was a pagan god of the geographical region which Boz comes from. He would have known that name, and so he slapped it on that persona because it was the closest thing in his mind that fit. But even that isn't what I'm trying to get at—it's more like—I don't know—he came up with the names *first*, and then created a personality to fit them. I think his 'warrior persona', the protector—they all have one, and so does Boz, I've seen mention of this in his data—is Khan, which again makes sense because his geographical region would historically have had to do with the Mongol Hordes and so of course a berserker warrior personality would have a name that might belong there. Other names reflect a Hungarian root, or a Russian root, and all of that is perfectly consistent with his geographical and cultural background. And then there's the one called Celeborn."

"Balkan, too?"

Stella gave him a swift side eye. "Fictional, mythological," she said. "One of the elves from a twentieth-century fantasy epic by someone called Tolkien. You must have seen the movies."

"So he might have seen them? Or read it?"

"Probably. They were huge at the time he left."

"So the name matched a personality and he used the name to indicate..."

"No," Stella said. "I mean he has an actual persona who appears to identify himself as Celeborn the elf. It's as though Boz was looking for molds—or *making* them—to pour his shattered self into when he was broken into bits like the rest of them. But the rest of them simply split along fracture lines and all of them somehow acquired a touch of life—as though the soul split into—oh, we talked about this when the *Juno* crew was given an explanation, just before they were allowed to leave—what did Joe say? The soul is like a starfish—cut it up and each part grows another whole, another soul, not necessarily identical to the original but still, alive, living, existing in its own right. With Boz..."

"With Boz, the original starfish withered?" Philip said. He grimaced, as though he had just swallowed something sour. "So does that mean that it isn't a question of a single soul per person in there that's in danger of being lost—it's a plethora of souls, it's an entire congregation, if you like? Or has the original soul been destroyed by this and I am no longer qualified to judge the situation at all?"

"And what about Boz?"

"Yes, what about Boz?" Philip echoed. "I don't want to force the issue there. But I am afraid for that man."

Stella stared at him with wide eyes. "So am I," she said. "Oh, so am I..."

It was unusual for a therapist to discuss a patient's situation with the patient herself, treating her as an equal and a colleague—but one of Alaya's fragments, Susan, appeared to have appointed herself as a practicing psychologist. That was not unexpected, perhaps, in that Alaya's medical training included a full psychometric module—but Stella was still startled the first time Susan emerged and insisted on crossing metaphorical swords with her, seated across the table in the common area of the crew habitat. This was the day after Stella's conversation with Philip, and she was still mulling around some of the things she had discussed with him. Susan appeared completely aware of the complexity of the situation that she was a part of and of her own role in it, and it turned Stella's head inside out to realize that she was actually discussing one of the most stubbornly difficult syndromes to offer assistance with and to understand... with someone suffering from that syndrome, in real time, from within, as it were. This was in one way the most insane thing she could possibly be doing because she was literally enabling what some schools of thought believed to be a strong patient delusion—and in another way it was the holy grail of therapy because she was gaining direct insights from the inside, as it were, as to what the syndrome was, what it did, how it worked, how it affected the patient herself.

"I had never met one myself," Susan said, leaning forward earnestly and resting her weight on the elbows of her crossed arms on the table before her. "I mean, I'd read about it. One does. It was *fascinating* stuff. I didn't spend too much time on it because—well—how likely would it be that it would matter? And now—this. Me. Here. Now. This."

"So do you consider yourself Alaya, in any way...?"

"Inasmuch as she was the one who did the initial reading on this subject, inevitably," Susan said. "Or you might posit that it was I who did the reading all along, because *I* carry the direct memory of this. Not any of the others. Joan might, at that, because she is just that kind of bookworm—but for her it was just a fascinating subject, not something that was worthy of study or exploration as a medical issue. I mean, some of the others are too young to begin with and would never have understood at all, but..."

"So how do you explain to them what's happening?" Stella said. "I've seen personalities simply *switch*, on the fly—who controls that, inside?"

"It depends," Susan said. "I sometimes make my own observations when it comes to my crewmates and I think that all of us have different methods of coping with what's going on in here." She lifted one languid hand and tapped her temple. "I think some of us are better at it than others."

"I'd say so, from my perspective," Stella said. "I mean, someone like Rob Hillerman..."

"Yes," Susan said. "He is still there—Rob himself, I mean—and I think very much in charge. His people emerge in a... controlled manner, if you like. It's as though there's a gate, and a gatekeeper, and a... what do you call them? Fragments? Personas?... one of the people inside... they have to have a password, or a secret handshake, or certainly *permission* of sorts to come out. With someone like Lily Mae... it's more chaotic. It's triggered by a situation or a context, sometimes, or even just by being in the company of one of the other personas. She—well, the part of her that is Diana—and Boris feed off each other—when Diana turns up, Boris immediately does. It's a double act. And it isn't as though those two particularly like each other. They've come to blows several times. I mean, just in terms of their physical bodies, he's got almost six inches on her and far more physical strength, but she makes up for it in agility and pure viciousness. Diana doesn't pull punches, or fight fair."

"Where did Diana come from?" Stella asked, diverted. "Lily Mae was never that kind of street child in her life so where is she pulling this from?"

"We talked, back when the crew was first assembled," Susan said. "Alaya and Lily Mae did, at any rate. From what I remember Lily Mae grew up in a big city—did she say she was born in New York?"

"Yes," Stella said, "but in a nice nuclear family, even though not a well-heeled one, and as far as could be ascertained fought hard to do well and leave all that behind her. And she did, when she was quite young. She didn't have time to be a Diana in the mean streets, so it isn't a personal experience. She got it from somewhere, but not from her own life."

"I think she said something about her grandmother being... but I don't remember, not in detail, and I don't want to make things up."

"What about you? Your people? You've got, what, nine on record? Ten?"

"That you know of," Susan said with a smirk. "I'd say, conservatively, maybe fifteen. Seventeen. Something like that."

"So how come only a handful get to come out?"

"Oh they *all* come out," Susan said. "Not all of them are sentient enough to be allowed out on their own but even they get a chance, under supervision."

"Is there one of those out now?"

"Of course not, I'm talking to you," Susan retorted. "I couldn't carry on a conversation like this with *two* of me peering out of my face. No, not now. But sometimes."

"How does that feel? To have two people in your head? Do you... think different thoughts?"

Susan considered this, her head tilted to one side. "N-no," she said at last, "or at least, not at the same time. It's a little bit like... having a pre-verbal toddler in your charge. You kind of let her blunder about and explore, but you stand ready at any time to snatch her up and put her away if she looks like she's about to hurt herself. Do you have kids? You know what I mean?"

"No kids, just a cat," Stella said, and an unlooked-for stab of missing the cat she had left behind on the premise that she would be away for only a few days brought a sudden prick of tears to her eyes. But she blinked them away and met Susan's eyes again. "I never had kids—I could say that I just haven't had the time, or hadn't considered it a priority, or even that I often find children a somewhat strange and alien species anyway. But I get it. It's a protective thing. But how young is too young? I know of several teenage personas amongst you lot, some young teens, some older, but you know teens, they all think they're all grown up thank you very much and you can just stop interfering with them—those—"

"Those fend for themselves," Susan said airily. "One of mine is seventeen. Another is twelve going on forty. You don't waste energy riding those with a tight rein. We all make mistakes and they're entitled to make their own."

"So what's the youngest that you know of?"

Susan's eyes hooded. "You know the answer to that," she said. "And no, Momo isn't about to be allowed outside alone with you, without the others."

"All right," Stella said, "although you know I would not harm her."

"That isn't the issue. You couldn't harm her, If you tried she'd retreat and it might be Grub you'd have to deal with—she's another teenager, but not a nice one—or even the Red Empress..."

"Is that your protector?"

"The Red Empress is the Red Empress," Susan said. "You can't hurt Momo. But you also can't have her. The young ones... are special. All of us have that child. And it's us... and it's more than us."

"I don't understand," Stella said patiently.

"Good," Susan said, sounding very satisfied with herself. "It leaves you some things to think about."

"All right," Stella said, lifting both hands up to signify surrender. "But tell me. It seems that all of you emerged with a whole muddle of different aspects—different people—but all of you have at least two personalities that are pure avatar—the child, and the protector personality, the inner warrior—do you think any of the others might map onto one another?"

"That's hard to say," Susan said. "There are similarities, of course—but I don't know that they are significant in statistical terms—they aren't made up of a bunch of building blocks that add up to some human cliché. They're all real, unique, and if they happen to resemble one another—different personalities from different origin people—that's just being human, it's not something you can make a thing out of."

"Except those children...?"

Susan stood abruptly, her brows pulling together into a scowl. "Leave the children alone," she said. "The children aren't for you. Not now, anyway. Not yet."

Stella continued to explore conversations with as many personalities as she could tease out, but despite the almost superstitious qualms she'd had about speaking with the *Parada* six she found that what she treasured the most were those rare occasions when she could connect with the person from whom all the others had split, any kind of an extended stretch when she could interact with or without the other personas singly or collectively chipping in or taking over. With some it was more straightforward than with others—Rob Hillerman was an easy one, when she could corner him; his brother was trickier; and the *Parada*'s captain was a prize, when she could rummage out the original personality and have a conversation with Hanford Millgar as fully and completely himself—the original Hanford Millgar, the man who had gone into the galaxy as the captain of the *Parada*. Stella would take what notes she could in the conversations she had with any of the multifarious personas that now inhabited the crew—but not when she found herself in the company of the captain. She would take no notes at moments like this, conscious of actually having a direct conversation with a great man she admired and respected, and she was taking no chances of triggering any interference at all.

"Did you know," Han Millgar said conversationally, on one of those occasions, "what the original name of the *Parada* had been, when she was first commissioned?"

"If I did see it somewhere in what's been written up about her, I don't remember," Stella said.

"They wanted to call her the *Leviathan*."

"So what happened?"

"Partly, me," Han said. "Call it superstition. It sounded far too close to *Titanic*, and I couldn't help wondering what kind of interstellar icebergs awaited out there. I made my feelings known—but I wasn't the only one to have that thought, I suspect, because they yielded on it far too easily."

"So what does *Parada* mean?" Stella asked curiously. It was an unusual name but she hadn't researched its origins and it hadn't occurred to her to try—now she wondered if there was some deeper meaning to it that might have colored its eventual destiny. "And who did give the ship that name?"

"Who finally chose it I don't know," Han said. "And as far as I know, one of the meanings of the word is exactly what you think it means, a parade—but whether someone had delusions of grandeur about what she would deliver, and called her after a celebration that hadn't happened yet, that I couldn't tell you. In some ways, if so, they were under a greater weight of hubris than if they had kept the original name after all—at least we were anticipating icebergs, with *Titanic*, unlike just expecting smooth sailing and a triumphant return to, well, a parade. But by the time the name was changed... it was getting too close to finalization, the whole process, and the name was what it was—once it was announced that was that and after that it didn't matter anymore. That's what the world knew her as, only that. There *was* no other name. Still, I wondered about it, once we crashed out there and drifted out in those oceans of stars. If there was an iceberg I steered the ship into, I never saw one, I never knew what I hit."

"You can't take all the responsibility yourself," Stella said.

"If you ask Boz, I can take no responsibility at all," Han said, "because he'll tell you he was the engineer and the drive was his problem and if things went wrong then it had to be his fault. He's single-minded on that, almost pathological about it. No matter that we all went out there knowing that we knew nothing—believe me, every single one of us was aware of the fact that we might have been painted as the heroes who blazed the way for the human race but that we were also, inevitably, six glorified guinea pigs being hurled out to see what would happen to us out there. Lily Mae said, and then bit down on it hard but it was too late, that she felt a little like Laika the dog, being sent to orbit the Earth, and wondered if the same thing didn't lie in store for us."

"What? Instant fame and then grim death? That was a little less than optimistic."

"She always had the knack of seeing the cloud inside the silver lining," Han said. "But you'll know all about that already."

Stella could feel him slip away. This was a different voice, a different tilt to the head. She recognized him: Hal. The young brash self-assured womanizing ass who could be counted on to hit on anything in skirts, and who had already demonstrated that Stella's own unprepossessing physical looks, or the fact that she was so much older than the 20 years he claimed, counted for nothing against the fact that she was female, and someone other than the limited candidates with whom he was customarily confined. Still, she could only hope that she could pull him back, somehow. If she could, perhaps the Captain might return... "How do you mean?" she asked, keeping her tone exactly the same as she had used hitherto.

But it was already too late. "Oh, you've met Mamie. Our Cassandra." His face had changed, a corner of his mouth lifting, a spark coming into his eyes. "I'd agree with her. Just for the hell of it. Because she'd be *so* grateful for it, and I'd collect my fee later. You *know*." He stepped a little closer to her, lifting a languid hand to smooth back a wayward strand of hair from her face. "But it was always so *difficult*," he said. "You know, when she'd suddenly go all feral street-child on me, and I'd go away with scratch marks on my neck like I'd been wrestling a spitting wildcat. And it was *never* against her will. Not when we started playing. Not ever." He smiled, in a way that a 20-year-old who thought the world of himself smiled when he was absolutely certain that he could not possibly be wrong about that. All the confidence in the world, and all the finesse of a sledgehammer.

Stella squirmed away from him. "No, you know the rules."

"Aw," he said. "If only you weren't so stuck on the rules."

"Are you sure the captain isn't still in there somewhere? Please?" Stella said. Sometimes that seemed to work, when the personalities became too agitated and started switching around too fast.

He considered that for a moment, and then his smile widened a little. "Nah," he said. "Don't think so. He's had his turn today. Now I'd like to play a little."

"Well, then, not with me," Stella said. "I'll catch you later."

He stuck his lower lip into a pretend pout, but didn't follow her as she backed away. She had already had to slap him twice—she, Stella Froud, raised her hand to Captain Hanford Millgar of the *Parada*—but young Hal sometimes had to have a point made physically obvious to him, and at least the lesson seemed to have penetrated. He didn't try to press his luck again.

Stella retreated, but Hal had the last word.

"Oh," he called after her, his voice far too innocent and guileless to be either, "I know what you want to talk about. And he knows more about icebergs than he's willing to let on."

"What do *you* know about them?" Stella challenged, a safe distance away.

Hal smirked. "Enough. I could tell you, you know, if you wanted. *Really* wanted."

But Stella had dealt with far too many boys who were using weapons they didn't really have to win a conquest, and who couldn't deliver on promises, after. All Hal knew was that *the captain knew*. He was perfectly willing to use that as bait. But Stella would not hear anything useful from Hal in pillow talk in the aftermath of dalliance, even if it was ethically permissible for her to go there at all or physically possible for her to forget that the body the gangly young would-be Casanova inhabited so loosely actually really belonged to a man who— in Stella's own cognizance—might have looked like a tall, well-built man in his thirties but was, to her, a two-hundred-year-old historical figure and a larger-than-life hero of her culture and her race. Leaving aside completely her role as a doctor in this context, young Hal and Captain Hanford were both far from being her equals to begin with, albeit in diametrically opposite directions—one of them too much of a child who thought himself man enough to make a play for a woman out of his league, and the other a man who was so completely out of that woman's league that they might have been different species.

"I'll ask him," Stella said, "the next time I see him. Gotta go now. You take care."

She edged away towards the door of the common area and Hal watched her go, Hanford Millgar's tall frame somehow folded into a gangly barely post-adolescent slouch and his eyes, under a pair of eyebrows lifted in open appraisal, looking her up and down in a manner which he considered to be properly lascivious.

Hal was a problem. Every time she talked to any of Hanford Millgar's people she usually ended up being chased away by Hal, who inevitably surfaced, sooner or later, and insisted on putting the moves on Stella as though he thought it was his bounden duty to do so. Hanford—the original Hanford—or one of the other personas sometimes emerged to quell him and restrict his access to outside contact—but the longer Stella spent with the *Parada* six the more divergent and self-identifying the various personas became, and the less certain she was that there could ever be a way back to a reintegration for any of them.

There were still only six adult human bodies penned up in the crew habitat, but the place was getting increasingly crowded with souls. It was as though the fracture, once it happened, was self-perpetuating, that the individual afflicted just didn't know how to stop the disintegration—or even, in at least one instance, wanted to try. Susan, the psychology-minded persona in Alaya's body, had a theory for that. Stella couldn't help feeling guilty about discussing anything about this subject with Susan, who was an integral part of the problem, but also, paradoxically, jumped at every chance when Susan emerged to talk about the matter. Philip had described the impulse as the rare chance a white blood cell had to talk about a bacterial invader, and Stella had been both offended and entertained by that comparison—but he had a point.

"It's simpler to delegate," Susan said, on the subject of the problem of Hal. "The burden of total responsibility is shifted. Now it isn't the single solitary central 'you' that is responsible for everything you do. Now you have individual fragments which are in charge of individual things, and it's each fragment that has the fragmentary responsibility for that single thing. The others can simply—if you like—throw up their hands and declare that it's not their monkeys."

"Their monkeys?... Oh. Not their circus, not their monkeys?" Stella queried

"Exactly," Susan said.

"But it's still a circus," Stella said. "And a more chaotic one than just keeping it all together in one personality. Now you have to fight internally to get access to the outside world at all. And if you don't get to..."

"Yes, but you see, that also helps," Susan said. "If you *don't* get that access that means it wasn't you who screwed something up."

"It still affects the body," Stella argued. "The body all those personas share. If someone screws something up, as you so elegantly put it, badly enough to hurt that body, it very much *is* your circus. You all suffer for it."

"Yes," Susan said patiently, "but we aren't all responsible for it. Hanford Millgar has a personality which is young, brash, invincible, and thinks he's irresistible to anything of the female gender—it might be something that was once part of Hanford himself and more or less successfully controlled, or hidden, or suppressed by a more 'evolved' part of his personality—and back when that part of him was only a jigsaw piece in the complete personality that was something he himself had to cope with, and deal with, and take responsibility for the consequences of his actions when he slipped up enough to allow it to control his baser impulses. Now, 'Hanford Millgar' is no longer responsible for the actions of the entity you know as Hal. If you talked to Hanford about that, he couldn't apologize for any of that, no matter how much that original identity might feel that he needs to or wants to. It quite simply isn't him who's doing any of it. It's Hal. It's a different person altogether."

"I thought you said you could communicate internally—I mean, between those of you living as part of the communal personality in a body that used to belong to any one of the *Parada* crew...?"

"We can—it depends on the coherence and cohesiveness of the fragments involved—but what of it?"

"Well, isn't there an internal, I don't know, consensus, agreement, in the end? Because otherwise—if every fragment is on its own and has individual wants and needs and plots for actions which deliver desired ends, aren't you all pulling in opposite directions? Is there a point at which that cohesion—the single-person origin—simply collapses... and what happens then?"

Susan considered that for a moment. "I don't know," she said. "None of us have quite got there yet. This may yet be a terminal disease—for the body, anyway—and if the body goes I am not sure what happens to the multiplicities of consciousness that now crowd the inside of it." She paused, pondering. "I told you, all of us are responding differently," she said at length. "Speaking for myself, all I can tell you is that I can handle it. For now. It's manageable."

"But you don't have a Hal."

"I have other issues," Susan said. "There's Grub, and there's Aidan, and there's Calamity. Any one of them could take actions that endanger this body, at any time. And I would have little to say in the matter if they were controlling the body at the time. It would be..."

"It would be their responsibility, yes," Stella said. "Can you... can any of you... actually *wrest* control, if you want to? Or need to?"

"Any of us can *hide* if we want to," Susan said. "And there are circumstances where immediate protection is necessary—which is why we have all got what you call a 'protector' figure, a warrior who can take over and preserve us in case of danger—in which case I suppose yes, that particular persona *does* get immediate control of the body and does what is necessary—I suppose you can call that as the protector personality 'wresting' control, if you want to. And certain personas are triggered by other specific situations. But if you're asking if any one of us can consciously step up and take over while another persona is in control of the body—absent external stimuli—that would be taking responsibility." Susan smiled, just a little, the corners of her mouth curving upward just the tiniest fraction, but her eyes stayed frighteningly serious. She looked at once smug and afraid. "That would mean consciously making the choice to subsume again, to cede control of the body's vehicle to a single driver. Some of us... might no longer be able to make that choice."

4.

"The things I talk about with these people..." Stella said to Philip, her voice dropping off. She was tired. They were eating a meal that passed for a late dinner, after another couple of days spent trying to get to a solid vantage point from which she could professionally assess, tabulate, and diagnose her six chaotic charges.

"What kind of things?"

"I got into conservation and climate change with a bunch of them," she said. "First I had to pick up the pieces when I talked about the ramifications of the sixth great extinction event with Alaya—that was still only beginning to have an impact, when they left. But now I had to tell her that it's been decades since the last wild polar bear was alive out there, or the last wild lion, or the last wild elephant, and we won't even talk about a myriad of lesser species that are less iconic and less cared about. Alaya went straight into Lilibet and I had to sit there desperately comforting the devastated twelve-year-old with a bunch of half-truths and optimistic happily-ever-afters most of which I was using as a Band-Aid on a wound that I had just inflicted myself."

She absent-mindedly put something in her mouth. She probably could not have identified it if anyone had asked her what it had been.

"Then Rob Hillerman started asking about global warming—again, something that we were barely beginning to get a taste of when they left—and I had to explain about Category Eight hurricanes. Then Boz—or at least, him in the guise of Leonid the Professor—began to ask really technical questions about things when I finally got through to him that we'd had a thriving colony base on the Moon and Mars for years. And then Jerry Hillerman was reading a book published the year after the *Parada* left, about the state of a particular group of low-lying islands. I told him that those islands have been under water for a hundred years now, and Jerry couldn't get his head around that. They can't just be gone, he insisted, and then wanted to have something more recent, and I had to look up stuff that has been published in the last twenty years or so just to get him up to speed—and then Han got into it, or at least Cap did, the 'bad guy' captain persona, and got Jerry to go all Fourth Wise Man on him...Have you noticed that only the twins have descriptive personalities? Everyone else has actual names, or at least personal nicknames—but only the Hillermans disdain that completely and go and *describe* the personality instead...?"

"That's enough coffee for you," Philip said, laughing. "You're starting to sound disjointed."

"There's so much disjointed stuff in my head that I am not at all sure I can ever connect all the dots again," Stella said, taking herself in hand.

"You're in danger of becoming them," Philip warned. "Did anyone ever tell you that you're entirely too empathetic for this job? You heal by understanding, by sharing, but sharing *this* could leave you in the middle of the briar patch with no way out. Be careful."

"I'm always careful," Stella said. She didn't consider herself to be lying although she knew she wasn't telling the whole truth either. There was something to what Philip had said—but empathy was partly why she was so good at what she did. If she lost that, she'd lose a vital connection with the people she was trying to help and heal. She brushed that aside and went on.

"The thing is, I feel as though I ought to be an expert in a dozen different subjects, in order to talk them through things. I mean, every time I think I've come to terms with it I collide with the fact that these people literally haven't seen this planet for two hundred years. It might as well be a different world, for all they know. And since they've been back—well—they were in *here*, haven't they? All they saw of Earth was a glimpse of the globe, perhaps, when they were being ferried down from the *Parada*—if they even showed them that much. After that, they've been locked away underground, reading books and watching vids and holos, but none of it seems real to them. The real world for them is the one they left behind when the *Parada* first departed. Everything else is just a dream to them. I don't even think that they have a clear geographical or historical picture about this place, why they are where they are—Alaya, at least, talks as though she thinks she can walk out of this place right now and be in her own neighborhood back home in Canada. I don't think she has the first clue that she's in Istanbul, on the cusp of not one but *two* wrong continents for where she thinks she is. They're lost, Philip..."

"They'd be a sight more lost if they were allowed out," Philip said. "Everything has changed from what they knew."

"And nothing," Stella retorted. "Sure, the details have changed. But people are still people."

"Two centuries does change even the people," Philip said. "You think that someone who left this world in 1700 and returned in the late twentieth century would have been able to come to terms with what they found?"

"Yea, I know, but that was different," Stella said.

"Not," Philip countered, with a grin. "Just the degree is. Not the fundamental change."

"It's academic at this point, anyway," Stella said, sniffing. "They aren't about to be let loose out there. Although—think about it—it's so *unfair*—the *Juno* people..."

Philip laughed. "You went on a crusade for the *Juno* people, but that won't work again," he said. "You have to come up with a bigger rabbit this time."

"I just wish I could show them," Stella said stubbornly. "This is still their world. And they went out to do errantry for it, and they came back and they got locked into a dungeon. When I first got here, it felt more like I had been transported up into a hermetically sealed spaceship than having the *Parada* crew brought down to me and transported Earthside. I mean, they literally haven't even felt the wind of home on their face..."

"How would they?" Philip asked. "They're the world's best kept secret. Their very existence is unknown outside these walls—except to the three members of the *Juno* crew and they've taken care of *that*. What did you expect—that they would put wigs on the *Parada* people and make them wear full latex make up so that nobody will recognize them? They can't take out six grown human beings and treat them like they were children on a kindergarten outing requiring close and constant supervision. Until such time as you clear them... they're stuck..."

"What if that never happens?" Stella said, and felt a stab of hollow panic. "What if I can't do it? What am I supposed to do—condemn them to death? Or to life in solitary confinement?"

"If you can't, then it would hardly be solitary confinement," Philip said. "As far as I know at least two of them haven't stopped fragmenting yet—a new and heretofore unseen personality popped up for Alaya just last night, one of the nurses said—and you don't know if they ever will. They'll always have the rest of themselves for company."

"That's not funny, Philip."

He sobered. "I know. I'm sorry. It's just that sometimes... there doesn't seem to be a way out of the labyrinth. And if you don't find something to smile about... But this Earth isn't a tame little back yard in which you can let them out to play, Stella. There would be damage, both ways. They neither belong to it any more, nor it to them. There's a delicate little balancing act involved, and it's just that..."

"Wait," Stella said abruptly. "Just wait a moment."

"What did I say?" Philip asked, his eyebrow rising into his hairline. He had learned to recognize the expression on Stella's face which meant that she had just had some sort of insight or inspiration, and she was wearing that expression now.

"The yard. The back yard. It *does* exist."

"What?"

"There's a garden, right at the top of this building," Stella said. "I know, because I've seen pictures of the bigwigs having parties up there—there's a rooftop garden, and because it's so private and so secluded... nobody would see..."

"You want to take your six-going-on-hundreds of people up topside to a bigwig garden party?" Philip said, amused and bewildered.

"*Yes!* I mean, no, not a *party*. God alone knows they'd make any party lively, the way they are now—good grief, can you imagine turning Diana loose on the diplomats?—but I don't want them to lay on the champagne and caviar, although if anyone deserved them it's these people. But the garden, Philip. The garden. *Open sky.* I could make a case for it, therapy, they absolutely need to see their sky with their own eyes. They *need* to. Look at the conversations I've been having with them, giving them bits of information, nothing direct, nothing with a real connection to the world as it exists now, today. They need to see this world, Philip—they need to *see* it—they need to reconnect to it, to know that it still exists—don't you realize? Everything we've been telling them sounds like just as much of a fairy tale to them as the weird stuff they keep feeding us sounds nuts to *us*. We've been talking past each other. We need to start building bridges..."

The idea had bitten hard, and to Stella it wasn't a question of *if* any more. It was *how*, and *when*.

She couldn't seem to stop talking now, her mind working furiously at the logistics of the matter.

"I had a strict father who insisted that a chain of command be obeyed, with him as the ultimate authority where the buck stopped—which was fine, except that all too often that meant that if my sister and I played by the rules we would end up faced with a blunt denial of whatever it was we wanted to do and that would be the end of the road," Stella said, apparently completely off the subject—but Philip listened with a grin, aware of what had to be coming. "My sister accepted that, and ended up living her life sitting silently and politely where she was bid, with her hands folded on her lap, and her eyes demurely downcast. She's married now with three children and as far as I know she's happy—but we haven't had anything to talk about for years. We exchange Christmas cards. If that. I couldn't even tell you for sure when my youngest niece's birthday is, we're that disconnected. We're just different people, and she lives her life, the best she knows how. As for me, I evolved a philosophy long ago that it is better to ask for forgiveness than for permission. You live with fewer regrets that way. My sister never understood that—but eventually my father gave up and learned to deal with me on my own terms."

"I'm beginning to understand you better," Philip said, his grin widening. "There are deep roots to all that you have done since you came to this place."

"*Carpe diem*," Stella said

"*Ego hanc ludum vincere omni tempore*," Philip countered. "Don't bandy Latin with a priest. You'll lose. All right. Let's assume I'm on board with this crazy plot of yours. How do you want to do this?"

"The bigwigs will be fine if they think it's all covered by a security detail, won't they?" Stella asked, her expression and her tone so bland that Philip was hard put not to laugh out loud. "So let's just get some security organized right from the start. I'll secure the living daylights out of this, so to speak. I'll just go and take care of that. You get them ready and wait for me."

"*Now*? You want to do this now? It's the middle of the night!"

"It's *not*. It's much later. What better time to avoid any attention? It's *carpe noctem*, at that." She grinned at making another foray into Latin, and her eyes sparkled with challenge as she locked gazes with Philip. "It's all good. We'd be alone up there and that's exactly what we can use to smooth it over with the authorities later when they raise their fuss. Besides, these people are practically *vampires*. Even if I could immediately lay my hands on six pairs of heavy-duty sunglasses and factor hundred-and-fifty sun protection—which I can't—you do realize that a sudden exposure to sunlight might make them all go up in a puff of smoke? My God, even Lily Mae is starting to fade to gray. These people haven't seen the terrestrial sun for a very long time. Moonlight, they can take. We *picked* this time, right? Very carefully?"

"Besides," Philip said, very softly and suddenly serious, "there's the stars. They now know the stars far better than they do the light of day."

Stella hesitated. "You think they might prefer *not* to be reminded...?"

"I think seeing the sky while actually standing on what at least passes for ground—even if it has to be a rooftop garden on top of a glass tower—might actually be exactly the kind of catharsis they need," Philip said decisively, committed to the harebrained scheme now.

"Fine," Stella said, grasping the nettle firmly herself. "I'll go deal with the security angle. You round them up. I wish I could make them all go into the Children's Collective for this—it would be just that much easier to keep them in a nice neat obedient group if they were all seven years old again—but do what you can. For the love of God try not to let Boris or Diana or Grub out. They might bolt and at the very least they might make the security guys feel very unhappy. Threaten to cancel the whole thing for the rest of them if you have to, if those types manifest."

"You're putting rather too great a weight on my ability to control the souls," Philip said.

"I have an inkling that if you... but maybe now isn't the time to experiment, just do your best. Get Han—if you can get him into an authoritative enough shape—or Rob to help you. For that matter, tell them I said it's bonus points if they all come *as* themselves. As the original themselves."

Philip snorted. "I think that might be pushing it."

"Perhaps," Stella said, remembering Susan's words about there not being much of a choice left for some of the *Parada*'s crew, wondering if there was enough of Boz Dimitrov left to even attempt to pull him together again in his original form. "Try. I'll be back."

She needed to thread a very fine needle here. She needed someone who could authorize unorthodox requests and provide access to forbidden places which were perks for the high-ranking officials who worked in the glass and steel tower in whose underbelly the quarantine quarters were situated, but not someone too high up in the hierarchy, someone whose flat 'no', uttered before she had been fully heard out on the matter, could scuttle the whole idea prematurely and permanently—and whose knowledge of the fact that the idea had existed at all would firmly put the lid on even the thought of any such notions in the future.

The fact that it was close to three in the morning unexpectedly worked in Stella's favor. Everyone who represented a higher authority had enough clout not to schedule themselves on this watch—and there was enough tedium in being rostered into a position where a high level of alertness was balanced by just the right amount of nothing worth noticing or acting upon ever actually happening that the officer in charge of the four-man security team on duty didn't dismiss Stella out of hand.

"You can't take them out of the quarters," the officer said, frowning, when Stella put forward her plan. "And certainly not all together like that. That would be above my level of clearance to approve, anyway. And I think..."

"I am their doctor, and I have clearance to treat them as best I am able," Stella said. "It's on my authority that this is done. I am not asking you for *permission*. Just for a security escort, and access to the garden."

"I don't have access to the..."

"You are really telling me that your literal authority is confined to a single level of this building?" Stella asked archly. "Here's what I need you to do. You can give me two of your men to provide escort; in addition, I will be present, and so will Father Philip Carter, another of our team. The rest of your men will secure an appropriate elevator, ensure that access to it is limited to our group for the duration of this excursion, and provide security outside the garden while we are in it and—if you consider that necessary—a discreet security presence inside the garden with our group. But I don't want these people hounded, bullied, or otherwise hovered over. I am a doctor in charge of their treatment, and I am giving you a direct order which states that the visit to the rooftop garden is an essential part of that treatment. Do what is necessary for that to happen."

"I would need to..."

"You can wake up the entire top command if you want," Stella said, hiding the crossed fingers of her left hand against her thigh, her chin held high and her eyes as commanding as she knew how to make them. "But they won't thank you for it, and it would cause considerably more commotion than this entire thing might entail right now, with the building empty of anyone whom you might not want aware of what is going on here in the basement. For the love of God, you've brought these people back from an impossible exile—you've brought them *home*—they've been shown the beautiful blue marble that is their home world—and then you've locked them away like prisoners ever since—and they've had nothing *but* blank grey walls... for literally years... There are good reasons for them being here. I'm not proposing we all go walking to the midnight souks in the city; I just want them to stand on dirt again. Anyone in their position would immediately feel the better for that, would feel reconnected to a world that they have to feel has washed its hands of them. What would you want for yourself if you were in their shoes?"

"There is a whole other security detail in the upper levels," the officer said defensively.

"So work with them. Or don't they even know that we are all here?" Stella challenged. "One hour. One hour under the sky with them. We owe them that much."

"I don't think..." the officer began again, but one of the other men stepped forward abruptly, the expression on his face set into something that Stella almost caught her breath at. It was a respectful defiance, but there was a wildness behind it that was wholly unexpected; Stella had no way of knowing what lay behind that, but all she could do was bless whatever it was that drove him.

"Sir," said the guard, "I volunteer. I will do whatever is necessary to perform this duty." He did allow himself to bite his lip, in consideration of what he was about to utter next, but he said it anyway. "I will accept any consequences for my actions."

"Sir, I also volunteer," said a second guard.

A third simply stood his ground, squared his shoulders and his jaw, and nodded.

The commanding officer shook his head.

"I cannot—I *cannot*—officially sanction any of this—I know you have a certain amount of authority, Dr. Froud, but I am not at all sure that it reaches to this level—but what you say is..."

"One hour," Stella said softly.

"On your responsibility," said the commander grimly.

"You were obeying orders," Stella said. "Absolutely. Now let's go."

The commander hesitated for one more moment and then grimaced, shrugged his shoulders, and barked out a sharp set of orders. Two of the other guards peeled off and headed down a secured corridor, on their way to the upper levels of the building. The other two and the commander himself fell into step beside Stella as she led the way back to the crew quarters.

"Wait here," she said to the security men, and slipped inside into the common area.

Philip waited there with the six *Parada* crewmembers, roused from their beds and waiting quietly in a tight knot, standing close to one another. Han stood between the two women, and the twins flanked Boz Dimitrov, the hands they both had on the engineer's elbows looking merely supportive but to Stella's eye it was obvious that the grip was equally well positioned to become a restraint if necessary. She met Philip's eyes, and he nodded slightly.

"They are who they need to be," he said. "On their recognizance. It may not be easy, but it's done."

"Rob, Jerry, you guys take Boz, lead the way," Stella said quietly. "Captain..."

"Yes, ma'am," Hanford Millgar acknowledged. "I understand."

Stella opened the doors, and—for the first time since they had returned to Earth—the entire crew of the *Parada* stepped outside of their confinement and back into their world. They had been taken out in small groups to use a gym, or individually for medical reasons, but that had always been briefly, and it had still been confined to the general area of where their quarters were. Now the commander of the security detail, scowling mightily, led the way down a corridor that led in quite a different direction. He was followed by Stella, then Han and the two women, then the twins with Boz between them, then Philip, then the other two guards. It still felt as though they were all being marched somewhere under armed guard but the atmosphere was quite different, and the air fairly crackled with the intensity. As each security checkpoint was passed Stella's heart leaped into her throat, absolutely certain that waiting beyond would be a wall of men bristling with arms who would deny further passage—but one after another they were passed, and finally the group emerged into a wider area, with two grey-doored elevators opening into it. One of the elevators was open, with one of the guards who had left earlier standing in the open doors.

"All clear, sir," he said to his superior officer. "This is a service elevator. It takes us to a staging area one level below the roof garden. There is a further elevator there. It has been secured."

"Access?"

"I have the code, sir."

The *Parada* crew were ushered into the elevator, towards the back; Stella and Philip took positions in front of them; the security detail closed ranks to form a wall between the civilians and the elevator doors should the elevator make any unscheduled stops on its way up.

It didn't. When the doors opened, two of the security rank-and-file officers stepped outside smartly and stood to either side of the elevator doors and the other two stood aside to let the rest file past them and into the elevator lobby area, closing ranks behind the group. In a tight knot, security before and behind, the *Parada* people and their two caretakers crossed the empty expanse of the utilitarian service area and then up a short staircase which led into a mezzanine area which boasted one more elevator. This one had its doors painted bright red, as though it wanted to signal just how forbidden it was. Another of the security detail stood beside it, and as the party approached pressed a swift key code into a pad beside the elevator. After a pause that seemed to last an eternity, the red doors swung aside.

"Take Ling and go up. Secure the exit." He hesitated for a moment and then asked, "Cameras?"

"Two, up at the next landing."

"Upon further thought...disable those."

"Sir."

"Send the elevator back down when all is secure," the commander barked, and two of his men stepped into the red elevator without a word. The red doors closed, and a red light above them blinked on. A few minutes later, they heard the elevator return to their level, and the doors whooshed open again, revealing one of the men who had gone up.

"Exit secured, sir. There is a stairwell leading to the garden level. I have the code."

"Let's go."

The red elevator was smaller than the service elevator which had brought them here, and it was necessary to transport the group up in two trips—first the captain and the women, with Stella, and then the twins and Boz and Philip, with the security detail commander bringing up the rear. Reunited at the upper level, they regrouped once again, security before and behind. It was immediately clear from their surroundings that they had entered a different world; soft lights glowed in sconces in arched alcoves and the carpet beneath their feet, patterned in curling leafy vines, was soft and deep. They walked across to the door which blocked the garden stairwell, also painted with a climbing ivy motif, and one of the security people punched in a code—Stella had already made a deal with herself not to even begin to wonder how or where these men had got hold of the necessary security codes to unlock all these doors. There was a whirring noise, and the door rolled back into the wall, revealing a short hallway leading to a set of stairs at the end of which stood a set of heavy double doors of bulletproof glass, with only darkness beyond.

The leading security guard punched in another code on yet another keypad. The glass doors swung open.

A curl of night breeze drifted in and caressed the faces of the people waiting at the bottom of the stairs. Stella could hear somebody's breath—one of the women?—catch on what was almost a sob. And then the guard stepped through the doors, took a quick recon of what lay beyond, and tossed his head at the rest of them, urging them to come through.

Stella led the way.

It broke Stella's heart to watch the crew step out into the rooftop garden—slowly, stealthily, warily, as though they expected every shadow to attack them. She remembered once seeing, back when she was very young and very affected by such things, old videos of dogs used in laboratory experiments back in the days when they still used live animals to test chemicals. A rescue group had acquired a handful of beagles which had been reared from very young puppyhood inside a laboratory—dogs which had never seen the outside of a lab, never felt the wind in their ears, never had their paws touch grass or dirt. They brought the dogs out into a patch of lawn in someone's back yard, and set the carriers out there with the doors open leaving the dogs to explore on their own terms. Stella had wept when she had watched the wary animals sit cowering for a long, long time in their carrier cages until one brave soul decided to put an experimental paw out—touch grass—pull the paw back in consternation and stare at that unfamiliar surface—then slowly, slowly, touch the grass again, put its weight on that foot, take another paw out and let it rest on the grass, trembling, its nose sucking in the new smells and questing for danger... and then, when one of the dogs had finally gathered enough courage to emerge, the others did, one by one, until they all stood on the grass in joyful bewilderment, disbelieving what their senses were telling them. Those dogs had ended up, in that video, racing around the grass with abandon, simply accepting the fact of their freedom and a sense of a new life that was about to open up for them as they danced, darted, rolled, permitted themselves at last to be touched and hugged by humans who loved them instead of using them as living records of scientific data.

Stella didn't know if that kind of a happy ending was even possible for the *Parada* crew—but she watched them stepping into the rooftop garden with the same wary anxiety as those captive beagles, as though they were touching grass for the first time.

The moon was full, and bathed the garden in a white light, casting sharp shadows. It was September, late in the season, but some lingering roses were still blooming, and a few of them—the dark red ones, black in the pale moonlight—were the ancient kind which still possessed the kind of rich scent that had once made them so beloved. The air in the garden was redolent with that perfume. Stars glittered palely in the sky but the tower rose above the city and the lights spilled a long way below on the ground washed out the brightness that might have been the glory of the night sky. Some stars were there, though, and Stella saw Alaya stand rooted with both feet flat on the ground and her arms straight down by her sides with both hands splayed out as though she were trying to keep her balance on a swaying ship, her head thrown straight back, her eyes gazing up into the sky, avidly, as though she was trying to count the stars that she *could* glimpse up there. Han Milgar wore a faint smile on his face, gazing both upward at the sky and outward across the lights of the city and, further out, the abrupt darkness that was open water.

"This must be quite the sight, in the light of day," Han remarked, directing the remark at nobody in particular.

This was his world, the world he had given his mind, his body, his life to. And all that it had left to give him in return was a glimpse of city lights, and the darkness of the night sea, and a scattering of faded stars. Stella felt a stab of something that felt strangely like guilt, although she had done nothing to claim responsibility for any of what had happened to the captain of the *Parada*.

Lily Mae, her eyes on the ground and not the sky, had padded over to the very edge of the garden and was gazing avidly out over the city; Stella's instincts tingled, and she was on the point of crossing to Lily Mae in case she needed some steadying attention, but just as she was about to move she felt a light hand on her elbow and turned to see Philip by her side, his eyes also on the slender woman standing alone in a tangle of moon shadows.

"I got this," he said softly.

Stella hesitated and then nodded,. Philip crossed the grass to where Lily Mae stood. Stella could see barely more than silhouette shapes at this distance but Lily Mae's head turned at Philip's approach, and then she and Philip leaned in towards one another engaged in a whispered conversation she could not hear.

She scanned the garden for the others again.

The moonlight glittered off Boz Dimitrov's cheeks, as though his eyes overflowed with tears. There was something about the stillness of his figure that suddenly made Stella think of emptiness—as though he was just a shell of a body, with everything that had once been inside that body now gone, fled... to the stars? She could not see where his gaze was fixed, precisely, but there was a sort of focus there, as though he were searching for something very specific, for the glint of passion in a lover's eyes. Stella felt as if she would be intruding on something close and intimate if she disturbed him—and she made the decision to rely on Jerry Hillerman, who still stuck close to Boz's side, silent, close enough to Stella for her to notice his nose flaring as the scent of roses wafted past him, to intervene if it became necessary. A few steps away, gazing at the sky in what looked like a more relaxed position than Alaya's but still revealed a tight focus on the visible stars scattered across the night sky, Rob Hillerman stood with his arms crossed across his chest, smiling faintly.

Stella drifted over towards him.

"You know," he said, apparently aware of her approach before she came nearly close enough to have been detected and certainly before she said anything out loud, "I feel like a boy again, staring at the skies washed by city lights, knowing that the stars were out there, finding it hard to see them—and tonight, with the city, and the Moon..."

"Are you okay?" Stella asked incongruously. This had seemed like *such* a good idea—and it might have been, if there had been six of her, one for each crew member, one shadow to watch each one of them and gauge their reactions and remember them and file them away and see how they responded to breathing the free air of home once again. She did stop to acknowledge the irony of wishing she had the gift of splitting herself up just like her subjects had done—if only to study their own fractures better. But even while keeping a corner of her eye on everyone, ready to react to the most minuscule of changes as soon as she could perceive it, she now found her attention focused on Rob. If he had been one of those beagles she had wept over, he'd have been the one to have had an ancestral memory of grass, dug it out from somewhere, buried deep in his subconscious, and he would have been the one to simply accept it, love it, take it as something that belonged to him and was rightfully a part of his world. He was relaxed, the word she was groping for was *content*—he just fit in this place, in this moment, as though the world had been shaped around him and bent so that he would find a comfortable place within it.

And yet. And yet...

When he spoke, it was in a voice Stella recognized, and shivered to hear.

"I remember this place," said the Poet in that rich, velvet tone that had raised Stella's hackles the first time she heard it. "When I was a child, I dwelled in a garden with high walls, and I was safe there, and contented, and protected, and nothing evil could ever happen to me there because this was home, and it was a happy place, full of light. I thought it was the whole world, and I was ready to accept that world, those walls, those boundaries, because they kept me safe and happy. It even perhaps smelled of these very same blessed roses, and the very same blessed faint stars twinkled above it. And I was young, and innocent, and I knew only that comfort that surrounded me and gave me value in the context of that place, and shaped me into that small young thing ignorant of all but only the things that I knew were real to me because I could touch and taste and smell them, and happy in that ignorance."

"Hey," said Stella, her voice a little unsteady. "We agreed..."

The Poet turned to look at her, those large luminous eyes glittering in the moonlight. "But I grew up," he went on relentlessly, still wearing that same faint smile that played around the corners of his lips. "I grew up, and I have passed the gates, and I have been beyond the walls. And I have seen the shadows that teem on the outside, the shadows with claws and with teeth and with terrible glowing eyes of hunger and covetousness, the shadows that would devour you. I have seen them and I have known the fear of them. But... I have faced them, and I have faced that fear, and I understand now—without those shadows, even just the stories of those shadows, the light in that childhood garden could never have been so beloved and so bright. I have stood outside the walls and they look so small, so fragile, from here—and yet I know, I remember clearly, how high and how strong they seemed to me when I still dwelt within them. I have left the garden of my childhood and I have walked the wilderness that lies all around it and I have fought its traps and its monsters and sometimes I win and sometimes I lose—but there is one thing that I never knew, before I stepped into that wild desert, and that is that the place is stark, and deadly, and beautiful beyond reason. It isn't safe. It isn't protected. But it's free, and its shadows sing, and the songs are sung with the voices of dark angels, and once you have heard those songs you are lost forever..."

His arms unfolded, his hands dropping to his sides, his breath escaping in a sigh. "You can never return, you know," he said. "You can never come home again, not truly home, you can never come back to that safe happy garden where you were a child. Because the wilderness leaves its seeds in you, and the seeds sprout no matter how hard you try to stop them, and something takes root inside of you and in the fullness of time it blooms—a flower that is dark, so dark, and yet it is velvet to the touch and it is full of stars, and its name is yearning—a yearning for what you know is out there, will always be out there, the knowledge that there is always *more*..."

He stopped, and fully turned to look at Stella, who stood speechless with tracks of tears on her cheeks. The Poet was gone; it was Rob Hillerman who stood there again, and it was he who reached out a gentle hand and wiped the tears from her face.

"I'm sorry," he said, and sounded genuinely regretful. "That was an ill way to repay a miracle. Thank you, for this. It means more than you can ever know. I suspect you will be made to pay for it, though."

"They called me here to try and understand what happened, to heal you," Stella said, trying to stop her voice from sounding thready with her suppressed tears. "That's all I'm trying to do."

"I don't think they meant this," Rob said, gesturing at the garden, at the Moon, with a wave of his hand. "I actually think... I haven't allowed myself to dwell on it, but tonight made me realize... that it is entirely possible that they will never let us go free. How can they? We are monsters now, the monsters who came back from the deep—and the deep has touched us and changed us. That is all that they will ever see, now. Everything else pales in the light of that. Even though it was all a comedy of errors, a chain of accidents, the possible folly of sending Jerry and myself out there together, for the Universe to find and for some intelligent part of that Universe to assume that the somewhat odd, almost schizophrenic, deep shared twin bond is the way the human mind is *supposed* to function and that maybe it is our fault that we..."

He stopped speaking, abruptly, but Stella's hair was standing on end although she still didn't completely understand why—all she knew was that she was hearing, for the first time, the truth behind what had happened to the *Parada*, and that there might have been more to that truth than anybody had imagined.

She narrowed her focus onto one particular phrase of what Rob had just said.

"Some intelligent part of that Universe?" she questioned softly.

His eyes had changed again, and what she saw there began to frighten her.

"Maybe you had better gather us up again," he said, and his accent had changed, broadened, became something out of an old-time gangster movie. "We all made a promise—but there are some promises you can't expect us to keep. Maybe it's too late after all." He glanced up at the sky and the fierceness of that look stabbed Stella to the heart— it was as though he was trying to gather it all up, pull it inside of him, treasure it there, a memory of something that he didn't know that he would ever see again with mortal eyes. "Thank you," he said, his voice tight. "Take us back. Now. While you still can."

It was something that was equal parts fear and instinct that made Stella clap her hands together and raise her voice, just enough for it to carry across the open space that was the rooftop garden.

"Glory! Momo! Jiminy! Coco! Gadfly! Gem! Over here, to me!"

Stella could feel the security guards tense, in the shadows, and could almost see hands shift towards weapons—they had all come here together and the group that the guards had escorted had been the crew members of the *Parada*—the guards did not recognize the names being called out, and an instant suspicion had reared up like a wall. There was a moment of real danger—a moment when Stella could not be at all sure of any of the people on that rooftop, and which way they would jump. And then she saw Hanford Millgar turn, and his body was Glory's, all overgrown and tangled and hard for him to control, to the point that he almost tripped over his own feet as he tried to obey the summons. When he moved, so did others—Jerry and Boz linked hands, and Gadfly and Jiminy stepped forward towards Stella. She could see Coco leave the garden's edge and begin to drift back towards the group in the center. Momo responded, as well. And, last, letting go of that final strange personality only with difficulty, Rob Hillerman's Gem.

Stella could see Philip edging over to where the captain of the security detail stood, and silently blessed him for defusing that situation, which she could not spare the focus and the energy to deal with. She left him to it, and turned to the assembled Children's Collective.

"All right," she said. "Remember me?"

"You're Doctor Stella," Coco said.

"We need to go back inside now," Stella said, "and it's really very late—so we all need to be very quiet because we'll wake everyone else up if we don't. Can we do that?"

"Yes," said a couple of them earnestly.

"But it smells so good out here," Momo said, pouting rebelliously and lifting her face up into the scent of roses.

"We'll take one with us," Stella said, loudly enough for Philip and the guards to hear. "One of these nice men will pick one and bring it. Now come along. Remember to hold hands so that nobody gets lost. Gem, you lead the way."

They obediently lined up—Gem, and Gadfly, and Momo (obediently but still with evident reluctance), and Jiminy, and Coco, and Glory bringing up the rear. Stella took Gem's hand and began to lead the whole daisy chain of them, aware of how incongruous it all looked from the outside, grateful of the darkness that covered the worst of it.

"There's steps, now. Be careful," she said, and led them out of the garden, back through the glass doors, down the stairs, across the plush carpet to the elevator. They waited there for everyone to assemble, and then Stella talked them gently into letting go so that half of them could go down in the first elevator load and the rest follow in the second, and then regroup into the daisy chain, making their way back along the corridors through which they had come earlier. Then, Stella's only thought had been the chance to allow that captive starship crew to steal a glimpse of freedom, to stand once again as free people under their own world's sky. Now, she was conscious of a terror that they would not make it back to the safety of the crew quarters in the underground quarantine area, that someone from the crew would break, would run, would be taken down without an instant's pause or regret. She had wanted to offer them freedom and now it felt as though somehow she had put their very lives in danger. She felt a heart-wrenching relief, coupled with an irrational guilt, that almost overcame her completely as they slipped back into the familiar secured corridors leading back to the underground holding area—something that so had her in its grip that she took a moment to realize that her hand was being tugged for attention by the first person in the daisy chain behind her. The hand was male, long-fingered, warm, solid, but the eyes that met hers when she glanced back were still those of the little girl who had control over that body at that point. Rob Hillerman's face; Gem's eyes.

"Illogon," Gem whispered.

"You've said that before," Stella said pitching her voice low, just for Gem's ears. "What does it mean?"

"That's its name," Gem said.

"Whose name?"

"It woke us," Gem said. "It came back with us. It is here with us now."

"*Gem!*" That was Gadfly, the next in the chain. "You're not supposed to..."

"She's a friend," Gem said sturdily, and the trust in her eyes smote Stella to the soul.

"Yes," she said. "Yes, I'm your friend."

"Ask Jiminy," Gem said. "That's where it lives."

They reached the crew quarters, and Stella opened the doors, leading the six crew members inside, still holding hands—but it was as though the familiar sight of the quarters where they had spent so much time acted as a sort of trip wire. The hands dropped from one another, as though they had suddenly found themselves grasping something searing or unpleasant.

"Mother*fucker*," Lily Mae said, shading from Coco to Diana in the blink of an eye. "What are you all doing out here? What's going on?"

"Bed," Stella said firmly. "Now. Yes, you. Especially you. I'll be by in the morning."

Diana glared at her from smoldering, hooded eyes, and then whirled and stalked off into her private quarters.

Boz still looked odd, weaving on his feet, and now that she had been pointed in his direction by Gem Stella suddenly began to see all kinds of telltale signs she should have noticed before. The body that had belonged to Boz Dimitrov had once been a slim, athletic six-foot-two frame—and yet somehow it had managed to melt away one insignificant piece at a time and when Stella looked at him now she could see how much weight he had lost, how long and thin his limbs were, how hollowed-out his face looked underneath sharpened cheekbones. He had always had very pale skin, which looked even more luminous underneath his shock of curly dark hair, but now the skin was starting to look almost transparent. Stella caught sight of the inside of his wrist as he slowly put down the hand which one of his companions had just released. She could see his veins stand out blue underneath the thin layer of skin stretched over wrist bones that looked like they were a size too large for him. He looked... as though something was hollowing him out, eating him from the inside.

Random thoughts about the man since his arrival in this place streaked across Stella's mind. The others never left him to sleep alone. The nightmares. The obvious loss of appetite. The oddness of his own personal response to the fragmentation of personality and soul that had afflicted the crew.

Tyrone Kidman, the engineer of the *Juno*, had had the same kind of obsessive passionate focus, had burned with a similar inner light— Stella wondered if the engineers of Earth's starships, burdened with so much direct responsibility for the miracle of the star-drives, were inevitably predestined for eventually buckling under the strain. It didn't feel like a coincidence that something seeking a safe space to exist would choose a mind like that, a mind so focused on a single thing that there were plenty of what looked like empty and unoccupied corners where sanctuary for a stray entity might be found—but a mind which was finely balanced, for all that, and a mind which this kind of intrusion would damage irreparably.

Was Boz actually aware of this... creature... this... *Illogon*... what was it Gem had called it... did he know it as he must have known the rest of the souls which inhabited his fragmented mind? Or was Illogon lurking on the edges, trying to keep itself apart? The children knew of its presence. Apparently *all* of the children did. What was it Gem had said—*It woke us?*...

Stella shied violently when she felt a hand on her elbow and snapped her head around, staring wildly into Philip's concerned face.

"Stella, what on earth is it? You did it—you did exactly what you planned to do, you won, and now you look like you've looked a Gorgon in the eye and turned to stone. They'll probably call you on the carpet for this but I'll back your play, I'll..."

"Philip—did Boz ever—did he ever tell you—"

"*What*, Stella? What is the matter? You need to speak to the security guys, they're waiting outside—the crew..."

"Yes. Yes of course," Stella said automatically.

She looked around the common area once again—it was empty, all of the crew having withdrawn into their own quarters, she had not noticed which one of them had quietly followed Boz into his for the first watch, but all the doors were now closed and she and Philip were alone in the open common room. Remembering that all of this was being watched on screen in the surveillance area, Stella shook herself and drew a deep breath.

"Yes," she said, "I need to talk to the security detail. I think I'd better give them a written statement they can produce if they're pulled up over this. Afterwards... I need to talk to you." If he didn't already know that the reason for this request was important, all Philip had to do was look into a pair of eyes that shone as though lit by fever, and the hectic flush on Stella's cheeks.

"What happened?" he said, very quietly, as they turned towards the door. "What is it?"

"Everything," Stella said, her breath catching on the word. "*Everything*. I think I understand."

The night was gone by the time Stella sent off the security commander with a written record exonerating him from any responsibility concerning the possible fallout of his actions and then, huddling with Philip over a table in the deserted cafeteria, laying out what she had learned and thought she understood about the true situation in which the *Parada* crew found themselves.

Philip sat ashen-faced, listening to her.

"You think there is an *alien entity...*"

"I know. Oh, I *know* there is. Now. How could I have been so utterly blind to all this?"

"But where...? How...?"

"I have every expectation of being hauled in front of a tribunal before breakfast," Stella said, her voice breaking in a laugh that had an edge of hysteria to it. "And oh boy do I have a story to tell them. They'll forget quickly enough how I came by it—but this is what I was brought here *for*, Philip, for me to give them a blueprint of what happened, of what caused any of this, and I may be able to piece it together now. But oh, I wish I didn't feel as though I am a wretched traitor to those people. Because if I spill this... they're just *done*. I have literally just given them the metaphorical final cigarette to smoke before the execution squad comes in, by taking them out to that garden..." She sat up. "The rose. I promised them I'd bring a rose..."

"I heard," Philip said. "It's okay, I took care of it. It's there. In the common room."

"Then they know already," Stella said. "The watchers. They'll have seen it. On those screens. I'll be summoned to explain myself any moment now. But before they drag me away to that—it's—I don't know what's going to happen next—go back to them, you go, go *now*, be there if they come to mind-rip them for this and I can't help—can you try and talk to Boz? Before they get to him? Before—maybe if we can tell them what they want to—if we can stop—"

He covered her hands with his own. "Peace," he said quietly. "Peace, peace. God will be with us all."

"I have never," Stella said, with a hiccough, "quite believed in God."

"I believe in Him more than ever right now," Philip said. "Those six people were in trouble, and God sent them you."

Stella unexpectedly burst into tears. When Philip stood up and came around the table, trying to comfort her, she pushed him away, although not in rejection. It was more a sense of urgency, of a need to have someone with the *Parada* six who was on their side and would take their part.

"Go," she whispered. "Go to them. I need to... to get ready."

"For what, Stella? You have no idea yet..."

"For everything. For *anything*. No, go. I'll be fine. I really will. I just need one more cup of coffee, and maybe somewhere to wash my face..."

"Forget coffee, you nutter, let's get you back to your place and you can wash your face if you need to and then try to at least lie down and close your eyes for a few moments. I know you don't pray, but do something like it. Just think good thoughts out at the Universe. I'll try and deal with the rest."

He deposited her back in her quarters, and left, promising to go straight to the crew area. Stella had only a couple of hours of peace before her tablet began an urgent buzzing which left no doubt as to its importance and the inadvisability of its being ignored. Stella dragged herself upright, caught sight of herself in a mirror and grimaced at the picture she presented, and answered the summons.

"You look like hell," Martin Peck said, without preamble. He looked grim himself. "I just read this," he said, lifting up a second tablet which presumably contained the note she had written and signed for the security commander. "You need to explain yourself."

"It's on me," she said. "Don't get him in trouble."

"That isn't for you to determine," Martin said. "I'll be expecting you in twenty minutes. Don't be late."

The connection was summarily severed.

Stella sighed, and tossed the tablet back onto her bed. She wondered if twenty minutes would be enough to snatch a quick shower, even if she didn't have time to dry her hair, and was already on her feet and halfway to the bathroom when the tablet buzzed again.

She considered not answering it. For a full second and a half. And then turned back with a faint snarl.

"Give me a chance, I'm on my..." she began, and then realized that it wasn't Martin Peck on the other end. It was Philip, and there was something in his eyes, wide and tragic, that stopped Stella in mid breath. "What?" she asked, after a long moment. "What happened?"

"You'd better get here," Philip said. "*Now.* It's Boz."

"I've just been summoned to Martin's... aw, *Hell*," Stella said. "He can wait. I'm on my way."

Shower forgotten, she barely took the time to drag a brush through her hair and straighten her tunic, the same one she had worn in the rose garden earlier that night and had just napped in fully dressed on her bed.

They were all up, when she burst into the crew quarters. Han and Alaya sat quietly together, not quite touching. Jerry and Rob stood on either side of Boz's doorway, like some strange honor guard. And inside, Boz lay on his back on the bed, staring up at the ceiling. One of his hands lay on his chest, a frozen gesture giving him the look of having been caught almost comically by surprise, and Lily Mae crouched beside the bed, holding his other hand against her forehead, drenching his unresponsive fingers with her tears. Philip perched on the edge of the bed behind her, one arm protectively over her shoulders; she didn't look as though she was even aware that it was there.

Stella froze in the doorway.

"What happened?" she whispered. "Is he..."

"I could find no pulse," Philip said quietly.

"They must have seen—has a doctor—"

"They had an emergency team in here, moments before you arrived. The medic said that he isn't dead. Not quite. But it's a coma of sorts, and by the looks of it a permanent one—he is completely unresponsive. And unless he is put on full life support immediately it won't be a long one. They..." he indicated the rest of the *Parada* crew, with a succinct toss of his head. "They said they were the closest thing he had to next of kin. And they don't want him hooked up on anything. The medic who was here only had a couple of assistants with him and he was outnumbered—he left, to get reinforcements of rank, perhaps, but he said he'd be back... that's when I called you..."

Stella stepped into the room, bending over the motionless body folded in silent grief over Boz Dimitrov's hand, and laid gentle fingers on Lily Mae's shoulder, softly saying her name. There was no response, and Stella glanced up at Philip who already knew the question she was about to ask and answered preemptively.

"She's been a couple of different people in less than five minutes," he said, "some of whom I've never seen before. But I don't know who she is now. She hasn't answered to anything at all for a little while, least of all to Lily Mae. She just sits there, holding him. She hasn't let go of his hand since I found them both here, like this."

"She was with him?"

"It was her turn," Jerry said, from the door.

Stella looked up, her eyes darting from one twin's face to the other's. "Have they—were they—"

"If you're asking if they were lovers, they may have been, once, but not recently," Rob said. "Not since we've been here, anyway."

"But this grief," Philip said, his voice catching. "She is breaking my heart..."

"We are all that's left," Rob said quietly. "To each other, we are all that's left. There is no deeper grief than knowing that what you lose is irreplaceable."

"I'm sorry," Stella said, some of the grief that Rob spoke of reaching out to hook itself into her own soul. "Was it—do you think that I did something, by this garden thing?"

"This isn't at your door," Rob said, with a faint smile of absolution. "I think we all knew this was coming. If anything, perhaps the only thing that you contributed tonight was that he went with his soul more at peace than he might otherwise have done."

"I won't be able to stop them," Stella said. "When they come for him. They'll want to..."

"We know," Rob said. "It's all right."

Stella stood, staring at Rob, trying to formulate a discreet question without revealing any knowledge that it might not be advisable to publicly show that she had.

"His... what happens to what he..."

"I don't know," Rob said.

"His body is a shell," said a voice from the doorway, and Han Millgar stepped up in between the twins. "But he will always be with us."

There was a final small exhalation of breath, as though Boz's soul was leaving his body, and then it seemed to be over. Lily Mae shuddered violently, and then stood up, shaking Philip's arm off and unfurling her long body, laying Boz's hand very gently on his chest. She still said nothing at all, but Stella finally met her eyes.

And quite literally stopped breathing for a moment as she became aware that she gazed into a soul that was very definitely not one that had been born on Earth.

5.

The medical team that had scrambled to attend Boz returned with reinforcements almost immediately, and the reinforcements included Martin Peck. As the entrance door of the crew quarters swung open to admit them, the frozen tableau in Boz's cubicle barely had time to react at all—Stella's wide eyes flew from Lily Mae's almost expressionless face to Philip Carter's who mouthed, only barely forming the words enough for Stella to notice and trying not to show too obviously that she should be paying attention, *Tell them nothing.*

Martin himself led the way, brushing past Hanford Millgar in the doorway, muttering a brusque "Excuse me" as he forcefully gained access to Boz's bedside.

Stella's gaze shifted to Martin.

"I'm sorry, I was on my way..." she said, incongruously. Even she wasn't sure if it was a real apology for disobeying his summons or a delaying tactic.

He made a swift chopping gesture with his hand, cutting her off. "I fully understand the circumstances..."

"I think he is dead, sir," Philip said evenly.

"What the hell happened?"

"He just... stopped," Philip said.

Martin rounded on him. "You were present?"

"At the extreme end of events, yes," Philip said. "But by the time I got here, Mr. Dimitrov was, according to the rest of the crew, already unresponsive."

"He was saying something," Martin said. "The surveillance..."

Stella's brows came together. She had never much liked the intrusive surveillance of the *Parada* crew at the best of times, and right now it seemed to have crossed entirely into the realm of ghoulishness.

"Yes," Philip said. "He was speaking. But he spoke too softly for him to be easily heard unless you were literally holding your ear to his mouth, which I am sure your surveillance would have shown you not to have been the case. And in any event what I did catch appeared to be in a language I did not understand. It is entirely possible that he might have reverted to his native language *in extremis*, and none of us here speak Bulgarian."

"But what happened? Was anyone actually with him when he began to deteriorate?"

"I was with him initially, after we all came back from the garden," Han said quietly, from the doorway. "He slept; he tossed and turned a bit but he was perfectly fine, physically. I've seen him... far worse. It wasn't one of his night terrors. I called Lily Mae to take over after about an hour, because I was myself feeling too restless and unsettled to remain there without waking him. But when I left, Boz was asleep. Only that."

Martin shot Stella a look. "We will discuss the garden later. Lily Mae, if you..."

But Lily Mae took this moment to simply fold into a dead faint, falling bonelessly to the floor beside Boz's bed. Philip caught her just before she hit the ground, lowering her the rest of the way, bending over her in concern.

"Medic! I need a medic in here, now!" Martin barked.

Han and the twins stepped away from the door as a medical team rushed in. A doctor felt for Lily Mae's pulse at the artery just below her jaw, and then pulled back an eyelid to peer into her eye—a movement that made Stella hold her breath. But the doctor apparently noticed nothing untoward because he lifted his head and looked up at Martin.

"She's fine, she's just passed out. I think it might just be the shock."

"She probably just needs to lie down," Stella said. "Her own cubicle is right next door. Could you carry her?"

"I think they all need to be..." Martin began, but Stella straightened and looked him straight in the eye.

"She is in no condition to be interrogated or examined right now," Stella snapped, "and you will just have to wait. The others clearly don't know much more than they told you—Han was only with him for an hour, and the others were not in Boz's presence at all since we all returned from the garden—where, I personally can state, I did not observe him in any particular distress. We can discuss the garden, if you want, you and I, but I don't think that it had any more to do with what happened here than the life in a fishbowl that these people have had to endure since they've been here. Quite aside from *anything* else that's been going on here, the psychological stresses and strains of that alone have been considerable. I think that they've had quite enough for tonight, don't you? I'm sure," she added, poisonously enough, "that you will be keeping a close eye on them via the cameras anyway. But can you at least leave them in peace to get some rest?"

Martin glared at her with frustration and resentment. "All right," he said, through clenched teeth, "we will take this up in the morning. But take Dimitrov," he said to the medical orderlies waiting outside the cubicle. "I want to know what happened to him. A report on my desk by noon tomorrow at the latest."

Stella heard a breath catch on something halfway between a sob and a wail in the common area just outside Boz's cubicle. Alaya, responding to Martin's command, to the implications of that command.

They are going to gut him like a fish, Stella thought grimly. And wondered if they would find any physical trace of the alien who had hitchhiked a ride within Boz's soul.

"Sir," the lead medic said, in response to the command. "Okay. Bring the woman..."

"I've got her," Philip said quietly, lifting Lily Mae with one arm under her knees and one folded under her shoulder. In this cradle, she looked like a child, a puppet, a floppy boneless body that weighed almost nothing at all.

"Into her cubicle, please. I will come in to give her a brief examination in just a moment. The rest of you—have you got the gurney? Bring it. We'll take Mr. Dimitrov down to the morgue now."

"You have a morgue?" Stella said, unable to stop herself. Maybe she should have known that, should have anticipated that. But it had still managed to take her by surprise. "You really planned for all the possibilities, didn't you...?"

Martin swept the silent *Parada* people with a swift glance, and then gimleted his gaze on Stella again.

"Gentlemen, and lady," he said "we'll talk later. Dr. Froud, with me, please."

He turned sharply and left the room, and Stella, trying not to look at Boz, followed meekly enough. She paused in the doorway, catching Rob's eye very briefly; something passed between them, something wordless, an acknowledgment of dangerous knowledge, promises offered and accepted, an almost invisible nod exchanged as messages were proffered and understood. It all took a fraction of a second. Then he turned and walked away towards his own cubicle. Stella, at Martin's heels, caught a glimpse of Han holding a sobbing Alaya in his arms and grim-faced Jerry Hillerman watching as the team inside Boz's room busied themselves with the body. Then she passed out of the doors and left the habitat, stepping outside into the corridor at Martin's heels.

The moment the doors closed after them, he rounded on her.

"*What were you thinking?*" he demanded savagely.

"I could explain that," Stella said, "but clearly you have already made up your mind on the matter."

"You presume too much," Martin said. "When you campaigned on behalf of the *Juno* men, I backed you. I thought you were magnificent, facing down the powers of the world, and I thought you were *right*. But that was by the book—at least you did all of that through the proper channels. It doesn't mean that you get to do whatever the hell you want and make unilateral decisions off your own bat, and just leave the chips to fall where they may. If they had..."

"If I had come to you and asked, would you have even considered it?"

"Probably not," Martin snapped. "For very good reasons."

"Martin, be honest, for once," Stella said. "They're prisoners. They've been prisoners since you brought them here. You never really had any intention of letting any of them out of here, did you? Is that why you're so angry? Because showing them outside this place—no matter that there was nobody to see—means that your bluff is called, and someone somewhere might figure out that they're here, and how they've been treated?"

"They have been treated well," Martin said. "They have received every care..."

"Every care... except even the merest possibility of being considered enough of a human being to even hope for rehabilitation and inclusion back into the human race," Stella said. "What were your superiors hoping for, that I would come along and certify them as irretrievably insane, letting you lock them up for good, and washing your hands of them? I can't, Martin. I can't do that. Granted, there are a lot more 'people' in that room than there should be if you just count the bodies—and granted, some of those 'people' are not very nice—but on the whole those entities whom I have met and interacted with, the entities with enough cohesion to be called a full personality, they are all just as sane as you or I. This isn't a disease you can classify or cure in terms of an insanity quotient. It was always going to be difficult. But you set out to make the bar high enough to ensure that any result other than the one you needed was impossible. Do you want to know why I really went out into that garden?"

"I would be inclined to say that it's because you seem to be unable to resist the urge to buck authority," Martin said. "You just don't respect the chain of command. You weren't the first choice for this assignment—we could have got..."

"Someone more tractable?" Stella challenged him. "I'm sure. But you apparently made the mistake of actually looking for someone who knew what they were about, when it came to this subject—and that got you me, even if I wasn't your first pick—and I'm a civilian, and the chain of command *doesn't apply to me*. When I signed your NDA agreement I only signed a paper stating that I would not discuss my work outside permitted channels, I did not hand in my enlistment papers, and if you had insisted on that I would have declined your invitation to participate. The reason I took them out into that garden, *sir*, is because I wanted to remind them of their humanity, of their original selves, their original souls. Has it occurred to you that keeping them locked up in isolation as you have done so far has actually *exacerbated* the problem? Have you never read any studies on solitary confinement?"

Martin opened his mouth to come back with a blistering retort, appeared to think better of it, and closed it again. His eyes smoldered.

"Fine," he said. "I want a full report from you, too. Today. And in the meantime I am going to have my hands full putting out the wildfires. You're right, we didn't particularly need the appearance of that group on CCTV footage in the most highly secured building in the world."

"Our security guy said to disable the cameras," Stella said, disconcerted, caught on the back foot.

"Not all of them, apparently," Martin said sharply. "And quite aside from anything else, this was a breach of my security, of the highest order, and I now need to re-evaluate our processes from the ground up. This can't happen again."

"Ever?" Stella said. "So you're telling me that I'm right, and you *are* just locking them up and throwing away the key? Should I tell them this?"

"Report," Martin snarled. "On my desk. ASAP. And until I receive it and evaluate it, you're barred from their quarters, Dr. Froud."

"No," she said, immediately, rousing. "No, that is not an option. For better or for worse, you got me into this and I have been trying to make a connection with these people ever since I first arrived here. I'm finally starting to make some headway—and you simply cannot cut us off from one another, not right now, not when they are in the middle of this loss—you do realize that you yourself have perpetuated the sense that those six people in there are *everything that there is*? And now they've just lost one of their number, and the psychological effects are going to be seismic—and you simply cannot leave them to fend for themselves, just like that, without any warning. At the very least, I need to go in there and tell them I will be absent for a while. I would like to think that you'd come to a quick conclusion. You will only do desperate damage on top of what's already there if you insist on this. You'll have your report, but first I need to speak to them. Right now would be best, actually."

Martin couldn't gainsay her. "Fine," he growled. "Get back in there and make what arrangements you need to. But I want that report, and after I receive that it is only on my say-so that you go back. Am I making myself clear?"

"Eminently," Stella said, unprepared for the sudden stab of loss that this severing dealt her. "You will have the report within the hour."

She turned back towards the crew habitat doors, before she could say something worse.

Her report would be an elegant lie. Even without Philip's warning, she knew that it would have had to be. Her exchange with Martin Peck had simply solidified Stella's impression of the intransigent attitude of the authorities towards the *Parada* crew—if she provided a report that told Martin the truth as she now knew it, she had a strong feeling that it would be devastating for the ones who were still left. She didn't know if any of them would thank her for commuting a death sentence to a life locked up underground while watched by unrelenting and ever-vigilant surveillance cameras, but she knew she couldn't be a party to murder, and murder it would be if she breathed a single word about the fact that there had always been one more entity in the quarantine habitat than anyone in charge of it had ever been aware of.

She refused to even acknowledge the fleeting thought that she and Phillip would probably also be too dangerous to be allowed to live.

Han and Alaya were still in the common area, sitting close together on one of the couches molded from the wall, much like the bed in her own quarters. Alaya sat gathered together in an attitude of acute distress, her feet raised on tiptoe on the floor and her heels against the edge of the couch, her knees raised and her arms wrapped around them, her head bowed, her hair spilling down to conceal her face; Han had his arm around her shoulders and was speaking softly into the general area where the fall of her hair might have concealed her ear.

He looked up as the door opened again, and met Stella's eyes. She did a quick shuffle through his personalities, and recognized that he was still himself, still Han.

"I owe you all an apology," she said, addressing him as the Captain. "I certainly didn't mean to make things worse."

"For what you did do, I, at least, am grateful," Han said. "I am no medical expert, but I can't believe that anything that happened in the aftermath was your doing. We might all have become a little agoraphobic after years of being cooped up in tight quarters but last I heard that wasn't something that could kill you."

"Did he say anything... when you went in..."

Han looked at her for a long moment, his face oddly closed, but then his eyes cleared and he shook his head minutely. "Nothing of consequence," he said. "Nothing that would have a bearing on events."

Alaya, who still hadn't looked up and sat crying quietly, gave a sudden gulp as she tried to catch her breath and buried her face deeper into her hands.

"Is she...?" Stella began, and then, more softly, "*Who* is she?"

"She was Alaya when she heard Martin Peck barking orders, and she knew what that meant," Han said. "She began to cry, and then Meggie came out and swore she was going to be just fine, but if Meggie is speaking you know she's lying about something. And then Lillibet came out and she's been sobbing her heart out ever since. Lillibet is only twelve, and is devastated. She knew Boz, and she also knew... well there are the children..."

"To her, it's like she's lost a whole bunch of friends," Stella said. "Listen, I need to tell you—I've been told to write up a report for Martin and until he gets through that I am not to be allowed to come back to you guys—so I might be away for a bit. Please let the others know..."

"Aw," Han said, and when he looked up Stella realized with a sinking feeling that it was no longer the Captain. It was Hal's glittering eyes, flirtatious even under the tragic circumstances, that looked back at her.

"Oh, not now," she said. "Please, can you remember to tell the others? *One* of you?"

"Sure," Hal said. "I'm going to miss you."

"Somebody better get Alaya... Lilibet... to bed, and it better not be you," Stella said. "Come here, Lil. Hal, go to bed."

"Will you come tuck me in?"

"No!" Stella said. "We don't have time for this. Go." She looked up, and saw Jerry Hillerman standing poised in the doorway to his quarters, watching. She stared at him for a moment, trying to match the expression on his face to the personalities that she knew, and found herself at a loss—it was himself, and yet not quite himself, as though she were looking at him as a mirror image rather than the original entity. In this enclosed little world where personalities shifted like water she might have expected to see something different on him, something perhaps even unfamiliar—but that was just it, this wasn't *unfamiliar*, just unexpected, as though she was not looking at Jerry but rather at...

"Rob?" she said out loud, weirded out, knowing that she was looking at one twin and yet somehow convinced that she was gazing on his brother.

"Yes," he said instantly, and it was impossible—*impossible*—this was messing with even the basic syndrome that Stella thought she knew. But she was faced with the reality of it—that one of the personalities that Jerry Hillerman carried inside of him was actually his twin brother Rob. *Some of me spilled into him*, he had said to her once, in a previous conversation. She had not understood, then. Did he mean this? That the twins were literally interchangeable?

Her mind was already spinning like a top and she had no room for this new impossibility, none at all—except that this was exactly what she needed right now. Rob was someone she trusted, and that she needed someone she trusted to deal with Alaya/Lilibet in a vulnerable moment.

"Fine," she said, shaking her head. She gently extricated Alaya—or Lilibet—from within the pouting Hal's encircling arm, and guided her first to her feet and then the reluctant few steps forward. "We can talk about that later. For now, help me. She's young and vulnerable right now—Lilibet—take her to her room. Just get her to her bed and put a blanket over her and make sure she's safe and cared for. Don't worry about anything else right now, just do that."

Jerry took the extra few steps between him and Alaya and put a gentle coaxing arm around her. "Come on then, Lil. Come with me. Gently now. Easy." He glanced back over his shoulder at Stella. "I'm on it. Thank you."

"Jer... Rob..." Stella stumbled on the names, still twisted by the whole thing, not knowing what to call him, what he would respond to. But that didn't matter. She said, quickly, "I'm sorry. I am really sorry. I can only begin to imagine what this means to you all."

He began to say something, and then changed his mind, and simply nodded, turned away, guided Alaya towards her cubicle.

When Stella turned back, Han—or Hal—had gone. But the door to Lily Mae's cubicle was still open, and Stella crossed over to peer inside.

Philip was still there, perched on a chair beside the bed on which Lily Mae lay apparently asleep, and he looked up with a tired smile as Stella entered.

"Is she okay?" Stella asked.

"I talked them into letting me stay with her for a while," Philip said. "She may or may not be really asleep, I'm no judge, but her breathing changes—and I think she's awake—but if I try and speak to her she won't respond, not to any of the names I know." His eyes warned Stella—*don't try the alien name. She might respond and then there will be hell to pay. Not now. Not yet.* "How are the others? I saw Han trying to comfort Alaya and I offered to come help but he waved me away..."

"That's because she was three different people at some point during the past half hour," Stella said. "I don't know that this hasn't changed the situation for the worse. There were six of them—and God alone knows how many hangers-on inside each of them—but they were there for each other, the only thing that any one of them had, this tight group of six which has gone through hell together and is now adrift in time and space, stuck here with one another and nobody else... they might be forgiven for thinking that there *is* nobody else, not for them, not ever again, not here. And now one is gone. And there's grief, and then there's something I don't even have a name for, an unspeakable loss of something or somebody that is literally irreplaceable. And now Martin wants to pull me from the group until he can stroke his ego back into place, with him as the controlling authority. *He* was put in charge here, and he takes that very seriously. He wants a report on his desk, and until he's finished 'assessing' it I'm not supposed to come back and talk to the crew. Now, when they need me... when they need *somebody*... the most."

"Do you want me to speak to him?" Philip asked. "I mean, I don't know how much it would help, but..."

"Hell, no, he's focused on me—don't get on his radar, he might ban you too and then where would they be?" Stella said. She drew a weary hand through her hair. "It's been a long night. And I'm supposed to be working on a report to top all reports. I have no idea when I'll be allowed to come back, but..."

"I'll keep you up to speed," Philip said.

Stella looked down on Lily Mae, lying very still with her eyes closed and her lips parted very slightly, giving her face an expression that looked like she had just seen something wonderful and had responded with an awed disbelief.

"Poor woman," Stella said, her voice very low, pitched just for Philip and turning away so that Lily Mae would not pick up anything. "How much did she hear, do you think? I wouldn't be surprised at all if whoever overheard Martin's commands is now no longer in any doubt that the only way out of this trap they're in is feet first through that morgue—and probably in pieces, at the end of it. Their souls are in tattered streamers, and now they're completely certain that their bodies are going to end under a hacksaw. And after all that, he pulls me out of here and leaves them to fend for themselves..."

"I think she really is just asleep," Philip said.

Stella caught his eye and tried to convey a warning—*she may be, but I saw what I saw and we both know that there may be more to this*—and then sighed, shrugging her shoulders.

"And now there's a whole new thing," she said, "and just when I should be getting to the bottom of it... Philip, Jerry Hillerman just turned into Rob. That's a new wrinkle."

"What, now?" Philip asked, rousing.

"Just what I said. Jerry was there, and then he was just Rob in Jerry's body..."

"Are you sure you didn't just mix them up? I mean, it's easy enough to do..."

"They're identical enough but I think I can tell them apart by now," Stella said. "They really are different enough on the inside for that to show. At least for someone like me. But in this total scattercrash of personalities... they have picked up... each other's?" She shook her head. "Damn. Damn it all. Every time I think I am a step ahead I get thrown right back into the quicksand. I need to go and think about this, on top of writing Martin's wretched report, justifying a perfectly justifiable decision in a way that's going to let his own self come out of this smelling sweet to his superiors..."

"God go with you," Philip said.

"You know I don't..." Stella began, but Philip raised a hand to stop her, the corners of his mouth lifting into a small smile.

"You might not but I do and it is a blessing to send you out with a blessing," he said. "Good luck, if you prefer. You do believe in luck, at least?"

"I drag my own with me," Stella said, with a quick tired grin, "and it's usually bad. But thanks for the sentiments. Appreciate it. You should get some shut eye too at some point—there is no good reason for you to keel over too, and I swear, at this point if I lose *you* I'll just throw in the towel."

Philip reached out a hand to gently squeeze her shoulder. "You don't lose me easily," he said. "Go, I'll hold the barricades."

By the time she put together a careful report which both blazed with truth and hid massive lies of omission underneath that blaze, Stella barely had enough juice left to send the document to Martin Peck before collapsing into bed to snatch a few hours of restless sleep. She woke raw, headachey, even less able than usual to suffer fools, and girded her loins for another round with Martin later that day. She was not going to allow him to let the *Parada* six... five, now, she corrected herself grimly... swing in the breeze without access to any support or assistance, and for better or worse she was that support. Philip was a good second, but he was a stopgap measure in this situation. He could hear their confessions. He could not help them—except through shared prayer, for whatever that meant to any of the crew—navigate the crowds they carried inside their psyches.

Even she, Stella, the professional, was finding it difficult to get a handle on this. Letting it all fall on Philip was fair to nobody at all.

She allowed Martin six hours to sit on her report, and then she presented herself at his office.

"He said that he wasn't to be disturbed," a young ensign in uniform who was hunched over a computer station in an outer cubby, functioning as secretary and access point guard, said as Stella swept into her presence, rising to her feet in consternation.

"Does he have somebody in there with him?" Stella asked levelly.

"No, but..."

"Then he will see me," Stella said. "You can tell him, or I can just wait right here. I have no other place to be right now. Your choice."

The ensign hesitated, and then tapped at a comm unit tucked in her ear.

"Sir," she began, "I have..."

"We need to talk, Martin," Stella called out from where she had taken station just outside the office door.

After a moment, there was a click, and the door slid back.

"Get in here, then," Martin Peck growled ungraciously. The hours that he'd had to digest all the information he had demanded and been given had apparently done nothing to sweeten his mood.

Stella, feeling the flush of adrenaline through her body that she had once dealt with when facing the committee deciding on the fate of the *Juno* crew, followed his instructions.

For all his love of authority, Martin Peck's office distinctly lacked grandeur—it was smaller than it needed to be, almost cramped. One entire wall consisted of a large built-in computer screen, on which now several windows with relevant information were open; other than that the room contained only Martin's workstation and a single other chair. Obviously he did not entertain crowds in here, and there was something about the expressed preference for the one-on-one that actually said quite a lot for his temperament. He didn't invite her to sit, but standing there made her feel rather like an errant schoolgirl called on the carpet by a stern headmaster so she walked up to the visitor chair and sank into it, her back very straight. Neither of them said anything for a long moment. Martin kept his head half turned away from her, studying the screen wall, but an odd rigidity in his shoulders and a forefinger that kept tapping rhythmically against his other hand where his hands were folded together before him made Stella aware that he wasn't actually looking at anything on that wall, just staring at that data in silence, making a point, and perhaps waiting for her to move first.

She didn't have time to play games. So she did exactly that.

"Do you remember the old-fashioned zoos?" she asked, without preamble. Martin did not respond, but he did turn from the wall and fixed that intense stare on Stella instead. Stella's left hand clenched into a tight fist until her nails dug into her palm, but she didn't let him derail her. "I do believe I talked of this in terms of a menagerie, from the first moment I walked into this place," she said.

"You did," Martin said, not looking around at her. "I think I disagreed with you."

"I remember seeing videos, reading about those zoos," Stella continued, undeterred. "There was a time they were really bad. Animals whose natural habitats were enormous—who would in the wild range for miles and control huge swathes of territory—would be locked up in a tiny cage so that visitors could gawk at them. And most of them simply went mad from it, and took to pacing the exact dimensions of their cages. And even if they were taken out of the cages afterwards to try to rehabilitate them it would often just not work. It was as though the size of those cages had become the size of their world and they could no longer comprehend that there was any kind of world outside of that."

"The *Parada* crew," Martin said levelly, "are hardly in a zoo. You are being theatrical."

"They were shown the biggest territory of all," Stella said. "We sent them out there, into the vast spaces between the stars, where there were no walls at all. And then we took it all away at a stroke, and here they are, locked into individual little cages and watched every minute of every day with cameras that feed into a surveillance room."

"There were walls," Martin said. "Even out there, there were walls. We sent a ship, we hardly sent them naked amongst the stars."

"The ship was a vessel, a protection, an arrow which was loosed and on which they flew," Stella said. "But the sense of freedom, that wasn't contained inside that ship. What you have in your cage, Martin, are six of the freest people you will ever set eyes upon, and they are the very people whom you lock away underground so that they are out of sight, and out of mind..."

"Five," Martin said, his voice flat and almost entirely without feeling.

"What?" Stella said, derailed.

"Five people. The sixth was thoroughly examined in a post mortem in these hours past, and is on his way to being quietly cremated as we speak."

A lump rose in Stella's throat. "What are you going to do with him?"

"We'll take him back to the stars," Martin said savagely, and broke. The iciness cracked and what was underneath boiled over. He turned to face her at last. "Do you think we are quite heartless? We know these people are a miracle. But you yourself have now had a decent chance to interact with them. Honestly, Stella. *Honestly*. Without any hedging, tell me, right now, what your recommendation is. Are they ready to be rehabilitated in any way? Returned to the world which they left two centuries ago and would find it tough to adapt to even if they weren't otherwise incapacitated?"

"I..." Stella wanted to rush out with a passionate defense, but he had trapped her with that 'honestly' and the words stuck in her throat. Of course the *Parada* people were not ready to re-mingle with the rest of humanity.

It was still not fair.

"The garden," she said, instead. "I wrote it up for you. The reason I did it... was simply... to unlock the cage. To let them know that they actually *were* back on Earth, and that it wasn't just an elaborate ruse being spun for them, a fever dream, a desperate wish, that they weren't really orbiting around some dead star somewhere and waiting to die and remembering the world that had sent them. It was important, Martin. It really was that important.

"You didn't think that it was important enough to involve me in the decision?" Martin asked, with deceptive calm.

"I didn't have time to argue the point with you," Stella said. "I strongly felt that providing them that anchor—letting them stand on the ground under an open sky—might bring them back to the people who once stepped off that ground to go up into those stars. Did you know that Joe White Elk actually carried a talisman into space with him, a handful of dirt from his home world, a few drops of her water? That it was this that kept him sane and centered while he was out there? Well, none of the *Parada* people had thought about that. They had no such bridge. They needed to reconnect—perhaps not to the society that's out there now but to their world, their physical planet, to... to *remember* that they were back. And it worked. It *worked*! For a moment, it worked perfectly—they came out with me as themselves, as the *Parada* crew, they kept everything else, all the other fragments, at bay... for the longest time... they stood there and they looked at the sky and my God, Martin, really, you should have been there to see their faces and the way their eyes opened wide to take it all in—and the roses, the scent of the roses, I wasn't expecting that but they smelled that and they knew they were home—and it was an unbelievable moment, out there..."

"And then what happened?" Martin asked quietly.

"I... lost control, a little," Stella said, with passionate desperation. "It was worth it, though. I think I made half a dozen breakthrough insights that stem directly from the garden experience. I think I begin to understand the beginnings of this phenomenon. And if I am right then one of the worst fears the authorities have—that this might be an artefact of interstellar travel—is something that isn't going to be a problem for future missions. So long as those missions don't include twins."

Martin leaned forward. "You think it was the Hillermans that triggered all this?"

"I would have to study more deeply to be sure but I think they may have been special even in the strange enough world that any pair of twins inhabits," Stella said. "When I was first told that they 'shared' personalities, I couldn't even begin to understand how that worked—I had never come across that before. But the fact that now— after the complete fragmentation that occurred—I saw at least one of the twins show an alternate personality that is *his brother's*—that's a whole different level. That is a connection that is over and above what I have already seen in this crew. And the oddest thing is not that the Hillermans are possibly the origin of this event—but that they are also, or at the very least Rob Hillerman is, the most intrinsically stable of the lot. It's as though they acted as carriers of this particular syndrome—but they themselves were, at least partly, vaccinated against it—immune, by virtue of being twins and already having a rich inner division between each self and its other half in the other twin. The others... they run the gamut. The Captain is strong, and can sometimes keep a tight control on things when he needs to—but he can also shatter into the most inconvenient fragment at the worst possible time. Alaya is full of completely stable individuals any of whom could function well in and of themselves—and one of her personalities is a psychology adept with whom I've actually discussed the syndrome, with input from the inside, as it were. Which is unprecedented. Lily Mae... exhibits some unusual fractures, which I haven't been able to completely map out to my satisfaction. Boz Dimitrov..."

"What about him?" Martin prompted, after a moment.

"I can't believe he is gone," Stella whispered. "You said they did an autopsy... did they find... how he..."

"They found absolutely nothing that they could point at as having caused his demise," Martin said. "He was a little on the undernourished side, to be sure, but nothing life threatening to the degree that it would kill him, certainly not as fast as his death happened. His heart was healthy, all other organs were perfectly functional. It was as though he suddenly decided to turn some switch off, inside of himself, and everything just shut down at once. According to the doctor who performed the autopsy, he died because his heart stopped. And we don't have the first idea why his heart stopped."

"He was happy," Stella said, her eyes welling with tears despite herself. "He was... different from the rest. His fractures were more... studied, somehow. As though they had been made up whole, from the beginning, rather than ignited by the same spark that broke the others. It was never as organic with him as it appeared to be for someone like Alaya. But up there, in the garden. For a little while, at least. He was *happy*. I could see it."

"You really have no idea what happened to Bogdan Dimitrov in between leaving his quarters to come with you to the garden and the time of his death not twenty four hours later?" Martin asked.

Stella lifted her hands in a gesture of defeat, and then buried her face in them.

It was only partly a gesture of grief. The rest of it was a good way to hide her face and her eyes from Martin's intense gaze—to hide what she had learned on the way back from the garden, the thing she could never reveal to him without permanently slamming the door to the *Parada* crew's cage and throwing away the key.

Stella's unilateral assumption of responsibility in taking the *Parada* crew up to the rooftop garden—perceived as a wound to Martin's own pride and position—had penetrated too deep to be reversed; at least a day had already been lost to Stella, as far as contact with the five remaining crewmembers was concerned, and this in the aftermath of the discovery of the new twin twist to the whole tangled story, something she was desperate to investigate further.

Martin appeared to give her an opportunity to recant, asking her if she would do the same thing again—but all she could do, looking him straight in the eye, was to reiterate that she would, and for the reasons she had already stated.

"I could replace you," he growled. "More than enough grounds." He sounded at once genuinely enraged and as though he was trying hard to rouse up enough anger to give his words the necessary depth and sincerity; Stella had to stop and consider the idea that analyzing Martin Peck was just as much her job as dealing with the *Parada* mess.

"You'd have to start again," Stella retorted, choosing to respond to the words alone and not the possibly complicated issues underlying them. "From the beginning. Building a relationship from the ground up."

"You may flatter yourself that you are irreplaceable," Martin said, "but really, you haven't been here all that long, and..."

"Long *enough*," Stella said. "Long enough to start making a difference. And now, with the garden night in the mix, long enough to have forged an understanding that there's somebody out here who's on *their* side."

"We're all on their side," Martin said. "Really, you make it sound as though we considered them enemy combatants or something."

"Worse," Stella said, suddenly very quiet. "If they were enemy combatants they would have their rights, and they would have some sort of notion that they were in a situation where—should hostilities cease— their captivity would end. But there are no hostilities, and their captivity is open-ended, and it's something predicated on a situation they don't have direct control over. They get that, Martin. You haven't sent these people out into space to represent mankind because they were stupid. They can see the shape of things and it isn't something that is looking good for them. They may very well understand—in their heads—that there is no real way out of this mess... but in their hearts they still might have had hope." She paused. "Until now. Until the garden night. When hope both blazed, and was put out for good. I showed them a glimpse of freedom, and Boz dying showed them that the key had already been turned in the door and they were on the wrong side of that door. They comprehend that at last, now."

"You are saying you gave them that comprehension."

"I didn't have to *give* them anything they didn't already have. All I did, perhaps, was to precipitate an acceptance. So yes, you could replace me. And in the end it wouldn't matter, because you've lost them anyway. But starting again, anew... I already have a body of knowledge,

I already have a rapport with not just the crew but with a bunch of the alternate personalities. All of that, you would just throw away. And for what? To punish *me*?" She snorted inelegantly. "Is it that necessary to 'teach me a lesson'? Why did you bring me here, then, if in the end it is going to come down to petty vengeance? Martin, let me work, or send me away."

He started a retort but she shut him off. "You cannot micromanage this," she said. "The situation is simply not one that has ever been encountered before. I have a good background knowledge of this syndrome—we have studies of plenty of cases where individuals occasionally disintegrate into multiple personalities for more or less well-defined reasons, but we've never before had a shipload of them fall apart, and you yourself, and your superiors, have instinctively understood this. I have to adapt whatever methods or knowledge I have—of other, less complex situations—to deal with this particular one. I did not define its parameters. I cannot—*cannot*—promise you to, what, 'be good' according to your lights. Not if you want your answers."

"We can't just let you do what you want," Martin said. "At least file a flight plan, before taking off into uncharted territory."

Stella smiled grimly. "You yourself said... if I tried to file this kind of flight plan it would just get me grounded before I had a chance to take wing at all," she said, taking a certain savage pleasure at wringing the neck of his metaphor before she handed its carcass back to him.

Martin closed his eyes in frustration, shaking his head. "Get out of here and go back to work," he said, after a long pause. "This was your last mulligan, though. I appreciate innovation and independence, but the next time you go off the reservation on your own say-so there will be no further stays... even if I *do* have to start all over again. And don't think you will get around that. Am I making myself perfectly clear?"

"Yes," Stella said. "*Perfectly.*"

She got up and left the office, managing to keep her expression schooled for long enough to be sufficiently far away from prying eyes—Martin's, or his ensign's—before she stopped and leaned against the wall to regain her composure. Strictly speaking, she had *already* broken the terms under which her return to the crew quarters had been sanctioned—because she had not told Martin the whole truth, and unless circumstances changed radically had no intention of rectifying those omissions. She would have to tread very carefully from here on, the ground under her feet not entirely firm, and she was acutely aware of this.

Perhaps it was that moment of not being quite in control that governed her response to her first impulse to go straight back to the crew and see if she could piece together all that she had missed through her Martin-enforced absence—something inside of her didn't feel quite steady enough to face a possible encounter with one of the stronger-willed personalities, if one manifested for her. Instead, she went halfway, and bent her steps towards the Surveillance Room. Part of her deeply resented the invasion of privacy represented by this constant covert spying, but right now it was a window into the *Parada* crew quarters that she guiltily welcomed, allowing her to check on her charges without having to directly interact with them.

Only Lily Mae and Jerry Hillerman seemed to be in residence as Stella slipped into the room. One of the people manning the screens looked up as Stella entered, and answered her question before she asked it.

"The Captain and the other two are in the gym," he said, pointing to a screen that showed Han Millgar bench pressing what looked to be an impressive set of weights, Rob Hillerman at a rowing machine, and Alaya McGinty running steadily on a treadmill. "They've got another half hour to go in there."

"Don't they usually all go together to sessions?" Stella asked, peering at the gym screen and then back at the crew quarters cams.

"Yeah, but Lily Mae's been feeling a little disinclined to leave her room since... since Boz Dimitrov died," the surveillance monitor said, indicating Lily Mae's screens with a toss of his head. "Seems to be sleeping a lot. Jerry stayed with her, this time. They don't seem to like being on their own—at least without having somebody else within earshot, anyway."

"Is she okay? Medically?"

"The priest was with her for a while and then the medic came back and checked her over again. They seemed to agree that she was physically fine, just suffering from shock and stress. I think the consensus was to leave her alone to deal with her grief in her own time. She was pretty close with Dimitrov."

"How close is close?" Stella murmured.

"They weren't lovers, or anything like that," the surveillance monitor said. "We'd have noticed something. But they sure seemed to knock those personalities loose in each other. It was a special connection—even if it was just screaming at each other."

"Yes, I know they tried keeping them apart and that didn't work too well," Stella said.

"She *has* been sleeping a lot, since... since Boz went. Maybe they gave her something."

"Maybe," Stella said, "although that would probably not have been something I'd have suggested. When did Father Philip leave?"

The surveillance monitor glanced at the clock in the lower right-hand corner of the screen in front of him. "I think he went off duty about three hours ago."

"Fine. I'll look him up later." Stella transferred her attention to where Jerry Hillerman sat with a tablet in his hands, apparently reading a book, and then yelped and literally jumped a full foot back when he suddenly looked up—straight up, straight at the camera, his eyes seemingly boring directly into hers—and bared his teeth in a feral smile. It lasted only an instant, and then he dropped his eyes back down to the tablet. "Jesus Christ! Does he know that we...? Can he *see*...?"

"Oh, don't worry, he does that every so often," the monitor said, perfectly tranquilly. "You get used to it. Of course he can't see out—but he knows where the cameras are and he knows we can see in, and at least one of his personalities has taken to doing that just to keep us on our toes. We expect it, now. Trust me, the first couple of times he did it we all jumped and screamed, too. Even though he can't see that I think he knows the effect. It gives him pleasure."

"Loki," Stella said. "The sort of thing he might do. Well. Looks like now might be a good time to go and tweak his nose about some things, after all. Lily Mae isn't going to interrupt and we mightn't get the chance again. Thanks, guys. Excuse me. I think I need to go have a little chat with Mr. Hillerman."

Stella almost collided with a janitorial cart right outside the entrance to the crew quarters, and skipped out of the way. The cleaner pushing it, an older woman with salt-and-pepper hair scraped back into a tight bun and tiny crow's-feet lines radiating from the corners of her deep-set dark eyes, tried to swivel it in the opposite direction to avoid her.

"I am so sorry!" the cleaner gasped, her English accented but fluent. "Usually when they go to the gym—the quarters are empty—"

"One of them isn't feeling well, and another is here with her," Stella said. "The others are at the gym, you're right. But not all of them went today."

"I can come back...?"

"I'm sure it's fine," Stella said. "Perhaps just don't disturb Lily Mae?"

"Of course. I will try and be quiet."

"Thank you," Stella said, peering at the cleaner's name badge. "Aisha."

Aisha flushed, looking pleased. "Ma'am," she said. It was conceivably a rare thing in this position for her not to be barked orders at or simply be ignored if she happened to cross paths with anyone above her station. Stella spoke to her as a person, registering her presence, even though her only role in this place was supposed to be to mop floors, pick up laundry, and empty the trash.

The cleaners had their own clearances in to get in and out of the crew quarters, and every use of that code was registered precisely with the exact times of entrance and exit and the identity of the janitorial staff. Stella would have simply punched in her own codes and waved the cleaner through but that would probably have got them both in trouble so she waited until Aisha had finished her protocol and gone inside before entering her own codes and quietly slipping in herself. Aisha had gone straight into one of the now-empty quarters, to begin her work, and Jerry still sat alone in the common area, staring down at his tablet.

"Hey," Stella said, sauntering over to him. "I got your message."

Jerry looked up, his expression carefully bland. "Message?" he inquired, putting the tablet down.

Stella mimed grinning up into an invisible camera, and then looked back down at him.

"You watch us, too?" he asked, still bland.

"No," Stella said. "And frankly if I had my way the rest of them would do it a lot less than they do. But you might have noticed that I have been gone for a day—that's because I had red tape to deal with, and I wasn't supposed to come anywhere near you guys until that was sorted out. And when it was, I just went up to glance in here, to see how all of you were, before I barged in here."

"Well, you missed everyone," Jerry said, shrugging. "Just me here, and Lily Mae who's asleep. Again. Still."

"People heal from grief in different ways," Stella said. "Let her sleep. And I'm glad it's just you. Because I wanted to talk to you. You, especially."

Jerry's eyebrow rose a notch. "To what do I owe the honor?" he asked, almost poisonously polite.

Stella shuffled through the personalities on record for him, something that had become an instinct every time she came up cold on one of the crew until she knew exactly whom she was talking to. Nothing really fit, this time, except Jerry Hillerman himself, which was just as well.

"I want to talk twinship with you," Stella said, settling herself more comfortably.

"Oh dear," Jerry said theatrically. "What have we done now?"

"Oh, it's worse than that," Stella reassured him. "It's what you *are*."

"Aw," Jerry said, managing to sound as un-contrite as possible when uttering that particular syllable. "Can't we keep *some* secrets? What's the point of being magical twins if we have to spill all the beans to everybody...?"

"Not everybody. Just me."

"Everybody," Jerry said, a touch of pure savagery creeping into his tone He aimed another gargoyle grin upwards in the direction of the monitoring camera.

Stella stood up and faced in that direction. "I am going to take Jerry into his quarters for a private medically necessary interview," she said, into thin air. "If I find that any record has been made of this through surveillance when I come back up there, I will make a noise about this. I hope we are clear on the matter." She spun away from the camera and stalked towards the door to Jerry's quarters. "With me," she tossed over her shoulder. "Now."

She didn't turn to see if he followed, merely leading the way, and only turned when she heard his footsteps as he followed her into the cubicle.

"They probably have cameras here as well," Jerry said conversationally, "but nice tantrum. However... follow me..." He passed through his cubicle, threading the narrow aisle between his bed and a computer station desk built into the opposite wall which, above the desk itself, doubled as a screen, much like the one in Martin's office. Of course, this computer was not connected to anything outside: they could not access current news or communicate with the outside world. They could watch movies or documentaries or have interactive holovids projected into the room. They had two hundred years of material to catch up on, to be sure, and they had been doing so diligently—but Stella could understand how this wall between them and the real world might start to itch and burn very soon.

Jerry ignored the screen, passing through an opening in the far side of the cubicle and into the tiny bathroom area which housed little else but a sink, a shower, and a toilet. He gestured grandly at that last, with the air of an aristocratic host inviting a guest into the most opulent of reception rooms. "Do take a seat," he said, himself leaning against the wall beside the sink. "They don't have cameras in here. I don't know about a microphone, but you have to take your chances with that. I guess you got your spy-free zone but it won't be for long. Go."

She nodded. "Take me through what happened again. Out there. Before the *Juno* found you."

His face changed, just a little. "You'd have to ask Boz," he said.

"Boz is dead," Stella said bluntly. "As you said, we don't have long. Talk to me. There are things I already know... already think I know. I have..." She glanced upwards, hesitating, and then decided to take the risk of assuming that she had been obeyed and that for a moment she had a blind spot. "I have given the guy in charge of this, of you all, a report," she said carefully. "That report was the truth, but it wasn't all of the truth. I dangled other truths in front of him in order to distract him from the bigger picture—but I need to know, Jerry. *I* need to know. And the truth I distracted him with... well... it's you. You and Rob. Jerry, you *were* Rob—right here in that common room—I saw you become your brother. Can he be you? Is that something that you and Rob can do? Independently of—of—everything else that's been going on here? When did it start? Before you left... or up there... or up there after you met with..."

She shook her head, still unable to articulate the things she needed to ask. She would have found it hard to do so if she were certain she was alone with the man who held her answers in a cave with the absolute knowledge that they were the last people on the planet, let alone in this place, where she simply could not trust the people she supposedly came here to work for not to spy on every word she exchanged with any of the *Parada* crew.

"You have siblings?" Jerry asked suddenly.

Stella tossed her head. "Sister," she said. "Older than me, by a handful of years. We don't have that much in common. Less and less every year, actually."

"So who was the favorite?" Jerry asked, ignoring the burst of confidence-sharing from Stella.

"I beg your pardon?"

"Which one did your parents like better? When you were growing up?"

Stella stared at him. "What kind of a question is that?"

"Well, figure it out," Jerry said, leaning forward slightly to make his point. "There are always favorites. In every family. For no real reason. If there is more than one child in a family, no matter how many more, there is always one that somehow manages to be the one whom everyone loves and no matter what any of the others do they simply never get to that rarefied height. They may be just as loved, but they never come *first*. And they can't. Not ever. The position, once occupied, is permanent, and the one in it cannot be dethroned."

"You're a *twin*," Stella said. "For all intents and purposes, the both of you are two asses jostling for position on the same pedestal."

"You'd think," Jerry said equably. "But there's always one ass that is first past the post. Always."

"And you think that Rob...?"

"I don't think, I know," Jerry said.

"How could they possibly tell you apart?"

"Oh, it was easy. Jerry was the one that made them laugh. Rob was the one that made them proud. Even when we did the exact same thing at the exact same time... Jerry would say something funny, and Rob would do something good. Jerry would get the pretty flighty girls, and Rob would get the keepers."

"I always thought that twins were inseparable," Stella said, shaking her head. "You're telling me that this whole situation arose because one twin was *jealous* of his *brother*?"

"Not strictly so," Jerry said. "I mean, you will never get me to admit that on the record. But... there's always a first time, a first time that opens your eyes to something. Yes, we are identical twins. And yes, that didn't stop our immediate family from being able to tell us apart. Except... except when I simply *became Rob*, that first time, and they all believed it, and they responded accordingly. And after that, it became easier, every time."

"Did Rob... does Rob... even know? Did he ever do the reverse?"

Jerry grinned, and the smile was frighteningly wolfish. "Of course he did. Once he figured it out—and of course he figured it out. We are twins, as you pointed out. There is very little between us that isn't shared in some way or another. But when Rob did Jerry, he did it to escape—*he* said it was a relief to just goof off sometimes and stop thinking long-term and distant-consequence and just live in the moment. We each... had our strengths. We were two sides of the same coin, to be sure, but we *were* different faces..."

"But you insisted on staying together," Stella said. "Even on this mission—you had a chance to separate, to be your own person, but you and Rob made it clear the only way you were going on the *Parada* was if both of you went..."

"The coin," Jerry said, "is *one*. You can't split the coin in half just because it has two faces."

"So, in the *Parada*... when you were up there when this thing happened..."

Jerry smirked himself into Loki; Stella saw it happen.

"When *our friend* dropped by," Loki said, his voice going very soft, so that Stella had to lean forward practically into his face to hear him speak, "it was the star-faring twins that it first encountered. The two-who-were-one-who-were-two-who-were-many. We already had parts of us woken up and functioning more or less independently, because of the fact that we shared so much, because of the fact that we had to build walls in order to separate out bits of us that we didn't want to share, you might say that the two of us were already a perfectly integrated set of multiple personalities—and the time spent in close quarters on the *Parada* didn't do anything to improve things. By the time it had met us, and stirred us up, and discovered that we were already too full of ourselves and of each other for it to find a place to safely exist, and left... I think it tried to get out, to go 'home', but it was already too late."

"Trapped," Stella said. "But it—are you saying *you* carried it first? You and Rob?"

Jerry tapped the side of his skull with a long forefinger. "Oh yes, it was in this noggin," he said serenely. "I think we drove it crazy. And then it went looking for another place to be, and there was nothing else out there, except... the rest of the crew."

"Bouncing from one mind to the next, trying to find an equivalence to you and Rob, and then creating that equivalence where it couldn't find one already in place. That's why everyone splintered. But wait. Wait. Are you saying this thing can just... *change hosts*? Just like that? Like it's... *airborne*...?"

"You make it sound like a plague," Jerry said. "It settled into Boz, in the end. It isn't as though the thing just danced around between us sipping us like cocktails. It wanted a permanent shelter, and Boz ended up being it."

"And then, when he died...?"

Jerry gave her a long, level look. "I don't think he took it with him," he said. "And neither do you."

Stella remembered Lily Mae's eyes, and blanched. "It *did* leave," she whispered. "I saw..." She blinked at Jerry, her eyes bright and almost feverish. "We've been looking for this, searching for this, for decades—for centuries. This is *huge*. This is first contact. I don't know if I have the *right* to keep it from the world. You brought a being from a different star back here. From a different *star*. And yet... and yet... if I say a word about it, you six... you five..." She swallowed suddenly, abruptly smitten by Boz's absence. "My instinct was to say nothing, because that would be putting you in danger, and I didn't want..."

"And now?" Jerry said, after a long pause. "Now that you have the story, what are you going to do with that?" He was Jerry again, Loki's brief flash suppressed. There was genuine interest, as well as brooding wariness, in his eyes.

Stella stared at him, her thoughts a flock of disturbed birds trying to find a place to perch safely and rest in peace.

"I have no idea," she said honestly.

6.

When Stella stepped back into the common area out of Jerry's cubicle, it was at the same moment when the cleaner, Aisha, did exactly the same thing, stepping out of Lily Mae's. Stella stopped, frowning at her, and Aisha met her eyes and then dropped her gaze guiltily.

"I thought I said you shouldn't disturb Lily Mae Washington?" Stella said. "She was feeling unwell, and she needs her rest..."

"I'm sorry, Ma'am," Aisha said softly. "She called out to me to come."

Stella raised an eyebrow. "She's awake?"

"Yes, Ma'am," Aisha said, her eyes still downcast.

Stella crossed the common area and Aisha stepped aside as she came up to Lily Mae's door, pausing in the doorway to peer into the cubicle. From her bed, Lily Mae lifted her head to glare at Stella.

"*Fuck*," Lily Mae said. "What the hell did they dose me with? My head feels like it's stuffed with cotton wool, my mouth is full of sand, and my legs are Jell-O. I just wanted some fucking water."

"Diana," Stella said, with a sigh. "Are you feeling better?"

Lily Mae/Diana answered with an eloquent snort. "How long was I asleep?" she demanded.

"Not sure," Stella said. "I was sort of barred from coming here for a little while. After... you know, the excursion."

"The garden," Lily Mae said, and the voice was different, softer. Not Diana any more, Stella thought, recalibrating on the fly as she had learned to do with the *Parada* crew. Perhaps Cassandra; perhaps Memorie. Maybe Lily Mae herself. "Oh, yes. Thank you for that."

"You said you were thirsty—did you want some water?" Stella

asked. "The others are…"

"At the gym, yes, the woman told me," Lily Mae said. "She got me some water, thank you." A sideways glance to her bedside shelf showed a bottle of water, about three-quarter-full.

"Do you need anything else? Stella asked. And then, with a glance she couldn't help in the direction of where she knew the surveillance equipment was, "Do you need to talk?"

Something flickered in Lily Mae's eyes—something that shuttered swiftly and then opened again, like a nictitating membrane moving too fast to properly observe, and Stella's hackles rose. The slow smile that began to curl Lily Mae's lips didn't help the sudden feeling of uneasy alarm that beat at Stella's instincts. But the whole thing lasted just a handful of seconds, gone almost before Stella had a chance to properly quantify having registered it at all. Then Lily Mae turned away again, curling back up on her bed. The expression on her face had hardened into something stiff, almost mask-like, and she had folded her arms across her chest, forearms crossed and braced in what almost looked like a fighting pose. The voice that delivered the response to Stella's question was flat, inflectionless, but the name it delivered was not the one Stella might have recognized.

"Alabastra does not wish to talk any more," Lily Mae said.

Alabastra. Do I know Alabastra…? Stella thought frantically, but on the outside she merely nodded.

"Another time," she said. *Another time, another personality…*

Jerry had followed Stella out of his cubicle, and stood in his doorway, leaning against the door jamb, arms crossed, watching as she emerged from Lily Mae's quarters.

"She okay?"

"I don't know," Stella said. "I don't think I met the current occupant yet. Who's Alabastra?"

"Oh boy," Jerry said, rolling his eyes. "She's in superhero mode."

"What, now?"

"Alabastra comes out when Lily Mae either wishes to disengage completely or if she's feeling particularly smug about having accomplished something difficult, dangerous, or forbidden," Jerry said. "Before I knew her name, Lily Mae drew her for me once, back on the ship. It really is her inner superhero, literally—Alabastra has a full superhero costume, something that Lily Mae can hide behind like a mask. The name is pure irony—alabaster is iconically white, no? But the Alabastra get-up she drew in her pictures is a black skin-tight catsuit, black cape, black mask. I think there is supposed to be an A on her forehead, picked out in jet crystals or polished obsidian or something, so that it throws out black sparks when it catches the light. The black woman, hot and all-powerful and pure black fire, coming in all unexpected if people who hear the name Alabastra expect something in cold white stone instead. Superhero sleight of hand. One of the things I liked about Lily Mae right from the start. She absolutely *never* does the thing you expect her to do. Zigs instead of zags every time."

"I've never seen this one since I've been here," Stella said carefully, knowing that there was something very important in what Jerry was saying but aware that she was fumbling the meaning while trying to grasp it. "Does this Alabastra personality come out often?"

"I've only seen her out once, since she emerged as her own entity," Jerry said. "Like I said. Lily Mae had carried the idea—but when the... the fracture happened, Alabastra gelled into her own thing."

"Once? What was the occasion?"

"On the ship," Jerry said. "It was... complicated. This was before the *Juno* got there, and we were in real trouble, and Boz thought there was something on the outside of the *Parada* that needed inspecting and adjusting, something he thought might help get us rebooted and back on schedule, and he couldn't go because he was dealing with those adjustments from the inside, on the computer. He needed somebody to suit up and be his hands and eyes and ears out there. Lily Mae *volunteered*. I'll tell you this, I did remember the Alabastra drawing then, when I saw her all sealed up in that white suit, the white helmet like a mask, watched her go into the back of the *Parada* where that useless tiny shuttle of ours lived, through the airlock, out into dead space, this crazy white spectral human-shaped... well, superhero..." He shook his head. "When she came back in—well, Boz's idea didn't pan out, in the end. But it wasn't through lack of pure raw courage. I tell you, I have never seen anything like it. She didn't go all smug and superior about it or lord it over the rest of us—but we all knew she had stepped up without pause to something the rest of us had hesitated over. There was something of Alabastra in her eyes, then."

"Something difficult, dangerous, or forbidden," Stella murmured.

"It was hardly forbidden, it was something that..."

"You said it. That's when the Alabastra persona took over."

"So I did," Jerry said. "And yes, difficult and obviously dangerous, potentially deadly, this. She didn't use this against us—but she never had to. We all knew very well what she had done. It isn't as if any of us could forget seeing her step out of that airlock. I hate to say this, to even think of it in those terms, but if I am honest we all ranked ourselves, in that crew. And she was in some ways the most expendable of us all—she was the mission specialist, the astronomer, the scientist, not someone essential to the existence of the mission itself, not like she was one of the command personnel or our medic or our engineer—if any one of us were to die out there without endangering the rest of us, it would have been her."

"So it was self-sacrifice?"

"Whatever it was," Jerry said. "She knew what we all knew. She still could have let someone else volunteer first, or waited to be designated by the captain, if it came to that. But she chose to grasp that nettle out of her own free will, and she never used that act to gloat over the rest of us. We knew she would be the first one to be expended if it came to that. We also knew that the most expendable one of us might also have been the most insanely brave one, too."

"Susan told me... one of Alaya's people ... all of you had a warrior or protector persona. I kind of thought Diana was at least partly that one for Lily Mae, but could this Alabastra persona have been..."

Jerry snorted. "Diana is lippy and doesn't hold back about telling you what she really thinks... in language that does make a certain class of adversary back off... but you never saw her and Boris square off. That was one of Boz's, remember."

A fleeting expression of a still-too-recent grief passed briefly across his face, but then he had his eyes and mouth back under his control, the grief veiled behind his usual sardonic smirk. "Boris and Diana... that was fireworks. But that was two mouthy kids squaring off. Diana could hold her own but she wasn't Lily Mae's warrior. And Alabastra isn't a protector. She's a *superhero*. Try and keep up. Count yourself lucky if you haven't had the occasion to meet Lily Mae's protector persona. You might easily confuse her with a superhero—she goes under the name of Stiletto and she's a seven-foot-tall black Valkyrie, as Lily Mae tells it—but she doesn't go in for heroics, like Alabastra might do. Stiletto's only job is keeping Lily Mae's hide intact. Alabastra might take on an army to do that—but Stiletto won't unless she is forced to. Her purpose is survival. You don't mess with that. And she doesn't talk much, at that. With Stiletto, what needs to be done is just done, in scary silence. You'd quickly figure out that Diana is all mouth and no ordnance."

Stella would have loved to pursue this—as always—but this time she was distracted by the return of the rest of the crew, delivered back to the habitat by their escort detail. Rob and Han greeted her courteously, Alaya even enthusiastically, and she spent a few moments talking to all of them—but then the three who had just returned from their workout excused themselves and retreated to their own quarters and Jerry used the opportunity to do likewise. Stella glanced in to Lily Mae's cubicle, saw that she still appeared asleep; she spared a moment to wonder if the way that Boz was never left alone to sleep was something to do with the alien entity he carried or it if was just that Boz himself was fragile enough to need the sentry while he slept. Lily Mae had barely been left on her own since Boz's death—Jerry had been left out of the gym session specifically so that he could be on hand for her, but he had not been sitting at her bedside when Stella arrived even though Lily Mae's door had been left open presumably so that Jerry could hear if she needed him—but although her door was still open all the others had retired behind closed doors into their own quarters, apparently leaving Lily Mae to her own devices. Or was that just something that would last for only as long as Stella was still there, and somebody would emerge to sit by Lily Mae as soon as Stella departed, the current status quo just a subtle invitation for her to go away?

She suddenly flashed on Martin's annoyed statement that the *Parada* crew were not in a zoo—but Stella had to wonder if the people in this habitat were starting to show signs of distress in response to the invisible bars of their cage.

There was still so much for her to do and to learn here. But it was clear that, for now, her presence was not wanted.

She took the hint, and left.

Perhaps it was partly due to the idea of captivity and cages that had begun to increasingly haunt her that Stella's instincts rose to rattle the bars of her own cage.

She had been a part of a team assembled to study the situation with the *Parada* and the *Juno*. The team had been split right from the beginning and Stella realized that she had no idea what, if anything, had happened to the civilian experts who had gone on to paw through the *Parada* itself, trying to figure out the role that mechanical or software issues might have had in what had happened to the ship—all that had been intimated was that they had all been whisked up to the shipyard station where they had parked the returning starship, if in fact it had not been spirited away somewhere else where it was less obvious and visible to unauthorized eyes. As far as Stella knew, they were all still up there. If so, then arguably that was a self-incarcerating situation, because the investigatory team was reliant on the people who had ferried them there to be so kind as to offer transportation back to the planet.

As far as the world-bound part of the team was concerned, though, the three of them who had been delegated to study the crews of the two starship—herself, Father Philip Carter, Dr. Ichiro Amari—they had just been immured in the same 'quarantine' that the subjects of their study were supposedly held under. But the *Juno* crew had been released—not least through Stella's own attempts to intervene—and at least one of the three outside investigators, Dr. Amari, had since departed, too, still bound (naturally) by the non-disclosure agreement he had signed not to ever discuss anything he had learned here with anybody, neither military personnel nor civilians who had no direct knowledge of the situation themselves.

Stella herself had bullied the security into a midnight excursion to the rooftop gardens for the crew who had remained behind.

There were personnel working in the base where the quarantine habitat was—but they couldn't all have been top-secret-clearance people who were locked down here until further notice. There were shifts that changed in the Surveillance room. There were people working administration duties. There were janitorial and medical orderly and lab assistant workers. They couldn't possibly all be military, subject to military disciplines. In other words, there were other civilians working here, besides herself. Other civilians, perhaps bound and trammeled by the same kind of agreement she herself had signed.

She had just been too focused on the starship crews to notice, or to think about it.

There was a security cordon around the deep underground base in which they all found themselves, to be sure—and there were probably security protocols imposed on everybody who set foot in this place, similar to what had been imposed on her such as when draconian control had been imposed on her own communications with the outside world. But was everyone who had any kind of job to do here literally kidnapped from the lives which they had led until that moment and permanently locked away in this underground bunker? Stella could not see how that could be managed, with the number of people who were required to run the place and take care of the captive crew. There were, as far as she knew, no secret staff dormitories anywhere—nor was the place (so far as she was aware) big enough to contain individual quarters for everybody who did even the most menial jobs here, unless there were numerous secret even deeper basement levels that she did not know about. These people had to be coming and going, under a gag order, to be sure, but still. Stella could not begin to understand what kind of threats or blandishments or direct intervention had had to be resorted to in order to prevent, say, a cleaner or an orderly from blabbing to friends or family outside about the things they had seen here—but something had to exist. Either such people were released from compounds otherwise kept under lock and key when their turn to do their work shifts came up, and marched back to those quarters when their shifts were done, and had no prayer of escaping this incarceration for the foreseeable future (if ever) if the government wanted the lid kept tight on the *Parada* story—or... or...

Or it was possible to go outside. And back in. And people had been going in and out ever since Stella herself had been immured between these walls.

She had not really had time to feel claustrophobic or trapped—but now, perhaps far more triggered herself by her brief escape into the garden than she had realized—Stella became aware of an itch to get out. Even for just a little while. To remind herself that a world outside of this habitat really did still exist.

She suddenly frantically missed the companion cat she had left behind 'for just a couple of days'. The cat might, physically, have been perfectly fine—but the government people could do nothing about the severed emotional connections, and the nerve ends of those were vibrating now with an unexpected pain.

On pure impulse, Stella retraced her steps back to Martin Peck's office. The ensign on duty in the anteroom was not the same one as had been there on her previous visit but the new one obviously knew better than to try and stop her. All she did, even while Stella swept past her and on to Martin's door, was to alert Martin about visitors incoming.

Martin looked aside from his screens as Stella stepped into the room.

"What now?" he asked, rather brusquely. "Something else has happened?"

"Things are happening all the time," Stella retorted, "faster than I can keep up with them. If I could publish any of this my career would be made..."

Martin looked down on her over the bridge of his nose. "You *do* realize," he said. A fragment of a sentence that left a whole lot unsaid, but it didn't need to be said. She did realize. Of course she realized. She made a frustrated little gesture with her hand, dismissing the subject.

"That's not why I am here," she said.

He swiveled in his chair to face her more fully. "Then what is it that I can do for you?"

"Am I allowed shore leave?" Stella asked.

"I beg your pardon?"

"This place. The… the bunker. Am I allowed to leave it? Go outside? Into the city?" She paused before adding: "And then return…?"

He stared at her, evidently a little nonplussed. Stella felt her hands ball into fists at her sides.

"You said, way back when, when I first got here," Stella said. "You said I had clearance…"

"Where do you want to go?" Martin asked quietly.

"I… nowhere. In particular." She gave a tiny helpless toss of her head. "I just want… to walk on a street again. To see… you know… faces of people I don't know." She paused, glanced around the room. "I've only been here such a short time, relatively speaking—but all of a sudden—the walls closed in…"

"Your garden escapade clobbered you, too, eh?" Martin said, sitting back and crossing his arms over his chest.

"Do people have passes?" Stella asked. "In and out? What happens to the people who just clean up in here? I mean… if all this is a deep secret… how can you trust anyone…?"

"Blackmail," Martin said.

Stella drew back, startled. "Seriously…?"

"There are no outside comms in here, except for people very high up on the totem pole, and even we have to go through regulated channels," Martin said. "I mean, I have access to the highest government and military people. But not their home numbers. They get reports, not social chitchat. People below those clearance levels, the non-military staff not under direct orders. Some of them do have residences in the city. Mostly they're people who have worked for us for years, people we absolutely know, have trusted for a sufficiently long time for that to be a factor. People who understand the first principles of working for an outfit such as ours. They don't last long, if they are not trusted. They have their very specific and particular codes and we know exactly where they are and what they are doing while they are here; when they end shift and go out, they are given a cover story to tell their people, should anyone ask."

He suddenly smiled rather warily. "But that's not what you came here to find out. You aren't a lab tech. You already have a high clearance, as you know, or you would never have been able to pull the garden thing. So what are you asking me?"

"What happened to Dr. Amari?" Stella said, apparently completely apropos of nothing.

Martin blinked. "So far as I know, he has returned to his practice and is out of our orbit," he said.

"And the others?"

"The others?"

"The ones on the ship—investigating the ship. The ones up *there*." She indicated the ceiling with a toss of her head.

Martin steepled his fingers and tilted his head, gazing at her speculatively. "The *Parada* has been moved from the shipyard station, if you have to know, and not much of use has been discovered from the work done on the ship so far," he said. "That part of the team is still there and still working—at least some of them are. One or two people are working at high-security facilities planet-side, coordinating data as it comes in. They haven't evinced any particular desire to go walkabout, the ones up there, if that's what you're asking. Nowhere much to go, out there. No gardens."

She winced. "All right. Stop. I took them to a garden."

"You want to go back there?"

"With them...?"

"Probably not," Martins said, and sounded genuinely regretful. "At least, not without... I mean, look what happened straight after..."

Boz. Stella swallowed hard and nodded.

"Not the garden, so much," she said. "Although I will admit that it did me a whole world of good to smell fresh air again, something that hasn't been recycled three times already before I got to breathe it. I just wanted... I don't know how to explain it to you. I needed to... be somewhere... that I could spread my wings a bit. I suddenly felt... trapped."

"That was hardly the object," Martin said.

"So I can go out?" Stella asked. And then added, once again, because that was an important issue, "And come back in again?"

Now that she had posed the question, she found that she yearned for permission to shake this place off and see something—anything—new and unrelated to the increasingly knotty problems she had come here to help solve, that the desire to leave the habitat area was a solid and palpable thing in the back of her throat, something she could almost taste. Martin pushed away his chair and stood up.

"How would you like a cup of real Turkish coffee?"

And she could suddenly taste that on her tongue, the hot bitter brew, the touch of the sugar cube to sweeten it.

"I..." she began, incoherently. "I mean—outside...?"

"In the city," Martin said. "Change back into civvies. I'll meet you at the security station in one hour."

Sufficiently nonplussed by the invitation, and grasping at the straw of permission from the top of the command chain to step outside of what had briefly become a suffocating air-tight prison, Stella didn't argue the point. She went back to her quarters and rooted around in the clothes she had brought here in her suitcase when she first arrived—that now seemed to be such a lifetime ago that she had to take a good long look at her own clothes in order to recognize them. There wasn't too much there to choose from but all of a sudden what she wore began to matter more than it had done since she arrived—and she even spent almost twenty minutes of her hour in front of a mirror, fussing with her hair and actually applying a smear of lipstick, even while repeating to herself like a mantra that this wasn't a *date*, that she didn't even like Martin Peck that way, that more often than not she actually resented the man and his being so much *in her way* when she wanted to accomplish something with the *Parada* people that was unsanctioned.

Finally, her hair down to frame her face and actually clutching a purse in her hands, she emerged from her quarters to hurry towards the security station where she had gone to chivvy the guards into making her garden outing happen, and almost ran Philip Carter down in the corridor.

He did a gratifying double take as he closed his hands around her shoulders and steadied her as he put her away from him.

"Whoa," he said. "You look... different."

"I looked exactly like this the first time you laid eyes on me," Stella said, a little defensively.

"Not quite, but I get the point," Philip said. "It's just that I haven't seen you wearing anything but those military PJs they gave us for quite a while. You look nice. Where are you going?"

She hesitated. "Out," she said, after a moment. "Outside. Topside. I've been promised Turkish coffee."

His face went still. "They're letting you go out? By yourself? Just like that?"

She flushed. "No," she said, unwillingly. "With... with Martin."

"Martin Peck is taking you out for coffee?" Philip said, sounding nonplussed. "Outside? In the city? What's going on, Stella?"

"It isn't like that," she said, not entirely sure what wasn't like what but wishing desperately that she didn't suddenly feel like some sort of a traitor—not just the obvious, abandoning the *Parada* crew to fraternize with the forces keeping them locked up, but also to Philip Carter himself. It was as if she were signaling that she was changing sides, even though there had been no real declaration of war made.

Philip's hand tightened on Stella's shoulder momentarily, and then dropped away. There was wariness in his face, even disappointment.

"You're going to tell him," he said.

"Of course not," she said, instantly and unexpectedly upset that he could have thought that she would betray the *Parada* crew, betray the friend and ally she had while working with them, betray the secret they both knew. It stabbed at her that Philip could even have thought that. It was just that this was an opportunity to get *outside*, breathe air just for a little while that hadn't been recirculated in and out of scrubbing filters and human lungs at least twice...

An opportunity that he hadn't been invited to share.

She clenched her teeth. There was nothing she could do about that, not at this point.

"Keep an eye on Lily Mae, would you?" she said deliberately bringing the topic back to the people both of them cared about. "I don't like it that she is sleeping so much. It's like she's creeping towards catatonia. And we know that she's the one who..." She stopped, suddenly very unwilling to utter anything at all out loud, glancing around the corridor for telltale signs of cameras or microphones. It was apparently that easy to kick up the dust of paranoia until it started choking free breaths.

"We'll be here," Philip said. His voice was perfectly calm and reassuring, something acquired through years of practice in his role as a priest. He was even smiling, ever so slightly, to underscore that reassurance—he radiated a sense of 'all-will-be-well' that was strong enough to glow in the dark. But underneath it all, Stella heard the unsaid, the reproach, something that might never have been there at all but that her own guilty conscience raised. *We'll be here. We aren't going anywhere.*

She hesitated, wondering if she was in fact just being selfish and self-indulgent, whether Philip was right, in his own inimitable sacerdotal way, to offer up that silent reproach. *Bless me, Father, for I have sinned...* But then, she wasn't Catholic. She had nothing to confess—not now, and not when she returned from this particular foray into the free world outside.

She had ties here. Interests. Responsibilities. She would do nothing to jeopardize any of that.

All of that required an hour's passionate and eloquent defense, or nothing at all. So Stella contented herself with giving Philip a small sharp nod, and slipped past him, taking long strides along the corridor so that she might put as much distance between them as possible in the shortest time. She didn't look back, but she knew that he had turned and followed her with his eyes. She could feel it on her back, an almost physical weight, light but definitely perceptible. She knew she would carry it outside with her, bear it like a burden with every step she took. She knew she shouldn't resent Phillip for this, but some tiny part of her *did*, damn it all—he had not precisely done or said anything to do it, not directly and not deliberately, but he had just put a drop of poison into the cup of sweetness she had dared to claim. Every small joy would now be shadowed by a thin ache of guilt in the back of it. A feeling of *I shouldn't be here, none of them can be, how am I supposed to enjoy this?*

Martin was waiting for her at the security station, but for a moment she didn't recognize him at all—he had also changed out of his uniform, and it was the first time she had seen him in civilian clothes. He couldn't help the short military hair—but he wore an open-necked short sleeved shirt and a pair of chinos. And sunglasses, pushed up to the top of his head.

Stella stopped, abruptly dismayed.

"What is it?" Martin said, having read the emotion that briefly altered her expression.

"I forgot sunglasses," she said, sounding awkward and gauche, like a child who had been promised a trip to the zoo and had let the excitement of it all drive everything practical out of her head.

Martin actually grinned, and it was something else that she could not remember having seen him do before.

"It's one of the things they sell in large numbers out there," he said. "We'll get you a pair. Ready? Let's go, then."

He punched in a code for the senior security supervisor on duty, and then gestured for Stella to precede him; she did, stepping through the opened security doors, and heard him follow before the door closed behind them with a decisive click. Martin walked around her, cupped her elbow in one hand, and guided her forward. Under this gentle propulsion she was ushered past another security checkpoint or two, into an elevator. Martin had a keycard which fit into a slot below the usual buttons; the elevator, obeying the instructions on the card, obligingly took them up from their subterranean level and disgorged them into a lobby with pale marble floors and lots of glass and shining polished metal. Stella narrowed her eyes as the light stabbed at them, and stumbled as she stepped out of the elevator. Martin took her elbow again.

"I feel as though I ought to tell you there are steps, just there, before you get down into the entrance hall," he murmured. "There you go. No, this way—this door. Come."

Heat and light enveloped her as they came out of the entrance to the World Government Building, its tall glass-and-steel façade at her back. Vehicles passed swiftly in both directions in the street before her. Beyond lay an open square with an abstract sculpture; on the far side of that, other streets, other buildings, a city spreading out. And above her, high above her, blue sky with a few puffy white clouds.

It was all something that she would not have thought twice about, only a very short time before. Now, it all seemed oddly miraculous. It was as though she was seeing her world through a whole new set of eyes.

And that thought framed precisely Philip Carter's words to her, the situation she had left behind in a space somewhere underneath her feet right now. She was guarding the knowledge that there *was* a whole new set of eyes down below.

She only became aware that she was holding her breath when Martin Peck's voice, oddly gentle, spoke from somewhere very close to her ear.

"You really needed this, didn't you," he murmured. "Come on, let's see about that coffee."

Martin steered Stella down one of the broad main avenues, making one quick detour to acquire the sunglasses he had promised her, but quickly turned into narrower side streets. It was a longer walk than she had expected or anticipated, the sun hotter and heavier on her shoulders than she remembered, and she was beginning to flag—but then, with an unexpectedness that made Stella stumble, they turned a corner and emerged into an area that broadened into a square, not paved but cobbled, filled with trestle tables under awnings fluttering with bright flags and lined along three of the four sides with round doorways which led down uneven steps disappearing into cool shadows. Martin pointed to a particular one of those.

"That one," he said, threading her along the outer edge of the trestles and then into the doorway of his choice. "Mind the step, take off the sunglasses, watch your feet."

Stella navigated the irregular stairs, taking a moment to let her sun-dazzled eyes adjust, and found herself entering a hostelry which was clearly not convinced that it had any obligation to cater to a tourist trade. Things looked honestly genuine, at times on the edge of threadbare, rather than a deliberate stage set that would lull a visitor into a vision of an Ottoman palace. The few people in the place glanced up as Stella and Martin entered, and then looked away again. They were not effusively welcomed, or made to feel like they were intruding; they were just two more people who had come in for a refreshment, neither more nor less.

"Don't be fooled," Martin said. "They know exactly what they are doing. And they make the best Turkish coffee to be had. And a few other things beside. Over there, the table by the far wall. I know you wanted out of below ground, but it's hot outside and these old stone walls were built this way for good reason."

Stella slipped into an alcove bench along the wall, pushing aside a pile of cushions, and Martin stepped away briefly to intercept a young man with an explosion of dark curls and the eyes of a falcon. They exchanged a few words, the young man nodded, and Martin turned back to settle alongside Stella amongst the cushions.

"I'm going to go out on a limb and say that you don't mind trying something different if someone you trust tells you it's good," he said. "So I ordered you something special."

"What makes you think I trust you?" Stella said, pushing her new sunglasses up on the top of her head, holding her hair like a headband.

Martin actually did a double take, and then gave her a tentative smile. "Well, you did let me bundle you down an ancient stair into an unfamiliar cellar based on nothing but a promise of a decent cup of coffee," he said. "A man just takes some things for granted."

They were sparring, and Stella found that she was actually enjoying it. Seeing her smile, Martin relaxed a little, letting a tenseness leave his shoulders.

"So," he said, "what do you want to talk about?"

"You," Stella said. "Who are you?"

Whatever Martin had expected, it wasn't this. He stared at her, momentarily at a loss for words. Stella tilted her head at him, and smiled.

"Martin Peck. You know everything about me. You know my background, my education, my experience, my home address, probably a good chunk of my super-secret passwords and the state of my bank account, my shoe size, even what kind of food my poor abandoned cat likes to eat. I know precious little about *you*. I know that they called you a doctor, although I don't know anything more than just the bald title, and that you're in charge of giving orders about anything to do with... with our friends, back there. I know for a fact that there are times you want to use a fly swatter on me. I know you've given me at least one final warning about what is going to happen next if I don't knuckle under and start behaving. And then you turn around and do... this."

She gestured at their surroundings with her hand. "You even smiled at me, back there. I don't think I ever saw you do that before. So. Who are you? You see, I've had a bit of a wild ride with trying to guess... which personality... I am talking to at any given time, in my... work situation. Maybe it's an occupational hazard, but I'm trying to work out right now if I am supposed to be doing the same thing with you."

"You are... something else," Martin said, shaking his head.

"I mean it," Stella said. "Who are you?"

"All right, then," Martin said, his lips curving into a ghost of a smile. "Yes, I am a medical doctor—I did my training while in the military, they needed a medical officer who was a ranking officer, and I made the cut. Yes, that was partly why I was put in place at... the base. You have no idea what kind of havoc it all caused when they... but that isn't a conversation we should have out here."

He paused. "I obey orders, but I respect spirit. I'm originally from

Philadelphia, my mother still lives there, my father died when I was twelve, I have no other family. My shoe size is irrelevant, but I'll tell you if you need to match it against forensic evidence. My hair is dark, and it curls uncontrollably when I don't have it almost obliterated, hence the style. And I don't have a cat."

The young man he had spoken to earlier chose this moment to arrive bearing a tray of hammered and engraved copper, dented and tarnished from much use but clean, and deposited a bright copper coffee *djezvah* on their table, accompanied by two small handle-less bowl like cups and a larger container piled with sugar cubes. He also put down a larger bowl in front of Stella, containing something frosted, shimmering, and dark pink, together with a long-handled spoon. The server ducked his head, smiled, and left.

Stella stared at her dessert bowl. "So what is it?" she asked.

"Try it."

She gave him a sideways glance, and finally sighed, picking up the spoon. It sank into the dessert, whose texture was something between a firm mousse and hard-frozen ice cream just beginning to melt, and she transferred a small experimental spoonful of the stuff into her mouth.

Martin laughed out loud at the expression on her face. "You like it."

"What *is* this stuff?"

"Rose water and pomegranate sherbet," he said. "They do... creative things with the taste buds, here."

"Pomegranate," Stella murmured, taking another spoonful, keeping her eyes on the bowl. "And afterwards, I get to go back underground. So did Hades woo Persephone."

"Only you," Martin said after a moment, taken aback. "Only you would come up with that right now. But sorry, Hades is a little above my paygrade. Shall I pour the coffee?"

Stella stuffed another spoonful of the cool sherbet into her mouth and nodded.

"This is nice," she said, a little later, the scraped-clean sherbet bowl to one side and taking genteel sips from the tiny coffee cup. "But now I feel guilty. Like I skipped class or something. Everyone else is locked up somewhere and working hard and I feel as though I cheated... Have you ever just... escaped... like this? Since... since that whole things landed on you?"

Martin hesitated for a moment and then nodded once, briefly. "I can't claim to be immune," he said. "Yes, I came out. Here, in fact. There's a reason I know about that sherbet."

"You didn't have any," Stella said. "Was that your guilt deference this time?"

"You're going psychometric counsellor on me, aren't you?"

"Isn't that why you brought me here?"

"Not for *me*," he said, with some asperity. "I'm perfectly sane."

For some reason, even as she laughed, that stabbed deeper at Stella than she expected.

"You think... I was needed because... others might not be?"

Martin glanced around, but they were almost alone in the place, the only other patrons being around a table in the corner opposite to themselves and having a loud boisterous conversation, in Turkish, punctuated by shouts of laughter.

"It's okay," Stella said. "I can circumlocute with the best of them. And I suppose we might as well discuss all of that in a place that isn't your office and doesn't feel like I have just been summoned to face the headmaster. It hasn't been that long, Martin, but there's a lot that's been stuffed into that short span of time already. I guess what I need to know is... what am I working with? Is there an actual time line? Is there a cutoff point looming that I don't even know about, a point after which everything will be stamped Too Late and I will be sent out to silent pasture for the rest of my life? What if there *aren't* any easy answers?"

"Stella, I *can't* just spill... yes, I suppose I am the headmaster, for the duration. I don't know how..."

"You said I wasn't first choice, for this," Stella said.

Blindsided again by the sudden change of subject, Martin blurted the truth. "You weren't. There was a list. You were on it. But not near the top."

"Who else did you ask?" Stella said. She didn't bat her eyelashes at him but her expression was definitely disingenuous enough to make Martin glare at her. "Ah, there you are," she said, in response to that. "I know *that* guy."

"If you have to know," he snapped, a little waspishly, "Istvan Ezsterhazy said he was way too old for this kind of thing at 80 and didn't want to meddle in it or start something he wouldn't be able to finish. Xi Huang's wife had just been diagnosed with a form of cancer that gave her a limited span of days on this earth, and he didn't want to waste any of that time on some government project. Vera Baruskov was herself in ill health. Michael Windermere simply declined—it was his choice, we didn't conscript people. Simone Ballantine had just got engaged—again—the woman's been married seven times but apparently she chose not to throw number eight under a bus before it even had a chance to try being, as it were, The One."

Stella's mouth was literally hanging open. She shut it with a snap. "You asked *all* the top people in my field?" she demanded. "And then you just ran out of candidates, and hauled in me?"

"One, nobody hauled you, we asked, and you said yes," Martin said. "Two, you're missing the point—you *were* on that list."

"It isn't a very *long* list," Stella said. "There aren't that many of us working on the kind of thing that you were obviously looking for in this instance."

"No, it isn't a very long list," Martin said quietly. "And you weren't the last one on it. But if you're thinking about yourself as a consolation prize, stop it—you aren't, and weren't, and anyway you've proved your worth many times over since you got here. Without you the—the—the other lot, the second lot, might still be down there." He flashed another rare smile, remembering Stella's turn before the tribunal that had gathered to discuss the fate of the three crewmembers from Earth's second starship. "Oh, but that was a moment," he said, savoring the memory. "For what it's worth, I don't think anyone else—on that list or not—who could have carried off what you did that day. What was needed was not only knowledge and experience, but pure passion— and you brought it all."

Stella flushed. "It damn near made my heart explode," she said.

"Stop it. Stop grinning at me. You look as though you'll never forget one wretched moment of that performance."

"I won't," he said. "As for the rest of your questions…some aren't going to be…" He looked up, caught the eye of their server, flourished a credit chit. "Have you actually seen the sea since you've been here? Let's walk."

Once they left the picturesque little cobbled square behind and gained a wider street, Martin flashed a military ID and quickly snagged a CitiCar to which he gave directions to a place whose name Stella didn't recognize. A short ride later, the car disgorged them at the requested destination, a park with signs that said it was called Bebek II, with trees and paved paths and a quay with small boats tied off alongside it, with benches strategically positioned to take in views of the sea, a suspension bridge, the turrets of an ancient fortress. Gulls fought over scraps on the quayside; pigeons strutted amongst the trees. It was still nearly four hours until sunset but the light was already beginning to change—or maybe, Stella thought, entranced, she'd just needed to be reminded of the translucency of sunlight filtered through leaves, or the scintillae shimmering on the water. The air was warm, but smelled of early fall, and of brine. Stella sighed deeply, and Martin, his hands stuffed into the pockets of his chinos, turned to glance at her.

"This world is beautiful," Stella said, in response to that look. "Even after we do our level best to wreck it. It still is. At least this part of it still is."

"I know," Martin said simply.

Stella looked at him, her eyes intense. "You see? You do understand. You were so *angry* when I took the… the others… to that garden. But you take me here, and it's the same thing, Martin. I needed to reconnect. So do they."

"It isn't as simple as that," Martin said. "You know it. But yes, I do understand. It's just that sometimes the pure comprehension simply doesn't give me the maneuvering space necessary to act upon it. You think I am a tin pot tyrant who rules with an iron fist and likes it. I didn't ask for this post, this command, this situation—but I am obeying orders, Stella. That is what one does, in my position. And you are a clear and present danger to those orders because you don't even see them and you just trample them underfoot, or you do see them and choose to ignore them and just shred them like confetti while you walk straight through them."

"There are times," Stella said, "that I'm perfectly certain you hate me."

"I don't hate you," Martin said, sounding oddly sad, perhaps at the necessity to formulate this response to Stella's statement. "You *exasperate* me. That's different."

"So tell me the truth. Tell me everything I need to know. Tell me before I ask, and I won't pester you by asking."

"Some things are classified," he said.

"So what isn't? Martin, I am not asking you for a blueprint from the ship, telling me that you found exactly where something flipped and sent them into this mess. I don't care about that. I don't even think *they* care about that, not any more, they're long past that. But I need to know the plan. The endgame. I need to know what I am working towards, if I can ever accomplish those goals, and at what point I begin to be a liability myself as someone who knows way too much."

"You signed..."

"I know. The agreement. And that's fine. I would love to publish some of the stuff I'm learning about this particular syndrome but I can live with the fact that I can't. I think I can safely say that this was not what the authorities might have been afraid it was—something happened out there, I don't know if your professionals dealing with the hardware and the computers will ever be able to nail down exactly what and why, but I think they will come to the conclusion that whatever happened was not a side-effect of starship travel. *Juno* proved that. The others... have been trapped in something that nobody could have foreseen or prevented. Now I think the most important question I have, here on ground zero, is how long. How long do you plan to keep this experiment running? How long does my involvement last? Where is this going? Where does it end?"

"You just used a whole slew of dangerous words without pause," Martin said, looking pained. "You see what I mean about rules?"

Stella lifted both hands, shrugged her shoulders at the space around them. "Who's listening?" she said. "Look, I'm sure you guys—the you guys of all that time ago—did everything you could to make sure that you covered all contingencies. But the problem with uncharted territory is that every contingency cannot possibly be covered. There were probably shields..."

Martin winced. "Stop," he said. "Nobody might be listening but we still shouldn't be spilling all the nuggets out here for anyone to pick up in passing. I can tell you this much—stuff was covered, from micro to mega—they had what was state-of-the-art shielding against potential microparticles, they had specific algorithms in place to avoid colliding with some stray world-sized rock; they..."

"What about in-betweens?" Stella asked suddenly.

"What?"

"Atoms and boulders. What about middling things?"

"What would they be trying to avoid, traffic?"

Stella blinked. "So what you're saying is that you built... a car... which sheds dust and can niftily avoid falling boulders, but you didn't give it brakes or bumpers or the ability to avoid another car?"

"There was another car?" Martin said, sounding bewildered.

"I didn't say that," Stella said, and it took a great deal of effort to keep her voice steady and light. She had not meant to get into these waters at all, it was skating far too close to the only thing that she did not want to discuss with Martin, the thing that she knew really happened to the *Parada* which had led to its crew's current predicament. She moved to refocus the conversation.

"We're getting distracted. I'm still asking you for a timeline. How long have I got, Martin?"

"That depends on you," he said.

Stella stared at him. "How?" she demanded. "Why?"

"Well," Martin said, "you might already have told me a lot of this. But I'm waiting for that final report."

"What final report?"

"The one in which you tell us that there is nothing more to be done," Martin said quietly.

"Yes...?" Stella said, after a pause. "The thing is, what happens *then*?"

"Well, then you get thanked for your expertise and you get returned to your life," Martin said.

Stella stopped walking, staring at Martin; it took him a moment or two to realize that she was no longer beside him, and he turned, a few steps away, to look back at her.

"What?" he said.

"Martin, I can't abandon them," Stella said. "Not now. I can't just sign off on them and wash my hands of it all and... and... just continue with 'my life'. They are part of that life now. Are you seriously going to classify me out of what happens to these people I have worked with, got to know, am interested in, care about—what are you going to do, disappear me or disappear them? Are you ever going to let them go? Are you even going to acknowledge their existence?"

"I can't tell you that," he said, a little desperately. "Partly because I don't know myself, and am not likely to be asked, about the details. At some point my command over a particular phase of a situation is as likely as not to get terminated, possibly passed up the chain. Stella, don't you understand? Neither of us owns this situation, or has any control over what ends up being the conclusion of it. We never did, right from the start."

"I should have said no," Stella said, dropping her eyes. "The others, on that list—they were wiser than I. It was pride—it was hubris—it was the very idea that someone had *sought my involvement*—I hadn't been told the whole story before I signed that agreement, none of us were, but I was told enough to intrigue me and then I was lost. But I should have known better..."

"We needed someone like you," Martin said. "They put me in charge because of the medical training. But I was clearly out of my depth there. I could supervise the physicals and make sure that they were in good health, as far as blood and bone and muscle was concerned. When it came to things of the mind, that was not my area. And it unraveled fast. We... I... needed help. Stella, *I* called for someone like you to become involved."

"Thanks," she said dryly.

He took the few steps back to where she stood. "I can terminate, if you feel..."

"*No!*" Stella rounded on him, eyes blazing. "You can't just dismiss me! I am involved now, and it might be simple enough in your military set-up to simply walk away when you're told to quit—but being a doctor doesn't just mean saying *Say aaaah* and prescribing an aspirin and then turning your back and pretending that you never heard of that patient before. I still have work to do here."

"Okay," Martin said, "what?"

Stella stared at him mutely, and he elaborated.

"You said you have work to do. What is it? What are you working on?"

"Now?" she said. "Here? All right, if you insist." She began counting off on the fingers of one hand with the other.

"One. Six people were involved in apparently the same triggering incident. I still haven't found out what exactly that was, only that it appears—from current evidence involving these... patients... and the control group from the other ship to have been a one-off and therefore not an issue as to pursuing further expeditions of a similar type. But I would still like to figure out what precipitated *this* round.

"Two. Six people involved in the same situation react nominally in the same manner—but every single one of them responds, within those parameters, differently. The one... we lost... was interesting because he stood out from the rest. They were more organic, and I could trace individual... fragments... to possible origins, in this one particular case they appeared to have been not created but manufactured, perhaps under duress, to take on a situation beyond the subject's control. They were artificial, they were characters in a play, they were even named and built around specific fictional characters the original subject was aware of.

"Three. As for the rest there's the situation of how specifically the twin identity factors into this, and there have already been things in this particular quadrant that have completely surprised me and I am sure that there is more here to find out. Four..."

Martin threw up his hands in a defensive gesture. "All right, you made your point," he said. "So how long?"

Stella, cut off in full flight, took a moment to regroup. "How long what?"

"How long do you need? To get all this research done?"

"How am I supposed to know?" Stella said, veering from bewilderment to outrage. "Research? It isn't just research. I'm trying to see if it is possible—and then it if is advisable—and then if there is a time line on which this might be accomplished—to consider integration to some degree. All right, in deference to your classifications I won't name anyone specific but at least one of my crew is almost there already, there is a situation, but he is in control of it and if you didn't know, you couldn't tell there was... a problem. One has reacted in unexpected ways to the loss of the one who is... gone... and apparently some sort of sedative was involved that I didn't know about and wasn't consulted on and she isn't dealing well with it. The others are on a range, some more likely to figure out how to cope with what has befallen them and some less so. *All* of them could be worked with to accomplish things, eventually, but I come back to my question—what is the endgame? If I am to prepare them for something, what is it that I am preparing them for? More of what they've experienced so far? Are they truly lost? I don't feel comfortable signing off on life imprisonment with no parole..."

And then, meeting his eyes squarely, she took a deep breath. "Is that midnight excursion to a deserted garden really going to be the last time they are allowed to walk under their world's sky?"

Martin winced. "God knows I don't want that."

"And then there's God," Stella said, picking up the gauntlet. "Father Carter has been a tower of strength and support but I think he is floundering in there, too. He isn't sure what his role is supposed to be. To report to Mother Church if these souls are permanently damned? Or which ones of these souls might be? Does he just answer to his superiors, or does he send you reports, too? Can you possibly make any sense of them?"

"That isn't in my jurisdiction," Martin said.

"But what about me?" Stella questioned, not letting him off the hook. "What about them... and me?"

"There will come a moment..." he began, and then she saw a tic begin in his cheek as he clenched his jaw together. "Stella, I cannot answer that. In the end, I may get the final word here now, but it isn't me who is going to have the final say. I respond to what is laid before me. To what you tell me. Why do I get the feeling that you aren't telling me everything?"

Stella abruptly lost color, and dropped her eyes. And then she steeled herself to look up again, meeting his squarely, and steadily. Her hands hung by her sides, and if one of them slid sideways a little, in what was something of a trademark gesture for Stella, to hide behind a fold of her skirt where she childishly crossed her fingers out of sight, Martin didn't appear to notice.

"What I can tell you," she said evenly, "I have told you. That of which I can speak with authority, I have shared. I didn't think the military would want half-baked intuitions and theories until I have distilled them into something more empirical... as empirical as I can get, under the circumstances. The things of which I am sure, you know. The rest..."

"So there is a 'rest'," Martin said.

"I am a scientist, and a healer," Stella said, drawing herself up to her full height and staring at Martin in challenge and pride. "That's why you brought me here. Do not ask me to put pieces together of which I am still not at all certain in a way that matches a pre-set agenda."

It was one of the hardest things she had ever done in her life, standing squarely in a lie she was choosing to give him, hiding the truth that was not hers to reveal underneath that lie, hoping she had it in her to conceal it well enough and long enough to prevent potential catastrophe for people she had come to care passionately about.

He held her gaze for a long moment and then closed his eyes and sighed.

"I was going to wait for the sunset," he said bleakly, "but it might be a long wait, under the circumstances. You want to stay? Or are you ready to go back now?"

"How long?" Stella said, inexorably. "How long have I got?"

"Until you give me a professional conclusion," Martin said.

"And if that conclusion is inconvenient...?"

For a little while they had stood together, and the shared moment showed that they could do this—but there was a wall between them now, and Stella didn't know if she could get past that again. She stood looking at Martin and could find nothing to fault him for—and yet she could not but see in him a sort of enemy, for herself and for those whom she was still, desperately, trying to protect from a fate whose exact details she could not find out but whose very undefined nebulousness frightened her. For his part, she could read on his face that similar emotions were at play inside him, too—that he was looking at her and trying to come to terms with the fact that there might come a time when anything, and everything, might have to be sacrificed in pursuit of a higher goal and that his might be the order to sanction that sacrifice... and that she, Stella, might quite possibly prove to be a part of what he might need to destroy.

7.

They made their way back to the World Government building in almost complete silence, with Stella thinking that she would always associate the taste of pomegranate with this now—brief joy, then hope, then a sense of loss so profound that she could not begin to fathom it yet.

Back in the base, past the final checkpoint, the two of them hesitated for a moment, finding it difficult to look at each other or meet one another's gaze. It was Stella who finally did it, sighing deeply and looking up with an air that was at once melancholy and defiant.

"Thank you for today," she said.

"You are more than welcome," Martin responded, and there was enough warmth and sincerity in his voice to make Stella's breath catch a little—but at the same time the words were distant, perfect and correct and polite and almost followed by some aspect of a formal address. They had been close, for a moment, up above what Stella had called the 'situation'—they had shucked their formal relationship and tried for something that transcended that, but they were back inside now. Martin was still wearing his outside 'civvies' but his mind was already back in uniform.

Stella hesitated, uncertain of how to take her leave, and Martin preempted her by giving her a small incline of the head and walked away.

She had meant to ask him if this experiment could ever be repeated. If she could have his specific, on-the-record permission to go out by herself. If she could get clarification on her own level of rank in the circumstances, or if being civilian personnel here on sufferance by the military and the higher government authorities meant that despite the small taste of freedom she really was in effect locked up and locked away and being treated as a potential infiltrator, spy, or enemy.

She admitted to herself that they had good reason for thinking that. She *was* keeping secrets, after all.

Philip intercepted her in the corridor so quickly after this, as soon as Martin was out of sight, that Stella actually recoiled in alarm when his hand closed around her wrist.

"Jesus," she said, appropriately enough, but not a little aggrieved, "were you spying on me?"

"Well, I want to know what happened," Philip said, "but no. I wasn't lying in wait. At least, not in the way you think. You must come. While you were gone..."

"What?" Stella said, abruptly frightened. "Is Lily Mae all right?"

"Still Sleeping Beauty. Which is not necessarily good—she doesn't seem to *want* to wake up. But while she's out of it—and well after Boz disappeared, and took himself out of that equation—the rest of the Children's Collective came out. What's left of them. Apparently even minus fully a third of their number they can still function as some sort of a unit."

"Did they say anything?"

"Not directly," Philip said. "But I have something for you. From them."

Stella stared at him. "Something *from* them?"

The expression on Philip's face was almost pleading, and Stella looked around with a furtiveness that she hated admitting to. And then, said, pitching her voice at just the right level to be overheard if anyone was listening, said lightly, "It was so nice to be able to take a walk by the sea. I brought something for you. A present." In an undertone, she added, "Okay. Your quarters or mine?"

He nodded in her direction, and she continued speaking in her to-be-overheard voice.

"Come by in a little while; I just want to grab a quick shower, walking in the sun took more out of me than I remember. It feels as though I hadn't done it in years, not weeks."

"I have something to finish up," Philip said, in a similar voice. "About an hour?"

"Sure," she said. "See you later."

Stella returned to her quarters, showered, and changed back into her base-casual wear from out of her civilian garb while feeling rather too much like she was peeling off a personality—one she didn't seem to know very well any more—and resuming a more comfortable identity with a sense of focus and purpose. The irony of her own persona's fragmenting under stress, albeit not nearly as radically as those of the people she had been brought here to study, was not lost on her, and it showed in her expression when a chime at the door indicated Philip's arrival at the appointed time.

"You look grim," Philip said. "I take it things didn't go all that well?"

"You don't look too happy yourself," Stella retorted. "No, in point of fact, things didn't. Oh, it started very nicely. Coffee and cool sherbet and picturesque old cobbled squares and a quayside by the sea... and then... but I'll tell you another time. What happened? What did the children do?"

"You didn't say anything...?"

"No, I said I wouldn't," Stella said, rather more sharply than she intended. "I think there are things he wasn't telling me, either, and that makes us even. The difference is that he is in a position to do something about things if he wants to and I just... have to keep secrets."

"More secrets," Philip said. "I have something for you. Specifically for you. *They asked me to give it to you.*"

"Well?" she said. "What is it?"

"Let me just tell you, first. I was there, in the habitat, and everyone was—well—it was situation as normal as it gets in there. I'm not sure who was in charge of whom at this point but Lily Mae was out of it, the others would all occasionally wander by and look in just to keep an eye on her, but other than that—Rob was reading, Jerry was playing some stupid juvenile board game with Alaya and gloating about winning, and Han was putting together the last of this three-dimensional puzzle he'd been working on for days now—when all of a sudden they all just dropped whatever they were doing and came and sat around the table in the common area. If they said something, I couldn't hear it, and I clearly wasn't invited—but then Han got up and went to his quarters and came back with a sheaf of paper, and with pens. And they all sat there for a while, like well-behaved little children, completely focused on drawing something on those papers. I wandered over and asked what they were doing..."

Stella frowned, and Philip shrugged defensively.

"Hey," he said, "I could have just sat and watched, I suppose, or left—but it was so... so startling. I kept on trying to figure out what the signal had been, if there had been a signal, but I couldn't remember anything happening that would have caused them all to change, just like that, at the same time."

"The children apparently always had their own rules," Stella said. "They showed you?"

"No, not then. They covered the drawings with their arms, like kids do, and Alaya told me to go away. So I did—I went in and sat by Lily Mae instead for a while. You ought to look into that, by the way, while we're on the subject. She sleeps, and she wakes thirsty, and drinks, and then sleeps again. That cleaner woman left a dozen or so water bottles in the bathroom for Lily Mae when she last came through, and she took almost as many empties away with her. If they have her on any medication, you should probably look at the side effects—this isn't looking good. Anyway, back to today—Rob came into Lily Mae's cubicle after about twenty minutes of this, and he was clutching a whole pile of paper in both hands, and I could tell he was still Gem, and he handed me the papers, very seriously, and said, 'Those are for you. And one of them is for Doctor Stella. You'll know.' And then turned and left."

"What were the drawings?"

"I don't even know," Philip said. "One of the orderlies took them. To be filed, he said. They must have been watching, and someone wanted to see what they had done—I don't know on whose orders, because Martin was clearly out there with you, he must have left standing orders for this kind of situation, or someone else took it upon themselves to step in. They came almost immediately, I barely had time to take the briefest look at the pages from Rob—from Gem—before I heard the habitat doors opening and they came marching in demanding the papers..."

"I have to go up to the library and get a look at this stuff," Stella said. "Damn it all. This is clearly in my bailiwick. *I* need to see, not some military brown-nose..."

Philip paused and looked at Stella with the beginnings of a slight sympathetic grin.

"What *did* Martin Peck do out there?" he asked.

"I have more questions than answers," Stella retorted. "He's just 'following orders' and that kind of attitude makes me itch to throw spitballs at it. Except that this time more is at stake than just me rebelling at a 'thou shalt not'. He was... actually... being nice. He *was*. But I got the distinct feeling that there were things he couldn't tell me. Wouldn't tell me."

"There are things I don't tell people," Philip said.

"You have the whole seal-of-the-confessional thing going for you," Stella said. "That covers a lot of ground when you want it to, I suppose. Martin has his 'orders' and if he wants to tell me that things are sealed or classified and I don't have the clearance, that's as good. What's my excuse, when I stay mum about things?"

"Doctor-patient privilege?" Philip suggested, after a beat.

"Hardly applies when practically all my interactions with my 'patients' are done under surveillance," Stella snorted. "But we digress. The drawings?"

"I have no clue. Try the library first. But they didn't get all of them."

Stella sat up. "Where is it?"

Philip fished out a piece of paper which showed attempts of being neatly folded as small as it would go but which had clearly been crumpled into a ball before that had had happened.

"Sorry," he said, handing it over, "I liberated that one before I handed the rest over, just balled it up and threw it under Lily Mae's desk a moment before the orderly came in and took the remainder of the pile. It was on top of the handful that Gem gave me and it was clearly the one meant for 'Doctor Stella'. I don't suppose you can ever slip it back into the library record now."

"What is it?" Stella asked, unfolding the paper, and then sat staring at a childish drawing of a creature which had a large head with a mane of what looked like wild hair spraying out in all directions from a hairline high on a domed skull, large inexpertly rendered black eyes, an elongated body with preternaturally long arms and legs, and an attempt at huge moth-like wings above and behind it all. The letters I L G were incorporated into the drawing—one above the creature's head, one shaded into one side of what appeared to be a high collar of some sort around its neck, and one dangling from its left hand as though carried by its handle. Incongruously, it had a speech bubble above it and inside that was—in childish capitals—the word 'Hello'. Stella raised haunted eyes to Philip. "You think this... might be...?" she asked haltingly.

"It might be," Philip said, staring at the paper. "I mean... I have no idea if an adult with a greater amount of artistic talent might give us a clearer picture, here—remember, this was produced by someone whose mind claims to be only seven years old, no matter what the chronological age of the hand that held the pen. But from what I am seeing... and being what I am... I am asking myself why God sent those people one of His angels."

On the morning after her return from her city excursion, Stella threw herself back into work. She checked on the crew, and discovered Lily Mae awake but not particularly communicative and the rest of them in a strange mood, almost expectant, looking up to find somebody's eyes on her at any given moment, as if they were waiting for her to say or do something specific.

Uneasy and oddly apprehensive, still unhappy about Lily Mae's status, she cut the visit short and made her way to the library to access Lily Mae's medical charts, pulling up the detailed daily reports for the period since Boz's death. Lily Mae had indeed been administered a light sedative in the immediate aftermath of that event, and Stella could not fault the medical response—the two were known to have been close, and Lily Mae had literally been holding Boz's hand when he died. It was an obvious thing to do, to help someone who could have been potentially deeply affected by something like that. The doctor who had prescribed the sedative could not possibly have known about the thing that Lily Mae now carried, the presence that she had inherited from Boz, and could not have been expected to factor in any kind of effect that the sedative might have had on that. Stella could not see anything there that she would have done differently or that seemed to be deliberately done as means to nefarious ends—but something definitely seemed to have been affected, and she had not even been consulted on the matter, despite being a primary care physician on the record. She gave herself a moment to resent this.

Stella could find no repeat dose of the original sedative, or any further medications which might have affected the patient, and yet Lily Mae had barely stirred from her bed since they'd lost Boz. Stella herself could count on the fingers of one hand the hours she herself had been able to observe Lily Mae awake and moving. Something was wrong, but unless Lily Mae had been given medication which had not been noted on her chart for some nefarious reason which was being carefully concealed Stella could not put her finger on what was amiss. There was enough silence and secrecy already about the *Parada* crew that she could not bring herself to believe that there was yet another layer of conspiracy underneath all of that—and in any event she didn't think that Martin Peck would have signed off on anything like this. He was nothing if not honorable in his own strict ways. Stella might not have official rank in his military universe but she was a civilian whom he himself had collaborated on putting in charge of the *Parada* people. She knew there were things he wasn't telling her—but those would be strategy and planning issues, not basic medical ones. He'd told her in so many words that he had been instrumental in bringing Stella herself—or someone else with her skill set who could have taken her place—into the *Parada* crisis; he would not then actively work, or collude in, plans to hamstring the contribution that expert could bring.

Stella abandoned that line of investigation, contenting herself with putting a warning note on Lily Mae's record that any further medications to be administered to the patient were to be run by Stella herself, in order to cross check potential damaging interactions with existing treatments that may have already been in place and that the patient's excessive lethargy and sleep patterns should be monitored closely. Then she turned her attention to other things.

She found the original Children's Collective drawings, the physical papers, in a folder in the back shelves of the library, and laid them out side by side on a work table. Without the one Philip had sequestered and brought to her, there were seven others, all of them executed with the kind of childish hand that was to be expected from the young minds that comprised the Children's Collective—and Stella had to consciously remind herself that this was a truncated Collective, at that, seeing as Boz's Jiminy was gone and Lily Mae's Coco had not participated in this particular conclave. None of the pictures were signed so there was no way of really knowing which one of them had produced which drawing; nor was there anything in these sketches to indicate why the Children's Collective suddenly assembled—apparently spontaneously—to produce them. And, indeed, at least five of the seven seemed... arbitrary. Stella discarded the one infested with butterflies—there may have been psychological interpretations of butterflies in this context, but Stella was inclined to believe that this particular one was just something done by Momo or Glory, two of the four little girls in the Collective. There was a complicated set of two drawings done by what appeared to be the same hand and seemed to be something of a storyboard, telling a kind of story that could be inferred from the inexpertly rendered images, something that involved flying masked superheroes ranged against serried ranks of almost comical bug-eyed monsters, which, seeing as neither side was rendered in anything much more complex than barely fleshed out stick figures, it was hard to take all that seriously. Stella suspected Jerry Hillerman's Gadfly as the author of those. There was an empty landscape consisting of hills covered with large daisy-like flowers (possibly Momo or Glory again). There was one which appeared to be no more than a graphically-rendered comic book 'BLAM', just nested stars that looked like an explosion from the center point of the paper; they'd had had no colored crayons, just pens, but Stella could vividly see this particular image as being passionately colored in in oranges and reds. But the last two drawings Stella pulled out of the pile and studied more closely.

They may or may not have been done by the same hand—and she suspected Rob's, or at least his Collective persona, Gem. At least one of them was definitely done by the same person who had drawn the one Philip had brought to Stella as a personal message. The first one was reasonably innocuous—just a child-imagined spaceship, with rocket flames coming out of the base below what looked to be spindly-looking landing gear but with the ship itself apparently suspended by itself in the middle of the page and surrounded by artlessly drawn stars. The spaceship had a window, and an attempt to portray a stick-figure-type person who was looking out of that window into the stars. Stella's own imagination improved the image as she stared at it, because there was something terribly huge and sad and lonely about the whole thing, and if it had been possible to see the face of the figure behind the window inside that spaceship, had the young artist been capable of rendering such a thing at all, Stella could imagine an expression with the downturned mouth of sadness, an endless sorrow in the eyes.

The second drawing, though, was the one which she stared at the longest, reading in it a message that she could not *quite* pin down but which seemed to gel perfectly with something she had thought about before... if only she could remember what precisely that was. It showed five human figures—again, little more than barely stick-men—ranged in a semi-circle at the top of the page. Behind each of those figures, like an echo or a repeat, many smaller similar figures receded away towards the edges of the paper. Below and in the middle of the page stood a sixth figure, which appeared to be holding hands with a child-sized smaller figure. These two were encircled in an irregular kind of balloon shape, lightly cross-hatched, as though they were in their own separate little bubble.

It wasn't a huge leap to assign the six figures in the drawing to the six individuals from the *Parada* crew. It wasn't even difficult to give them identities. One of the top five figures was shown as having longer hair, and it was clearly supposed to be Alaya. Two of them were a little removed from the others, towards the left of the page, and they seemed to have been rendered so that the position of their limbs was an almost exact mirror image of one another's—Rob and Jerry, the twins. Of the remaining two, one was depicted as a shade bigger than anyone else on the page, which indicated authority, and thus Han; the other, positioned slightly further from the rest at the far right hand side of the page, had pointillist hair, and that pointed to Lily Mae's own close-cropped tight-curled hair.

Which left the isolated one at the bottom as Boz, the engineer. The one who died.

Was that the point of the bubble? A childish rendition of death?

The ones on the top all had repeats of themselves, shadows of shadows of shadows, attached to the primary figures and disappearing into the distance—the fractured personas? Was it supposed to be a depiction of what had happened to them all—the multiple people who now inhabited each individual body?

If so, why was Boz depicted so differently? Simply because he was gone?

Who was the child figure?

Stella stared at the drawing, feeling the itch of something... something... something others had said to her. Something she herself had said to other people.

Boz. Boz had always been different. She had seen it herself. She had commented on it.

The personalities of the others had always felt organic. Parts of the original whole, peeled away from the core, acquiring their own individuality along the way, becoming as real and alive as the original, as any other persona in the shared body. Boz... what was it she had called him? Artificial? As though he had created his own fragments to order, perhaps first picking names for them and then crafting the personas to fit...?

But what was the child figure...?

It called us out first.

That thing, in the secret drawing, the one only Stella had, not part of the collection. Illogon. The alien entity. The thing that called out *the children.* The Children's Collective. The thing that had potentially caused this entire situation, the thing that had taken six human minds and shattered them.

Six minds. What if it had always been only five? What if Boz had never been truly afflicted?

There had been a loneliness about him. An isolation. The others had always protected him, had always been close, had never left him alone. As though they knew—as though they felt that he was different, that he needed the support of the Many, which all of them had, to strengthen him while he carried the heaviest weight of all, the One, the alien mind itself.

What had been different? Was Boz just the most stubbornly sane of them all? The most completely focused, to the point that there was no room in his brain to spare for creating entire personalities to carry aspects of his self? Had he been the key to it all... and now he was gone...?

Stella pushed aside the drawings and turned to the computer screen, calling up Boz's file and all the personalities they had had on record for him, staring at each of the names and trying to remember exactly what it was that had distinguished that particular personality from the rest. And then, squaring her shoulders, she began to type in search queries for every single name on Boz's list, cross checking with Boz's own biographical data.

This was going to take a while. But the picture was coalescing in her mind. And it was no longer the same picture she had constructed from the pieces that she had been given when she had arrived here, no longer the picture which she had believed so unquestionably to be true.

Philip found Stella in the library, hours later, still at the computer, concentrating so hard that she didn't even realize that he had come in until he touched her shoulder gently and she jumped, swiveling her head around and staring at him for a long blank moment before the recognition came.

"Do you plan on eating anything today?" Philip queried. "Also, did your mother ever tell you that if you don't stop staring at a computer screen for at least a little while every day your eyes are going to turn square and stay that way?"

"I have something," Stella said, ignoring his attempts at levity. "I've been taking way too much for granted, or at face value. It seems like I just wasn't seeing what was right in front of me. For whatever reason, the Children's Collective has decided to give me a nudge. Here, if you didn't have a chance to look at those drawings when you got them handed to you, take a good look now. That one. The one with the semi-circle of those figures on the top. Do you see? Do you *see*?" She hooked her finger over the page and tapped on the solitary figure at the bottom of the page. "That. You know who that is?"

"Is this meant to be them? The six of them? And if they are—then is that one... Boz?"

"I should have done this as soon as I started getting a sense that he was *different* from the rest. I told you that, remember? That I thought he—that his people—were more, I don't know, *artificial* than the other five's fragment collections? That it felt more like he picked out a name, and then whittled out a puppet character to inhabit it? Well, how about, characters to *pretend* to inhabit it? Philip, what if he was the only one who was not fragmented at all?"

Philip lifted his eyes from the drawing, and they were haunted. "But why?"

"Because of..." Stella glanced around, wary. Of all places, the library might have been wired, and she didn't want to blurt out things she didn't want known. "Well, I haven't figured it all out yet," she said, instead of what she had intended to say. But she smiled at Philip, and he understood the unspoken perfectly well. The *Parada*'s alien guest was very much present for both of them. And Philip was the one who voiced the irony of it.

"Protection," he said.

Stella nodded, her expression intense. "They are extremely bonded," she said. "And when... whatever happened... happened up there... oh, it must have been appalling, for Boz. He was the only one who didn't..."

"I take it you think all these other figures are the other fragments? The other souls?"

"Well, but souls are your department," Stella said. "The other personalities, yes."

"But if the numbers are accurate, there are more than we know...?"

"Don't take it too literally," Stella said, "I don't think the seven-year-olds who drew that were concerned with accuracy. What was intended was the idea be conveyed, not the details."

Philip tapped the smaller figure beside the Boz-character. "But then what's this?"

"There was one," Stella said. "One true one. One true fragment. Jiminy. I heard it said—I *heard* it, and I skated right over it—they were the first to come out. The children. The Children's Collective. *All* the children, from every one of them out there. Whatever caused their sense of wonder to snap loose and break apart from them and assume its own—if you like—soul... that's what the children were, Philip. That wonder. The awe. The endless astonishment of it all. The empty cups waiting to be filled. They're real, all of them—yes, even Jiminy. But Jiminy was the oldest of the children—even that. Jiminy was the wariness within the wonder. Jiminy was the most adult of the Children's Collective. And when the rest of them kept going, peeling persona after persona off and giving each one life and existence, Boz and his mini-me, the Jiminy soul, they... they couldn't follow. They stood back, and they watched, and oh God, Philip, I don't know yet, I can't tell you exactly, I don't know whose idea it was in the end—but he just *made it up*—to be like the rest of them...each of them contained multitudes, in the end, but Boz, Boz was always alone..."

"But there were others—I know, I think I spoke to—"

"You thought there were. Because there were the others in the rest of the crew, and so you saw... what I saw... you saw multiples in Boz, too. But now that I think back over every interaction I had with him..."

"You wondered once if there was anything left of the original Boz inside of him," Philip said. "I know you said that. And now you're saying that it was *all* the original Boz, and that everything else was—what—an act?"

"Of desperation, perhaps," Stella said. "Look, look at this—" She swiveled back to the computer and enlarged one of the several windows she had open on the screen. "I went back to the list of named personalities we had on Boz and I did a search on the names. And look—I can map them all. His 'professorial' persona, Leonid—Boz did his Masters degree under the dual supervision of a Dr. Lionel Winger, at Cornell, and a Dr. Leonid Adamov, from Bucharest. Hence Leonid. He just took the name. The thuglet with which he always faced Lily Mae's Diana—Boris, a name of Russian origin that maps onto the personality of the bully, which works in the known cultural context. There was a well-known and very ambitious local regional politician in Boz's time with the name of Imre—hence his Imre Imperator persona. He has what I call a 'saint' persona—"

"Konstantin. Yes, I think I actually spoke to that one."

"You would have done. He created it for you," Stella said.

Philip reared back. "He what?"

"You were a priest. He felt as though you might want to communicate with... someone you might relate to."

"Where do you get that from?"

"Look it up. The first time Konstantin appeared as a named personality arrow in Boz's quiver, it was when he first spoke directly to you. There was no mention of him before that."

"I don't... I don't know what to say to that," Philip said, looking dazed.

"You created a saint," Stella said. "So to speak, anyway. That would be quite a feather in your cap to take back to your supervisors."

"If what you say is true, I faked a saint, which is not the same thing," Philip said. "You said they all had a warrior or protector persona—did he?"

"I believe so. Named Khan, and again, that fits, because that region remembers the Mongol invasions and they were their history's bad guys, warriors, cold and ruthless, and I guess that he invoked one to 'protect' him, that would fit with making history pay its debts to him."

"But what about—there was this pagan God persona—"

"Perun? I don't know. Possibly he was running out of ideas by that stage. The others all had at least ten personalities and he was starting to show some which he could not fully substantiate. I 'met' someone— just once—who claimed to be a young gypsy boy. But the name was not Romany, and although the boy claimed to be able to play the violin, he also neatly precluded being put in a position to prove it by saying that he hadn't been able to do so ever since a nebulous 'they' broke the fingers of his right hand. He..."

Philip sat up. "But wait. There is at least one other persona out there with a god-name."

"What? Who?"

"Jerry. Loki."

"Yes, but you see—that makes sense—Jerry had that personality all along, the trickster persona, the edge of selfishness, and Loki was a name that fit that persona. Whereas Boz then—ah, maybe he was even inspired by this!—plucked a name from a pantheon that he felt more culturally comfortable with, and then created a persona to match it. It's exactly the opposite to what Jerry had done—a mirror image, almost."

"I believe you, even though I don't begin to understand what you are talking about," Philip said helplessly. "And Jiminy, then—how was Jiminy different?"

"Jiminy was real," Stella said. "That much I can bet on. *Everything* else Boz claimed to be was a fabrication."

"The question then is, were the others fully aware of this? I mean, did they really *know*? And if they did know, why did they say nothing— and if they didn't know, how come they couldn't tell?"

"That might be something I can, carefully, talk to some of the others about. All kinds of questions arise. And they aren't exactly saying nothing any more, are they?" Stella indicated the tell-tale drawing Philip still held with a toss of her head. "I can't believe it took me this long to see..."

"We've been re-enacting the three wise monkeys story," Philip said wryly. "If you weren't seeing, I wasn't hearing, and they certainly weren't talking."

"Well, we all are now," Stella said. She swiveled back to the computer. "I checked the others, too. Look. Some of the personas aren't given a name—Rob's Poet, for instance, and Alaya's Red Empress, and, well, Han's evil twin just goes by Cap which would be short for Captain—but for those that are named, the names are random, Philip. They don't map to anything that I can directly find in any of their backgrounds. Jerry has a den mother persona named Edwina, and unless he's projecting the dimly remembered personality of some long-gone kindergarten teacher, I can find no Edwina in his personal record. Lily Mae has a bunch of named personalities—Billie, Mamie, Diana—and I can't find anybody by any of those names in her past either. Rob's named personas include Simon and Eddie—again, no matches. Han maps to Hal, to Raff, to Charlie—no matches. Alaya has a psychology guru by the name of Susan, who has nothing to do with her past. All of these new people, the named ones, they just... knew themselves and named themselves and the names fit. Not one of Boz's ever did that."

"Except Jiminy."

Stella paused. "There was something about Jiminy... something different about the Children's Collective." Stella chewed on her lower lip. "Damn. If I had figured this out earlier maybe I could have pushed Boz out of the fugue state. He was still whole, Philip. He was himself. He could have helped us figure out the others. Maybe he could have been rehabilitated, released..."

"Maybe that is why it all fell out the way it did," Philip said quietly.

"What do you mean?"

"Think about it," Philip said quietly. "And—again—it isn't something you haven't said before. There are...were... six of them, Stella. Only six of them. The rest of us are all strangers from a different century, a literally different world from the one that they left—remember the discussions you've had with them concerning all the stuff that happened while they weren't here? Everything they knew is changed—everyone they personally knew, family, friends—it's all been dust and ashes for a hundred years or more. All they have is one another—and then, when they came home, they got locked up in that habitat area *with* each other and forced to interact with that tight little group of people—that's all they've got. You can't just randomly pick and choose which of them you think might be 'releasable'—it would break the only whole thing they have, the only thing they know—the cohesion of that little group. Themselves." It looked like he was about to say something else but caught himself in time. He shook his head in a small frustrated gesture. He couldn't talk about the alien presence and how that might have changed the game, not out loud, not here, and Stella heard the silence and understood.

"I have to talk to Martin," Stella said. "This does change the prism I'm looking through."

Philip gave her an urgent look and Stella nodded.

"I know. Go away, Philip. I have a report to write and it's going to be a tough one. And before I take it to him, there are a few other things I need to check up on."

"Eat first," Philip said, smiling, but obediently getting up to obey the dismissal.

Stella grinned back at him. "Meet you for dinner later," she said, and swatted at him. "We can talk more then. Now go. Let me work. Keep an eye on the crew for me."

It took Stella another couple of hours to pull everything into an urgent report for Martin, even dutifully scanning in the drawings from the Collective although the report itself contained a thinly disguised rebuke for those drawings, which were clearly in Stella's own remit and should have gone to her, instead of being hijacked by someone plainly under separate orders. Stella had to stop herself from starting that part of the report with 'As you already know...', but she was pretty certain that the drawings had been seen by Martin before they landed in the library, and there hadn't even been a notification for Stella herself that they existed. It was only through Philip that she had learned of them at all.

When she finally copied the report onto her personal tablet and signed off the library computer, pushing her chair back and knuckling her blurry eyes, she remembered Philip's admonition to eat something and became aware that she was in fact starving; her stomach rumbled in confirmation. She texted a note to Philip to ask if he felt like meeting her at the cafeteria imminently and while waiting for a response took a quick detour to the *Parada* quarters to check on Lily Mae.

She was not pleased to find that Lily Mae was asleep again, curled up on her side with her hands folded underneath her chin in a vulnerable and almost fetal position. Beside the bed were two water bottles, one empty on the floor and a quarter-full one on the bedside shelf; another half-full bottle teetered precariously on the bathroom sink, and the shrink-wrapped pack of twelve wedged into the bathroom, which Aisha the cleaner had brought the day before, only had three full bottles left in it. Stella looked around briefly for any detritus to account for the rest of the pack, but when she glanced at the door it was to see Rob Hillerman standing there, his hands folded primly in front of him. It was a feminine gesture but it didn't look like he was Gem; Stella did the usual mental shuffle, looking for the personality that matched.

"Ruby," Rob said, recognizing the blank look of non-recognition and supplying a name politely but with thinly disguised exasperation. "I'm *Ruby*."

"Have we met?" Stella said carefully. "I'm sorry if I'm being rude."

"Course we have. Leastways I think so. I had a few things to say every now and then." Ruby sniffed, looking around Lily Mae's cubicle with disdain. "I know she can hardly do anything with this one in here all the time, sleeping and lollygagging, but still. You'd think this Aisha woman would do a better job. Just *look* at that. She carted off a whole bunch of empties just this morning, and now there's all this lying around. Wouldn't happen if I was on the job."

"What job's that?" Stella asked, picking up the empty bottle on the floor which had been the object of Ruby's scorn.

"I've been cleaning for twenty years," Ruby said, sniffing, "and I can tell you I don't leave no rubbish bobbing about in my wake."

"I may have told this Aisha not to disturb Lily Mae if she's asleep," Stella said. "It may be my fault. I do wish Lily Mae would shake herself loose from this, though. I don't like it."

"Too many voices," Ruby said, crossing her arms and leaning against the doorjamb.

"What was that?" Stella said, suddenly paying attention.

"It was clear... before. Now, there's too many others. Too many voices. If they're all talking at once, *inside*, it's too hard to deal with the outside world at all. So she sleeps. At least nobody talks to her then or tries to get her to make sense of things. And it's just getting worse."

"Is there anything I can do?"

"It's trying to find a place," Ruby said, and it sounded completely incongruous, but Stella felt the cold touch of something at the base of her mind, staring at Ruby's earnest eyes. "Things were easier... before... it had settled, and it could have space...but now... too crowded. No room. No room for quiet and sense and sanity." She sniffed. "I am a cleaner. I know what I see. There's too much clutter. Something has to be cleared away in order to make room to breathe. Easier if you can just make the silence you need."

Stella found a giddy moment to wonder about what the watchers in the Surveillance Room would make of this gibberish—all of which was beginning to make perfect sense to her, now.

Illogon had jumped from the clear spaces of Boz's sane, clear, singular mind... into the welter of personalities that now existed in all of the others. It was not, in the end, surprising that the entity might have started to lose its own marbles—and in a sense Stella was grateful that Lily Mae's response had been to go semi-catatonic rather than into a screaming banshee mode. She remembered Jerry's description of Lily Mae's protector persona, Stiletto, and counted herself lucky that Stiletto hadn't emerged to protect Lily Mae from perceived threats... which now pretty much might be anything, and everything.

"Has she... any part of her... talked to anybody here? Directly?" Stella asked, choosing her words carefully. "Do you know this, or are you assuming...?"

"It can make you feel... alone." Ruby said. "And they would be... afraid. They wouldn't understand." Her eyes slid to Lily Mae where she lay curled on the bed, and then she added, very softly, "And she's one of us. We will keep her safe as best we can. And all that she carries within her."

Stella had to fight the urge to cast a desperate look at where she thought the nearest camera surveillance equipment was, like Loki did, and stick her tongue out at it. The sense of having someone constantly eavesdropping on every conversation she had with the *Parada* people violated every tenet of her training—and she felt increasingly hamstrung by not being able to ask real questions she needed real answers to just because doing so in the open might reveal more to those who sat watching over this place than Stella was ready to offer up to them. She closed her eyes for a moment, heaving a huge sigh, and then looked up at Ruby again.

"Is there a good time to come by when Lily Mae's usually awake?" she asked. "I understand that she won't be eager to. But if I could just get... some..." Aware that she was floundering, Stella closed her mouth with a snap. "All right," she said. "I'll be back later."

Ruby plucked the empty water bottle from her hand. "Fine," she said, her tone bland and completely conversational, as though she had said nothing unusual or untoward at all in this conversation and it had all been just about the presence of unsanctioned trash on the floor. "I'll just get rid of this for you, then, shall I?"

There was a message from Philip on her tablet by the time Stella walked out of the habitat, and she made her way to the cafeteria to meet him. It was busy, with a number of tables occupied by various personnel—a shift-change in progress, with the day people going off and the night crew just coming on line. Philip's table in fact already had another ensign sharing it, which meant that for at least a little while Philip and Stella had to content themselves with small talk and inanities, until such time as the inconvenient ensign finished her quick meal and excused herself. By that stage things were starting to thin out a little and nobody else approached their table, so Stella finally leaned in closer.

"Just been talking to Ruby," she said.

"Who's Ruby... all right, which one?" Philip said, resigned. "Every time I think I know them all someone else crawls out. Is there a limit to how many they can segment into?"

"I don't know. There are way too many things here I don't know. But I am getting an inkling that while that sedative might have started it all, it isn't the medication that's strictly speaking affecting Lily Mae adversely. Ruby, another of Rob's, says that the whole thing is something along the lines of a self-defense mechanism. That there's too much of a clamor inside Lily Mae's head and... things... are loud and complicated. So much so that parts of her can't hear the other parts of her think. So she chooses not to exacerbate things by communicating externally and adding more noise into the mix. That... makes sense, but I have no idea how to fix it."

"Have you told any of this to Martin yet?"

"I was going to but I went by the habitat first and then I came here," Stella said, tucking into a square of moussaka on her plate. "You were right about eating, at that. I feel better already. So no, not yet, I was planning on delivering the report in person but I might have to wait to do that tomorrow morning."

"Just... be careful there."

"Oh, I am," Stella said, sounding faintly smug. "I took a moment this afternoon to comb through my own contracts, and the statements I signed. I can't talk about any of this with anyone outside this place, anyone without a certain level of clearance, that is. But I *am* allowed to call on civilian authorities if I feel as though the military is overstepping on something. And those drawings... that was a deliberate attempt to cut me out of the loop, at least until such time as the military could inspect the things. If he tries to stonewall me on this, I might just call in the civilians, at that."

"But he still has authority," Philip said.

"Yes, and he threatened to pull me off if I overstepped the mark—as he saw it—again," Stella said.

"That's the *worst* thing that could happen..." Philip began, rousing.

"I am no use to them at all if I can't do anything to help them," Stella said. "I'm here for them. First, and only, them. Martin said he might have been instrumental in bringing me—or someone like me—on board in the first place, but that doesn't mean that he gets to give me orders. That isn't something I was paying nearly enough attention to, until now. I might need to... I don't know... pull civilian rank."

"You'd need to contact them first," Philip pointed out, "and you know that Martin and his people control the communications channels. What if he just clamps down on it all?"

"I don't think he can just batten down the hatches that completely and if he tries then he'll have his own superiors on his case asking why," Stella said. "And if they ask, I *will* give them some answers they might not like. And Martin damn well knows that."

"Impasse?" Philip said, with a faint smile.

"I don't know. We'll see. But in any event, I'll talk to him tomorrow, first thing. A couple more hours won't hurt anything. Maybe Lily Mae has the best idea—let's just sleep on it. We seem to be in a bit of a holding pattern and I'm pretty sure things are going to get worse before they can get better. It can all wait, for a little while longer. Maybe I'll come up with some other bright idea by morning."

But the Universe was done with waiting.

Stella had found it hard to go to sleep, her brain in overdrive, tossing and turning for at least two wakeful hours on her tumbled bed before she finally managed to doze off—and then apparently fell far more deeply asleep than she realized, coming awake with difficulty at the insistent summons of her tablet. She batted around for it sleepily and responded, yawning.

"Yes?" she said, and then glanced around at the clock and sat up, irritated. "It's four in the morning! This had better be important!"

"Ma'am," said an immaculate young ensign from the tablet, "You're wanted in the *Parada* quarters."

Suddenly very wide awake, Stella clutched at the tablet. "What is it? What happened?"

"I'm afraid it's one of the crew," the ensign said. "Lily Mae Washington."

"*Is she all right?*" Stella demanded, her voice raw.

But she knew the answer before it came back, after a small hesitation.

"I'm... afraid she's dead, ma'am."

8.

Stella barely paused for long enough to pull on sufficient clothes to make her acceptable to appear in public before stumbling out of her quarters and racing towards the *Parada* crew quarters at a dead run. By the time she got there, it was to find the rest of the crew up and awake and standing very close together in a tight and quiet cluster a little away from Lily Mae's quarters. There was an orderly standing in front of Lily Mae's door, firmly closed; he looked fierce, as though he was guarding treasure, although it wasn't entirely clear against whom. He was no match for Stella's glare and stepped aside to let her pass.

Lily Mae's room was crowded. A duty medical officer and a nurse were already in there, the nurse tidying away medical paraphernalia as best she could in the cramped space which wasn't meant to hold this many adult human bodies. The doctor, who had been bending over Lily Mae, straightened as Stella stepped into the room, and from the expression on his face he had clearly been expecting somebody else. Martin Peck, perhaps.

Stella took advantage of his disconcerted pause and moved forward until she stood toe to toe with the man; he was nearly a foot taller than she was but she managed to give the impression of glaring directly into his eyes.

"Report," she said sharply. "What happened here?"

"We... there was an emergency call. To the duty nurse. I got here as fast as I could..."

"How long ago?"

"Forty minutes...? Maybe?" The man hesitated, collecting his wits. "I should be reporting directly to..."

"You are reporting to me," Stella snapped. "I am a primary caregiver on record. I was quite possibly the last person to leave notes on this woman's medical chart. I want to know exactly what you found when you got here. Who called you? Who was here when you arrived? What was the status of the patient when you got here?"

"The Surveillance crew put in the call to the medical staff on duty," the doctor said. "They called me."

"What did you find?"

"She was gone when I got here," the medic said. "No pulse. I called it, almost immediately."

"Who was with her when she died?"

The medic blinked. "She was alone in here."

"The rest of the crew. Nobody was in here with her?"

"Not when I got here," the medic said. "Surveillance will know..."

"Did you exclude them?"

"I beg your pardon?"

"There's a guard set outside this door. Was that to prevent the rest of the residents from coming in here? Are you even aware of the situation? Of the connections between these people?"

The man looked bewildered, and raised his hands as though to defend himself, but Stella lifted her head and indicated the door to the room with a toss of her chin.

"All right. You have done your job. Now get out of here and wait outside. Both of you. Both of you, and the guy at the door. Send the rest of the crew in."

"Ma'am..."

"Now," Stella said. "It is not your province to isolate this woman from the only people left whom she might have called family. Out. And open that door."

"I have sent for..."

"I know," Stella said. "I am expecting him to come through that door imminently. You may go wait for him outside. He may be the designated commanding officer but I am still the senior medical officer on site. Out, now."

The nurse, who hadn't said a word, collected a medical kit which she had tidied away and smartly obeyed the order; the doctor might have argued further but another glare from Stella quelled him, too, and he meekly stepped outside, tossing his head at the orderly at the door in an unspoken instruction to follow him. Stella peered out of the doorway just long enough to catch Han's eye across the commons and gesture for him to bring the others through. The captain, his arm around Alaya's shoulders, guided her forward; the twins fell in behind.

Stella stepped back into the room and carefully leaned over Lily Mae, lifting one of her eyelids to peer into her eye. It was blank, lifeless, blind; the body was nothing but a broken and abandoned pupa. If there had been anything inside it—one soul, or many, or anything more—it did not seem to be there any longer. Where it had gone, that was another question altogether.

Illogon. If Lily Mae had gone—if the vessel was dead—where was the alien? Did Lily Mae take it with her?

Stella turned, her heart thudding painfully, as the rest of the *Parada* crew came up to the door.

"Is there anything you can tell me?" Stella asked. "I'm sorry. I'm so sorry. I don't understand, I don't know what I could have done to prevent this. What happens now to... to..."

"None of us were with her," Han said. "The first we all knew of this was when *they* all raced in here. They wouldn't let us close."

"I was in here earlier," Alaya said quietly. "But I left—maybe an hour before... before they came. And before that..."

"I was there, for a little while," Han said. "Before that. Mine was the early watch."

"What were you watching for?" Stella asked.

"Just over her," Han said. "Just so that there would be somebody—if she woke."

"I had the next stretch," Rob said. "But I was late. I met Alaya, coming out; she said Lily Mae hadn't woken or spoken to her while she was there. I sat with her for a little while, and then I stepped out briefly to answer a call of nature. By the time I returned... I could not see her breathing. And then the medical team came, and they pushed me out of her room—and after that, I don't know."

"So she was alone...?"

Rob was looking straight into Stella's eyes. "Yes."

"When was the last time any of you spoke to her?" Stella asked desperately. "When you did... who was she?"

It made perfect sense in context and it was answered at face value.

"Alaya and I both spoke to her, before we all went to bed," said Rob. "She did not say anything that seemed unusual. The last time I spoke to Lily Mae... I spoke to Lily Mae."

"It may have been Mamie," Alaya murmured. "I am not sure."

"It was Alabastra," Jerry said sharply.

Rob and Alaya both turned to look at him, clearly surprised.

"After she turned away, after she started for her own quarters," Jerry said. "I was over there, across the table. She turned, once, just before she went inside. It was Alabastra who looked back at me, who met my eyes."

"Are you sure about that?"

"I'd know that look."

"Out of my way." The voice that cut in from behind made the *Parada* crew part before it, Rob and Alaya to one side and Jerry and Han to the other, and Martin Peck strode in as if through an honor guard. "How did *you* get here so fast? Don't answer that. All right, let me see."

"She's gone, Martin," Stella said. "Your medico already pronounced."

"I was looking at her chart," Martin said, turning to stare at Stella. "I saw your notations. What did you think was going on here?"

"I couldn't find anything I could hold responsible for her status," Stella said. "But I was worried. I was going to come and see you in the morning—I have something I need to discuss with you. But it's nothing that would explain this, or give me any reason to suspect that it might happen."

"Was this what happened to Boz?" Martin asked, staring at Lily Mae.

"I don't know," Stella said. "How could I know?"

"Well," Martin said, after a pause, and glanced back at the other four, who hadn't moved from their positions. "I'm so very sorry," he said, his voice formal.

"Could we sit with her for a while?" Alaya asked, in a low voice.

Stella's heart lurched at the sense of something profound—it was loss, but it was more than that, it was too many things, it was resignation, and anxiety, and expectation—that emanated from the remaining quartet, but before she could speak Martin cleared his throat.

"I don't think that would be such a good idea," Martin said, even managing to sound sincere in his regrets, but in a tone which brooked no argument. "It's probably best that she is moved immediately to a more appropriate place."

"It's *late*," Stella said, stepping up to him. "It isn't likely that you are going to get any of the answers you're looking for until morning. Can't you let them have this?"

Martin hesitated—very briefly—but then shook his head. "I don't think so," he said, with what might have sounded like genuine regret. "It doesn't help anyone," he added, more gently. "What purpose..."

"Saying goodbye," Stella said, and choked on the word.

"Very well, do that," Martin said, after a beat. "And then we'll make appropriate arrangements." As he turned to leave, he caught Han Millgar's eyes and held them for a long moment, and then nodded once more, a short, sharp motion. "I'm sorry," he said. "I really am. Stella," he added, over his shoulder. "if you don't mind, a word."

He stepped out of Lily Mae's quarters, through the same *Parada* crew gauntlet as he had entered by, and Stella, after a pause, made to follow him.

She felt a piece of paper thrust into her hand as she brushed past Rob; she had no more time than to glance at him and see him give her the briefest of nods before she was past him and he turned to follow Alaya to Lily Mae's bedside.

Stella closed her hand over the paper and took the few steps to where Martin waited for her.

"Is it about those drawings?" Martin asked, without preamble, as she came up to him.

She lifted her eyes and glared at him in a moment of pure defiance. "Yes, damn it, and if Philip hadn't been literally handed them, and then had them taken from his hand, I wouldn't even have known about them until... whenever..."

"You said you were going to come see me in the morning...?"

"Yes, but only *because* of those drawings! I went hunting for them, after Philip told me what happened—"

"You and that priest are entirely too close," Martin snapped.

"It's because we don't work against one another," Stella said sharply. "We don't treat each other as though we're constantly keeping secrets and trying to spy on each other's activities or being paranoid that if the other found out anything we knew it would make the world come to a crashing end. We trust each other. That kind of helps a lot."

She glowered at him. "Also, our responsibility is to the *Parada* crew, and not to a 'chain of command'. We don't work for, or find ourselves constantly responsible for reporting to, someone else of a higher rank—we don't justify our existence with every breath we take. We work for the people we have been brought here to help and to understand. Which makes *our* understanding of material like those sketches, with all due respect, far more relevant than yours."

"You would have got them," Martin said tightly. "In the morning, in fact."

"Oh, but as I said I went looking for them already," Stella said. "And I found them in the library. *Nothing* that the Children's Collective does is completely random, Martin. These things have meanings—did you see anything in them? Did it matter so much that you saw them first? Has the military wing of this project so completely stopped trusting the civilian experts that you're willing to sabotage what we are here to find out, just so that you can get *incomplete* information before anyone else does?"

"All right," he said, after a beat. "There are standing orders that any materials that might emerge from those quarters..."

"Those things should have come to me, or at least I should have been informed through channels," Stella said. "At any rate, there's something in there that made me re-evaluate the Boz situation completely."

"What is it?"

"I'll be at your office *in the morning*," Stella said. "In the meantime, if you really want to get your answers, work with people who can help you get them. Go get some sleep, and think about the fact that you *are* getting new information in the morning, instead of twenty four hours or more down the line—given what happened here tonight would it have even been a priority to let me know about the existence of some scribbles the 'kids' threw into the mix while I was away? And one more thing—"

"What?" Martin managed, glaring at her.

"I need to know what happened to Lily Mae," Stella said. "Please don't make me go looking for that information in the library a week from tomorrow."

She turned and left him standing there, in the grip of such righteous fury that she completely forgot that she was holding onto that piece of paper that Rob had thrust into her hand until she was well out of the habitat area and halfway to her quarters. She'd had her fist clenched around it and it had not even been remotely near the furious roil of thoughts that whirled inside her mind. It was only as her fist flew open and she stretched out her hand in a gesture of pure frustration—and the paper slipped through her fingers and fluttered down to the floor—that she remembered its existence. She stopped, glanced down, suddenly remembered what the piece of paper she had just dropped actually was, and stooped quickly to pick it up.

It was crumpled into a ball, and she smoothed it open as best she could, peering at it. There were only three words written on it, in rough capitals: *Ready. Tonight.* And then, in a different pen and what looked like a different hand, *Four.*

Stella stared at the paper stupidly for a long moment, all other thoughts suddenly fled from her mind.

The clock in her room had showed 4:13 when she had been roused from her bed.

Lily Mae Washington had died minutes earlier.

Ready. Tonight. Four.

The man who had handed Stella the cryptic note was locked away in a place that was probably still a hive of activity and teeming with other people. Above and beyond all that, and the tragic circumstances which had precipitated it, there was the fact of the pervasive surveillance cameras which would have made any direct interrogation about that note impossible if Stella wished to keep the answers she received private.

She would have to think her way around that. But in the meantime—and she hated to take a leaf out of Martin Peck's playbook by going straight to 'that priest'—Philip Carter was the one ally in this place that Stella could trust with new information. There was also, no matter what the hour, the simple fact that she couldn't let him find out about Lily Mae from someone else when he woke in the morning, or find her bed empty when he went into the habitat. He'd been there when Boz had died, but he had not been present this time—they would probably not have called him, not if Lily Mae had been pronounced dead at the time of the doctor's arrival. They would have seen no need for a priest. Stella paused in the hallway, hauling out her tablet, pulling up Philip's contact, waiting while the call connected. By the time he sleepily answered the call, she had still not arrived at a reasonable alternative and so she did simply give it to him straight.

"Are you awake?"

"I am now," Philip said. "What *time* is it?"

"Early. Late. Depends on from which end you're counting. I have to see you, I'm on my way right now. There's trouble. It's Lily Mae." She hesitated, but there was no easy way to say this. "She's dead, Philip."

There was absolute silence on the other end.

"Philip?"

"Here," he said, sounding flat and strange, almost robotic. "I'm wide awake *now*."

By the time she had reached his quarters, Philip had made himself presentable and opened the door almost before Stella had time to announce her presence. They stared at one another for a long moment over the threshold, and then Philip dragged one hand through his hair in a gesture of helpless frustration and stepped aside to let Stella in.

"What happened?" he demanded, as the door closed behind her.

"I got summoned," Stella said. "I am given to understand that the sequence of events began with the surveillance crew observing something amiss, and calling in the cavalry, who pronounced her dead when they arrived."

"Was anybody..." Philip began, looking white and shaken.

"Lots of people, at various times," Stella said, "but she was alone when she slipped away. The one on duty was Rob—but he had apparently slipped away briefly to obey a call of nature, as he put it, and when he came back, she was already gone. But he did... manage to slip me this."

Stella fished out the note, and handed it to Philip. He took it, almost automatically, and stood staring at it with a blank expression.

"What is this?" he asked, after a moment. "Where did it come from? Who wrote it? Are you telling me that Lily Mae—she's dead? Planned? *By her own hand*?" He shuddered, hunching his shoulders, bringing his free hand—not the one holding the note—up to his face to cover his eyes. He was still a priest, and the idea of suicide genuinely shocked and horrified him. "I cannot believe—I would never have thought—I can't even begin to—"

"That's hardly a suicide note," Stella said.

Philip looked up, with a sudden flare of what was almost hope—something that faded as quickly as it had come to him as he thought out the ramifications. "Are you talking *murder*? Who would kill..."

"None of the crew. I don't know, Philip, I can't think straight. It makes no sense. *Rob* slipped me that. Secretly, as I was leaving. He looked as though he was trying to tell me... something... but you know how it is, in there, and it was worse than usual at that point, with Lily Mae lying there and the medical team hovering there, and Martin..."

"Martin was there?"

"They called him. Of course they called him. They would have had to."

"Does he know about the note?"

Stella shook her head mutely.

"So where did Rob get it? What does it mean?" Philip stared at the piece of paper again, willing it to say something else, something different, something that made sense. "This looks... like a *plan*. A communicated plan. Where did Rob get it? Did *he* write...?"

"I didn't get the impression that it came from him—that it was something he originated—but if he found it—then who—" Stella dragged both her hands across her face, frustrated. "I haven't the first idea about how to figure this out—if anything happened to Lily Mae, we have no way..."

"Yes," said Philip suddenly, "we do. Of course we do."

He met her gaze and held it and she stared back, puzzled at first, and then, suddenly, straightened.

"The Surveillance Room," she said. "They'll have a record. Good God, I never expected to be grateful that they spy on that place so closely. Let's go."

"Now?" Philip said, startled.

"Now."

Philip handed back the note, grabbed his tablet and stuffed it into the pocket of his tunic. "Lead on," he said grimly.

By now it was close to half past five, and shifts would change in less than an hour. The two people on duty in the Surveillance Room had apparently had quite an exciting night, but things had quieted down a bit and they weren't expecting company at that hour; their response to the arrival of Philip and Stella was an almost guilty start, as though they had been caught goofing off on the job. When Stella demanded to see the surveillance footage of the habitat for the last three days, she was obeyed with alacrity—and then they took care to keep out of her way when she keyed up a spare monitor and loaded the data.

There were vast stretches of tape where it was worse than saying that 'nothing happened'; what *was* happening was so mundane, so repetitive, that even Stella herself was being lulled into being sleepy again.

"This has to be the most boring job in existence," Stella muttered to Philip, watching with her chin cupped in her hand, propped up by her elbow as though to keep her head from lolling. By mutual consent they were fast forwarding through sections where they could see that nothing noteworthy was happening—but even with that, they found themselves mired in mundania.

The *Parada* crew were on tape eating, napping, reading, talking amongst themselves or to other people; the habitat was on tape as being cleaned while some or all of the crew were at the gym for their daily workouts; all the things that had been happening as a matter of routine ever since the crew had been immured in their quarters after their return to Earth.

"You've been there a lot," Stella said, oddly touched, watching as the tape showed Philip spending hours in the habitat—talking with the crew, or simply sitting quietly with the sleeping Lily Mae while reading something on his tablet to occupy his time.

"That's possibly the only reason I am here," Philip said quietly. "There, that's when they did the drawings. See? They just upped and slipped into the Children's Collective and then they started drawing the stuff—and there's Rob, handing them to me—"

"Yes, yes, we already know that," Stella said, a touch impatiently. Mere hours ago she had been thrilled at the insights that the discovery of those sketches had given her—but now that was old news, already covered by a report she had in her tablet, overshadowed by the enormous loss suffered by the crew in the aftermath of that.

But the sudden unheralded appearance of the Children's Collective was pretty much the only notable thing that turned up on the footage. Stella had her finger on the fast-forward button for a lot of it simply because this really was routine, repetitive stuff—so much routine, in fact, that both of them almost missed the obvious—just as everyone else had done, apparently, because no alarms had been raised at all.

"There's the cleaner again," Stella murmured.

"Doesn't that woman ever take a break?" Philip asked, almost sleepily.

Stella turned her head fractionally to look at him. "A break?" she echoed. "What do you mean?"

"It's the same woman as the last time," Philip said, and yawned. "Isn't it? It's *always* the same woman. Does she have exclusive duties in that precinct or something?"

Stella sat up, suddenly alert. "You're right," she said. "Wait, you're right. Go back...?"

They watched the footage again. Carefully, and paying close attention to the janitorial segments, which were arguably even more boring and unimportant than the rest of the repetitive routine stuff, and therefore probably the reason that nobody had bothered to take any real notice of them. The watchers in the Surveillance Room simply tuned out when someone was picking up the trash; that was not the kind of thing they were there to notice, or care about.

The cleaner on duty was Aisha. Almost every time. No matter what shift was supposed to be on duty.

Aisha faithfully performed her cleaning duties in the whole of the habitat area, but something that she had apparently taken on as a special responsibility was to ensure that Lily Mae's supply of bottled water was kept up, taking care to remove the empties every time she replenished the stack in the bathroom with replacement bottles.

She was very careful about how she went about this task, something that Stella was suddenly and exquisitely hyper-aware of, and but for one moment of clumsiness on her part and, now, a heightened focus on Stella's, it might have all passed unremarked—but once, just once, Aisha had picked up an empty bottle without taking care to shield it from the surveillance cameras with her body before stuffing it into the garbage bag where she emptied all the rubbish from the habitat. It was a glimpse that Stella caught—just the barest glimpse—but it was enough. Suddenly very wide awake, she glanced at Philip, asking a question with her eyes. He nodded, silently. Stella, glancing over her shoulder with a carefully casual motion to make sure that the monitors on duty were not paying too close attention to what she and Philip were doing, went back over it all, doggedly watching it from the beginning, peering closely at the screen whenever Aisha was in the frame, just in case, just to see if she had missed anything.

She could only nail down seeing it happen once. But once—with the evidence of the note now folded away into Stella's pocket—was enough.

In one of the empties, there had been a slip of paper.

Just like the one Rob had handed to Stella.

Lily Mae and Aisha the cleaner had somehow—thumbing their

noses at the whole surveillance juggernaut that loomed over the *Parada* crew's living quarters at all times—managed to establish a secret communication. Not only that, but they had apparently put together a conspiracy.

A conspiracy that had ended... with a very carefully timed death.

"Are you sure," Philip said, very quietly, just as Stella herself arrived at this thought, "that Lily Mae was really... dead...?"

"Get a copy of the stuff we just watched," Stella said. "We'll take it with us."

"Is that strictly by the book?" Philip queried, but he'd already plugged in his tablet.

"I don't think we're doing anything by the book anymore," Stella murmured. "I don't think there is a book. And I want to have *that* available if I want to look at it again. Are you done? Come on."

"Where are we going?" Philip asked, as they shut down the monitor they had been using and signaled to the people on duty that they were leaving.

Stella waited until they were outside the Surveillance Room with the door safely closed behind them before she answered.

"We're going down to seek the dead," she said. And then grinned. "Yesterday, when Martin took me to that coffee place, he fed me something with pomegranate in it and I made some comment about Persephone. I didn't think I'd be chasing the newly-departed to the underworld in real life not twenty-four hours later."

Neither of them had really known that the subterranean habitat they were in boasted a morgue—it had not been part of their zone of operations—but they had found that out back when Boz died, and the powers in control of the place had whisked his body away to the post-mortem with almost indecent haste. It had seemed morbid and irrelevant to go looking for the morgue facilities just to visit them, at the time, but now the same had been done to Lily Mae, by Martin's express fiat, and Stella and Philip turned to the facility maps on their tablets in order to locate the place where her body had been taken.

There did not seem to be a place described as a morgue in those maps.

"That's ridiculous," Stella snapped, after a moment. "I know it isn't exactly a popular destination, but they *have* it, I heard Martin name it, and they put this map together and it shows the location of every toilet in the place but it won't tell you were the morgue is?"

"Do you suppose it's some kind of special access?" Philip asked, looking up.

"I *have* 'special access'," Stella said, miming sarcastic air quotes. "I'm supposed to be a top-level medical specialist. Fine. We'll go down to the labs and we'll find out there."

"What makes you think they'll know?"

"Well *somebody* took the bodies there and there were medical orderlies involved. There will be records. And I will have records shown to me."

"Don't count on it," Philip said. "It's not yet six in the morning. There may not be anybody there who is in a position to dish out classified information."

"How is the location of a morgue classified information?" Stella asked sharply.

She stalked off, and Philip smothered a grin and followed.

There was only one person in the lab area when Stella and Philip arrived there, the nurse who had been in Lily Mae's quarters earlier, and her eyes widened as Stella pushed the lab doors open and walked in.

"Ma'am?" the nurse said, warily.

"So, this morgue," Stella said. "I take it you have already transported the body there. I need to see Lily Mae. Where did you stow her?"

"She... I mean... there isn't..."

"Martin Peck called it a morgue but there isn't such a thing on the maps," Stella said. "Please point me to the correct facility."

"It isn't... there's an operating theater. And there is a cold storage facility. That's where we took..."

"Take me to Lily Mae, please. Now."

"Yes, ma'am," the nurse said. "This way."

She sidestepped past them and back out into the corridor, deserted and empty except for the shrouded shape of what looked like a cleaning cart. Stella and Philip followed as the nurse led the way to a sturdy door with a keypad lock, a small light glowing red along the top. She slid in a key card along a slot just above the light, which promptly turned green, and pulled the door open. They entered a vestibule which led, through an archway to the right of the entrance, into something that looked like a staff locker room. It opened up to the left onto a surgical scrub-in area with a storage closet, door ajar, that seemed to contain spare sets of clean scrubs. A large window above the scrub sinks offered a view of a small operating room beyond; it was currently empty, with only a few dim emergency lights on, glinting dully off polished metal fittings and a stripped-down steel slab in the middle.

The nurse absent-mindedly pushed the scrubs closet door closed with an elbow as she stepped past it. "It is a surgical theater," she said, glancing through the window, "and that platform is used as an operating surface—for minor surgery—we aren't exactly set up for a heart transplant here but it also doubles as..."

"As the morgue," Stella said, a little grimly, staring at the steel table. "Good enough for a post mortem. Have you already cut her up?"

"We are going to perform a post mortem... on the deceased... when the day-shift comes on line," the nurse said. "The doctor is due in at oh-seven-hundred."

"Where is Lily Mae now?"

The nurse pointed. "Back there in the cold storage area."

"Show me."

"Sterile conditions..."

"You aren't going to be opening up anything living that could be contaminated," Stella snapped. "And I'm pretty sure the area would be properly prepped before any actual surgery, so this isn't an issue now. Show me the body."

"I don't know if I am ready for this," Philip murmured.

The nurse glanced over, perhaps hoping that a dissenting voice might give her an option to wriggle out of the situation, but Stella's expression told her otherwise, and she dropped her eyes again and turned away.

"This way." She pushed open the doors to the surgery.

They crossed the small operating room and the nurse turned the handle of a massive chrome door that closed off the cold storage area. As she began to pull it open, Stella stepped up and took over, and the nurse retreated, with a distinct air of relief at having any responsibility for this taken off her shoulders. Stella pulled the door open the rest of the way, gasped a little as the cold air from inside the room washed over her, and then stood there in the doorway, quite still, staring inside. She was blocking Philip's view, and the nurse was now behind the door, so neither of them could see what she was looking at—until she turned around to skewer the nurse with a stare as cold as the air that pulsed against her.

"All right," Stella said, very softly, but Philip—who knew her—snapped to attention when he heard her voice. There was as much cold steel in it as there was in that operating room behind them. "So, then. Where is she?"

"What?" the nurse said, looking genuinely bewildered.

Stella stepped aside and gestured with her hand. "I can see the gurney. Where is Lily Mae?"

The nurse peered into the room, and lost color. "She was there," she stammered. 'I swear, she was in there. I helped wheel that gurney in myself. Lily Mae Washington's body was on it."

"When was this? Exactly?"

"M-maybe an hour ago," the nurse stammered.

"Has anyone else been in here?"

"Shouldn't have been," the nurse said. "It's just the skeleton crew, the night shift, and we all stepped down within the last hour or so—I am just here to sign in the day shift, when the first one arrives, and then I am off too—there was nobody else here who..."

"When do the facilities get cleaned?" Philip asked quietly.

Stella shot him a questioning look, but he didn't acknowledge the glance, his own gaze focused on the nurse's face.

"Once a day, and then as needed," she said.

"Once a day when?"

"Usually during the quiet times—when there are fewest of us working in the lab—it minimizes disruption," the nurse said.

"Right about this time?" Philip persisted, and the nurse looked down at her shoes.

"During the night shift, yes."

Philip turned his head a fraction and caught Stella's eye.

"I'll look in that locker room," Philip said. "And shut that door. She's not there. No point in all of us being frozen into cold storage."

Stella slowly closed the door to the cold room.

Behind her, torn between the departing priest and the still very much present superior medical officer, the nurse was beginning to babble.

"Ma'am, she was brought down here—it wasn't long after you left, upstairs, in the habitat—Dr. Peck said that the others could have a moment to say goodbye, but then he gave the orders to bring her— he wanted her here, prepped and ready for the morning—there are questions about... I know she was here, I saw her laid here myself... I don't understand how..."

Stella looked around the operating room, completely empty of places a grown human being could hide—even if there had ever been any reason to hide inside this room. Lily Mae's body was clearly missing.

"Let's go find Father Carter, shall we?" Stella said, turning the nurse with one firm hand on her shoulder and propelling her back towards the exit.

They stepped out into the scrub-in area, just in time for Stella to hear Philip urgently calling out her name. Abandoning the nurse in her wake, Stella lengthened her stride and crossed to the entrance of the locker room.

"What is it?"

"Over here," Philip called.

"Is it Lily Mae?" At the entrance to the locker room, Stella turned around and faced the nurse. "Stay right there," she said. "Don't move until I get back."

"Y-yes, ma'am," the nurse stammered, saucer-eyed.

Stella slipped through the archway, and into an area that opened up larger than she had expected. A locker wall divided the area into two separate sections. The front one, almost directly in line with the archway entrance, was empty. Stella made a sharp right and slipped past the middle locker section, peering past it into the back area. At first all she saw was Philip crouching over something in the far corner, and for a horrible moment she thought that it might be Lily Mae's body left folded up and abandoned there. But as she came closer Stella realized that Philip was not concealing Lily Mae's' corpse... but, instead, a living woman whose eyes were wide with shock, the pupils black holes which had almost completely obscured her irises, and whose face was streaked with tears. She sat on the floor, her arms around her knees which were drawn tight against her chest, and her feet, clad only in a pair of blue socks, pigeon-toe folded against one another with her toes curled under.

Stella dropped onto one knee beside Philip, reaching out for the woman's hand. It was icy with shock.

"It's her, isn't it," Philip said softly. "The one from the surveillance video. The one from Lily Mae's quarters."

"Aisha," Stella said, gently, as though she were addressing a lost child. "Aisha. Look at me. *Look at me.* You know me. It's all right."

"She's terrified," Philip said.

"I know," Stella said, without turning to him, still keeping her eyes on Aisha's face. "Aisha. What did you see? Tell me what happened." She reached into her pocket and pulled out the crumpled note that Rob had passed onto her. "Did you send Lily Mae this? Aisha, we know about the bottles..."

Aisha's breath caught and her hands flew up to her face, covering her mouth and nose.

"Aisha. Where is she? What happened to Lily Mae?"

Philip glanced back towards the scrub area. "Stella, that nurse said the day shift is about to come in. We need to be out of here before then. If they don't find the body..."

"I know. We'll be the ones they will be asking questions of. But

I can't leave her here. Help me." Between them they leveraged Aisha upright, and then Philip stood beside her, a steadying arm around her shoulders, while Stella turned back towards the archway that led out of the locker room. "I'll take care of the nurse," Stella said evenly. "We'll call this a need-to-know thing, and she does not need to know it. When I call you, follow me out with Aisha. We'll get her out of here and somewhere safe and quiet where we can calm her down. And maybe we can get an answer out of her."

"Stella."

Stella turned, mid-step. "What?"

Philip, his own face white and drawn, gazed back at her over Aisha's bowed head.

"She looks like she saw a ghost," Philip said.

"She may have done," Stella said, after a moment, the pause sharp with the shards of shattered secrets. "She may well have thought that she was just doing a good deed, helping a young woman escape from what really does look like jail, no matter how luxurious, on the face of it, the cage is. But if Lily Mae is not as dead as we thought—if she's alive, and moving—then it is entirely possible that what's driving her... is no longer... human..."

Stella left Philip talking quietly and soothingly to Aisha and went back out to the vestibule area where the night shift nurse still waited, as ordered, looking almost as wild-eyed as Aisha.

"Right," Stella said to her, "this is what you are going to do. The last time you are perfectly certain of anything, that was back when you came here—with others, who will corroborate that—to bring Lily Mae Washington's body down here, and put it into the cold storage area awaiting the arrival of the day shift medical staff whom you understood would be performing an autopsy in the morning. *That was the last time you were in here.* We were never here, Father Carter and I, you never brought us to the morgue, you never took us to show us the body, you don't know anything about the body not being where you left it. Go back to the lab, wait for the day shift to come in and hand over, they will want to know about what happened last night, keep them out of here as long as you can by simply telling them about the things you did see and do know. Then go. Go off shift, sign out, get as far away as you can, leave them to find out what they will find out all by themselves when they get here. They will want to ask you questions, no doubt, when you come back on shift but that will be a long time from now and who knows what else will have happened before then which might make you and what you know obsolete. But your best and safest course of action is, go, and say nothing to tie yourself to this night. Do you understand me?"

"Yes, ma'am," the nurse said, very quietly, and Stella saw her tight shoulders relax just a little.

"Try and give me as much time as you can. Go, now. And thank you."

"What are you going to do?" the nurse asked, unable to help herself.

"What I have to," Stella said quietly. "I will not fail a woman who was my charge, my patient, my responsibility. I will find out what happened."

"Ma'am," the nurse said, giving Stella a small nod of respect, and fled. The door of the surgery suite closed behind her, and before it had finished doing so Stella had turned and hurried back into the locker room area.

"Hurry," she said, speaking as she rounded the central locker wall. "We don't have much time."

"I think we're out of time altogether," Philip said, looking up as Stella stepped into the back locker aisle. "I'm trying to calm her down, to get her to tell me what happened—but the most coherent things I've got so far is 'she took my shoes'..."

"Just the shoes?" Stella asked abruptly. "But she must have been left down here prepped for that post mortem in the morning—probably naked on that gurney, covered with that sheet that was still on it—but what might she..." She checked herself. "The closet was open," she said. "There's scrubs—she must have taken a spare set of scrubs—or Aisha got them for her—but there weren't shoes to go with it, and so she took..."

"She also said something about a phone—but it isn't hers, I found that back there in the corner. She might have procured one for Lily Mae, as part of this scheme. And she repeatedly mentioned someone who—as best as I can make out—is her nephew... she mentioned two names, Arslan and Emin, and I don't know which, if either, is the nephew, but I am guessing it's to one of those that Lily Mae is heading, out there..."

"That doesn't give us much to go on," Stella said grimly. "I don't know who Lily Mae was manifesting when she came to—or took this woman's shoes—but whoever it is, that persona is not going to find anything she can make sense of out in that street. She has no money, she doesn't speak the language, and she is lost in an unfamiliar city."

"Maybe not completely—one more thing—there's that phone. It might be a preloaded burner loaded with necessary information, and Lily Mae is tech savvy enough to make use of that, even if it's just a map to take her to a pre-appointed destination. And if this Arslan, or Emin, is expecting her—they may have resources waiting. And Aisha's own phone—I just glanced at her contacts, and there's a name—Arslan Ilhan—"

"Bring the phone," Stella said. "That'll help. Lily Mae has a head start, but not a big one. She's out looking for this Arslan—and if she can find him, so can we—come on, we need to..."

"Stella. We can't do it."

"We can't do what?"

Philip indicated Aisha with a terse nod. "She is in no shape to be moved. At best, she will be a dead weight; at worst, she will resist and struggle and scream and she will get whoever tries to help her nailed to the wall by security within five minutes flat."

"I know, but we can't just abandon..."

"Her best protection might be precisely the state she is in," Philip said. "And I hate myself for saying that. But it's the truth. We may be doing her more harm than good if we try to haul her out of here—and we are not going to do any favors to ourselves either. We can't save everybody..."

Stella stared at him, her eyes big and haunted. "I hate this."

"I know. I'm not happy. But what do you want to do? Whatever it is, do it now—because every moment that passes you will not have again. And I truly think it would be worse if they found *us* in here right now, than if they just found her."

"But we can try and save Lily Mae," Stella said. She took a last long look at Aisha, still sobbing and trembling, and closed her eyes, clenching her hands into fists. "All right. Put her down. Maybe it was just Alabastra that scared her, at that, and not anything... else..."

Aisha whimpered at the name of Alabastra, as Philip eased her back down onto the floor, and curled up again into the same tight little ball of terror and misery that she had been when he had first found her.

"I'm sorry," he whispered to Aisha, as he straightened. "I don't know how else to help."

"I'm going after her," Stella said abruptly.

"Going after... after who? Lily Mae?" Philip said, turning his head sharply to stare at her. "How...?"

"If you want to go back and lie low, I will understand," Stella said, already turning away. "But I'm going out there, after her. She was given to me to care for, to understand, to help. I will not abandon her."

Philip, after a last anguished look back at Aisha, turned to follow, lengthening his stride to catch up with her.

"What are you planning to do? If you find her? If you don't?" Philip demanded. "Think this through for a minute."

"They took a hit, with Boz," Stella said. "They survived it. They took another, with Lily Mae, and when this all spills out—and it will, it has to—and the *Parada* crew find out that she isn't dead, that she is gone, it is going to *wreck* things up there. They were a tight-knit cohesive group—of necessity—and it's all starting to unravel—they are losing everything, and how they respond may be borderline catastrophic for everyone. But at least... at least... they still have each other, those four up there. Lily Mae is now on her own. She hasn't been on her own for a very long time. She may not... handle it well."

"None of them are alone," Philip objected. "Not really. Not carrying twenty people inside of them. There's always... company."

"You'd still be talking to yourself," Stella said. "They may present as differentiated but in the end all those twenty people are still *you*. It isn't that simple."

"But there's the other thing. Which... as far as we know... is still with her."

"Yes," Stella said. "I know. That is not something I forget. Not for a minute."

"But maybe it would even be best if..."

Stella came to a sudden stop and Philip braked hard to halt beside her.

"Do you think for a moment," Stella said evenly, "that they will *not* go straight out looking for her themselves, the minute they find out what has happened? And what do you suppose will happen if they find her first? Do you think they might stop to ask questions...? And if they shoot first and ask later... what is going to happen... to that thing you are worrying about? What do you think is going to happen to this city if they find out—after she's dead—what they might have released out there?"

"It isn't a plague," Philip said. "It's a single..."

"Panic doesn't pause to examine facts," Stella said. "Don't you think a part of me doesn't take fierce joy in the fact that at least one of them is out there, is free, as they should be? Even if it has to be in secret, incognito, and uncelebrated, which she should so rightfully be...? God, if I could ignore this, let her go—let her go free—and if I knew that the others would not be penalized for it in some way—I'd go back to my quarters right now and curl up under my covers and cover my eyes and ears and insist I know nothing, nothing at all... but I am terrified. And in the face of that fear, I'll go look for her. Because I may yet be the only thing that can stand between her and disaster."

"You may be," Philip said, after a beat, "but how do you expect to...?"

"I read up on a lot of stuff," Stella said grimly, "back when I was doing my research in the library. When you gave me the drawings. Now come on, if you are coming, we are wasting time."

Philip said no more, simply falling into step beside Stella as she moved off again.

It was with a sense of déjà-vu that he saw her heading for the security station where she had already led him once, to demand access to a roof garden for the six dispossessed star-farers in her care to reconnect to the earth and the sky of their world. This time, the stakes were much higher. But the woman who bent her steps towards this obstacle in her path wore an expression of someone who would not be denied, and Philip spared a moment to consider Stella Froud as the personification of the irresistible force which assailed the immovable object of Martin Peck's security arrangements for the underground base they were in and through that challenging the entire monolith of the military and government administration system that underlay it all. He almost felt sorry for the officer in charge who was about to have to deal with the onslaught.

Three security officers looked up in alarm as Stella flung open the door to their station room, sized up their insignia in one swift glance, and turned to the highest-ranked officer.

"I need immediate clearance to topside," she said. "Right now. Don't bother calling anyone for confirmation or permission, my name is Dr. Stella Froud and I am on record as a senior medical officer of this facility. I hold no military rank but I have looked up the regulations that would apply and as senior medical officer I have the authority to overrule anybody else in the case of a medical emergency. And I am stating for the record that I am invoking a medical emergency right now, that time is of the essence, and that any time you spend delaying me or putting any impediments in my way could have life or death consequences for the patient under my care. One of your men will accompany me through the checkpoints, with all the pertinent codes and passwords, and I am to be escorted to an exit right now. Immediately. Make it happen."

"Wait—what—what medical emergency? I haven't been given any instructions—"

"An emergency doesn't always leave time for a proper briefing," Stella said. "That is by definition the nature of one. And I am the person qualified to inform you that such an emergency is ongoing."

"What is the emergency?" demanded the security chief stubbornly.

"We could call it an unexpected resurrection, if you insist," Stella said.

"Resurrection?" the officer echoed, looking almost offended. But he happened to glance sideways, and caught Philip's eye, and Philip nodded gravely.

"I concur," he said.

Stella shot him an almost disbelieving look, but he managed to keep his expression suitably solemn. She turned back to the officer.

"You may register your reservations on the report that you will be required to submit on this matter. Until that opportunity, do as I tell you. You have already wasted precious time."

"But I don't—"

"Now," Stella barked. "If you won't delegate an officer, then it's you." She stepped to one side and indicated the door with a sharp gesture. "After you. I will give you my own personal security clearance codes to back up my authority. You may discuss it with whomever you wish after you return from escorting me through the perimeter. And you—staying behind—" She glared at the other two officers, who stood there slack-jawed. "You will do nothing further about this matter until my escort returns from having delivered me to where I wish to go. After that, you may report the incident wherever and to whomever you feel the need to do so. Am I understood?"

"Yes, ma'am," said one of the two officers she was addressing. The other merely nodded, looking like he was fighting an impulse to salute.

"Go," Stella said.

The senior officer reached for a communications tablet, looked up to meet Stella's gaze, glanced at the two frozen men in the station with him, and dropped his hands to his sides in resignation.

"Bring an emergency credit chit," Stella said. "I will require one. Now let's go. Move."

The officer moved. Stella followed. Philip nodded politely to the two still motionless men left behind in the security station, and fell in behind.

"You can still..." Stella began, but he flung up a hand to stop her.

"I can, hell," he said, sacrilegiously. "I'm coming with you."

9.

Stella and Philip followed the security officer through the checkpoints, but not the same route that Stella and Martin had used to gain access to the streets of the city. Instead, they ended up in the same staging area that they had been taken to when Stella took the *Parada* crew up to the rooftop garden, with the two utilitarian grey-doored service elevators opening up into a wider vestibule area. The security guard ushered them into one of these, and the elevator disgorged them into the vastness of a parking garage—still underground, by the looks of it, but something that clearly had egress to the outside world. It was cavernous, and mostly empty, except for a bank of the ugly squat lime-green little CitiCars, the communal automatic self-drive vehicles that were used as convenience transport in the streets, plugged into their charging stations across the huge expanse of unoccupied parking spaces. The guard pointed across to them.

"You have access to those," he said. "They'll take you out to where you need to go."

"Fine," Stella said. "That'll do. Thank you."

The guard handed her a couple of credit chits, still looking very unhappy, as though he had more to say. He seemed to decide against it, on reflection, and abandoned the two of them there, stepping back into the elevator and letting the doors close on the unspoken words. Stella strode across the garage towards the cars. Philip, pausing to glance in what was almost bewilderment back at the elevator as though he couldn't believe that they had just been left to their own devices like that, scrambled to follow.

"Wait," he said, "but if we plug anything specific into that car, they'll know immediately where to..."

"We need it to get out of here," Stella said. "It's the fastest way. And once we're in the city... we can make other arrangements. Come on."

They reached the nearest CitiCar, and Stella touched the activation pad, waking it up; the car turned on its lights, retracted its charging umbilical, and opened its doors, awaiting passengers and instructions. Stella and Philip climbed in, and Stella tapped in something on the launch screen; the car doors closed, and it nosed out of its parking space into the central aisle of the parking garage, heading for the exit ramp.

"Where did you send it?"

"Outside," Stella said. "it wanted a destination—I gave it the park that Martin took me to. But once we're out in the street... I'll override. We can find this man that Aisha mentioned—this—Arslan, was it?— and get another CitiCar to go there, an arbitrary one from out in the streets. One they can't immediately trace. Okay, hang on—look, there's the exit ramp. Almost there."

The car paused at an exit checkpoint and Stella typed something else onto the pad. The ramp rose, and the car edged forward—up another short ramp—into a wide entrance area that fronted into the street. As soon as the car, pausing to check for oncoming traffic, turned into the street itself, Stella brought it to a halt.

"On our own now," she said. "I'll send this one on to the park. With luck, if anyone tries to follow us they might waste a bit of time chasing that down. Give me a second."

Philip climbed out of the car and stood patiently on the sidewalk while Stella finished doctoring their destination. Then she stepped out, the CitiCar's doors closed, and it slid off into the street and out of sight.

"Right," Stella said briskly. "Did that phone of Aisha's have an address? No? All right. There's Net out here. We can find the address by name and phone number if we need to. Lily Mae had to have been told, and if anything was transferred from Aisha's phone we should be able to find out. We need a public terminal."

Philip was gazing at the building behind them, the one from the bowels of which they had just emerged, with a strange expression.

"Wow, that thing is impressive," he said. "Particularly in this light..."

They had emerged into pre-dawn light, and the sun was just starting to come up above the horizon. The sky was a vivid shade of pale yellow shading into bronze and gold, clouds being painted by the light into citrine and orange and patches of reddish pink.

"Lemon drop sky," Stella said, gazing upwards. "It's been a while since I've actually seen a sunrise. And I think it's going to be hot again. And bright. And dammit, I came out without my sunglasses again." She glanced back at the building, its steel and glass façade reflecting the colors of the dawn until it blazed with golden light, and gestured with her hand. "The main entrance, there? That's what Martin picked for his exit, on the excursion. No postern gate or a little green CitiCar from the bowels of the place for him."

Philip's eyebrows shot up at this, and he measured the marble staircase, the gleaming brass railings, the high glass doors. "He must have wanted to impress you," he said.

Stella glared at him across the bridge of her nose. "Well, he succeeded," she said. "The inside of that place is amazing—remember? You must have walked in through there, when you first got here. So did I, to be sure, but I'd forgotten just how carefully calculated that lobby is, designed to make an impression, until Martin reminded me of it all over again. But there's no time for that now. Lily Mae simply can't be that much ahead of us. It's going to take her a little while just to navigate the city—this is not her city and not her world, not any more. There's too much here that she might think of as familiar but it won't be like the things she remembers, not quite, and it'll slow her down. Unless Aisha gave her specific and explicit instructions, in which case we may already be too late. Stop gawking and come *on*, will you? Where's Aisha's phone?"

"Copied the name and number onto mine," Philip said, passing the item to her. "Here."

Stella grimaced. "I should have thought to bring my own," she said. "It would make looking things up all that much easier. I've just got my habitat tablet and that's no use out here. Well, but we can try to use your connection—if we can find a network—"

"Do you think they might be able to trace that?" Philip asked quietly. "Do we want them to know what we are looking for?"

"You have a point. Maybe it would be better to do it from a public terminal, after all. Right. Arslan Ilhan," Stella said, reading off the phone screen. "Lily Mae had a direct line straight to him—if that meeting was essential for her getaway Aisha must have given her a map straight to his front door. It's going to take us a little longer."

They found the public terminal they sought only a few blocks away, and it yielded two addresses on record for an Arslan Ilhan. Stella hesitated over them, knowing that if she picked the wrong one Lily Mae might well be out of their reach by the time they got back to the one that mattered. By the time she made her decision, the sun was up, and the streets were already heating up; they had the option of calling a CitiCar to take them to where they wished to go, and the advantage of its cool air-conditioned inside and its tinted windows that kept out the worst of the glare, and they gratefully took it. Stella paused to spare a thought for Lily Mae—admittedly she had the advantage of the cooler pre-dawn hours but she had to have walked this route. She wouldn't have known how to use a credit chit, or how to hail a CitiCar and program it—there had been no time for Aisha to give her instructions on how to function in the streets of a city two hundred years older than the one Lily Mae has left behind on Earth when she had departed from it.

It was entirely possible that Diana had taken over—and if Lily Mae needed to charm this Arslan into giving her assistance, Stella hoped that the Diana persona hadn't gotten her in trouble before she'd had a chance to get any. And then it occurred to her that she was out here chasing Lily Mae but that part of her was actually rooting for her and hoping for a clean getaway.

Stella snorted, and Philip glanced at her. "What?" he asked.

"I was just being... irrational," Stella said. "Are we there yet?"

Philip grinned. "Well, we just turned into another street narrower than the last. I don't think the car is going to be able to take us much further."

As though it had heard him and responded, the CitiCar came to a halt. The map on the navigator screen showed the solid red line that indicated their route from the start of their journey to their designated destination, and a length of red line—no longer solid but dotted— remained; the car informed them that CitiCars were not permitted in the narrow cobbled streets of the Old City and riders were advised to 'complete the remainder of their journey on foot'.

They obediently disembarked; the car's doors slid shut and it reversed out, returning to circulation in the busy streets of the modern city. Stella looked around, at the neighborhood awakening around them, people coming out of locked doors of their shops to put up awnings and bring out display wares, offering polite greetings to Stella and Philip if they caught their eye.

"That way," Stella said, pointing. "Hurry."

The address that they had for Arslan Ilhan, when they finally arrived there, didn't look promising at all—it belonged to a hole-in-the-wall cobbler's shop, in front of which an old man sat cross-legged on a threadbare piece of carpet on the ground, bent over a half-finished shoe. Stella spoke to him, but he merely glanced up with narrowed and clearly short-sighted eyes, shrugged placidly, and returned to his work. Stella clicked her tongue impatiently.

"I don't have a translator bud and I know he doesn't," she said. "This could be a tricky..."

But Philip had ducked into the shop, and beckoned her inside. "Maybe there's someone else here."

There was; a young woman was bent over an incongruous computer screen in the corner of the traditional shop, its blueish light washing across her face in the semi-darkness of the small cluttered room. She looked up as Stella and Philip ducked in, and this time Stella was ready. She had a photo of Lily Mae on her tablet screen, and she held it up to the woman.

"We're looking for our friend," she said, and pointed to the screen with her other hand. "This woman. She was sent to Arslan Ilhan to get assistance... we are looking for Arslan Ilhan..."

The woman stared back impassively, keeping her expression

carefully blank, but Philip nodded at her in an economical little motion.

"*She* has an earbud. She understands just fine," he said to Stella. "Look," he continued, focusing on the silent young woman, "we mean no harm but we have to find her. It's important. She..." He glanced up at Stella, apologetically, and then looked back at the girl. "She may be sick. She may need help. The person who sent her to Arslan... it was Aisha, Aisha sent her... but Aisha didn't know everything. And now she has sent us. Have you seen this woman...?"

The silent girl still hesitated, but Stella held the tablet in front of her steadily and the girl's eyes flicked back to Lily Mae's face and then back to Stella's, and to Philip's own earnest one. After a long moment, she dropped her eyes back to her own computer, but she made the faintest of motions with her head—towards the back of the shop, and what looked like a curtained-off area in the rear.

"Thank you," Philip said, and grabbed Stella's wrist. "That's as much as you're going to get. Come on."

He pushed aside the curtain—of some thick hand-woven stuff—and ducked behind it, and through into a dark corridor beyond. It was short, and ended in a T-junction with a blank crudely plastered wall right in front of them. To their left was a closed door, with a small and not very clean window of yellowish glass set high into it allowing just a shaft of pallid light to stir the shadows of the corridor; Philip tried it as he stepped up to it but it was locked. Opposite the door a flight of uneven steps led upwards, its destination invisible from the foot of it. Philip hesitated for a moment, but there was little choice in the matter—and he turned right, and started up the stairs. Stella followed.

They emerged into a room which was strewn with rugs and cushions, with one low table along the wall which—by the evidence of the smells and sounds coming in through the row of windows set into it and left ajar—faced out into the cobbled street from which they had just entered. An open archway led out at the far end, curtained off with similar stuff to that which hung down in the cobbler's shop. Stella looked at the room with what would have been Lily Mae's eyes and was conscious of a sense of recognition and relief—the room was familiar, even old-fashioned—nothing in here spoke of the two centuries that separated Lily Mae from the world in which she was now adrift. There was little technology here, no computer, no screens, no climate controls. This room looked like it might have existed unchanged since the day it was built, a timeless place. Just as the lobby of the World Government Building had been engineered to impress and even intimidate, this place might have been carefully arranged in this way in order to keep a certain kind of client, dependent on technology to the point of feeling queasy without it, unsettled and wrong-footed enough to be more easily manipulated by someone who made it their business to keep them that way. To Lily Mae it might have had exactly the opposite effect. Perhaps that might have worked in her favor.

Unless she brought Diana in here with her and allowed her to run riot.

"There is nobody here," Philip said, and began moving towards the second curtained doorway.

"Wait," Stella said, reaching out a hand to stop him.

At exactly that moment, theatrically, the curtain was pushed aside and a man came through the arched doorway. He was tall enough to need to duck as he did so, straightening to his full height as he entered. His face was thin, chiseled into sharp lines, with a hooked beak of a nose and glittering obsidian-dark eyes under a pair of bushy black eyebrows. His hair curled riotously around his head, falling to just below his jawline, and his angular jaw bore a carefully manicured Mephistophelian beard to match the thin moustache that arched above his upper lip.

"I believe you were looking for Arslan Ilhan," he said, speaking in a clipped and elegant accent but in a language that did not require the translation earbud Stella and Philip did not have. "How may he be of service to you?"

Stella retrieved Lily Mae's photograph to her tablet screen and lifted it towards Arslan.

"We are seeking this woman," she said. "Her name is Lily Mae

Washington." She paused for a moment, waiting to see if that name brought a sign of recognition—either because of a recent encounter or because of a memory of a woman by that name who had been briefly and incandescently famous two centuries before. But Arslan's face remained tranquil, inscrutable. Unsure of just how much he knew and how much of what he might not know she should reveal to him, Stella ploughed on. "We know she was sent here for... for assistance... by the woman called Aisha, who works... in the place where this woman was held, and who conspired with her in order for her to gain her freedom from that place. We need to find her. It is important. Aisha released her into the world without knowing...important details. This woman may be in danger if we do not find her. We are only hours behind; she may have barely left here."

Arslan courteously took the tablet and gave it his complete attention for a long moment. Then he looked up again, with a little smile.

"Aisha is my father's sister," he said, "and she is very dear to me. If she asked it of me to give aid to someone she called friend, then that is not something I would refuse, such as I could, even if I am just a lowly merchant in the Old City markets. But I could not speak of such things to strangers. What I may or may not have done..."

"Please," Stella said. "Have you seen her? There may be others who come looking for her, and they may not have her best interests at heart, they have their own agenda. If we find her first, and soon, then I may have a chance to defuse the situation..."

"It may be life or death," Philip said.

Arslan lifted an eyebrow. "You can be sure of this?"

"Yes," Stella said, shooting Philip a quick glance. "You don't know everything either, and because we need your help, I am going to tell you the truth. That woman was born on this Earth more than two hundred years ago."

That got a hit; Arslan's brow folded into a frown. "What is this you say?"

Stella glanced at Philip briefly, met his eyes, saw the very clear *I hope you know what you are doing* that was reflected there, and then looked back at Arslan.

"She will be sought," Stella said, quietly and steadily. Arslan's dark eyes lifted from the photograph and met hers. Stella could not read them—it was like looking into glittering obsidian mirrors—and she shuffled the information in her mind, pulling out what she could share, the knowledge of psychology and instinct and reaction that led all the tangled threads of this situation to this moment. "We are friends. We are trying to help, to keep her safe, but to do this we need to find her first. Before others follow, others who have... other priorities, whose orders to protect carefully kept secrets would override any concern for her own wellbeing or possibly survival. Let me put it this way. While she was held, she was a treasure. On the run, she is a potential liability. Steps will be taken to remove that liability."

"And you are in a position to prevent this?" Arslan said, sounding polite but a little unconvinced. Stella instinctively lifted a hand to push her hair back in place, aware that she had not come here looking like any sort of authority at all.

"I have known Lily Mae Washington's name all my life," she said, "but I only met her a very short while ago. I am a doctor; I was brought in to help heal her. That is still my responsibility. Because I know that you are an honorable man... even if I had it to offer, I would not offend you by trying to offer you money for information... except, possibly in the shape of the warning which I bring and which I lay at your feet right now. We came here. We found you. There is every possibility that they will get your name from Aisha, and there will be others coming in our wake. Forewarned, you may take... what steps you need to in order to protect your house and your name. But before the others come...please tell us where Lily Mae has gone. Help us reach her before anyone who might wish her harm." Stella paused, swallowed. "She is my responsibility," Stella said. "She is my patient. She is my friend."

Arslan held her eyes for one long moment, and then reached out to hand back the tablet he still held. His expression did not change, but his voice did, dropping into what was almost a whisper, so that Philip instinctively leaned forward to catch what he was saying.

"All I know," Arslan said, "is that I had word from Aisha that a refugee needed assistance—the right papers—to help her leave the city.

Those, I could provide. It is a small thing I can do for those who come to me asking for help. Your friend carries a temporary refugee passport, in the name of Maryam Senai, an Ethiopian woman who no longer requires those papers. They look enough alike that the paperwork won't be questioned, at least until she reaches a second staging post, the location of which she has. A man I know there can provide a more permanent secondary identity for someone who has cause to flee a difficult existence. You are correct, she left here less than an hour ago. I myself placed her in a vehicle which was programmed to take her to a rendezvous point which would take her further."

"Where?" Stella asked.

"There is a ferry that departs about an hour after sunrise," Arslan said. "Someone will be meeting her on it. I put your friend on a CitiCar whose itinerary I can control and then erase—yes, I have access to a handful of those," he said, as an aside, registering the reactions of his companions to what was a direct admission of something that was not only illegal but that was thought to be nearly impossible, with the CitiCar software being so carefully controlled by authorities. "If you will give me one moment..."

He turned away and reached out to slide a hand behind a small woven tapestry hanging beside the curtained doorway. In response to a hidden switch, part of the rustic wall shimmered away into oblivion, revealed to be a holographic projection. Behind it, a sophisticated electronic bank was revealed, and Arslan bent his head over a screen to scan a readout, and then frowned, and bent closer, taking another, longer look.

"This is not right," he murmured.

Stella's stomach knotted. "What is it?"

"The car. It did not go to where it was sent. It was overridden. Do you think your friends who are searching for this woman may have already intervened?"

"Where did the car go?"

"According to this, it was taken only a very short way from here, and then it was abandoned there, "Arslan said.

"How long ago?"

"As I have said. Less than an hour."

"Will you give us the location?"

Arslan hesitated for a moment, and then turned in a decisive motion and reached out in an imperial gesture in Stella's direction. "Give me your tablet."

Stella passed it to him without a word. Arslan 's free hand swiped and rearranged something on the screen of his own computer, and then touched the tablet to it, tapping to transfer the data he had isolated in a single window on the screen into Stella's device.

"The car is here," he said, passing the tablet back. "Whether your friend still is, I have no way of knowing."

"Thank you," Stella said.

Arslan's hand slid back behind the tapestry hanging, and the holographic wall blinked back into being, hiding the console behind the rustic wall in a room that looked like it had been untouched by centuries of time.

"I will be ready," Arslan said, "for whoever comes in your wake. Thank you for the warning. I hope... any assistance I may have rendered has not made it harder for you to find your friend. It was not my intention." He hesitated for a moment, and then added, "One thing I need to ask—Aisha, my father's sister—you speak of people who may be ruthless in pursuit of their goals. You know much of what has passed, by which I have to assume that you have spoken with her. But now I have to know—is there reason for me to think that Aisha may not be... safe...?"

"I don't think she will be physically harmed," Stella said, with a confidence she wished she was more fully certain was the truth. She didn't think that Martin Peck or his outfit would do anything to hurt a clearly terrified cleaning woman but she knew that Aisha would be closely and perhaps brutally questioned. That she was sure of, and how much would come out of that Stella had no way of knowing.

Caught between loyalties, she unwillingly offered up a little more. "Those of whom I speak... they have their own honor, rules under which they operate. They may hold her, until they are sure that they have learned everything they think she might know—but in the end

I think they will be obliged to release her. When they do... it may be best if she finds another place of employment."

Arslan's eyes glittered again. "I understand," he said. "I will make appropriate arrangements. May God go with you."

"And with you," Philip responded, automatically, even though the God being invoked was of another faith.

"The door at the bottom of the stair," Arslan said, "it will be unlocked. Leave by that door, not through the shop. It will take you into a courtyard, and on the other side of that is a gate that leads into the street beyond. Turn left, and if you follow that street you will quickly come to the arch that is the Old City gateway. Beyond that, you will be in your world, not mine."

He bowed to them, very slightly, an aristocrat taking his leave of honored guests, and stepped back behind the curtained doorway through which he had first made his appearance.

Stella closed her fingers around Philip's wrist in a grip of iron and pulled at him. "Come on. We need to go. Now."

They hurried down the stairs, and found the door Arslan had spoken of not only unlocked but ajar. Everything beyond was as he had described it, but Philip, turning around to gaze back at the narrow streets of the Old City as they stepped out from underneath the arched gateway that demarcated the edge of it, snorted in disdain.

"His world. He made it sound like he owned that place. And as far as that goes, that rig of his was pretty far from Old City Traditional when it comes to interior design..."

"Less than an hour," Stella said, apparently not listening to him at all, focused on her own thoughts, her eyes darting about for a CitiCar she could commandeer as soon as they stepped into the streets where those were permitted to go. "Less than an hour. If we'd moved just a bit faster..."

Philip looked as though he was about to say something else, and then reconsidered, keeping close to Stella as she finally flagged down a CitiCar and frantically fed it the coordinates Arslan had given her before she settled down into her seat.

"Stella," he finally said, after she turned from the console and sat down, "just what is it that's driving you so hard? Why is it so important to you that you find her? I mean—I know about Illogon, and that's a factor—and Lily Mae is not..."

"Because it may be my fault," Stella said, very quietly, staring straight ahead of her, her hands folded in her lap in what looked like repose until one took a closer look and realized that her fingers were knotted about each other with a white-knuckled intensity. "I may have... precipitated this. I may have given her the idea."

"Precipitated it? How? Are you still agonizing over that garden thing?" Philip asked. "And anyway—given her what idea?"

Stella turned very slowly to look at him. "I keep thinking—I said it, I know I said it, and she was asleep or she looked like it—I have no idea what she heard or how much she heard or what it triggered in that shattered mind—I, of all people should have known better than that!—but I said it in her presence, and that's exactly what she did..."

"You said what, Stella?"

"That they may have got the idea, the *Parada* people, that the only way out of that cage of theirs was by way of the morgue," Stella said. "And that is what she did, what she literally did—she found a way to get her body out of that guarded habitat and into a place from which she could... somehow... walk away. But I said it, Philip, and she did it. Now if they find her she's a liability, and oh *God* if anything happens to her it will be my fault..." She turned to Philip and her eyes were unexpectedly full of tears. "I want her free. I want them all free, all of the *Parada* people—but not like this—I wanted them free because they didn't deserve to come home to be locked up like that. I don't want them free as... as *fugitives*, free only as long as they keep running. And you're right—they don't even know about the whole Illogon thing. If they did, they would be after her with a flamethrower right now. As it is, I'm afraid of what might happen if they catch up with her and she refuses to go quietly. If they knew about the real truth...!"

"You want to find her but you don't want to find her," Philip said. "Look, don't do this to yourself. You can't possibly hold yourself responsible for a phrase you might have uttered in passing above somebody you thought was asleep or unconscious. And even if she *did* get the idea from you, Aisha was all Lily Mae. You had nothing to do with that at all. It was Lily Mae—or whichever personality was ascendant—who struck that deal, and then fled to Arslan and his own tender mercies..."

"Arslan," Stella said, catching her breath on a sob she couldn't quite hold back. "That man. I can't believe he and Aisha are actually even related—one is like a little brown hen, and the other is a raptor— just about the only thing they have in common is that they share an anatomy which features wings."

"Nice bit of reverse psychology on that one," Philip said. "Treating him like the prince of chivalry rather than a hoodlum for hire..."

Stella grimaced. "I had an ex who responded to exactly a similar kind of approach. He was an ass, and we both knew he was an ass, but if you approached him hinting that he really was a better man than he appeared to be... occasionally he rose to the challenge," she said. "Eventually it became a question of diminishing returns, so I cut my losses and divorced him."

Philip stared at her. "You were *married*?"

Stella actually laughed out loud. "Don't sound so astonished," she said. "Yeah, I was married. We were both too young for it at the time, probably, anyway. But I grew up. He didn't. He didn't seem to be planning to, either. I gave it three years, and then I bailed. I had a whole life before I turned up in the habitat to hover over the *Parada* crew, you know."

The CitiCar slowed, and came to a stop. Its doors opened, and Stella, her attention back to the problem at hand, all but fell out in her haste to exit, and then froze, looking up at the building in front of which they had been deposited.

"A train station?" she said. "I have a bad feeling about this."

Philip, following her out, glanced about and pointed. "There's another CitiCar. Lily Mae's? Do you want me to check?"

"Yes," said Stella, distracted. "I'm going in to see what I can find out..."

There was nothing of potential interest left in the abandoned CitiCar, and after satisfying himself of that Philip hurried back to the station building, back to Stella. He found her standing inside, at a window that looked out over the tracks, her expression bleak.

"The guy at the counter says there were three trains that stopped here within the last hour," Stella said. "One going south, one going west, one going north-west. He doesn't remember seeing Lily Mae, but she could have been on any of those trains. Maybe one of her crewmates could track her, from here—there are connections there—but this is the end of the road, for me. I have no idea where she is, where she went, where she is headed." She looked over at him, and her eyes were quenched, defeated. "I lost her, Philip. I lost her."

"What do we do now?" Philip asked, after a moment of silence.

Stella responded with a helpless shrug. "I may have lost *all* of them, by doing this," she said. "In fact, I can almost guarantee that I have done that. Martin did warn me and I did defy him. If he went crazy before, when I pulled the garden stunt, just think about what he is going to do now. I'm going to be burned out of there. With fire. And I may have done more damage than I wanted to. And you..."

"What about me?"

"You're tainted by association," Stella said, with a wan little grin, looking him up and down to acknowledge his presence beside her. "You're here. With me. Now. You're an accessory. You'll always be an untrusted accessory from now on."

"I would really love to tell you that you are being silly about this," Philip said, "but I'd probably be lying. But what was I supposed to do...?"

"You tried to stop me," Stella said, offering him a way out. "You came along hoping to keep me under control. That's the story you ought to tell them."

Philip smiled but said sturdily, "I came of my own free will to help you."

"Great," Stella said. "Then they may just have lost both of us. The *Parada* people. What is going to happen to them now?"

"We still know more than the people in charge of all this can ever..."

"Yes, and we haven't told them what we know, and we can't tell them, and we won't tell them," Stella said. "So Martin can pull rank on my pulling rank, and he—he said that he could kick me out, and he would if I put him in a position to—I don't know, actually... the idea did cross my mind that the easiest way to keep this secret a secret was if I never left that place, any more than any of the *Parada* crew did. For the same reasons. Because it would be easier to keep a tight lid on it all if people who know more than they ought to were somehow kept quiet. Permanently."

"What are you saying?" Philip said, sounding genuinely appalled—and at the same time trying to deal with the fact that the thought had crossed his own mind, and he was far from surprised by it. Still, it was something that sat ill with him—that he could even have considered this as a possibility—and there was something defensive in his tone even though he could not have said what it was that he was feeling defensive about. "You think they would *kill* to protect that little project? You told Arslan that Aisha would be safe—and now you're standing here telling me that you think that Martin would order murder?"

"I have to go back," Stella said. "There is still the question of that last report that I have for Martin. If I can at least plant the seed that it isn't as bad as they fear—that it isn't contagious, that it is possible for even people closely connected to the phenomenon to remain unaffected, unshattered, like Boz seems to have done—there might still be a key left in the lock, for them, after that, no matter what happens to me. I failed Lily Mae, I can't fail the rest of them. But you..."

"What about me?"

"I hate this, I really hate to even think of abandoning those people to silence and to solitary, or at best a whole new poke-and-prod crew whom they would need to learn to trust—but you know... what I know. You also know too much. About Illogon."

"Stella... what *do* we know about Illogon? Really?" Philip asked quietly.

"Enough that if they knew about its existence they would have their hair on fire already. And we learn new things every time we turn around. We didn't really know that it could jump vessels—jump bodies—until it leaped from Boz to Lily Mae. I don't have the first idea if that's because it had already made a niche for itself in the minds of these particular people, or if it can now make that transfer anywhere with anyone—and if that is the case, and it's out there right now and loose, you can imagine how much Lily Mae's life might be worth at this moment."

"If they kill the host body won't they risk a random transfer?" Philip said. "Wouldn't that keep her at least alive? I mean, if anyone believed that the moment of physical death the alien entity—parasite—whatever it is—simply jumps into the next available living vessel—well—would *you* shoot...?"

"I wouldn't shoot in the first place," Stella retorted.

"There's only one of it," Philip said. "It's hardly an invasion..."

"But they'll say that they have no idea what happens next, or how it might reproduce, or what it can do now that it has an unfilled ecological niche out there on planet Earth," Stella said. "The only thing that might protect Lily Mae's life might possibly be that—as far as they know—this thing is a little like a spider carrying its young on its back and when they shoot Lily Mae it'll just make her explode into a scurrying mass of babies going off in all directions, impossible to contain, and then they'll have to nuke the place from orbit or something."

Philip stared at her. "You really think that this thing is going to..."

Stella spread her arms out in a helpless gesture. "I don't believe it, not for a minute, if that was the way it was going to go wouldn't it have done it already? What would it be waiting for? From everything we've seen so far this thing doesn't seem any less trapped than any of the rest of them in there, the humans," she said. "Remember the way this whole planet lost its collective marbles when they found that Europa squidoid when they poked into those weird oceans, sixty years ago? *Those* things could not share the same space as a human being long enough for them to be any possible danger to us—the conditions they need to exist in would kill us long before the aliens got at us. But the world freaked out at the whole idea. It's past due for another frenzy, and just think what could be built around the very idea of an alien not just extraterrestrial but from some incomprehensible place from half a galaxy away... and one that is demonstrably able to exist in the same space—hell, the same *body*—as a human being. It could be a fluffy bunny, incapable of anything except a loud purr, and we'd still freak out over it. It's in our nature. We're afraid of what lurks in our own shadows... but then, I am no xenobiologist. My strength, if you can call it that, is that I know what people think, how they will think. And there are some minds that will respond to anything they see as a threat with immediate violence."

"What are the alternatives?" Philip asked, sounding miserable.

"Possibly worse," Stella said, bowing her head. "If they get her alive—and they know about what she is carrying inside her—she might not even get to go back in with the others. It might be permanent solitary, until the day she dies a natural death, and she is still a healthy young woman. Barring purpose-inflicted hurt or accidents, that day is a long way away for her. But it would be that, or a swift demise under controlled sterile conditions where they can hack her up in safety and make *sure* they got that terrifying alien thing, where they can lock it up inside a test tube or a force field and watch it squirm and *die* before their eyes..."

"You're a ray of sunshine today," Philip said, after a moment.

Stella managed a smile. "Sorry. I wish I felt better about all this. But I can't see the silver lining for the black cloud, not today." She glanced up at him. "I've probably burned my last bridge, and it just remains to see what they will do about it. But you... is there any way you can make an official getaway? Get your Church to pull you out of there?"

Suddenly breathless, Philip managed a small sharp nod. "I could arrange it. I would need to contact a friend..."

"Don't do it on anything that you can get traced on," Stella said.

"There are the public terminals back in the city," Philip said. "I could use... what time is it? It's still early... but Rome is an hour behind, it would just be coming on Prime back there... they will be up and at prayer, but it's a Minor Hour and Father Cabrera should be back from the chapel soon, and I can try to see if he'll take a call... or he'll check his messages..."

"Do it," Stella said. "And then we'll go back and see what kind of fallout we left behind." She turned to look one last time at the stretch of empty rails which unfolded towards the horizon from the small station. "Your God alone knows where Lily Mae is right now."

"The CitiCar is still here," Philip said. "At least the one Arslan sent Lily Mae out in is. We can take that back into the city. Arslan will know exactly where we take it, if he's telling the truth about how he can control those things, not that it matters at this point..."

"Let's go," Stella said, turning her back on the rails and starting briskly for the exit.

Stella programmed Arslan's hacked CitiCar with coordinates that took it back to the inner city—but stopped the vehicle before it reached that destination and stepped out with Philip before sending it on its way to its programmed end point. Philip didn't comment, but Stella gave him a tired little smile.

"I know. At this point being concerned about who knows what about where we are seems a little paranoid, given that we're going back to the eye of the storm of our own free will anyway. But still. It comforts me to cling to the idea that I can still do something independent without being accountable to anyone at all."

"I said nothing." Philip glanced searchingly around him. "My concern right now is finding a public terminal I can place a call from."

Stella pointed across the street. "There," she said. "It's a VirtRealCafe, and they'll have terminals. They'll have access to the Net."

"It'll do," Philip said. "Let's hope Father Cabrera is there. It'll save a lot of time if I can just talk to him, directly. He is, he's always been, a friend."

Stella hesitated. "Philip... we've always said... we can't tell Martin and his cronies about the... about Illogon... what are you going to tell this priest...? Are you—do you have to tell them—tell them the truth about, the real reason behind everything—"

"I have to tell them enough to justify pulling me out," Philip said grimly. "I have to tell them something. Perhaps my best bet is to hint I could tell them more if I was out of here. But I'll have to do penance for this. I'm lying by omission and the vow of obedience is already dust at my feet."

"But there's the crew."

"Yes, there's the crew," Philip agreed. "Stella, it isn't simple, with us. With me. I can't just tell them, oh, I've had enough, get me out of here. We go where we are sent, where God wants us—we do what we do not for our own greed for success or wealth or power. *Ad majorem Dei gloriam*—for the glory of God—somebody asked for a priest, and the call came to my order, and one was sent. Me. Now the priest that was sent is asking the order to rescind that sending, to second-guess God. I'll do my best. But I have no idea what Father Cabrera is going to think about any of this. He has the power to send in that recall— he is First Secretary to the Father General, and he certainly has the authority to do this, or at the very least initiate the process—but he also has the responsibility to kick it further up the ladder. If I *do* manage to get myself out of this particular frying pan we are both in, well, I don't know about how you get to land out there, but as for me, I might be climbing straight out into a holy fire."

"Do you think that you should stay?" Stella whispered.

"All I know is that once I get a moment to myself I will have to pray about this," Philip said. "I cannot believe that God would make a plan that would end up like this, I cannot believe that those people in there are doomed to die in that underground warren. There's a part of me, too, that hopes Lily Mae stays free... but I don't know God's mind. Something about what you are saying feels right, and I have to assume that I am hearing God speaking through that. So I am going to try and do this thing. But a part of me is recoiling from it and calling me coward, right now, and if I leave that place, and those people, behind me, I may carry the guilt of that all my life..." he shrugged. "There are no good choices left," he said. "Not really. Now, if you will excuse me, I'll try and see if I can make Father Cabrera understand enough of this to help me through it."

"Do you want me to..."

"No," he said, abruptly, sharply, and then softened as he saw her flinch. "Sorry. But no. You can't help me here. I need to do this on my own. In private. In as much of a private way as I can manage to accomplish under the circumstances."

"Okay," Stella said. "I'll go find a place to buy another pair of sunglasses. And I'll wait for you here, after."

When Philip re-joined Stella at the corner where she was waiting for him, eyes hidden behind a new pair of dark glasses, his face was set and pale.

"All right," was all he said to her, "I'm ready. Let's go face the music. Do you have any idea how we're going to get back in there? I am assuming the back door they let us out of is not likely to respond to an open sesame from you..."

"I wouldn't think so," Stella said, with genuine regret. "I mean, there is a distant possibility that they might have a patrolman pacing up and down outside the garage entrance there but I doubt that they'd want attention drawn to it in that way. No, we go back through the front door."

"Isn't that drawing *more* attention...?" Philip asked, letting the question peter out into silence, but Stella shrugged her shoulders.

"We'll go knock," she said. "How much attention we draw depends on how they decide to react to that. We'll go into the front lobby—the one you said Martin wanted to impress me with—and I'll call him from there. Let's see how much of an impression he really wants to make."

"You cannot possibly be as calm as you look," Philip said, staring at her.

"Neither can you," Stella said, "but here we both are, calm as a clam. I guess that's as good as it's going to get." She smiled, a little grimly, and held out a hand in front of her, fingers splayed. There was a tremor there, but a very faint one; Stella stared at it for a moment, and then let it close leaving a single pointing finger. "Thataway. We can walk. It isn't far, and we can use the delay."

They walked in silence, side by side, until they turned the final corner and faced the wide stair of the World Government Tower sweeping out onto the street and the plaza beyond. Philip halted, and

Stella, beside him, took another couple of steps before she became aware that he was no longer moving and stopped to turn back to look at him.

"Second thoughts?" she asked softly.

He shook his head, and thrust his hand into his pocket, coming up with a slip of paper. He offered it to her, and she reached out automatically to take it.

"I created that, just now, after I finished my call," Philip said, in a low voice. "It's an email account. It isn't encrypted or anything secure, it's just a generic webmail one, but it's mine. Direct. If things go badly—if we get split—if you are out there, and on your own, and you need to get in touch and you don't want to wade through the halls of the church trying to get them to acknowledge I even exist—that'll work."

"Philip," Stella said, "isn't this a direct action against..."

He stepped up and closed her hand around the paper. "Take it," he said, with a trace of urgency in his voice. "I need to know you have it. I need to know that if there is... anything I may need to know... and if you are free to tell me... you can find me. You and I and Illogon—that's the only connection there will be. Nobody else will know that this line of communication exists. And I'll ask God for forgiveness, later. This isn't something His Church needs to know."

Stella nodded, just once, abruptly, and stuck the piece of paper into her own pocket. "All right," she said. "Thank you." She hesitated. "For everything."

"You sound like you're saying goodbye already," Philip said.

"I kind of am. Once we get in there... I may not have another chance. Listen. I will draw Martin's big guns. If he isn't focused on you—if he doesn't sic a security detail putting us both under direct arrest, and he may, because he might just be that angry—if you are able, let me stand against it. You slip away, before they notice that you are there. Go to the crew. Warn them. Tell them... I tried. Tell them I'm sorry. Tell them I wish... things had turned out differently. I may not be able to tell them anything myself, ever again. Will you do that for me?"

"Yes," Philip said.

"We, who are about to die..." Stella said, the ancient gladiatorial salute, and managed a smile. "Well, here goes. Follow me."

The white and gold foyer of the World Government Tower was not crowded when Stella and Philip walked inside, and Stella murmured something about that being 'a pity', because things might have been more easily camouflaged if there had been a crowd in the hall. But things were what they were, and Stella paused a few steps inside the door, toggled her tablet until she found Martin's contact, staring at it.

"I'm not sure that this will work out here," Stella said, frowning at the tablet. "They specifically use these on the internal system. I wonder if Martin will answer if I..."

As though she had invoked him by saying his name out loud, the tablet in her hand vibrated to indicate an incoming message. Stella gasped softly, and then tilted the tablet to show Philip.

Go to the elevator bank. Take the last elevator on your left. Hit the last subbasement button. You will be met.

Stella glanced up at Philip.

"Oh yes, he's mad," Stella said.

"How did he know we were here? Does he have a camera monitoring the front door of the Tower?" Philip muttered.

"This thing probably pinged a tripwire in the building," Stella said, weighing the tablet in her hand. "That means they knew exactly when we left the place. To the minute."

"We still have to clear security to get back to those elevators," Philip said, "don't we?"

"I think you'll find they'll know to let us through," Stella said, pocketing the tablet and walking forward.

One of the security men on duty at the front desk actually peeled off to meet them just in front of the scanner gate, and opened up a small side gate beside the main arch, waving them through that instead. Stella gave Philip a significant look under one raised eyebrow—*I told you so*—and obeyed instructions. The security guard who had escorted them in followed them as unobtrusively as it was possible to be followed by security in a place like that, and waited until their designated elevator came for them; Stella could see him standing doggedly in a place where he could clearly observe the two of them right until the elevator doors closed. She pressed the lowest button on the elevator display and the cabin descended five levels below ground before the doors opened again to disgorge them. They were, as Martin had promised, met—by two security people who worked for the *Parada* habitat. Stella recognized one of them, from the garden excursion. He would not meet her eyes. One of the men turned smartly and walked away, gesturing for Stella and Philip to follow him, while the one whom Stella knew waited until they had exited the elevator and fell in behind them.

"Are we being arrested?" Philip asked, softly.

"Not yet," Stella said. "But watch this space."

Two security checkpoints later, they were back in the smooth grey corridors of the *Parada* base, and Martin waited for them as they stepped through, standing with his feet planted wide apart, his hands clasped tightly behind his back, his body rigid and his shoulders tense, wearing his full dress uniform. He had somehow managed to keep his expression calm but his state of mind was betrayed by the incandescent fury in his eyes and the tic that gave away a tightly clenched jaw.

"*Doctor Froud,*" he said, with emphasis, the words barely passing through his locked teeth.

"All right. Here's what I know so far." Stella said, stepping forward, leaving Philip at her back. She couldn't afford to pay attention and see if he would take the chance and slip away as she had asked him to do, but she was determined to give him that chance. "We were all blindsided by what happened to Lily Mae last night. Early this morning, I guess. You ordered her body taken to the morgue. Something occurred to me, afterwards, and I wished to examine that body before you handed it over for the autopsy when the day shift arrived to report for duty. So I went looking for that morgue you spoke of. When I reached it, I discovered that Lily Mae was no longer there. There was a cleaning woman barely coherent in the locker room area adjacent to the space that you are using as the morgue facility. All we could get out of her was the fact that Lily Mae...was in fact, somehow, improbably, alive.

Also, that she had slipped the facility—possibly using this cleaner's own codes, and wearing the woman's shoes which she had taken off her feet. Alive, and loose out there in the city in the pre-dawn hours—it qualified as a medical emergency. Frankly, it qualified as a medical miracle. And I was well within my rights to follow. As it happens, I was less than an hour behind her, all the way. Unfortunately, what little head start she had proved enough. By the time I caught up to where she was last seen... she was gone."

"And just where," Martin spat out, "was *that?*"

"She had arrived at a small regional train station literally about forty minutes before we got there. Unfortunately, in that time, three different trains had come into and then left the station. I had no means to track her further, not in three possible directions. The only people who might have had an instinct about where she went from that station—and why—might have been her crewmates, back here at the base. There is a connection between the members of that group that is very real, and not something that I can easily explain. But they were here, and she was out there. Lacking such a connection I returned here."

She snapped her mouth shut and roused up to face him. "I was within my rights according to the regulations!" she said. "I know. I checked. There was no time to roust out the high command, in the shape of your good self. By the time I could explain, she might have been anywhere. If I had been only a little faster in following, in fact, I might have caught up to her in time, in which case I doubt we would be having this conversation at all because I would have come back successful. But I failed, and now you can blame me for that. Fine. But in one way you laid the breadcrumbs to this, yourself."

"*I* did?" Martin said, sounding vaguely astonished.

"Pomegranate freaking sherbet," Stella said. "I made the Hades and Persephone remark as a joke. I didn't know I'd be chasing down the steps into Hell for someone newly dead only hours after you fed me that pomegranate seed."

"This is about you flouting the established chain of command again," Martin snapped, "and don't try to be precious about that. I warned you. I *warned* you what would happen if..."

"I came back, Martin, because as you may remember I said something the last time we saw each other—in Lily Mae's quarters, over what we both believed was her dead body—about a report I had for you. There are certain conclusions that I have come to which you may be interested to know about. I came back to do my duty to you, damn it. I came back to do my duty... to them all." She blinked furiously at the hot tears that threatened to flood her eyes. She could not cry right now. *Could* not. It would wreck everything, even beyond the wreckage she was already standing knee deep in.

"Well, then?" Martin said, his eyes boring into her.

"It's on a need to know basis," Stella snapped. "If you think everyone in this hallway needs to know, then..."

"My office," he said. "Now."

He whirled and stalked off, not bothering to see if she would follow. She did, stealing a glance behind her at last. Philip was gone. Stella felt a pang of regret—he had probably done as she had asked, had gone to the crew, and it was extremely unlikely that Martin would permit her—in his current mood—to see any of the *Parada* people again, not even, if he did banish her from here, to say her goodbyes. She had acted purely on instinct, trying to save Lily Mae for them, but she had not succeeded in accomplishing that and now she had lost them all.

She bit her lip, and lifted her chin in a gesture of defiance, and walked slowly in Martin's wake.

He was waiting for her in his office, standing in front of his desk in much the same position as he had greeted her in at the entrance."

"Well?" he demanded, as the door began to close behind Stella.

She dug out her tablet and rooted around for the report that she had prepared. "I'll transfer it to your screen," she said.

Without taking his eyes off her, Martin reached out behind him with one hand and slapped it against something on the surface of his desk; his screen wall woke and illuminated, several windows open, at least one with scrolling data active on it. After a moment the screen blinked, and a line of red writing blinked on at the top of the screen.

Martin finally tore his eyes off her face and looked around at the screen, zooming in with a gesture of his hand, opening the file that had just arrived. Stella's report unfurled, lines of writing scrolling rapidly down the screen. Martin scanned them through narrowed eyes, fairly cursorily, and then he turned a little more fully towards the screen and slowed down the screed, paying closer attention.

At length, he turned to face her again.

"You're telling me Bogdan Dimitrov *faked* it. All of it."

"There is no way to prove it. But yes. I believe that."

"So the rest. They can be cured of this too?"

Stella tossed her head in an impatient gesture. "There you go again with 'cured'. They don't have chickenpox. I believe they can function—have been functioning—with this. Some deal with it better than others do. Looking at the ones currently in that habitat, I think that Rob Hillerman is by far the most stable of them all—"

"You mean he is reintegrating?"

"Not necessarily. Just learning to exist in a new form, encompassing all of his new voices. But he can... to a large extent... control it. So can Alaya, but she is by far the more vulnerable of them—some of her personas are more than capable of holding their own but too many are too fragile to serve her. Han is too... erratic. For someone who was put into a position of leadership and command, as Captain of that ship, he doesn't seem to be able to control his personas in a way that I would call useful—I've seen him change mid-sentence, sometimes, from one soul to another, and it isn't something that seems to be under his conscious control at all. Jerry Hillerman... is odd, and I don't want you to take this the wrong way because I don't mean it in a threatening way, but he is the most dangerous of them all. He's got some of Rob's control but the people who now live inside him seem to have... far fewer inhibitions than Rob's crowd does. I don't know how far I would trust those transformations, if it came to a crunch. He is... selfish, I suppose, would be the word. If it came to protecting himself—any of his selves—there would be no question that he would have absolutely no scruples about abandoning anyone else to whatever fate awaited."

"And where would Lily Mae fall on that spectrum?" Martin questioned, dangerously softly.

"She has... aspects of all of that," Stella said. "If you are asking me if she can function by herself out in this strange world that she has no real true ideas about, not any more—all I can tell you, she's doing very well so far. She hasn't let the culture shock throw her off. She seems to have the ability to focus, and to accomplish what she sets out to do."

"And what," Martin asked, "do you think she set out to do?"

"She's free," Stella said simply.

Martin shook his head, as if in pain. "They are not being kept—"

"Tell *them* that," Stella said grimly. "I think you'll find it hard to convince them. For heaven's sake, Martin, one of them was content to put herself through the appearance, at least, of *death* in order to get herself out of there. What does that tell you?"

"You said the others could find her?"

"I have no idea," Stella said. "I said that it is possible. Perhaps even likely. Someone who has spent time with her—like myself—could try and predict which way she'd jump—but obviously I didn't do that successfully. It just wasn't *enough*. But...I don't know how else you'd go about looking. She's a little drop in a big ocean now."

"She has no papers, no legal standing," Martin said. "It will only take a single mistake, and she will make one, sooner or later. You already said that she was in a strange world unfamiliar to her. Her picture is already disseminated—in a discreet way, of course—to security personnel in the city. She could..."

"She's already out of the city," Stella said. "Any one of those trains, she could have been on."

"Or she could have wanted you to think that."

Stella snorted. "We're being a little conspiracy-theory here, aren't we? I told you she apparently functioned in this strange brave new world she found out there—but that doesn't mean she can negotiate it with that kind of finesse. You yourself said that it's only a matter of time before the first mistake—but you think that she thought *this* part out so carefully?"

"Maybe she got lucky, here. But she'll make that mistake."

"Martin... what are you going to do...?"

He began to answer, and then caught himself, and roused up to his full height.

"That is no longer any of your concern, Dr. Froud," he said. "I told you what the consequences would be the next time you discarded the rule book, and now you have, and I am standing by what I said. As of now, you are no longer a part of this team. You have an hour to pack your bag and you will be escorted off the premises. Please ensure that you take nothing with you that has any bearing on this project. Your baggage and your electronics will be subject to search. You are not to contact the *Parada* crew again in any way, and it may not be necessary for the two of us to speak again. Am I being perfectly clear?"

She had known this was coming, but it still kicked her in the gut like a mule. Suddenly short of breath, she could barely muster enough of it to utter a single word.

"*Perfectly.*"

"Dr. Froud."

Stella turned back from the door of the office, to which she had taken the few steps after turning her back on Martin.

She turned now to look at him, her chin on her shoulder. Voiceless, her hands gestured the question *What?*

"Do not fail to remember," Martin said, his voice flat and edged with a dangerous steel, "the agreement that you signed upon entering into this project. Make no mistake, you *will* be monitored. And there will be zero tolerance for any flouting of either the spirit or the letter of that document. Again, am I being clear?"

Stella nodded, turned away again, and stepped through the door as it opened for her. She stood for a moment just outside it, as it closed behind her, aware that tears were streaming down her cheeks although she could not remember starting to cry.

She could only hope she hadn't given Martin Peck the pleasure of having seen her do it.

10.

Stella found that she had very little to pack. She stripped off her *Parada* unit gear and left the tunic and the pants on her bed—she didn't bother checking if her ID plate was still showing as valid—and changed into her own clothes, stuffing the things she wasn't wearing willy-nilly into her small suitcase. The base-issued tablet she left on the desk in her quarters, retrieving her own personal phone which she had not been using since she had got here and slipping it into an outside pocket of her bag—they said they would search her tech, but they wouldn't find anything of interest on that phone. She contemplated calling Philip, on the institutional tablet, to bring him up to speed, but in the end refrained from doing so—she had nothing new to tell him, anyway, and it might not be helpful to have calls from the resident persona-non-grata on his record right now. The secret personal email address he had given her she had already memorized, and the little slip of paper it had been written on had been ripped up into pieces and flushed down the toilet. She contemplated making her way to the library, to see if she had left anything there, but she figured that there was nothing in that place that she would have been allowed to take. She would have liked to have been allowed copies of the drawings from the Children's Collective, the ones that had precipitated her insights about Boz, but she doubted that Martin would see fit to allow that.

In the end, the hour she had been given to pack proved to be entirely too much time. Stella wondered if she should take her small suitcase and make her way to the security checkpoint, and wait there for whatever was supposed to happen next, but Martin had said that she would be 'escorted' off the premises and Stella refused to escort herself. If they wanted her out they would have to come and get her. And so, her bags full, her soul empty, she sat down on her bed and waited for the people bearing her marching orders to arrive.

She did not expect to have her door chime at her to announce a visitor. That did seem rather more polite than necessary under the circumstances. She glanced at the bedside clock, noted without thinking too much about the situation that considerably *more* than the allotted hour had gone by, and then slipped off the edge of the bed, her legs feeling stiff and leaden, and made her way slowly to the door, toggling it open.

Of all the people she might have thought she would see standing there, Martin Peck was perhaps the very last. She stood and stared at him owlishly for a long moment, in absolute silence; there was something about his face that was strange, a new line etched deeply into his forehead and another slashing down from his nose to the corner of his mouth, but it was his eyes that held Stella. There was something in them that she wasn't expecting. A tinge of resentment, yes, but that would have possibly been the last vestiges of the fury he had rained on Stella earlier—but over and above that, there was... defeat.

"May I come in?" Martin asked at last, breaking the silence.

"I thought you had rendered that question rather obsolete, earlier," Stella said. "I am hardly in a position to invite you... but, hey, sure, yes, of course."

She moved aside, gesturing him into the room and Martin stepped across the threshold. The door closed behind him. The two of them stood there for a moment, with Martin half turned away from Stella so that all she saw was one rigid shoulder and the tight jawline of a face mostly turned away from her. And then Stella sighed, and crossed her arms across her chest.

"Did you come to make sure I left without making trouble?" she asked.

"No," Martin said.

"In that case, what can I do for you...?"

He turned, at last, and faced her. Stella's eyes widened a little at his expression, but she stood her ground, and in the end he echoed her sigh with one of his own.

"We have to talk," he said. "Sit down."

He reached for the chair tucked under the desk, turned it around, and collapsed into it. Stella found a perch elsewhere and folded her hands in her lap, waiting.

"Did you know that Father Carter...?" Martin began, glancing up at her, and then his lips tightened. "Of course you know. I just want to know how he got around the... never mind. Either way, he's gone."

"Gone? Already?" Stella blurted. She hadn't quite got that far in her planning. Philip's absence was not something she had thought about as yet; she was still in the *Parada* base, and because he had always shared it, had always been right there and beside her, had shared all the revelations, the fact that he was gone and she was suddenly on her own here felt as if she had stuck her tongue into a tooth with a raw and open nerve. Even if it had been partly her idea that he should go, she could not help but feel briefly abandoned—and very, very alone, sitting there under Martin's scrutiny.

Her choice of words had betrayed her prior knowledge of Philip's departure, however, and Stella curled her fingers against her palms in her lap. *Tactical error.* Martin's presence here in this room at this moment had unnerved her more than she had realized. She braced herself for an attack on this point, but it didn't come. Instead, Martin reached up to drag one hand through his hair in a gesture that Stella couldn't begin to interpret.

She took the initiative instead.

"How is the crew?" she asked. "Did Philip, at least, manage to say goodbye to them, even if you won't let me speak to..."

"Oh, he managed," Martin said, and there was something raw and savage in his voice.

Something had unraveled—something big—something that Philip's departure had precipitated, or been an inadvertent part of, something that had been happening during this last endless hour that Stella had spent cooped up in her quarters waiting for her ejection from the habitat.

She bit her lip, waiting. Martin was going to have to spill this one on his own terms, in his own time.

"*They* called *me*," Martin said abruptly. "Jerry Hillerman just... stood up, and looked straight up at the camera, and demanded that I come and see them. It's as though he..."

It's as though he was suddenly in control, Stella thought. *You're not used to being summoned to explain yourself, not by people you consider to be below you on the totem pole. Chain of command, eh...?*

Martin shook himself. "I didn't watch the surveillance footage before I went in," he said stiffly. "Mistake. I would have not been blindsided by it if I had done so. But there was no time—everything just happened at once, and I was still too damned angry."

"At whom?" Stella asked, unable to help herself.

"You. Then the good priest. Everybody." Martin buried both hands into his hair at the sides of his head, in a gesture that was pure frustration.

"What did they want?" Stella asked, after a beat.

"What?" Martin said, dropping his hands back down and looking briefly disoriented, as though he was startled at his surroundings.

"You said they called you, the *Parada* people," Stella said. "What did they want?"

Martin bared his teeth in a feral smile. "You, actually."

Stella sat up, astonished. "I beg your pardon?"

"Philip Carter had got there first," Martin said. "If it had been up to me—well, they didn't know about Lily Mae. What had happened. Not yet. I would have chosen a better time to tell them—to explain—you can imagine, the news landed like a hand grenade."

"That she was alive? That she was out there?" Stella inquired. "I would think so. Who talked to you?"

It was an odd question, but in the *Parada* context it was always an appropriate one. Martin took it in stride. "Han dithered between Hanford Millgar himself and the Cap alter ego," he said. "Alaya... was Susan, I think. I don't think I have met Jerry's current persona before. It has aspects of Loki, as we have charted that persona, but it wasn't quite that. And Rob didn't say much at this point. He could have been anybody." He sighed. "That was when I got there. And then... and then they all went into the children."

"The Children's Collective? Again?"

"It is damnably difficult to deal with a bunch of seven-year-olds," Martin said sharply. "They don't..."

"They don't respond well to military bullying techniques," Stella said.

Martin shot her a look. "Give it up."

"Never," Stella said softly. "So. What did the children want?"

"I told you. They wanted you." Martin threw his hands up in the air. "You had to tell them, didn't you?"

"Me? I was sitting in this room," Stella said primly.

"You sent your minion," Martin said savagely. "Don't think I don't know that the two of you are always whispering something. You and that priest."

"I would hardly call a Jesuit priest my minion," Stella snapped back, "and I think the Church might take a dim view of that too. What did Philip tell them?"

"What you told me," Martin said. "That you couldn't find Lily Mae, not alone... but that they can possibly help. And..."

"And what?"

"And they're *willing* to help," Martin said. "But... you. They'll only work with *you*. If not you, then..."

"Then what?" Stella said, her heart thumping against her ribcage and a flush rising to her cheeks.

"They're basically giving me an ultimatum, the lot of them," Martin said. "And I'm supposed to sell this to my superiors. The fact that a bunch of *children* have me backed into a corner and demanding I countermand orders or they will suspend all cooperation. What they are basically threatening is that from here on they intend to speak to nobody, on absolutely anything to do with their situation. The... children... told me that they couldn't help it if we sat there watching them all the time... but that they'll just stop playing with us at all in any other context. It was the equivalent of name, rank, and service number. Unless *you* were our representative."

"But I am not," Stella said, far more calmly than she felt. "You asked me if you made yourself clear, and you did. Crystal. I don't have it in writing—yet, anyway—but my verbal marching orders were unequivocal. What are you telling me now?"

Martin leapt to his feet again and prowled the small sitting room like a caged tiger. "Damn it," he snarled. "Damn *you*, for being apparently far too good at what we brought you here to do—get their confidence, get their cooperation. And now here I am—and I have to—" He appeared to literally choke on his words, the lines on his face etching even deeper.

"What do you want me to do, Martin?"

His head snapped up and he stabbed her with a sharp gaze from bloodshot eyes. "Ideally? Go tell them not to be a pack of juvenile..." He stopped himself, but not before the word got out, and Stella had to bow her head to hide a quick smile. "*You know what I mean,*" Martin snarled. "I want them to behave like adults, like people I can communicate with—"

"People you can give orders to and expect them to be obeyed," Stella said.

"I never demanded that!" Martin said. "I am a doctor too, remember? Medically trained? These people were my responsibility as much as they were yours. But more than that—"

"More than that, they were cogs in a military machine," Stella said. "And they knew it, Martin. They are hardly stupid, any of them. You kept on trying to pull the wool over their eyes, spinning the story they were told, but all *that* collapsed when the *Juno* people left. They got the message—those people got to leave. They didn't. And then Boz. And then... what Lily Mae pulled off. And now they're done pretending to believe that any of this is for their benefit. Am I close?"

Martin stopped abruptly, and turned around to face her. She had never seen him look more haggard, more trapped, than in this moment. Despite herself, she felt a pang of something almost like pity for him. It was difficult to see any place where he could jump and salvage the operation, at least from his point of view. It was almost certain that this turn of events had sabotaged his own military career irretrievably. Anyone who had lost control of the situation as comprehensively as Martin seemed to have done would be extremely unlikely to be considered for a command post in the future.

"Will you help me?" Martin said hoarsely, his hands hanging helpless by his sides.

Stella stood up, and was astonished at how absolutely calm she felt.

"Of course," she said. "Let's go talk to the Collective."

The Children's Collective was still out when Stella and Martin returned to the habitat, sitting around the table, disconcertingly quiet for self-identified seven-year-olds, but Stella could read their presence from the posture and the attitude of the four adult human bodies who literally occupied the seats.

"Hello, Stella," Glory said, the youngest of the ones remaining in the Habitat, the least inhibited. The smile the little girl put on Han Millgar's chiseled face lit up his eyes, and Stella instinctively responded with one of her own.

"Hey," she said.

"We're glad you're back," Momo said, with an engaging dignity.

"I'm glad I'm back too. It's good to see you all. But now I have to ask you a big favor. Can you let me... let Martin and me... talk to your other people for a little while? The big folk? I promise, I will come back later if you want me to. And then we can spend some time together. But now I need you to go back and call your original big person. We need to tell them something, something that it's easier to talk to them about."

Gadfly looked rebellious. "But it isn't fair. We know all about..."

"You know a lot of things," Stella said. "I know I learned a whole lot from all of you. I never got to say thank you for those drawings you sent me, but they were beautiful. And they helped me figure out a whole lot of stuff."

"We know secrets," Glory said, beaming.

"And now that I'm back, if you want to, you can tell me later. But now—please let us talk to the others? At least for a little while? Trust me." Stella glanced at Martin, and then back at the *Parada* group. "I'm not going anywhere."

She heard Martin suck in his breath, but he didn't interrupt. The other four gazed at her from four sets of childlike eyes, their heads tilted, considering her promise.

"Okay," Momo said, after a moment. "We'll see you later."

"I'll never get used to this," Martin muttered as he watched the faces and eyes change, all around the table. Alaya was still wearing the smile she had on her face as Momo, but it was demonstrably the smile of a grown woman now; Han sat back and crossed his arms; Rob folded his hands on the table before him and gave Stella a small nod of welcome and recognition; Jerry...

"*Loki*," Stella said. "Not now."

"It's actually so much easier when you aren't here," Jerry said, sounding a little aggrieved, wiping the mocking glint in Loki's eyes and stepping back into his own original body. "Other people don't instantaneously classify us. I can play other people along for a while, and it's so much more fun."

"I dare say," Stella said dryly. "But for once it isn't about you. I gather Philip told you? About Lily Mae?"

"Yes," Alaya said. "They are all right, you know."

"I know," Stella said, a little too quickly, hoping that Martin wouldn't notice that she was heading this particular idea off before Alaya could get into details. To Stella, the 'they' meant so much more than Lily Mae's cohort of resident souls. It meant that one extra one, the one that Martin did not know about. Must not know about. "I knew that you guys would know. If you could—"

"Wait," Martin interrupted, suddenly rousing. "Wait. If you know that—if you can tell *that*—then you must have known... that she was not really..."

The reaction spoke of an epiphany, a flash of understanding that Martin had reached before Stella had done so, and she frowned, going back to the chaotic night of Lily Mae's death. She ran the memory through her mind's eye, looking for things she might have missed on the night. She had been summoned by a piece of blunt and shocking news, and she had been focused—perhaps hyper-focused—on Lily Mae herself. But now she retrieved the other members of the crew and their reactions, and something suddenly stood out for her that had simply not done so at the time.

The rest of the *Parada* crew had a quiet and coherent story to tell of the events of that night. A story that—in twenty-twenty hindsight—sounded remarkably cohesive, remarkably calm, almost rehearsed. There had been sorrow there, certainly, and it would have had to be there because Stella would have been expecting it... but she suddenly realized with supreme clarity that she had missed one very important detail.

They had been sorrowful. But what they had not been... was surprised. What grief there was, in the face of this second death from amongst their rapidly diminishing ranks, was not the same grief that had been there when Boz had died. There had been something real, something raw, in the aftermath of that death. Lily Mae... might have taken a bite of a poisoned apple, and was waiting for the kiss of the appropriate prince to wake her and send her back, living and laughing, into the world.

"You put the thought into my head," Stella said slowly. "*You* did. The way you looked—the way you spoke—that thing that sent me looking for..."

Rob held her gaze for a long moment, and then looked down at where his hands lay folded on the table before him, his eyelashes, long and curled like a girl's, veiling his eyes.

Stella stared at all of them in turn, one after the other, lifting a peremptory hand to silence Martin when he would have spoken. And then her lips thinned.

"All right," she said, her voice a knife. "I do believe it's time I asked some rather pointed questions. You said you would work with me—well, you'd better start. And Martin... a word." She beckoned him away from the table and he followed, clearly annoyed that he was being summoned in that manner.

"Well?" he said in a low voice, his back turned to the crew table, standing by the door of the habitat.

"You asked me to help you, and I am willing to try. But if you want me to do that... you need to go *away*. They will not talk to me with you here." She paused. "Or under your surveillance. They *know* every move they make, every word they utter, is on record. Now they've pretty much told you that's done."

"What are you trying to tell me? That a complete surrender..."

"Were we at war?" Stella asked sharply. "Look. They told you their terms. Me. They told you they would work with me. And I will work with you. Think about me as the bridge across the chasm. Now go away, and *turn off the cameras*. I will come straight to you when I am done here."

"Ten minutes," Martin said, biting the words off. "I will turn off the surveillance sound system. For ten minutes."

"You will turn off the whole system, and you will give me more than ten minutes, damn it," Stella said. "In fact, it is entirely possible to make a case of it staying off. I must say, I've recently had cause to review some footage of the surveillance that you have gathered from the habitat, and for the most part all that you are accomplishing is accumulating an endless loop of repetitive routine. You are not learning anything from any of it—not when the people you are watching know they are being watched. You can stop. Mothball the whole effort. Starting now. If they don't choose to tell you something, you won't learn it by voyeurism or by eavesdropping, that should be abundantly clear by now. And by your own word—they are not here as prisoners who need to be constantly guarded at all times. Not everything can be crammed into military time or context."

"But I need..."

"Martin. You asked me to help you. I said I will. But *they* have information you might want." She glanced back at the crew, none of whom were carefully looking in her direction. "I think they're willing to share it. Some of it. It's still your court, but it's their ball now. Play the game, or call it quits."

Martin's eyes spoke volumes—*whose side are you on?*—but he clenched his teeth to keep an intemperate response from coming out.

"That is not my decision," he said instead, after a moment to

gather his thoughts. "But I will take it under advisement. As for now...
you have half an hour."

"Martin."

He paused at the door, about to stalk out, to glare back at Stella.

"You *will* do this. I need your word. I am invoking whatever
doctor-patient privilege I can at this point. You will let me talk to
them, in private, and I mean in private—if you won't turn off that
surveillance, at least temporarily, then I am afraid that we will all
just have to go pile into the nearest non-surveilled bathroom and
see how many grown humans can fit inside that shower, until we are
done discussing this."

Martin yanked his tablet out of his pocket, toggled in a contact,
barked in an order, and then opened up a screen on the tablet
and handed it to Stella. It briefly showed an image of the habitat,
with all of them at the table—the view of the surveillance cameras,
exactly what the people on duty in the Surveillance Room were
seeing. As Stella watched, the image blinked, and died. The screen
went black.

"Keep that," Martin snapped. "So long as you can't see anything
on that screen, neither can anyone else. You'll know when you're back
on view."

Doors weren't built to slam in this place, but Stella had the
distinct feeling that this was the one time Martin might have wanted
to slam one in his wake. But that was all the time she had to spare
for him at that moment. If he was being straight with her, she had
less than thirty minutes to get to the bottom of what was suddenly
looking like it was a dizzyingly deep well she hadn't even known
existed until mere minutes ago.

This time, when she turned back to the crew, every single pair of
eyes was on her. Waiting.

Taking a deep breath, she made her way back and took a seat,
leaning forward on the table, pushing Martin's tablet with its blank
screen out into the middle so that they could all see it.

"All right," she said, "so long as that's blank, they're not watching
or listening. Talk to me."

"You trust him? On this?" Jerry asked cynically. "He turned it off... just like that?"

"Not just like that," Stella said. "There will be a price to pay for it. But I will pay that, not you. First. Tell me, and tell me the truth. *Did you know that Lily Mae was not really dead? How did you do this?*"

"We had... help," Han said carefully, eyeing the tablet without a great deal of conviction.

"Yes, let's speak of that help, at last." Stella said. "Where is it now? Still with her?"

"That is why she needed to go," Rob said, and the intensity of his voice rocked Stella. She looked over at him and his hazel eyes were glowing as he gazed at her, leaning forward to emphasize his words. "It was... necessary. And they weren't ready to let her go. Any of us go."

"On your word, maybe," Jerry said.

"With all honesty," Stella said, and she really meant it literally, "none of this is my decision. All I can contribute is a professional opinion. And I don't know if any of you are ready to deal with that outside world right now, or ever will be—I believe in your right to do it, bitterly, and I fought to get the *Juno* crew to be released, but they never—*never*—had to deal with what you have had to face here. They came back from the stars with just their own souls intact, not splintered into the dozens of people you all carry. All of you... except Boz. I'm right there, am I not? He had Jiminy. Jiminy was real. That was all. Everything else... was a stage dressing. So that he would fit with the rest of you. Especially after you returned here. And there was space there, inside, for... for what you brought back with you. But then Boz died, and it had to go... somewhere. And you're telling me that Lily Mae is not alone out there." Stella grimaced. "Where is she supposed to go? What is she supposed to do? Why did you send me down there after her that night?"

"We—she—had a plan," Rob said. "But if she needed help... we needed someone there whom she would trust. Just in case things went badly."

"You do know that poor Aisha—the cleaner—is compromised, sedated, probably won't be able to shake this, even if they ever trust her enough with knowledge of any of it to let her go free without any major consequences? And me—you knew I knew things I had not told anyone else about. I kept your secrets, trying to understand—trying to protect you—because I was afraid of where such knowledge in the wrong hands would leave you—and you led me straight to a place where I had to make the choice to go against the rules and regulations—that, or run to someone with higher authority with everything I knew. How could you possibly be certain that I would not do the second thing?"

She swallowed, looking around at them. "They want her," she said. "They want to find her. I told them that only you—what remains of this crew—have the necessary connections with Lily Mae to be able to track her, to have any idea of whether or not she is alive or dead. Now you told them that you don't want to work with anyone except me. Just what is it that you want me to do? Do you *want* me to go looking for her? I can't do it—I can't do it alone, not unless you tell me right now where to go and find her, or without at least one of you in close enough proximity to activate those connections I know you all have, and lead me to her. Do you want me to find her? Why?"

"Why did you run after her?" Rob asked gently.

"Because I knew what I knew. Because I was afraid of what *they* might find out, and if they learned what I already knew the military might not have bothered weighing their options before they took steps to eliminate what they would consider an unacceptable risk. And I could not help them to—to—do you have any idea what sort of mayhem could have gone down here? Why would you take such risks to help her flee, and now be ready to help someone go out there after her, ostensibly to bring her back here? How can you even be sure that she can survive out there, right now, alone? For how long?"

"But she is not alone," Alaya said.

"And that," Stella said, "is the heart of the problem. If we—if I—turn around and tell Martin Peck that Lily Mae can survive out there right now and why, my fears of the consequences of that remain exactly the same. I cannot possibly tell any of them out there—tell Martin—your truth, not without condemning you all. So here's the situation. I think you have a very clear idea that the authorities are probably never willingly going to allow you to leave this place and go free—however much I myself passionately want to see that happen, and to have you recognized out there for everything that you have done, and been, for Earth."

She looked intently at each one of them for a long moment, then went on. "That suddenly mattered enough that you were willing to risk everything on one throw of the dice to let one of you—possibly the most important one of you, given the circumstances—escape from here. And now you're telling me—what? That you are willing to help those authorities—or not those authorities, but just me—track down the very person you did so much to help to leave this place, and bring her back here?"

"But you wouldn't bring them back," Han said. "Not in obedience, not because of duty. Yes, Father Philip told us."

"He talks too much, for a priest," Stella growled.

Han smiled. "But we knew that already. The children knew that. The children helped put it all together. Don't blame the good Father for talking out of school. When Boz died... everything changed... with Lily Mae it was just not that simple to begin with, and then it got even more complicated, very quickly. But they had to go. And we all did what we could to make that happen. The children knew that you would help us. That you understood it. The odds were against us, against any of this working, when we came to the conclusion that Lily Mae had to get out of here we had no real notion about how to go about it—but then Lily Mae made the connection with Aisha, and Aisha *offered* to help. We—the rest of us—don't know any more than that. We don't know where Lily Mae went. We don't know if she is safe, or if she is for how long she will be. You yourself have been telling us that the world is very different from the one we knew—and we have no idea if Lily Mae is going to be able to find her way in it..."

"But I trust Alabastra and Diana to get her through the rough spots," Jerry interrupted.

"I think it was Alabastra that scared Aisha witless," Stella murmured.

"She has that effect on people," Jerry said, with a touch of smugness, as though Alabastra had been his idea.

Han glanced at the still blank tablet. "Assuming Martin is telling the truth, we don't have much more time unobserved," he said. "Jerry, stop distracting us from the issues at hand. Stella, we do want your help to find Lily Mae."

"I thought it was more about me needing your help," Stella said.

"That, too," Han said, smiling.

"But I still don't understand - why? *Why*? If I—if *we*—don't track her down, and she is lost, then you have accomplished nothing at all. If we do find her... what do you expect me to do?"

"You can't help us, not anymore," Rob said quietly. "But you can... help her. We need you to help her. And we will do everything we can to help her, even buried in this bunker and cut off from her. Of all the people who have touched our lives since they brought us back to Earth, aside from Father Carter, you were the only person who saw us as more than the problem to be solved, more than a curiosity, more than a potential disaster if our very existence was revealed. Even after... you learned just how much of a disaster it could become. If we find Lily Mae... she needs our one friend. She needs you. The rest of us..."

"The rest of you have lost everything," Stella said. "You've lost Philip, He might be replaced but you'll have to start all over again and you might never really trust another priest to be the same kind of man that Philip is, able to wrestle demons and come out on the side of right even when it cost him half his own soul. And one way or another... you lost me—I was on my way out of the door, Martin kicked me out of here, and whether or not he would have replaced me with anyone else from my field to continue to study you... you remaining four... you were already even more alone than you were before. What did you possibly accomplish by all this that was worth the price you have already paid, never mind what you will continue to owe...?"

"They are free," Alaya said softly. "At least one of us... came home."

"Okay," Stella said, walking into Martin Peck's office, "we've talked it through. This is how we think this is going to work. There *is* a connection between the crew, something that I couldn't begin to explain to you in empirical terms—a very solid and specific link which is something that I, despite my affinity with them, utterly lack. In theory, they can use that to connect, to track Lily Mae out there— to figure out where she is, how she is getting there—but they cannot do that from in here. If you were hoping that their cooperation would boil down to them sitting down with you over a map and pointing to a location to which you can send your men to surround Lily Mae and bring her back here—it doesn't work that way. If you want her, we're going to have to go hunt her."

"We?" Martin said. "Who's *we*?"

"I will go," Stella said. "And one of them—one of the *Parada* crew— will come with me. And I believe you and I already spoke about this. If it is to be anybody, it has to be Rob Hillerman. I don't think... any of the others are ready for this."

"But you believe—in your professional capacity—that he is?"

"I believe he can handle it, yes," Stella said sturdily.

"And he agrees to this?"

"He is willing."

"So we hold the six of them here because we didn't think that any of them were 'ready for this'," Martin said, "and then one of that crew dies—one is out there God alone knows where and doing God knows what—and now I have to loose a third one into the mix, unleash more chaos to salvage the chaos already unraveling...? If I..."

"You still have three hostages left," Stella said, acidly enough. "What's more, if this goes down as I have just said, you have more than that—you're going to be splitting the twins. Jerry and Rob would have turned down a trip to the stars if they hadn't been allowed to go out there together. By asking Rob to take this on you're basically asking them to separate, now, here, after all that—after the initial reluctance of a bonded twin pair to be pried apart, after the subsequent superglue applied by the *Parada* misadventure, after their return to Earth and to *this* particular circle of hell you have created for that crew here."

Martin bristled at that description, but Stella ignored that and pressed on. "*You're asking them to separate.* It's a big ask, Martin. A *big* ask. And even if you don't trust the connections between Lily Mae and the rest of the group... you have plenty of evidence to know that the connection exists between the twins. You aren't 'loosing' anything, you're unspooling a leash, and you're holding the other end. And don't think that the two of them don't know that."

"What are you proposing, exactly?" Martin said after a moment.

"I will take Rob to where I last knew Lily Mae to have been," Stella said. "That trail may be long cold, but it's a starting point—and the sooner we leave, the better the chances that Rob might be able to pick up on *something*. Give us a direction to go in, at least. And hopefully the closer we manage to get to her the better able Rob will be to help us find her."

"I'll send a squad of men with you, they can..."

"Don't be ridiculous," Stella said sharply. "You have spent an inordinate amount of time and effort keeping the very existence of the *Parada* people from being even whispered about. The whole thing is so shrouded in secrecy and is so... so... *classified*... that you have non-disclosure agreements damn near signed in blood, with everybody involved, from the top down. And now you want to throw a bunch of Marines out—to what? Hunt someone who doesn't exist? The whole idea about enlisting the crew's cooperation and me leading that particular dance was that we should keep the whole thing quiet and under the radar. That will be exceedingly difficult to do if you have a small army racing around pointing machine guns at everybody. I thought you wanted to find Lily Mae...?"

"I do!"

"And then do what—*shoot* her? If not, what's the firepower for? What are you thinking of—Rob in front like a pointer dog, me as the obedient handler trotting in his wake, and a dozen armed men—do you want them in full battle uniform?—arrayed around us so that absolutely nobody who might be within shouting distance of all this is left in any doubt that a dangerous situation involving lethal force could erupt at any point? Do you *want* to cause panic out there? We need to go quickly and quietly, not armed to the teeth—Lily Mae isn't a wild boar that needs to be brought to bay..."

"I can't let you go out there without escort!" Martin snapped.

"Philip and I already..."

"Yes, and that turned out to be a magnificent success, didn't it," Martin said, his tone acid.

"Not because we didn't have a... *squad*... on our side," Stella said. "If anything, it would have gone worse had we done so."

"You aren't going out there without an armed guard," Martin repeated.

"What happens if Lily Mae won't come out with her hands visible when they call her—would you see her dead?"

"Of course not."

"Then what are the guns for?"

"For your protection," Martin said. "*And* hers, if that should prove necessary. And because I am responsible for the whole operation, and it is being carried out, still, under a military command and military discipline."

"You won't get the results you want with an army out there," Stella said. "No matter how small an army you make it. It's still going to be a question of sending out armed men to hunt down a single unarmed and probably thoroughly disoriented and frightened woman... who has basically done absolutely nothing wrong."

"Nothing wrong, except..."

"Except escape your custody, yes," Stella said. "Throwing guns at the problem won't help."

"Escort," Martin said stubbornly.

"We don't need s squad of..."

"Six men," Martin said.

"Send one security officer if you have to—but—"

"Five," Martin said.

"Are we *haggling*?" Stella said incredulously. "I am telling you that the presence of even one trigger-happy trooper who might fire without any real reason at someone who hasn't done anything..."

"All right," Martin said through clenched teeth. "I will accept two, armed only with sidearms. But those two accompany you. Or none of this happens." His voice was flat, his tone absolutely final. "I am done surrendering ground. Two armed guards go with you to watch your back. That is the only way this goes ahead at all."

"*Fine*," Stella said, after a beat. "I am not going to sit here arguing about it. The longer we delay, the less likely it is that we can actually pick up..."

"So when do you want to leave?"

"As soon as some basic supplies have been acquired."

"What do you need?"

"To start with, some street clothes in which Rob can leave this place," Stella said. "Dressed as he is, he'd hardly be inconspicuous. Definitely a hat of some sort, for him. At least a preliminary supply of strong sunscreen for those bits of him that are going to be exposed to a sun he hasn't seen in a *very* long time. Heavy duty sunglasses. And I strongly suggest that we step out of here towards the close of day. I don't know what Lily Mae did to protect herself—at least I hope she knew enough to know that she might have a problem with at least some aspects of the physical world out there—it's hotter than she remembers, than she knows, and it may well have caused her issues—but even she first ventured out there in the pre-dawn hours, and had the advantage of not having to deal with the power of the full midday sun."

"That means you'll be going into night operations," Martin said clinically.

"Initially," Stella said. "I don't expect that we will find her in a matter of hours. Tomorrow will be a whole new day."

"So you're leaving in..." Martin consulted his watch. "Shall we say, nine hours from now?"

"Approximately," Stella said, fully aware that the imprecision of her decision drove Martin's neat military mind into fits of impatient exasperation, and at this particular moment reveling in that. "But mostly... it is going to be up to Rob. When he is ready, we will leave. Before we do, he has things he needs to take care of here."

"What things?" Martin demanded.

"This will be the first time in literally years that he is facing an existence without his brother at no more than an arm's length. And if that isn't complicated enough for you... all the personalities that are in play here are now awake and aware. With Rob being taken out of that habitat, they're down to literal half strength—three remaining, out of the six who went out. They've been hammered with losses already. They need... to come to terms with this new situation."

"Why am I thinking you sound like you are planning to run for the hills...?"

"I don't know, why are you?" Stella riposted. "If we are still talking Greek mythology, let's think about Orpheus. I'll return to the lands of the living, as it were, from the expedition to retrieve one of the dead... so long as I remember not to look back." She stood, and gave him a parting nod. "I'll see to the necessary requirements. When Rob is ready, I will let you know."

Cheering crowds had greeted the first steps onto the surface of their own world that the crew of the *Juno* took as they returned to Earth from their journey into the depths of space. No such crowds waited in the street as Rob Hillerman, navigator of the *Parada*, crossed the threshold of the doors of the World Government Tower and stepped out onto the top landing of the wide stairway leading down to the street below. There was only Stella, standing beside Rob as he paused to lift his head and stare into the deep of the sky, to see the strange white shadow around Rob's mouth, his eyes hidden behind his dark glasses. He looked like a wild creature, wary and focused, poignantly still, aware of the moment.

It was the first time in two hundred years—or more than three years—or what may have seemed like endless weeks of captivity in a sealed sterile environment separate from everything that was real and solid and genuine and true—it all depended on how one measured time—that he had had a chance to feel a part of his world again, and Stella could see the awareness of that in the set of his shoulders, the way his hands hung half-curled at his sides as if he were afraid to clutch too tightly lest the substance of the world should seep between his fingers like sand.

"It is hot," he said, almost too quietly to be heard, almost as though he was merely speaking his thoughts out loud, speaking only to himself, taking the time to treasure this unlooked-for instant of release. "It is way hotter than it should be, isn't it? And it smells... I was going to say, the same as I remember... but that's not true... it doesn't smell the *same*, but it smells..."

He breathed in deeply, and Stella could see his nostrils flare, as he tried to gather in the scents he was talking about, classify them, learn or maybe re-learn them. "It smells like city. Like people. Like *Earth*," he said at last, and glanced down at her with a small smile playing around the corners of his mouth. "Sorry. I am not being entirely quotable."

"I'd quote that," Stella said, returning the smile.

One of their escort—the same Lieutenant Lydia Marsh whom Stella had met on her first day on the job here, the day she met Martin Peck—stepped up to Rob's other side, a little impatiently.

"Should we get moving?" she said. "We're losing light."

"Do you need a CitiCar?" the other member of the security detail asked. He had been introduced, very briefly, to Stella as Lieutenant Oleg Gryshenko, and the soft Russian vowels still informed his accent. "Where are we headed?"

"Yes, grab a car," Stella said. "We're right behind you."

Oleg ran lightly down the stairs to the street level, casting about for a CitiCar he could commandeer, and Stella touched Rob's elbow.

"Come on," she said.

He glanced up at the sky one more time, his expression, from what Stella could glean of it behind his sunglasses, rapt. "All right," he said. "But oh... that light..."

Stella could sense the shiver of transformation, a potential emergence of the Poet, and she could not blame Rob for that—it was a shattering moment for him, and if any occasion was going to trigger his fragmented personalities offering up the one most able to cope with it being presented in order to do so, it was right now, as he stood bathed in the light of the first sunset he had seen for a long, long time. But she couldn't let it happen, not here, not right now. Her fingers tightened on his arm.

"Rob," she murmured. "*Rob*. Stay with me."

He shivered, as though someone had just woken him from a dream. There was a bad moment as he fought for control and Stella braced for the possibility of damage control—but then he had it in hand, and merely sighed deeply, looking down at his feet, deliberately dragging his eyes from the sunset-painted sky.

"I'm fine," he said quietly. "I'm fine."

"Car is here," Oleg called from the curb, a lime-green CitiCar idling beside him with its door open.

Rob allowed himself to be steered down the stairs towards the waiting car, Stella at his side, adjusting her small army-issue backpack. Lydia brought up the rear. Stella was aware of Lydia's eyes darting around as though she half-expected—or perhaps half-hoped—for some enemy to come hurling themselves out of the deepening shadows of the street, so that she could take actions she deemed appropriate. But nothing untoward showed itself, the presence of the four roundly ignored by the city that eddied obliviously around them, and Lydia settled herself in the seat nearest the door as the CitiCar closed up behind them.

"Where to?" Oleg said, from beside the car's console.

"Let me," Stella said, and leaned over to tap in their destination.

This wouldn't do—this wouldn't do at all—and she was thinking furiously about her options as they all sat in silence while the car took them all towards the Old City. Arslan Ilhan would not thank her for bringing the weight of the establishment down on him—but if he was able to help Lily Mae with the logistics of her escape, Stella could only hope that he was also able, and willing, to help Stella and Rob with their own.

"It's stopping," Oleg said, as the car slowed and then came to a halt.

"Yes," Stella said, "we go the rest of the way on foot."

The Old City was starting to be loud and busy with tourists and visitors, its cobbled streets full of people eagerly chattering to one another in a dozen languages, the shops and tiny food-selling establishments looking exotic and inviting under colorful awnings and with period streetlights or raw flame torches in sconces casting flickering shadows everywhere. Lydia was on high alert, her hands loose at her sides, as though she was just waiting for an opportunity to draw her weapon; she and Oleg kept close to the other two, one at Stella's elbow and the other at Rob's, until Stella wanted to stop and demand to know just who they expected to attack them out here. When they finally wended their way to the cobbler's shop where she and Philip had gone—was it really less than twenty four hours before? It felt like a lifetime to Stella, suddenly—Stella came to an abrupt halt outside it, causing Lydia to literally tread on her foot as she came crowding after.

"Are we here?" Lydia asked, looking around. "What is this place? Why are we here?"

"For some information," Stella said. "And you are going to have to wait here."

"We are here to protect you," Lydia said. "We go where you go."

"You are here to protect the mission," Stella snapped, "and the mission is to find a missing person. In order to accomplish that I need to get information from someone inside this shop. That person is not likely to speak to me at all if he sees two gun-toting lurkers at my back—is likely, in fact, to have maybe already fled the premises if they are paying any attention to what is going on—and at best, if you are present and that person is still here, I am likely to get misleading information. Like it or not, you are not an intelligence gathering team."

"We have our orders," Lydia said stubbornly.

"Lieutenant, I may technically be a civilian but in this situation I outrank you," Stella said, drawing herself up to look Lydia in the eye. "I paid very close attention to my papers. If I need to, in certain situations, I can pull the rank that is at the very least the equal of Martin Peck's, and is definitely higher than yours. I'm changing your orders. *Wait here.* Guard this door, if you have to make yourself useful. Rob, come with me."

Without waiting for another word, she turned Rob with one hand and pushed him through the door and into the shop, letting the door swing closed behind them.

A young man at the counter looked up with first interest and then consternation as Stella put a finger on her lips, demanding silence, and lifted the curtain over the inner archway. At a sharp gesture from her, Rob obediently slipped under and through. She followed.

The corridor beyond was lit by just one dim yellow light in a sconce on the far wall, illuminating the door to one side and the stairway to the other.

"Up there," Stella said. "I just hope he's here."

Rob raised an eyebrow but said nothing, going where she indicated, emerging into the room that Stella had been in only that morning. It was lit by two small lamps, and what light washed through the windows from the street outside; and it was quite empty. Stella hesitated, wondering if she needed to make some sort of sign of their presence, but even while she was thinking about that the curtain on the far side of the room lifted and Arslan Ilhan stepped into the room, a faint frown on his face.

"I have to apologize," Stella said, preempting anything he might have said, "because I may have brought trouble to your door. But now it is I who need your help."

"You did not find your friend?" Arslan inquired solicitously.

"We are still searching. She has... apparently taken matters into her own hands. I don't think she was there to meet the person you sent her to meet. This is why... I have brought this man. He is close to her, he may be able to tell us where she went, where she is going, help us catch up with her before she runs into... real problems... but we have to shake an escort to do that."

"The people waiting outside my door?" Arslan asked.

"Can you let us slip out the back way, as my friend and I did this morning?" Stella asked. "And at least delay them?"

Arslan gazed at her, with his head tilted a little to the side, in silence.

Stella spoke again, into it. "And one more thing, if that is in your power." She fished around in her pocket for her tablet, and brought it out. "I have a pretty good idea that anything I do as myself on this thing is somehow traceable and trackable," she said. "I have a personal phone, but that can also be used to track me, if I switch it on or use it in any way. I need another phone, something I can use to contact someone without anyone else being the wiser. I am not, of course, implying anything... but I think you may be in a position to help me obtain one."

Arslan smiled, very slightly, only the corners of his mouth curving upwards.

"It amuses me," he said, conversationally, "to play this game. Wait here."

He ducked out of the room again, and Stella folded her hands over her tablet, tense, doing as he asked. After a few moments Arslan returned, holding a somewhat battered smartphone tablet a generation older than Stella's own in one hand and a couple of loose garments draped over his other arm.

"I believe this will serve your purposes," Arslan said, handing Stella the phone, "and when you are done with it you may discard it at your pleasure. It will be traced neither to you, nor to me. You will be wise to abandon the phone you do not wish to be traced by, at your earliest convenience. I just ask, as a favor..."

"Not at your own doorstep," Stella said. "I understand."

"As for the other... these will change your silhouettes."

Rob was closest to the arm holding the folded cloaks and accepted them as Arslan let them slide down his forearm. Rob shook one out, handing the other to Stella.

"Thank you," he said gravely.

"What is she to you, the woman you seek?" Arslan said, holding Rob's eyes.

Rob hesitated for a moment, and then said, "She is like a sister to me. We have been through much together."

"Then I hope you find her well," Arslan said. He flicked his eyes over to Stella as she settled her hooded cloak around her, the small backpack underneath giving her a curious hunchbacked shape, and then gestured towards the doorway they had entered through. "Your door will be open. Go with God. I will take care of the rest."

Stella gave him a grateful nod, and then gestured to Rob. He pulled his own hood up over his hair as they both turned away, and skittered down the stairway to where the outer door stood ajar in the yellow light.

"Go," Stella said. "Through there. Quickly."

They slipped through the door, one after the other, and Stella closed it gently and quietly behind them. Then she led the way across the shadowed courtyard beyond, and through into the far street; they slipped out of the courtyard's gate and melted into the crowds out in the street. Stella closed her hand around Rob's wrist and pulled him after her in the direction of the boundary of the Old Town, back towards civilization.

Incongruously, she heard Rob laugh—an exhilarated chuckle that made her turn to look at him, disconcerted.

"Back when I was just a boy," Rob said, "I used to do these role-playing games—they grew out of stuff they used to call Dungeons and Dragons, back in the day. This... feels like I just stepped back into that time. I feel sixteen again. And you—you're just..."

"I'm just *what*?" Stella said, a little breathlessly, slipping between two large knots of laughing people and through into the shadows beyond. She had her phone tablet in her hands, working at the back of it, as she walked; it popped open at a seam, and she extracted the battery from its innards, only barely pausing to drop it furtively, in passing, into a garbage receptacle by the side of the street.

"They used to have alignments," Rob said, easily keeping up with her and speaking just loud enough for her to hear. "If you ever thought Jerry and I were completely identical, think again—I was lawful good, the righteous knight, acting out of duty and honor and compassion, and Jerry was more of a neutral evil, absolutely out for himself, the mercenary who switched sides if someone offered him something he found more valuable than what he already had in hand. You... you're total chaotic good."

"What are you *talking* about?" Stella said, pausing with her back against a wall, turning to stare at him, her fingers sliding the data card from its slot inside the phone.

"That would be a character who will absolutely do what is necessary to make things better," Rob said. "Even if it means riding roughshod against any otherwise well-meaning bureaucratic behemoths that stand in their way. Perhaps sometimes even because they will have to do that. Against... well... against someone like Martin Peck, I guess."

"And what is he, in your hierarchy?" Stella said, aware of a certain urgency to be away from this place but finding herself fascinated—in a professional capacity—with this glimpse into the working of Rob's mind.

Rob considered for a moment. "I would guess he comes closest to a lawful neutral," he said. "Someone who, you know, follows orders. Someone who believes that there is an organization that he is part of, that he is bound by order, rules, tradition—adhering to the absolute letter of the law, no matter what it costs..."

"And Lily Mae would be...?" And then Stella shook herself. "We don't have *time* for this, not now. Come on. There's a lot we need to do before they realize that we're gone and they start looking for all of us. This time, Martin might send out his Marines. And Lily Mae is still out there, alone."

11.

It was full dark when Stella and Rob arrived at the train station where she had lost track of Lily Mae that morning. The station building was locked, and a fence prevented easy access to the tracks, but they could easily see the rails which showed crisp and dark in the light of the waxing gibbous moon in the sky, unspooling off into the distance in both directions. Stella stood with Arslan's cloak pushed back over her shoulders, so that it draped only across the backpack on her back, her hands laid lightly on the fence but her head turned so that she could watch Rob. He was frowning at the rails, she could not tell if in displeasure or just furious concentration—he had finally removed his dark glasses and she could see his unconcealed expression, but it was ambiguous in the moon shadows, and she could not quite read him.

"Well?" she said at length, after a period of silence. "Anything?"

"I don't know what you were expecting," Rob said. "Any of you. There's no telepathic umbilical, if that's what you were hoping for. Even if it were Jerry, I couldn't stand here and point in a direction and say, there, that is where he has gone. There is a *link*, yes. A tenuous one. And that link... and my gut... says *that* way."

He pointed to where the rails ran south, curving to southwest out of sight.

"Well, we can follow, but I don't want to bring anybody down on us by looking up a train schedule on anything I am not sure that they can't trace and I have no idea when the next train is due out. Other than, if they run daily, early in the morning—the one that Lily Mae herself took from this station. But that would mean staying here until then, and there's a good chance that they might come looking for us here, after they get done playing hide and seek at Arslan's place. And anyway—if we wait here for hours... Lily Mae could be anywhere by then..."

"There's still the link," Rob reminded her.

Stella hesitated, and then made a decision. "We'll walk," she said. "We'll follow the rails. Next station down the line, we wait for the next train that is going in that direction. And then we'll see what happens after that."

She glanced at Rob again, and he was not looking at the rails at all, but up, into the sky, at the pale moon.

"I know this is going to sound bizarre," he said softly, "but it feels like I'm seeing that sky for the first time again. It is almost impossible to believe that I have been out there, that I have returned from... from *inside* it. That I have looked back here, from the other side, as though from the wrong side of a window."

"You brought some of it back with you," Stella reminded him, and then gave him a light push. "That way. Start walking. And while we're out here... I think you need to tell me now."

"Tell you what?" he asked, falling into step beside her and tilting his head to glance down at her.

"The truth. Everything. Everything you have been holding back on. And when you're done, tell me why you were holding back on it."

"If I tell you that it was terrified when it crossed our path, terrified and desperate, will that help?" Rob asked quietly. "I don't know which one of us it touched first, I can't remember, but if I wasn't that first contact then I was very close after—I could sense it inside of my brain, trapped and bewildered, almost insane and very nearly driving all of us there too. It was not... a gentle presence. But it was not a malicious one. I don't believe it meant to harm us. It just couldn't help it. Boz had a theory..."

"About this... what did you say its name was... Illogon?"

"Illogon isn't its *name*," Rob said, frowning. "When sentients meet others out there among the stars they lead with species, not names. We did exactly the same thing, centuries ago, when we first sent out our feelers—we sent images of ourselves, we held out a hand to be shaken and said to the Universe, here we stand, we are Humans. This creature who crossed our path out there... its people are Illogon. To be perfectly honest, I never understood its name. When that creature first tore a strip of us all apart, it was the children who came out— the children, which were the form our sense of wonder took at this whole thing, and the children just thought of it as Illogon. But that's its species. Its race. There was a name attached to the world that it originally came from—I only ever heard it, never saw it written down, and I may be getting this completely wrong—but their name for their world is something like Illaguund Rah Hasha which at my best guess at interpretation translates literally into 'The World of the Illogon', it would be as if we described our Earth as 'the World of the Humans'."

He lifted his head again from where he'd been keeping his eyes on the path before him, watching for obstacles, and glanced up at the star-scattered skies above him. "I wonder which of those is its home."

"You call the thing 'it' all the time. They aren't gendered?"

"Yes, they are, but only at times—we got this in an encapsulated encyclopedic form, just inserted into our minds, no actual knowledge, just information," Rob said. "They don't separate into the reproductive forms until conditions are right for that cycle—and the female form will bud off something that for what of a better word you might call an egg sac and the male form will internalize that, and recombine it with its own genetic contribution, and then carry it until the progeny—as I understand it, usually twins—is ready to emerge. You can imagine the kind of gutter-level ideas that the whole thing would have put into Jerry's mind. And then..."

"Twins?" Stella asked sharply. "Is that why you and Jerry were so interesting?"

"It might have found us similar enough to have jumped to the conclusion that we might have been the young," Rob said. "That doesn't really explain..."

"I don't understand *how* it happened in the first place. You said Boz had a theory—what was it?" Stella interrupted.

"It was looking... for something alike to itself," Rob said. "Boz thought it simply didn't expect to find a physical form out there. And that confused it, initially—it may have tried to break us out of our personal shells, just like it was spilled out of its own shell."

"Rob," Stella said gently, "you aren't making any sense."

Rob sighed. "I know. It's hard to explain. I carry the memory of it inside my DNA now, but it's really hard to put into words."

"What do you mean, shell?" Stella said. "It had a... it was a *space lobster?*"

Rob laughed out loud. "Nothing so literal," he said. "Stella, they don't... travel out there like we do. They have solved our perennial problems of life support—food and air, necessary for the bare existence of a physical human body—and gravity issues, and space radiation protection, all of that by simply... not sending a physical body out there. When the Illogon go out among the stars they send out, well let's still call it a shell, but it's a vehicle. The vehicle is literally operated by... by a..."

He broke off, obviously struggling to put it into words. "The best I can get my head around it, the body of their space traveler is safe on their world, in some sort of an induced sleep, while the spirit of that traveler inside this tiny vessel that's out there in deep space. You might say they send their minds out—they almost literally download their sentient core into a machine—to remote control their spaceships, at least the exploratory ones like the one we met. The ship holds the connection."

"Quantum connected?" Stella asked, curious.

Rob stared at her. "What was that?"

"Doesn't matter, I don't know enough about it to make a complete thesis," Stella said, waving her comment off. "I just remember—back in college—reading something—there was something Einstein said—'spooky action at a distance'. Two separated particles somehow connected and acting in unison."

"Was that applicable to living entities or to quantum level particles, though?"

"I don't know," Stella said helplessly. "The Illogon never tried to explain...?"

"This entity is an explorer," Rob said. "If it had been someone like, say, Alaya who had got tangled up with one of their ships, she couldn't have explained how our starships work either. Perhaps this particular unit... simply didn't have that kind of specialist knowledge. Or didn't care to share it. Or didn't know how."

"Sorry. I distracted you. This is a whole new can of worms, a discussion for another time," Stella said. "And perhaps for entirely different people. About this collision. You were saying?"

"Yes. I mean, I don't know how it happened. All that we could piece together was... that the Illogon ship crashed into something...into us? I don't know. Whatever, when it did, so did the connection to its shell. I don't know what happened to the body, back on the home world, but that part of it that fell amongst us, a disembodied spirit... it didn't die. It found us. It thought that we were somehow alike, it could sense a sentient spirit inside... inside a vessel... but it wasn't thinking in terms of living bodies which still held their sentience tightly attached... and while it bounced off our walls and tried to find something to attach to... it ripped us up, inside."

He was silent a long moment. Stella didn't interrupt. Finally he went on. "I think... Jerry and I... had an early grip on it. When we first started to meet the... fragments... that were coalescing out of the wreckage left behind from that very probably completely inadvertent and violent first contact... we could deal with it, because we'd already had the experience of having lived inside each other's heads, in a way, so it wasn't so much of a wrench. And because Illogon had us there... as prototypes... it might have assumed that it was okay, that it was normal, for more than one 'mind' to exist inside one of our bodies. And so it went looking—for the one which it thought it could communicate with, bond with, find another shell to share with... Han and Alaya...and Lily Mae... had no protection against any of this. They had always been sane single human minds. Sharing their brain pan with Illogon *broke* them. They were sliced open with a psychic knife, and they fell apart, like orange segments. It was the children who held us all together, in the beginning. The children, whose curiosity and acceptance and sense of awe simply took the impossible for granted, and allowed all of us to come to terms with what we had become. For a little while, it was the children who ran the *Parada*. The rest of us were mostly incapacitated. All of us responded to that in the way that you saw, when we came home. All except Boz."

"Why him?" Stella asked. "Why *not* him?"

"I don't want to say he was the strongest-minded of us all—but perhaps the most focused and single-minded, yes," Rob said. "Illogon fled to him last. Whether because it was exhausted from battling with the rest of us, or whether it simply found the space for the calm haven it needed, I don't know. There was enough left there to carve off Jiminy—but there was no more for it to cut out of Boz. So instead of the multitudes that the rest of us came to carry, Boz had... himself, and Jiminy, and Illogon. And we could deal with that. But then... the *Juno* came."

He paused a long time, remembering. "We had to face humans again. If five of us came back as fractured as we were, and one did not... it was the children who came up with it, in the end, again. It was the children who told Jiminy what to do. Create his characters. Pretend. Put up a stage set. In one way, he had it the hardest of all of us. With myself and Jerry, with Han and Alaya and Lily Mae... we had to deal with keeping our other selves from overwhelming us. With Boz... he was always on guard. Always. He could not for one moment relax, knowing he was always observed, knowing that one slip up and it would be out. He was, in the end, freaked out by being the only one who was 'alone'—he saw the rest of us split apart before his eyes and for a while all he knew was that he was different, that he was a solitary, that he was on his own. Aloneness frightened him, in the end. That's one of the reasons we never left him by himself in the habitat. The reason he always had someone in the room when he slept. Because he could wake up and see one of us there and know that he was not alone, that he would never be alone."

"But then... when he died... what happened? What happened to Illogon?"

"Its shell became extinct," Rob said. "It needed another. And Lily Mae was close to Boz. And she was there, when he died."

"So it can—just—*jump*—from one human to another?" Stella said. "That alone would be enough to have freaked out everyone."

"Exactly," Rob said. "Even though it only did that intentionally... that one time, going from Boz into Lily Mae, for sanctuary." He glanced over at her. "I didn't need to tell you it had done that. You already knew. You are possibly the only one outside of us six who has... seen it. You saw it, didn't you? You saw it in Lily Mae's eyes."

"That's why I ran after her," Stella said. 'Because I knew. Because I could not just sit and do nothing. Because I could not tell anyone else what I knew, because if I did, the consequences would be dire. For her, and for all of you. Once you start keeping this a secret, it only gets deeper..."

"As for keeping Illogon's existence a secret... that was initially something that the children bound us to," Rob said. "Their instincts. And then, once the rest of us—the rest of the personas—had a chance to think about it, we came to agree. There was only one of it—only the one lost and adrift Illogon—but it was inside of us all, bits of it were inside of us all, that is the very core of that link on which you are relying right now—I am not sensing Lily Mae out there, that sliver of Illogon left inside of me is sensing the creature she now carries within her, that's what is keeping us connected. But it was a deeply, deeply alien thing. And although we knew—we six—that it was not malignant, that it had no evil intent, and that it was not really capable of wreaking any havoc even if it wanted to... we knew that we'd find it hard to persuade humanity of it. So we...protected it."

"You told me," Stella said. "*You* told me. Well, Gem did, anyway. But Gem is part of you."

"The children decided that," Rob said. "As for the grown-ups in the hive..."

She looked at him, startled, and he let out a sharp little laugh. "Yes, that's what we called ourselves in the end. The hive. All of us connected to all the others. Six bodies, and so many, so many souls, and always more coming... and some silent, and in the background, and would never speak to anyone outside their own core mind, and others who interacted with other fragments much as any human would interact with another… and we evolved a way to do it, and remain sane…"

"The authorities didn't think so," Stella said quietly. "That's the very reason they called in someone like me. To basically confirm to them that… you were no longer what they might consider sane."

"But you refused to do that," Rob said.

"Because they were *wrong*," Stella said sharply. "But I didn't know about the trigger, when I came. About the fact that inside all the spilled human personalities there was one which was… not."

"If they had known that," Rob said, "there is at least one part of humanity that would have responded by the absolute conviction that the only way to combat such an infection would be to cauterize it and completely sterilize the wound. Humans… when they encounter even other humans, whom they may not understand, things have not gone well. Look at all of our history. When we encounter things we don't understand we react in two ways—we make that thing into a god, or we demonize it. When it comes to encountering other humans we don't understand… what does that leave? Recognizing them as 'superior', triggering either servility or resentment, or as 'inferior', and therefore exploitable and destroyable. That just doesn't set a good precedent. What of the alien? We couldn't take the chance. Especially when any knee-jerk instinct of 'destroyable'… would have destroyed us, as well."

Rob paused. "We all still carry it," he said. "The seed of it, the memory of it. None of us will ever be quite free of it. And I suppose that in itself would be enough to terrify some people. But it isn't here to start an invasion, Stella. It isn't here to steal bodies and wreck minds. When it encountered us—the *Parada*—out there, it panicked, at first, and that was when most of the damage was done. But afterwards… when we had all had a chance to take a breath and things calmed down… Stella… this particular explorer might have been young, or inexperienced, or simply, unluckily for us, particularly inept, but it still carries within itself a certain amount of history, of knowledge, of racial memory. In the end… it knew us. It recognized us. Its kind… have encountered us before."

"*What?*"

"Another one of their explorers," Rob said. "It was here. Observing Earth. They have some of the data stored, from that. Our Illogon 'remembered' it once it had a chance to allow itself to think. And then it told us."

"Told you what? What data? When?"

"It's hard to say, exactly, I am not altogether sure how their 'years' correlate to ours. But I got a sense of—well—a couple of thousand years ago. There were definitely people here. Humans. That may have been why it 'remembered' us, in the end."

"But that would have been... well before we had any capacity to... we were being watched like specimens under a microscope and we knew nothing about it?"

Rob laughed. "You sound so *outraged*."

"I kind of am," Stella said, but had the grace to laugh at her own response. "Hey, I was on Martin's back all the time because he had *you* guys under such close surveillance every hour of every day. The idea of my entire world having been under that sort of microscope... by some weird alien intelligence, at that... you're surprised I'm losing my marbles over this? So what did they learn, about us, then?"

"If I understood correctly, they never really completed the study," Rob said. "It would appear that some disaster happened to the scout. What transmissions they received came to an abrupt end, with a catastrophic failure of the shell—the ship. What became of the Illogon inside it... they have no way of knowing. The body, the physical body back on the home world, died; the ship was gone; there was no way of communicating back to its home world. And apparently there was never any attempt to find our world again."

He looked at Stella and gave a 'Jerry' grin, She smiled wryly and asked, "So what could have happened to it? That original entity?"

"It either perished with its ship or it..." Rob shrugged. "This is me, extrapolating, now. Now that we know that it can do what it did— with Lily Mae. If it managed to—I don't know—eject in time from a flaming wreck... if you can talk in those terms when it comes to what is in effect no more than a disembodied *presence*... it might have found a sanctuary inside some oblivious human mind, and all that anyone down here might have known about that was that the human being so possessed had suddenly gone insane, or became a hunted criminal, or became a saint. Too long ago now to know, too far away to trace, lost in time, and lost in space. If only it were to be..."

Stella woke to the rising cadences, and reached out to shake him by the upper arm. "Not *now*. I can't have the Poet waxing lyrical now. Rob. Rob, come back."

Rob stumbled, reached out a hand to steady himself on the fence, stopped to shake his head sharply. "Sorry. It's difficult."

"I know," Stella said softly.

She allowed him a moment to gather himself again, and was startled by the words that came out of that brief silence.

"Okay. Your turn."

"*My* turn? At what?"

"You tell me something *I* don't know."

She actually laughed out loud. "Like what? I don't carry any secret alien souls inside of me."

"Yes, but they brought you out here—and you came—because of what? What was it that made you come to us?"

"Well," Stella said, after a beat, "I don't think I've ever had someone in my charge ask me why I was treating them before. This is a first."

"Were you treating us?" Rob asked, persisting. "What did they think was going on? And what about the *Juno* people? You were the thing that set them free. Your word. Your insistence. But you didn't speak for us."

"Are you rebuking me?" Stella said. "Really? You need me to spell this out?"

"I'm here," Rob pointed out. "Now."

"Yes, and Lily Mae is out alone," Stella said. "But there is a reason it's you out here, now, and not any of the remaining three. The *Juno* crew were... whole. They could be released into the world and forbidden to ever tell anyone about you. The world would lionize them for a brief shining moment and then they would reintegrate into it and they would not stand out and be tripped over every time someone remembered their names—none of you, *none* of you from the *Parada*, could hope to accomplish the same thing. Even you—even you, the one I freely described to anyone who wanted to know as the closest there was to being able to function out here in the real world—even you are sliding back into your fragments when the moment takes you. Twice already I've had to yank you away from the edge of becoming the Poet, and that's just moments I knew enough to *recognize*. And you can—I don't know—marginally *control* it. Han can't. Jerry won't. Alaya... has too many difficult and vulnerable personalities to deal with. With the best will in the world—and trust me, I had plenty of that—I could not tell them that you all would be safe to release, as they released the other crew, and trust you to survive out there without supervision and care."

"Lily Mae..."

"Yes, and why do you think I raced out after her?" Stella said sharply. "She... I will admit that she is a difficult one. She has less control than you do, but she also has specific triggers, and if they aren't tripped she can handle being Lily Mae for long enough for it not to be a problem to anyone she... *damn*, there's enough material out here for a career. And I signed away my rights to write any of this up and publish it, when I came on board..."

"That's all you regret? Sorry to be so inconvenient," said a voice from the shadows, and Stella's head came up. It was Rob's voice, but the tone of it...

"Jerry?"

"Who did you expect?"

"I left your original back there for a reason," Stella said. "Back off. I need Rob out here with me..."

"Because you think you can control him?" Jerry said acidly. "How are you going to write that up, madam doctor? That you're actually afraid of me—afraid of the rest of us when they come out to speak?"

"I am not afraid of you!" Stella snapped. "But this attitude—the arrogance and the selfishness and the self-absorption and the pure unadulterated sarcastic snark—is precisely the reason why Jerry Hillerman was never a candidate to come out here with me—because he would never be an ally, would never help me, would only be looking out for his own betterment. Now get out of Rob's way and let him back in there."

"Oooh, scary," Jerry said.

Stella paused for a moment to center herself, annoyed that the Jerry personality had goaded her into losing her temper.

"If you cared anything for Lily Mae, and I think you did, go *away*, Jerry. Rob, come back."

"Low," Jerry said, and then the silhouette by the fence straightened again, and it was not Jerry any more. "Sorry," Rob said, sounding tired. "This is taking more out of me than I realized."

"And you still want to know why I advocated for the *Juno* crew to be released but not you guys?" Stella said quietly.

"I'm fine now," Rob said. "Let's keep moving."

They walked in silence for a few long moments and then Stella turned her head towards him again.

"Was it you, who drew that particular drawing—the one where Illogon was drawn as an angel?"

"An angel?"

"That's what Philip called it. The winged creature."

"Oh. Yes. That was one of Gem's efforts."

"Does it... really look like that? Did you see it like that?"

"I don't know," Rob said slowly and then tapped his temple with an index finger. "In *here*, I did. That's the image I have. I think. It's really hard to say. I don't think we *saw* it—directly—and if we did then it would be something that we would all—is that what they really look like, themselves, the sleeping bodies back on the home world, or is it just an image their downloaded and disembodied souls saw fit to project for us? How would we know?"

"I seem to remember a long-lost tale of some early astronaut looking outside his capsule and seeing an 'angel'," Stella said. "You think it was one of your guys? Was the one who originally came here still floating up there just above our atmosphere or something?"

"I don't think they can survive just 'floating out there'," Rob said. "It isn't a question of just existing. I mean, it isn't as though it would absolutely need air to breathe or food to eat—that is why they *send* out these downloaded minds instead of the physical bodies, the ability to dispense with needs like that—but what it *does* require, as far as

I can understand, is... is something to exist *in*. It's like, if it doesn't have something solid around it, to contain it, the mind inside would simply... dissolve into the cosmos. It would be like pouring sugar into a cup of hot water—it would—it would stop being sugar, and the water would just get the sweeter for it. For want of a better way to put it."

Stella could hear his voice change as he grinned. "You sure you don't want the Poet out here? He'd be able to explain in much better language..."

"Yeah, and leave me weeping at his feet wrapped in woven word dreams," Stella said, without thinking, and then flushed deeply, grateful that Rob could not see the color that flooded her cheeks in the moonlit shadows that played on her face.

"Thank you," he said, unexpectedly.

They walked in silence for another few minutes, a silence made a little awkward by that last exchange, and then Rob sighed.

"Nothing turned out the way I thought it would," he said, conversationally enough, almost a complete non sequitur to what had come before.

Grateful for the change of direction, Stella gave him a sidelong glance. "Why do you say that?"

"Well," Rob said. "Look at us all. To be perfectly honest with you... when we left in the *Parada*... I almost never expected to come back. At all. Not for the reasons that things eventually went wrong—that was unlooked for, the collision with the Illogon and all that came after. But just. You know. Going out there. I almost looked on it as... a one-way ticket. And then suddenly we were returning, and I thought about Earth again, and I wasn't sure what I was expecting to happen when we got there." He paused, mulling over the thoughts that were struggling to come out. "I never really wanted... the adulation," he said. "The reception you say the *Juno* people got. I would have probably run away from that, hidden somewhere where they couldn't find me. If I felt anything at all... it was... there was just a quiet happiness that I was, improbably, unbelievably, against all odds, coming home, home to Earth."

"And then Earth showed you its teeth," Stella said quietly. "I mean, Martin, and the habitat, and the lies, and the surveillance, and everything else that follows from those things."

"You think I'll ever end up back there?" Rob asked unexpectedly. "With the others?"

"You think you won't?" Stella asked.

He glanced at her, and shrugged. "It just seems... unlikely, at this point. I mean, we did basically ditch the guards they set on us, and those people were sent to watch us for a reason. I don't know what Martin will do next—maybe you do—but I don't think that he'll take that in any other way except that we've plotted an escape and accomplished one. I think—I'm sorry, my dear doctor, but I do think—that you're as much of a fugitive as any of us might be right now."

"You're probably right," Stella said, bowing her head. "But we all made our choices."

"I know—even the good Father was caught up in that net," Rob said. "What happened to him, anyway?"

"He said he would go hide back under the Jesuit cassock somewhere, for a while at least," Stella said. "I thought... we both thought he would be safer there. If they ever found out that he knew about... about the Illogon situation. He went... he went home, I guess."

"Home", Rob echoed. "How we all want to go home. In the middle of the greatest adventure of my lifetime, out there, I could only think of my world—this ball of dirt I stand on now, which hurtles around an insignificant little star we called the Sun and made the center of our little universe at least until we learned to look beyond it—of my Earth, my planet—as 'home'. And the pull of it was vast, much greater than you can imagine, much greater than I can ever convey to you in words alone. But at least I got to do that." He paused, lifting his head to gaze up at the starry sky again. "In the end, I think that's all the Illogon really wanted to do too. Just go home."

"I don't blame it," Stella murmured. "I've only been away from mine for such a little while, comparatively speaking, but so do I—"

"Which, of course, is the one thing it can never..." Rob broke off, realizing that she had stopped speaking entirely too abruptly. He turned to look back at Stella who had stopped moving and stood frozen and focused a few steps behind him. "What?"

"Home," Stella said. "*Home*. Of course. That's exactly what she is doing. That is exactly what I would have done. That's the only familiar thing she thinks she knows. I know where Lily Mae is going, Rob." She closed her eyes for a moment, conscious of a surge of hope and relief, and then opened them again, her expression newly determined. "First... let's hole up for a couple of hours, until we can go and try and find some place that will give us some kind of an early breakfast. And then... I need to send a message. We're going to need some help. We're going to New York."

Stella found a CitiCar to take them back into the hub of the city, and left the vehicle at a random corner, casting about for a VirtRealCafe or some other place with a public terminal. She eventually settled on one with a falafel shop next door, reluctantly left Rob there by himself to get something to eat, and slipped back to the café and behind a public terminal, tentatively typing in the email that Philip had given her. She encapsulated her situation very simply—*We need help*, she wrote. *In the city. Not alone. Call me. I don't have a number for you and my phone is dead but you can call...* she had to consult Arslan's phone for the number, and typed it in.

She had to hope he would be checking his email regularly—but she didn't expect her phone to ring less than twenty minutes later, just after she had returned to collect Rob from the falafel shop.

"Where are you?" Philip asked, without preamble. And then, as an afterthought, "Are you safe? Is it safe to talk?"

"For now. It would take too long to explain in detail—but—Martin okayed a Lily Mae search. I took Rob with me. We were saddled with an armed escort but we... lost them. And then I realized..."

"Lost them? What did you do?"

"I left them for Arslan to deal with," Stella said, deadpan. "That isn't important right now. What's important is... I can probably chase after Lily Mae, now that I have a good idea of where she's going, and there is always a possibility that I am currently over-estimating her ability to accomplish this, but somehow I don't think so—not with...

not under the current circumstances. So I will assume she will get to where she is headed, and it will just take her a little longer to arrive there."

"Where do you think she's going?"

"Home, to America, to New York," Stella said. "And I am not sure that she'll find what she thinks she is looking for—things aren't what she left there, those two hundred years ago. That's partly the reason I want to get there first—for someone she might know to be there to make that hard landing easier for her... But even if she succeeds immediately—she won't just walk onto a ship, it won't be that easy—I'm going to give it, what, maybe three weeks before she can get to the east coast of America... and I need to be there first. Is there any way you know that can get me to where I need to be, fast?"

"Yes," Philip said instantly, "but it will cost."

"I don't know if I can access my accounts, but I have some emergency savings that I can..."

"Not money," Philip said. "Favors. Do you need money, by the way?"

"We're okay for now. I have the emergency chits, still, and that'll take me through a couple of days, at least."

"Where are you, exactly?"

"In the city. Back in the city."

"Well, get *out* of the city. Try and do it without leaving a trail any wider than you need to, but if you can get yourself to anywhere in Italy in the next few days—is that possible? I can have you picked up there." He hesitated. "So. You. And Rob. And is Martin after you with everything he's got now? How did you get out of—what were you planning to—what happened to the... Stella! I knew I should never have left you on your own in that mess. What did you get yourself into the middle of now?"

Stella gave a shaky laugh. "I have literally no idea. I am doing this one step at a time. I can't think beyond the next goal, and my next goal is finding a way to pre-empt Lily Mae."

"What do you plan to do with those two poor waifs when you gather them in?" Philip asked. "Lily Mae and Rob? I am assuming that you aren't contemplating a meek return to Martin's tender mercies...?"

Stella snorted. "That... is not looking likely, is it? Believe it or not, I didn't *plan* any of this. Not really. It just... became inevitable."

"Are you under your own names? Is he likely to close the port against you?"

"It's been less than twenty four hours. If we move fast, we might make it."

"Call me again as soon as you are able. Use this number. What are you using for a phone? Can you safely save it?"

"Philip," Stella suddenly said urgently, "I've burned quite enough bridges over here. Don't do anything that will get you even more tangled up with..."

"Stella. I hesitate when I am speaking to someone of your profession to say that I 'hear voices' because you will probably have your own ideas about that—but if I have *ever* heard God speak to me, it was now, when I prayed about what happened back there, with the crew. If it should happen that the answer to one's prayers is taking matters into one's own hands, I will do that, and make what amends I need to, after. I know you don't believe any of this, and it doesn't matter. I have been asking God to keep you safe—I didn't think that He would toss you out into the world alone."

"I'm not alone," Stella said. "I have company..."

"Yes, but until Rob Hillerman finds his feet again on this world, you're the one in charge of that game," Philip said. "I will continue to say those prayers, no matter how little faith you have in them. It can't hurt, and if God has had your back thus far I know He won't abandon you now. Trust in that, and trust in me. Do what you can to get here, I have to believe that you can, and you will. In the meantime, I will try and get a few things arranged."

"You can do all that? It all sounds so... important. You sound like you're rather higher in the church hierarchy than you led us to believe," Stella said.

"Not that high," Philip said. "But I was never just a simple monk, either. Now go. Don't linger, and don't wait. Get out fast and get out dirty if you have to."

"Okay. On our way."

Stella stuffed the phone back into a pocket and beckoned to Rob, whose dark glasses were back on his face, hiding his eyes from her.

"We need to move," she said.

"Was the good Father in on all this?" Rob asked, slouching into step beside her.

"That depends on what 'all this' is," Stella said. "I'm *thinking*. It would be best on a ferry, but they might have locked those down already—we might find it easier, but we might be able to find a boat, elsewhere. Someone who can take us to a place where they may not be looking for us."

Rob laughed. "It all sounds more and more like those games I told you about, that I used to play," he said.

"Well, remember what you used to do back then to figure out what to do when the world is against you," Stella said. "But it's no game. It's going to be tough enough. You have absolutely no ID on you—which on the one hand is good because that means they can't really track a man who doesn't exist out here, but it also means that you might have trouble at a border if they get overzealous about things. And it also means that you have no access to anything—no information, no money, no points for transportation or for food—and my emergency chits are just that, emergency chits, they'll stretch only so far. We may have to save most of that for passage."

"You keep talking about shipping," Rob said. "Flying is faster—why wouldn't Lily Mae have tried to..."

She gave him an appraising look. "I keep forgetting you haven't been around for a while," she said. "In your day, flying *was* faster, and easier, and far more commonplace. But it's been a while since any but the wealthiest have travelled by air, other than chartered corporate travel or emergencies. I mean, they flew *us* out here, the people they brought out to study you guys, but that was through a high World Government order. And even these rare flights are by stratoplanes now, skating out there on the edge of the atmosphere, and not the jet fuel beasts you will remember. The fuel crisis took care of a lot of that, and then the climate change repercussions that followed... There is no flight for Lily Mae to get on. I think she will try and go home—the only way home from here is a ship—she'll figure that out fast enough, and then she'll have to figure out a way to get on one..."

"You think she will?"

"She is not alone," Stella said.

"That may not... be entirely an advantage..."

"Call it a gut feeling. But I think I know exactly where she went, what she is doing. She's likely to be making for Greece, too. There are a couple of ports there where she can pick up a ship, even if it's just to get her across the Mediterranean, and into a place like Genoa, or Marseilles, or if she's lucky some port past Gibraltar—or even, if she takes the first thing that turns up, to Alexandria, and through the Suez, and maybe out to the west coast of America—that would leave her with the continent to cross if she lands in California, but she'll likely feel more comfortable traveling in a place she is even marginally more familiar with. It can be anywhere—but I think she is going to get on whatever ship she can find, and by the time we get to where Philip wants us to be Lily Mae may well be on her own way..."

"But what can Father Philip do?"

"He didn't say. Exactly. First, we have to get to a place where he can find us. My geography is sketchier than I might like. Is this antique of Arslan's able to pick up a free network? I miss my tablet..."

The phone obliged by providing cursory information, and Stella extrapolated from that, finally enlarging the tiny map on her screen and pointing to one spot.

"There," she said. "Izmir. I like that idea. They may not expect us to jump in that direction. I don't want to go too far down that route, it leads down the gullet of the Middle East and we're already going to have trouble with you and potentially disastrous sun exposure without going into that anvil, before you're even properly acclimated out here—but as a jump off point..."

Rob reached out to stop her scrolling the screen, and pointed. "It could work. Is that a bus schedule? Look, there's a bus to Izmir from the city, we can pick it up at about half past nine tonight, and it's an overnight,"

He peered at the tiny type on the screen. "Best I can make out, that looks like it takes some seven hours to get to Izmir, which also takes care of us trying to find a safe place to sleep."

"Nice catch," Stella said, grinning.

"I was a starship navigator," Rob retorted. "Give me credit for being able to find my way around."

"Okay, then. We just need to lie low for a bit before we can get on that bus, and at least try to keep you out of the sun for a little while. Which leaves us a bit of time to kill. So what do you want to do? You're the man who fell back to Earth. Anywhere you want to go?"

"I missed... water," Rob said, considering the matter. "If you think it's safe, if you know of a way, I wouldn't mind a glimpse of the sea."

"Izmir is on the coast and if any of the plans I have tumbling around in my mind come to anything you'll see more of the sea than you might want to," Stella said. "I'll call Philip when we get to Izmir. Maybe he'll have ideas. In the meantime... we could go to a park, I guess..."

"What *are* you planning?" Rob asked abruptly.

"At the moment I'm just trying to stay a step ahead," Stella said, giving him a quick smile. "How are *you* doing, anyway? Does it still smell... of Earth?"

"Oh, yes," Rob said. "I'm more tired than I thought I would be— but maybe that isn't so unexpected. I haven't walked this far, anywhere, for a very long time, except perhaps on a treadmill which isn't quite the same thing; the muscles in my legs kind of remember this but they're waking up under protest."

"Well, then. We'll do what we can. We'll have to leave the rest in the hands of that God of Philip's and hope that he stays on our side."

"I thought I would just rest my eyes and maybe snatch half an hour of a nap," Rob said, rousing in his seat and looking out of the window at his right shoulder, "but it's hard to tell from *that*... how long was I out?"

"Couple of hours," Stella said, her head tilted back against the headrest, her eyes closed. "Doesn't matter. You needed it."

"Are we there yet?" Rob asked, mimicking the iconic whiny child on a road trip, and Stella grinned, turning her head to look at him.

"Getting there," she said. "We have a full recharge now, so we won't be stopping again until we reach Izmir. I have some more of those energy bars in my backpack, if you get hungry—there, under the seat. They said they have food on the bus but it won't be anything substantial. We'll get something real to eat when we get to the other end."

Rob's eyes wandered around the capsule-like cabin of their vehicle. "When you said 'bus'," he remarked, "I'm not sure what I expected but this... is weird."

"You had electric vehicles in your day," Stella said. "Why is it weird?"

"I guess we did. In towns, on municipal routes. I just never really went on a whole road trip in a plug-in bus before. Did you get any sleep?"

"Not really, it was my watch," Stella said tiredly.

It was Rob's turn to grin. "Well, you're relieved," he said. "I'll just sit here and watch the world go by for a while."

"You can't see anything, it's dark. Anyway, easier said than done," Stella said, squirming a little, trying to get comfortable. "I never could sleep sitting up in your average public transportation seat. It just makes my back lock up."

Rob gazed at her with a touch of unexpected tenderness, and then lifted his arm and patted his shoulder with his other hand. "Come here," he said. "I can be a pillow for a little while."

She hesitated, but only for a moment. Sighing deeply, she kicked off her shoes and lifted her feet up onto the seat underneath her, curling up against his side, letting her head fall on that freely offered shoulder, sensing his arm fold around her until she was held comfortably snugged against him.

"Thank you," she murmured sleepily, feeling a tenseness in her shoulders relax, slipping into somnolence.

Rob pushed a wayward strand of Stella's hair from his mouth and chin, smoothing it back against her head. "It's little enough," he said softly, only partly for her benefit.

Stella started back awake almost three hours later. Rob felt her position shift as she began to sit up, and released her from the circle of his arm.

"Where are we?" she asked.

Rob pointed to a graphic on the screen embedded in the back of the seat in front of him, showing a route, the position of the bus marked as a flashing red dot. "There, I think," he said. "As best as I can make out we don't have that much left to go."

"The sun should be coming up soon," Stella said, yawning.

An attendant leaned in over them, smiling. "Breakfast?" she inquired.

"I was starting to obsess about those energy bars," Rob said, sitting up. "Breakfast would be good."

They were served little black plastic trays with pots of yoghurt and cold croissants, and they both tucked in with gusto. The attendant thought they were about forty five minutes out of Izmir, when Stella inquired about an estimated time of arrival. Stella used her phone to tap in a text message to Philip, telling him that they were well out of Istanbul and that she would call him and let him know their location as soon as they got off the bus.

The message got an almost instant response.

There have been developments. Find the nearest church to wherever you end up getting off, get inside, call me from there. I'll have a safe place for you to go by then.

Rob turned sharply to look at Stella, aware that her shoulders had gone rigid.

"What is it?"

"Trouble. Maybe. Maybe nothing. We need to be ready for anything, apparently." She glanced at the screen in the seatback in front of her, tapped it with a finger. "There. The bus makes a stop, just before we hit Izmir. I think we should hop off there. We can always make our way into Izmir later by some nondescript local jalopy—but if they're watching long-distance routes, we're better off doing the unexpected."

"Was that Father Philip? What happened?"

"He didn't say. But it was a warning." Stella bent over to drag her backpack from under the seat in front of her, Arslan's cloak folded up and tucked under a strap. "Just be ready."

Only one other person stepped down from the bus at its last stop before Izmir, so there was no opportunity to use crowds to disappear—but it was still a dark pre-dawn hour, and Stella managed to find a shadow to slip into, and then a side street into which to dart. The area in which they had alighted didn't appear to be particularly holy and finding 'the nearest church' proved to be rather more of a task than might have been expected. The sky was lightening appreciably in the east by the time they did. The front doors of the church were locked, but when Stella tried the little side door it opened, and they slipped into a small shadowed vestibule, with the flickering lights of votive candles faintly illuminating the transept. Stella pulled out her phone and tapped in the number Philip had left her, and the call was picked up on the second ring.

"Where are you?"

"About twenty minutes out of Izmir," Stella said. "More specifically, in, as you suggested, a church."

"All right. Don't go into Izmir proper. I am texting you an address—it's a little hostelry, in a less fashionable outer suburb. There'll be a room for you. Go there as fast as you can—get a taxi, if you can—and wait."

"For what?" Stella asked, mystified.

"I'm on my way."

"*You* are? Philip, what's going on?"

"When I get there," he said. "When you get to your room, let me know. Just leave a message on this number, if nothing else. Stay down."

He broke off the call, and Stella lifted her head to look up at Rob.

"I have no idea what is going on but it seems *he* is coming here to get *us*." She checked her phone again. "There's an address we need to go to. And wait for him there."

"Did they get Lily Mae?" Rob asked, very still.

"I don't know." She hesitated. "We can take a moment to look at the news headlines once we're out of sight somewhere. Let's do what he said."

A soft voice behind them made them both start, and turn to face it. A thin, wiry priest with a shock of dark curly hair stood in the nave of the church, a few steps away from them, looking at them in a manner that managed to be both wary and serene all at once. They appeared to share no complete language in common, but Stella finally managed to communicate a query about the address she had been given and somehow she and Rob found themselves in a somewhat worse-for-wear car that had seen better days and may or may not have been an official cab, the driver shook his head when Stella offered payment as he dropped them off outside an unprepossessing house with chipped and peeling shutters. The front door was sturdy and looked firmly closed, but it opened when Stella tried it; it let into a tiny hallway bisected by a desk which left an even smaller space behind it, barely enough for a single small human body to squeeze in. Such a body, in the shape of a woman of indeterminate age who was barely taller than the desk itself, presented herself before Stella had a chance to fully close the door behind her.

"I... believe... we are expected?" Stella said, unsure in which name the room they were supposed to claim had been booked.

But the woman seemed to understand perfectly. She reached out to a board on the wall behind her where a handful of old-fashioned keys tagged with wooden numbers were hung, took down Key Number Two, and motioned them to follow.

She showed them up a flight of stairs and into a small second-floor room at the back of the house, looking out into a compact square garden with an incongruous fountain in one corner where a classically draped plaster woman poured a trickle of water from an ewer into a chipped basin below. The walls around it were high, and the young sun had still not risen enough to spill real light into the shadowed square—but it touched the window of the room, which faced east, and a brightness was spilling inside. Stella chose to take that as a good sign. She tried calling Philip, standing in that light by the window where the signal was best, but he wasn't answering; she texted, as she had been instructed, a message, simply, We're here.

When she looked up, Rob was smiling.

"What?" she said.

"You. In that light. Anything looks possible."

Stella flushed. "Don't be so sure," she said. And then her features drew into the faintest of frowns, and she looked at Rob a little more closely. "You keep asking if they got Lily Mae. Is there something you aren't telling me?"

He hesitated. Too long. Stella straightened, sharpening her gaze. "Talk to me. If there is something I need to know, talk to me. Now. For the love of God, look at us—we're riding the ragged edges out here, and it all started with the Lily Mae incident. No. With Boz dying. What suddenly *broke*, Rob? There was—I don't know—a stasis there. Things weren't exactly wonderful but you six—or however many of you there are, by alternative counting methods—were hanging in there, but there was... a balance of sorts. And then—Boz, Was the transfer into Lily Mae planned or was it an accident that tipped the scales? Was it me? Things were hobbling along and then I waded in with both feet and dragged you all out to that rooftop and *everything* fell apart after that—was it my fault?"

"Oh, no—*no*—don't ever think that," Rob said passionately. "What you did for us went a long way towards healing wounds we didn't even know were there. And we all knew, we were all very aware of the fact that you were willing to go to the mat for us, no matter what. But you may be right, that may be what tipped things for Boz—although I don't know, I can't be sure, it isn't as though we ever *talked* directly to the Illogon, not as such, how could we? We had no way to communicate in any kind of language."

"So how did you communicate?" Stella said, diverted.

Rob gave a helpless shrug. "It *thought* at us. It *felt* at us. It put a sense of something into our minds and our brains that would translate that into a human metaphor that we could understand. Oh, it worked well enough. You can think of us as a glorified translator bud in your ear. The Illogon could think itself lonely or in danger and that feeling would be translated and put into words by whichever of us had it inside us. We all spoke for it, at some point, aboard the *Parada*, when we first met it."

"What, like it was a ventriloquist and you just opened your mouth and out came whatever it wanted to say?" Stella said, sounding appalled. "That's one hell of a lot of control."

"No, it didn't have its fingers in our jaws, or in our mind, flapping our mouths at its will," Rob said, with a touch of impatience. "I am doing a really bad job at explaining this. It needed a safety shell, so it sought one—none of us were what it wanted, what it had to have— our minds were too crowded even though it might well have been the Illogon's own doing that they became so. Boz was the closest thing to its having its own space, its own shape, its own body—but even Boz was already fully Boz, it wasn't as though it was a blank mind, with no life experience or memory there, something that the Illogon could simply overwrite like a palimpsest. It is an ethical being, in its own way. It needed... it *needed*... but it couldn't simply take what it needed, with no regard for other sentience or other prior claims."

"So Boz..."

"Maybe Boz tried to give it that," Rob said quietly, a world of pain in his voice. "Maybe in the end they reached an agreement—maybe Boz was willing to give it space in his mind, maybe the Illogon gained what it required, consent. And maybe, somehow, it all went horribly wrong and when Boz...died...or maybe killed himself, erased himself to make room... there was nothing left there for the Illogon to take over. Maybe that fully adult human body and human mind weren't able to divorce from one another, either at all, or fast enough for the Illogon to take the proper control. We'll never know now, will we? But I think the crossing into Lily Mae wasn't planned, I think the Illogon was *hurt* by it, I think Lily Mae was changed by it, and I think that a whole different price needed to be negotiated... and it could not be paid, Stella, not with us in that place, not with Lily Mae in controlled captivity—the Illogon inside of her would have doomed her, would have doomed us all..."

"Why didn't you tell me any of this?"

"I can't tell you *now*," Rob said desperately. "I have a vague idea of the direction in which she ran, because you are right, the Illogon link is sufficient for that. But what I don't know—what I have no idea of—is *how* she is, or if the Illogon, now free and in a body which it can manipulate and control in its own ways up to a point, has done anything at all to affect a transformation that it needed, to her body, to her mind. There are times I think having the Illogon with her is only going to help her because its survival instincts are strong and those will inevitably work to help Lily Mae survive, too. But the flip side of that is... she has the Illogon in her. And I don't know where that is going to end. And if Philip's news is anything about her—if they found her, caught her, took her back, then they are all in danger. All of them. All that remains of the crew. And I—I feel as though I cheated, somehow, to get out here—to be—"

"We're all damaged," Stella said quietly. "Stop it. If we both start wallowing in our various guilts, we won't be any use to anybody. Maybe Philip has the answers. How long is it going to take him to *get* here?"

In the end, there was little to do but wait.

When, finally, a soft knock sounded on the door of the room, both Stella and Rob flinched, as though they had been expecting death itself to come calling. It was Stella who stepped up to the door to open it... and it was Philip.

He was dressed in full Jesuit kit, black cassock hanging all the way down to below his ankles, a short cape over his shoulders, his hair cropped shorter than when she had last seen him as though he had made it a penance to undergo a particularly violent haircut after he pulled out of the *Parada* habitat. It made him look a little alien, sufficiently *different* from the man whom Stella had come to look on as ally and equal while they were working together with the crew that she found herself unable to speak out loud, her voice fading from her lips even as she opened them to speak. Instead, she merely stepped aside, offering him space to step into the room.

He did, apparently fully aware of the reasons for her silence, reaching out to lay one hand on her shoulder as he stepped past to give her a reassuring squeeze. His other hand held a black duffle bag, which he dropped as he came inside. He paused as Stella softly closed the door behind him, and his eyes found Rob, who was perched on the edge of the armchair by the window, his back rigid and straight.

The two men looked at each other for a long moment, and then

Rob got up out of his chair and stepped up to Philip. They both reached out instinctively and gripped each other's forearm in an almost antique greeting, one that might have been exchanged between two noble knights in the age of chivalry, holding one another's eyes; Stella blinked back a sudden sting of inexplicable tears.

"I almost didn't recognize you, in full battle dress," Rob said.

"I almost don't recognize *you*, outside your four grey walls," Philip responded, with a faint smile.

"As for that," Rob said somberly, "there's still an echo of that back in those walls, Jerry is still there, after all." The unspoken words that followed that hung between them in the air: *And may never leave.*

"I didn't want to risk anything I didn't know about, and you said you were coming, but now you're here, and I'm starting to get really spooked," Stella said. "For the love of God, what is going on?"

"*Is* it Lily Mae?" Rob asked, softly, intensely.

Philip dropped Rob's arm and reached for a tablet in the pocket of the cassock. "Not specifically," he said. "But... there's this."

He found what he was looking for, scrolling down the screen with his finger, and then turned the tablet towards Stella and Rob, who both craned their heads to look.

WHAT HAPPENED TO THE CREW OF THE PARADA?, a large headline screamed at them from the top of a tabloid page.

Stella sucked in her breath, looked sharply up at Philip. "When did that land?"

"Yesterday," he said grimly. "It's still just the more lurid press, the tabloids, the more out-there news sites—but there's a conspiracy theory being whirled together as we speak."

"The truth is, it was...is...a conspiracy," Rob said with sudden savagery,

Philip simply nodded and went on, "I am told that Martin Peck's superiors called the Father General demanding to know if I had spoken to anyone about my sojourn in the 'quarantine' quarters. They were able to swear that I had not been in contact with anybody who was outside the contract I had signed like the rest of you when I got to the habitat. But I'm afraid that by that stage *your* flight was already known, and they're now focused on you, Stella."

"But it *wasn't* me," Stella gasped. "I spent the last forty eight hours first racing around Istanbul trying to figure out the Lily Mae situation, and then getting Rob and myself out of there, we've been on that bus all last night, I didn't have *time* to blab to anyone even if I had wanted to which I wasn't going to blunder into doing before I thought..."

"I know," Philip said. "I *know*. But it does mean that you might find it difficult to slip out of sight now. There's an alert."

"Are they watching *you*?" Rob asked.

"Why would they? I am a priest who goes where he is sent," Philip said serenely. "And there's a way I can both get you two out of here, *and* get you to where you want to go—America—but I'm very much afraid I'm going to have to get you both ordained to do it." He nodded at the duffel bag by the door, ignoring their startled reactions. "There's a cassock in there for you, Rob, and one of my spare dog collars. And one of the good sisters from a somewhat conservative convent in Rome—one where they still wear habits—has parted with hers, for you, Stella. There's a chartered flight leaving from Rome for Chicago in four days. We are all going to be on it."

12.

The cassock intended for Rob Hillerman fit him reasonably well, although he looked sufficiently uneasy wearing the clerical dog collar that Philip made him keep it on after trying the whole garb on for size so that he could get used to it. Stella's new habit proved to be the cause for some wholly unintended hilarity, though, since it was clearly meant for someone rather larger than Stella and it both hung untidily off her slender frame and was too long by several inches, the hem pooling around her so as to completely hide her feet.

It was, incongruously, Philip who undertook the necessary alterations. Stella kept giggling every time she caught sight of him sitting in the armchair by the window, patiently plying the needle at the adjusted hem of the habit, and it was infectious—even in the midst of the drama in which they found themselves embroiled they couldn't seem to stop smiling at one another when they caught each other's eye.

"What?" Philip said equably, biting off a thread with an expert familiarity. "You think we have seamstresses at our beck and call? I've mended my own rips many a time. And, with all due apologies, these things don't come off the rack—I had to guess at the size, at that. For what it's worth, it's a compliment. You've so much presence that I obviously believed that you were taller than you are. Here, try that on and see if it's any better."

It was, in terms of length, but even if Philip's gifts ran to more intensive alterations there was no time to spare for them—they would just have to hope that a good cincture and the protection of a nun's persona, which meant that nobody would be caught staring too openly at her, would do to protect Stella from being unmasked.

"You'd better not speak to anybody, though," Philip said. "There's going to be forty people on that flight, and not a soul on it would believe you to be a professed nun if you opened your mouth to them."

Stella roused up to glare at him, outraged at the implications, and both men grinned. "Oh, and refrain from doing that, either," Philip said. "Look anyone in the eye with that kind of defiance and it's over. Can you hope to stay meek and silent for the five or six hours it's going to take us to fly there? You're wearing that rosary at your waist—pretend to be praying, or something. Or maybe I should just let it be known that you've taken a vow of silence. Or one of the two of us has to hover over you at all times, to head off..."

"Oh, so I'll make a terrible nun, but Rob is going to do just fine as a preacher?" Stella demanded, still annoyed.

"She has a point," Rob said equably.

Philip raised his eyes—to the ceiling of the room, and above. "Lord, help me get them through this," he said, only half-jokingly. "Rob, for once, use the gift that this alien gave you. I remember talking to you, back in the habitat, once, and you were... you were someone called Abraham. You were no slouch at arguing with me about God, back then, as Abraham, at least. Can you bring him out, for the journey, at least? Can you control it that finely? Can you handle being... who you need to be...?"

Stella, suddenly all too serious, glanced from one man to the other. "That is so dangerous," she said quietly. "It'll be playing with fire. And if you're really telling me to be seen and not heard, there's very little I can do if you suddenly switch to something... less appropriate..."

Rob's grin had faded, and he looked a little grim. "I never thought I would have to... use this... as a charade," he said.

"I'll be there," Philip said. "For what it's worth. I cannot hover over both of you at once all the time and, Stella, you are going to have to hand over the reins for this one. Trust me. I really need you not to draw too much attention to yourself. There are going to be only two other female clerics on that flight—one other sister, and a female anointed priest from a wholly different denomination—it is probably going to be natural for at least that other nun to want to be in your company, but I'm going to have to pay way too much attention to protecting Rob, you *are* going to be on your own, can you handle it?"

"It's the only way out," Stella said, very white around the mouth. "Believe me, I appreciate that you had to have pulled a lot of strings for this—this is likely to cost you, even if you aren't completely found out—and if either of us slips up—"

"It might cost me a non-negotiable trip to some distant chapter house for retreat and contemplation of my sins," Philip said, "or maybe a couple of years' service in some particular post that nobody is greatly eager to be called to serve in. It could be good for me, at that. Curb unwholesome ambition, if nothing else. But it isn't going to be..."

"Ambition," Rob said. "You never did really tell us why they sent *you* to us."

"One of you asked for a priest," Philip said, shrugging his shoulders. "So we were told."

"A priest," Rob said. "Not a prince of the church."

"You didn't *get* a prince of the church," Philip retorted. And then his lip curled into a small self-deprecating smile. "Only a minor aristocrat. My family has deep roots in the Church—to hear my French grandmother tell it, hers was the family that paved the road for the Pope's move to Avignon in the fourteenth century. When it was my turn to step up to take vows, I ended up as one the under-secretaries to the Father General, and the worst that could happen to me is that I will have to face him while he tells me how disappointed he is in me. But even that—Father Lorenzo Garibaldi, Father General of the Society of Jesus, is a hugely pragmatic man. And I've known him for way too long not to have an understanding of that, and him having a decent idea that I am aware of it. You need to be, perhaps, in that position."

"Were you groomed for it yourself, then?" Rob asked, with a faint smile.

"I don't think anyone ever looked at me as a candidate for that— and if Father Garibaldi had any ideas about it, from my pedigree, before he met me, he probably found me wanting anyway. I have far too many faults, as a Jesuit monk."

"You're a good priest," Rob said, "but I do think you make a lousy monk. No offense."

"None taken. I sometimes agree with that so much it hurts. Neither of you is aware of the kind of spirituality we are supposed to practice, in my order—but one of our basic tenets is to regulate our lives in a manner that allows us to make decisions that are free from any inordinate attachment to anything. Anything except the greater glory of God, of course."

Philip bent a glance on both his companions, and it was a wholly open one, completely vulnerable—he was trusting them with some deeply personal things, but it didn't seem to be unwarranted. There was a bond between them now almost as strong as the bond that an alien soul had forged between the *Parada* crew. Stella honestly felt choked with love for these two men, and their willingness to sacrifice for the greater good. It seemed only natural that they were both dressed in the garb of men of God—with all that this implied—even if she, Stella, had openly told Philip that she believed in no part of the creed which he so cherished and tried to live by.

"And look at me," Philip said, shrugging. "How attached am I now to things that are not directly of God? Here I am, doing what I am doing, freely and under no duress... and under Jesuit rules I am an abject failure. It is a question of loving God and loving Man and I am supposed to make a proper distinction between them—but sometimes..."

"Sometimes there's a light of God inside Man," Rob said. "And what you do, gives honor to both."

"See?" Philip said, moved despite himself but managing a grin that had enough self-deprecation in it to disarm the moment. "I knew I could trust you. You'll hold your own just fine in the company of thirty-odd men of God. They might learn something from you, if they listen, at that. But Stella—I reiterate—you are not to..."

Stella hit him with a pillow, with a very undignified squawk of exasperation. Philip fended it off, laughing, and allowed that moment of pure release to take them all, perhaps the last such moment they would be given before embarking on a risky venture which would have them all on their guard every waking moment, probably without much chance to even let off the edge of the tension by speaking freely to one another. But then he stepped away, serious again.

"We should go," he said. "It'll take a little time to get back to Rome, from where the flight is leaving. We don't want to be late for that. The next one might not be for a while, and not even I have the clout to arrange a special one just for ourselves. Are you ready?"

"We won't let you down," Rob said.

Stella smoothed down the bunched folds of the too-large skirt of her habit, spreading them to their best advantage. "My tongue," she said, "will be held. I won't blow this, Philip."

He smiled at her. "I have no doubts on that score, Sister," he said. "Let me make sure everything is square with the house, below, and then we can be on our way."

On the journey back to Rome, Philip drilled his two new 'initiates' with the basic responses they needed in order to communicate with the others on the flight they were joining. Rob sucked in his breath sharply as they finally approached the stratoplane, a sleek machine which made the round-bodied passenger jet planes of his own era look positively bulbous and clumsy by comparison, and Philip glanced at him.

"Don't lose it now," he said urgently. "What is it?"

"I keep on being surprised when I have it rubbed in my face that I live in the future now," Rob said. "Sorry. I'll be fine."

"Just tell them it's your first time on one of those," Philip said. "You wouldn't be the first to say that, and it isn't even a lie. And you can indulge your astonishment as much as you want. In fact, one way to keep you out of harm's way with the rest of the ecclesiasticals would be to develop a nephew with an interest in the technology of the craft, and you can probably get one of the attendants or even one of the pilots to tell you all about it."

"Can I come and listen?" Stella asked plaintively. "To keep *me* out of harm's way?"

"Sorry, Sister. That would probably lead to precisely what I want to avoid. Someone's going to pat you on the head with enough paternalistic dismissal that you're going to go all anti-nun on us and put them in their place..."

"If only I wasn't a pious holy woman, I'd stick a tongue out at you right now," Stella said.

Philip bent his head to hide a smile. "It's only a few hours," he said. "Keep it together."

The rest of the passengers were finding their seats, a low respectful murmur of background noise indicating polite apologies for being in the way or stepping on toes while trying to get settled. Stella found herself seated next to a tall hatchet-faced man who wore all the trappings of a Vatican Monsignor; he gave her a polite but perfunctory greeting, and Stella closed her eyes in relief. Such a one would not wish to indulge in small talk with a lowly nun, so she was safe from a potential situation developing. She saw Philip two seats away next to the female priest, who was already engaging him in earnest conversation while he tried to be polite and respectful and respond while at the same time keeping an eye on his two dangerous traveling companions, and Rob, sitting silently with his eyes on the hands folded in his lap, one row in front of her across the aisle. She could not see who his seatmate was. She closed her eyes and even though she had said on so many occasions that she did not believe in God she could not help formulating what was very nearly a prayer to *some* deity, whoever was listening, to get the three of them to where they were going in safety and with all speed. And then the gleaming machine was on its way.

The stratoplane rose up through the sky until it was on the edge of black space, and it was quite easy to make that final step and sever the final umbilical, seeing the blue glowing globe underneath as Rob must have seen it when he first left it behind to journey to the stars. Stella suddenly wanted nothing more than to find him, to be near him, to hold his hand if he needed that, because this would be a reminder of so much—even if Philip hadn't thought about invoking one or another of his fragmented personae, this event, this sight, might have been quite enough to trigger that on its own. But from what she could see, trying to steal glances in his direction every so often without being obvious about it, he was almost serene, quiet, sitting in his seat wrapped in solitude, speaking to absolutely nobody. They were served a meal, and Rob barely roused enough to accept his tray, but Stella could see that he hadn't touched the food. She wasn't feeling so hungry herself, stretched so tight and tense that she could almost hear herself vibrating.

Philip had said it would be about six hours—roughly the same time Stella and Rob had spent in the bus from Istanbul to Izmir—but it seemed endless to Stella, and she was about ready to burst into tears, for want of a better reaction, when they finally announced a final approach to Chicago. The stratoplane landed uneventfully, the clergy began to file out into the terminal building, and Philip waited until Stella's monsignor had got up and inched his way towards the exit before dropping back to where she was still sitting, awaiting further instructions.

"One more hurdle," Philip said. "Come on. Stick close."

"Is Rob all right?"

"He seems fine. I hope he can hold it together for just a little longer."

Rob was quiet when they collected him, too quiet; Stella's glances towards him began to be increasingly concerned. He allowed himself to be guided, directed, and otherwise manipulated without raising any demur, just murmuring responses to direct questions if asked. Philip finally managed to get through the red tape and shepherded the two of them unobtrusively through the terminal and towards the exit and into a self-drive taxi cab hovering at the edge of the curb on the ring road. Finally free from the possibility of incriminating lapses, Stella turned to Rob and picked up one of his hands in both of her own.

"Are you okay?" she asked urgently. "Rob...? Anybody?"

He sat unresponsive for a moment or two, and then shook himself, curling his fingers around hers. "Yes. Yes, I'm fine. It just... it reminded me..."

"I know," Stella said. "I know."

"I just thought... Jerry..." He shook his head sharply. "I can't think about that now."

"How about Lily Mae? Do you think you can still find her?"

Rob lifted his eyes to hers.

"You're asking a lot of that link that you believe Illogon seeded in us," Rob murmured. "It is true that it exists, but remember what we just did—what's left of the *Parada* crew is locked up back in the habitat, Lily Mae is God alone knows where somewhere on the open ocean, and here you and I are, on a different continent, in a land that's empty of all of them—it's going to be a hard enough job trying to reconnect with Lily Mae if and when she lands here. Tracking her down with pinpoint accuracy is going to be almost..."

"Maybe we need help," Stella said slowly.

"Help? Who would..."

Stella turned to Philip. "I have to ask you to pull one more string," she said. "If you're right and they think I'm the one who leaked the *Parada* story and they're watching for my name to pop up somewhere... the last thing I want to do is draw attention to the fact that I am trying to contact Joseph White Elk. I swore, after all, that I would have nothing more to do with the crew of the *Juno* after they escaped from the habitat, or seek any of them out, and—well—if I am not to technically break my word, will you find him for me? Tell him I need to speak to him. Tell him it's important. Tell him he has to do it without anyone knowing that he's agreed to do it. Set it up."

"Didn't they get released only on pain of taking a hypnotic block on the *Parada* matter?" Philip asked. "A memory block? An inability to speak of any of it? How is he going to take seriously anybody who..."

"I put it in," Stella said. "I also put in a release word. Tell him that, and he will remember. He will remember it all. Just tell him... *starfish*."

He came, of course, as Stella knew he would.

Philip had done his duty as messenger, and had pulled back, after that; he waited with Rob, until Stella called them in. But she met Joe White Elk alone, first.

"Thank you for coming," she said, reaching out a hand.

Joe took it, his grip firm and dry, his eyes never leaving her face.

"I did not think," he said, "that I would see you again."

"Circumstances...change," Stella said, dropping his hand, inviting him to sit—they had chosen a busy café for the meeting, right out in public, seeking safety in the crowds. That had been Stella's choice and she had held out for it even in the face of Philip's worried dissent, his urging that the encounter should take place somewhere far from prying eyes. She was counting on the relative anonymity of a high-volume coffee shop, with its constant stream of patrons, to keep at least the initial meeting from being conspicuous. So far it was working—nobody seemed to be giving the two of them a second look.

"You released it," Joe said. "All of it. I remember everything and I am no longer constrained if I choose to say... a certain name out loud."

"I need your help," Stella said. "Of the... six of whom you are thinking... one of them is dead."

Joe's eyes dropped for a moment, and then lifted again to her face, steady. "May I ask who?"

"The engineer," Stella said.

Joe nodded slowly. "I am sorry to hear it. My own engineer colleague would take it hard. When we first returned... I know he wanted to meet his counterpart. Very much."

"Of those that remain... three of them are still where you left them, and as things stand they may never be free of that place. But one of them... is out here with me, now. And I have to tell you—you will already have realized that, I could not even be seen to contact you directly, myself—we are very much fugitives ourselves, because we left without sanction, because the one who accompanied me is helping me... look for the last of their number. Who is lost, and out there by herself. Alone. Having done what you might consider unconscionable things to free herself."

"I have seen rumors about... the crew," Joe said carefully. "I have seen... certain headlines. I was wondering what happened. Does this...escape... this woman's or your own... happen to be the basis of all that? After all that they did, with us, with my crew, to keep it all quiet?"

Stella sighed, looking down at her hands wrapped around the coffee cup on the table before her. "It was not I who had anything to do with that, although it is easy and convenient for them to believe that," she said.

"I believed, even before I myself was silenced, that this story would eventually rattle loose, somehow," Joe said. "I confess that I am not altogether unhappy that it has. I just hope the leak doesn't have unforeseen consequences which could be... catastrophic. Who do you think broke the story?"

"I have my suspicions," Stella said. "The one who escaped—whom we seek—she may have used what she knew, information, as currency to purchase her passage back here. If that is true, it is even more important that we find her, and soon. There is a connection between these people—and oh, there is more here than I can tell you right now, but I will—but the connection... may not be strong enough. I remember, back when we first spoke, that you said to me that on your first encounter... you could hear children. On the other ship."

Joe nodded slowly. "Yes. I said this. It is true."

"You have a connection, too," Stella said. "We need to find Lily Mae Washington. We think she is on her way back to the place she once called home—the city of New York. I know that she has to be running on fumes, and it may be that the sight of the city—now—as it is—so very different from what her memories of it must be—it might be enough to push her right over the line. We need to find her—I need to be there to help her. I know that you need to know so much more—and I will give you whatever information I have—but right now—I need to ask for your help. Whatever your connection might be, added to Rob's, it might be what gives us that advantage we need."

"Rob—this is Rob Hillerman you speak of? The navigator?"

Stella nodded.

"Are their souls still... what did you call it... shattered into new fragments of people?"

"Yes," Stella said. "I believe it may be contained—to an extent—and it would be different for every single one of them—but I do think it is irreversible."

Joe reached across the table to touch her hand where it folded tightly around the curve of her cup. "What I can do, I will," he said quietly. "Of course I will. You said Rob Hillerman is with you? Is he... all right?"

"He is possibly the best adapted of them all. He is here—all of the personae who are him are here. But he can mostly handle them, now, and stay himself. He has a measure of control over it all."

"And the other one? The one you are trying to find?"

"Less so," Stella said, almost unwillingly, but there could be nothing less than truth here now. "I think she may be capable of it—but I also think she is more susceptible to triggers and if she is faced with one without warning then the appropriate entity will respond, displacing her basic identity. This could be dangerous. Extremely dangerous. To herself, and possibly to others, to people who might get in the way of what she needs, people who will not understand. And if *that* happens... that is a weapon that plays straight into the hands of the people who have already held them for so long. It will be the proof they have always wanted, if Lily Mae succumbs to something that is beyond her control and they can point to that and claim that they were right to lock these five remaining people away permanently."

"I do not think anything you are able to do at this point is going to change that conclusion," Joe said. "If you win this race—if you succeed in finding this young woman first—you may have a hope of finding her shelter, of controlling some of the narrative. But if it goes wrong, or if they find her first... If you can challenge their story at all, then, it will be that much harder to prove anything that you might consider to be true. Especially if the people who wished to keep the entire situation a secret would want known."

"So," Stella said. "You understand. It is utterly important that I find her—that we get to her first."

"The others—they do not know where she is going?"

"They may. They may not. Martin Peck is more than capable of coming to a similar conclusion as I did. And he has far more resources than I do. If he goes to his superiors with this and they consider this whole thing essential to keep from public knowledge—the World Government has the resources to cast a tight net. They could put a cordon around the city, until they can tighten their grip enough to get Lily Mae back."

"If they do so—and you are inside—will they not capture you too?"

"The life I used to have is over anyway," Stella said soberly. "Win or lose this, I seem to have cast my lot with the survivors."

"You will not be alone," Joe said. "Rob Hillerman... may I speak to him? We never got the chance to meet, back at the... facility. We found the six of them out there, we brought them back from the edge of an abyss, and then we were severed from them. It has been one of my most profound regrets that all we were able to exchange with those people were messages across the empty spaces between us. There are things I need to say to this man."

"He is waiting to speak to you too," Stella said. "We should leave as soon as we can—when can you be ready to join us? On the road to New York, Philip and I will make sure you and Rob have your chance to say all that needs to be said."

"I am ready now," Joe said. He indicated a small backpack that he had brought into the coffee shop, which rested against the back leg of his chair. "Everything I need is here."

"It takes about twelve hours to drive to New York. Philip has a car, and at least he and I can drive—I am not sure I'd trust Rob with it right now. We can do it driving right through, in shifts."

"Three drivers," Joe said. "I can pitch in."

Stella picked up her phone and thumbed a text message into it. "Philip is waiting with Rob," she said. "I'll bring them here. You and Rob—we can give you the time you need. You probably would prefer to make it less public, for this—but there will be plenty of time, on the road, for more conversation. I just want to give you a chance... to meet. Without anyone who doesn't share your connection muscling into the moment. When you're ready to go, Philip and I will be over on the other side of the place—just give us a signal, and we're going to be ready to leave as soon as you are."

"Thank you," Joe said.

Stella stood as she saw Philip and Rob slip into the coffee shop. Philip peeled off towards the counter and Rob made a slow and careful approach to the table where Stella had been sitting. Joe rose to his feet also as Rob came closer, his eyes steady on the other man.

"Joseph White Elk, of the *Juno*," Stella said, as Rob came to a halt a couple of steps away. "Robert Hillerman, of the *Parada*. You are two of the bravest men I have ever known. It is time you got to shake each other's hand."

There had been a clear option of a self-drive which Philip could have procured, a modern car with the option of simply setting a destination and then allowing the vehicle to take them there choosing the fastest and easiest route and operating without a human at the controls, but Stella had balked at that. She'd been taking pains to use and quickly discard CitiCars within Istanbul, during the first stage of the flight from the habitat, because they were so tied into the grid and could feed exact movements into whoever might be looking for the people in them, and it would be that much more difficult to do that in a car somewhere on the lonely stretches of road that lay between Chicago and New York City.

"I don't want to be any more of a bug under a microscope than I can help, right now," she'd said, even faced with the prospect of a twelve-hour drive with an awake and aware human driver at the wheel of the car at all times.

"But we wouldn't have to..." Philip objected, but Stella would have none of it.

"Old-school," she said. "We do this old school."

"Old school it is," Philip said, resignedly. "It might take a little longer."

"We have a little time," Stella said. "You hopped us over on a stratoplane; Lily Mae is still somewhere in the middle of the ocean. You have a bit of wiggle room there."

"I know somebody in Chicago," Joe said unexpectedly. "Well, close enough to it, anyway. One of my best friends from medical school and his wife lived near here; he died a few years ago but I am still in touch with Amelia, his widow, and I am certain she could spare a couch for us for a couple of days. About the vehicle... might I be able to help?"

"You three can go to ground there for now," Philip said. "I am staying in town, at the Bishop's residence. I have to show my face, after having crossed the pond in such a manner. There are people I have to speak to, up there. Go to your friend, and give me the address. Joe, at this point, it is entirely possible that it would be either you or I who would be the only people with the credentials to obtain any kind of legal vehicle at all—and it might well be that you could find us a jalopy somewhere that matches Stella's requirements—but let me try it first. I think the Church might prove an easier way to source something that might not be directly attributable to any one of us. If I get hold of a car, it might not be under my own name—and they might not know which vehicle taken by which agent and going in which direction might be the one they are looking for. It's a layer of protection, perhaps. Leave it to me—I will come and find you when I've got something in hand."

"The Bishop's residence?" Stella asked, a little alarmed. "Are you sure you're going to be safe...?"

"From what?" Philip asked, shrugging. "I have absolutely solid alibis for anything that anybody would want to accuse me of. And I came in that aircraft with fellow clergy, not any potential fugitives from any potential justice. So far as they know, Stella, you and Rob are still knocking about the Aegean somewhere trying to put together an exit. It hasn't been that long, not nearly long enough for anybody to start widening the search area all the way over here."

Joe's contact, the widow, had initially been astonished to hear from him but had, as he had predicted, been happy to offer her house as a bolt-hole for a couple of days. It was an ordinary small home in a leafy suburban street, indistinguishable from its neighbors, a perfect place to lie low; Amelia welcomed them to it, apologizing that the quarters would be tight—there was a spare bedroom which was offered to Stella, Rob bedded down on a futon in the study, and Joe took up residence on the sleeper sofa in the living room.

Amelia took an interest in her visitors, without being prying; when Stella announced that she desperately needed some basic necessities—because previous luggage had been minimal, or mislaid along their travels—Joe gave her his own credit chit to put it on, and

Amelia offered to take her shopping. It was pleasant—relaxing, even—
to be doing something as prosaic as this, buying a change of clothes
for herself and for Rob, tossing necessities like new toothbrushes and
a shaving kit into a shopping cart just like normal people did every
day in ordinary lives—even stopping for a cup of coffee and a break
along the way. Amelia did not ask any nosy questions, but it was
clear that Joe's entourage interested her; it was, obscurely, that very
reticence that made Stella trust her. She explained, in broad terms,
what they were about, without really revealing the *Parada* angle, but
it was impossible to even begin the story without implying that there
was a cohesive group which was somehow deeply connected, that both
Rob and Lily Mae were part of it, and that she, Stella, had held in
some way a position in which she was in some way responsible for
their wellbeing. If Amelia connected any of this with the fact—which
she could not help knowing—that Joe White Elk had been part of
the *Juno* crew, she did not fish for information. She did focus on the
people involved.

"Your Rob," she said. "He just has an air of... I don't know...
errantry."

Stella laughed. "How do you mean?"

"He has the protective instinct," Amelia said thoughtfully. "I've
seen him watching *you*. You said that he was part of this group that
you were concerned with helping—and that may have been true,
then—but the dynamic must have changed since you both left that
group. Because now I sense that somehow he is feeling responsible for
you rather than the other way around. There's a... tenderness."

"That isn't really..." Stella began, a little disconcerted, but then
stopped. There was a certain amount of truth to it. If she wanted to
pinpoint a moment where she was first aware of it, there was the time
that he had offered her a shoulder as a pillow on a Turkish bus. But
even before then—even when he was just one of the *Parada* six—it
had been Rob—it had been him or one of his fragments—who had
been the one to reach out to Stella. To trust her, first. To give her
information. To commit to *her*. Perhaps it was in the hope that she
would come through for the rest of them, for his family—but there

was more to it than that. There was a warmth. Of all the *Parada* six, he had been a special case. There was... what was it Amelia had called it... a tenderness.

In a way Stella desperately wished that Amelia had not drawn her attention to this, because even though she tried hard not to let this new awareness color her relationship to Rob she could not help it now. There were times it was easy to just put it aside and focus on other things but they had established a camaraderie. She had napped on that shoulder more than once, she liked the sense of comfort and safety that she got from having his arm around her. But in the hours after she returned from her outing with Amelia, she was hyper-aware, wary, and she knew that he noticed it and didn't know the reason why and would never ask.

Joe noticed, too. He had offered to take up a number of small chores in return for their board, and it was thus that he ended up wrestling Amelia's excited Golden Retriever, Ash, at the end of a tangling leash on his way out to take the dog for a walk.

"Do you want to come with me for company?" he asked Stella, and it was just a perfectly ordinary question, but there was an undercurrent in it that made Stella hesitate just as she was about to demur. The same instinct obviously touched Rob, who said something about the collection of books in the study being fascinating and asking permission to hole up in there and catch up on his reading. Amelia said something about dinner. Stella abruptly nodded, and followed Joe and the dog out of the front door.

"I do not mean to pry," Joe said, as they sauntered along the sidewalk underneath street-side trees already very nearly bare of leaves, "but... what is the end-game here? Did you come here with a plan?"

Stella gave him a somewhat bleak look. "I haven't had time to *plan* anything for a little while," she said. "Things just kept on running away with me. Right now, I have a plan to try and find Lily Mae before... before anyone else does so."

"And then?"

She shrugged helplessly. "I suppose I don't have much to offer in terms of protection or support," she said. "But I have to find a way to help."

"I said I could perhaps be of assistance in finding her," Joe said. "If there is a way I can offer anything—after—you need to tell me. How certain are you that she is going to be in the place where you are seeking her, though?"

"Not very," Stella said. "But it is the best extrapolation that I have. Home—the place she thinks of as home—is the only destination that I can imagine her consciously trying to get to. If she went anywhere else then it is truly random and I don't have a prayer of ever seeing her again." She managed a smile. "But don't ask me what I am thinking of doing after. I don't even know if there is going to be an 'after' to worry about, right now."

"It is not just Lily Mae. There is Rob, also," Joe said gravely. "I think he is a little bit lost—lost, and grieving."

"I know," Stella said. "I can feel it, and there isn't much I can do except hold out a slim hope. If that doesn't come true—or if things go really wrong—Joe, you have only the beginning of an understanding of what the *Parada* crew was, how much of a cohesive unit they were, never mind the extra bond between Rob and his brother. And yet he gave that up, to come out here with me, to help me find Lily Mae. You have only just met Rob; I may have spent more time with all of them, but even I don't have all the answers, and I have a feeling that Rob is still holding onto things he hasn't told me yet."

"I think he trusts you, but he does not quite believe you," Joe said. "He wants to. And a big part of him clings to that because if it does not prove to be true then he has lost more than he can bear to think about. It would mean that his own escape from that place was for no good reason, that he left his brother back there with no hope of a 'rescue' while he himself is 'free' out here. If this does not pan out... the guilt will come. And it will be ravenous."

"I know. But there is something important here, about Lily Mae, important enough for him—for all the *Parada* people—to have accepted this disintegration of that tight unit that they returned to Earth as. When I find out what that is, then I'll have a plan." She shrugged her shoulders. "When I know," she said, "I'll tell you. I promise."

It took Philip a couple of days to find a vehicle that matched his criteria, but in the end he managed to obtain an incongruously baby blue and somewhat aged minivan. It came with a GPS system, but one that could be turned off if desired, even though Philip roundly told Stella that he thought the action might be rather more palliative than actually efficacious.

He brought it round to Amelia's house mid-morning of the third day that Stella, Rob, and Joe had found a perch there.

"You're going cross country in that thing?" Amelia had asked, surveying the minivan with a raised eyebrow. "There has to be a better way...?"

Philip met Stella's eyes, and gave a huge resigned shrug.

"Old school," he said.

The four of them left Chicago towards the end of the day, looping out of the city with the sun setting at their backs, intending to use the hours of darkness for their journey—as they had left the sun setting when they departed, so the sun would greet them as they reached New York City at more or less the time that it would rise. They had no set plans about what would happen when they arrived there; Rob did raise the inadvisability of attempting to drive in the city itself, but given that human driver hands-on-controlled cars were illegal in most such places, Philip could quite sincerely reassure him that he had no intention of doing so. The idea was that they would leave their vehicle on the outskirts somewhere at a place where it was possible to pick up New York's version of the CitiCar to reach the places they might need to be. But all that was still up in the air, seeing as it all depended on how, where, and even whether they could actually find Lily Mae in the city—and they couldn't plan for that until they were close enough to find out if Rob, bolstered by Joe's own potential affinity to the *Parada* crew, was able to use the Illogon link to pinpoint Lily Mae's location with any degree of certainty.

Philip and Stella spelled one another at the wheel every few hours, spending their off hours grabbing a quick catnap on the folded-down rear seat of the minivan or helping Rob continue filling in Joe White

Elk on the reasons behind their race to New York.

They had not really talked of the Illogon before, especially not at Amelia's place where they could have been overheard, and it was only now that Joe learned some of the details of Lily Mae's escape. Joe didn't say much, listening and absorbing—he was so silent, in fact, that Stella interrupted the account at one point to ask if he had any questions and he lifted a hand to stop her.

"When I have put them into the proper words, I will ask them," he said. "But so far I have gained several answers to questions I already had."

It took just over twelve hours to reach the outskirts of New York City, and then another half a day to find a place to stay, and a manner in which they could find their way to the Bronx address where Lily Mae had lived before she left Earth for the stars. It was the apartment she had grown up in as a girl, which she had inherited on her parents' death and which she had always considered her home base.

"She's going home," Stella said, "and if she's going home she'll be looking for this place. It's the childhood home we all want to return to in this kind of crisis. And if I'm right and it's all tied up with the Illogon's desires, then that's going to be the place she instinctively seeks out—the place of origin. The first home. The beginning. She'll be here."

But although she exhorted both Rob and Joe to listen, to reach out, to keep looking for any sense of Lily Mae anywhere near, they seemed to have struck out completely. Days passed without so much as a sign, and the days lengthened into a week, and then longer.

"She couldn't be here yet," Stella said. "She might still be on her way."

"How long do you intend to give her?" Philip asked quietly.

"She'll be here," Stella said, stubbornly, absolutely certain of that fact for no reason that she could actually articulate. She annoyed even herself because as a scientist she should have been working with some kind of empirical evidence that she could have offered up as proof of her hypothesis—but she had nothing, nothing except that burning certainty, a knowledge, the provenance of which she had absolutely no idea of. All she knew was that she was willing to lay down her life in defense of that idea.

It began to seem hopeless, though, even for her, until the morning Rob rose abruptly from a chair, his shoulders stiff, his head turning, as though he was a hunting dog with a scent of quarry at last. Stella began to ask him if he was all right, but then read her answer from the too-bright glint in his eyes, from the expression on his face that was a mixture of disbelief, astonishment, and the dawning of a fragile joy too tenuous to be completely trusted but nonetheless desperately clutched at.

"I think..." he said, choosing his words very carefully, "I think... she is here."

Stella took control of the situation, and they all deferred to her—it was as though she was the searchlight, the guiding light, the seeker. It was Rob and Joe who were the only guides who could hope to take them directly to Lily Mae, but it was Stella who had been the compass pointing to the place where they were to look. All Rob could tell her at that moment—and Joe could only quietly add a word of agreement, that he too could sense something coming closer—was that the presence they had come here to seek was close. But it was Stella who chose, of all the possible places, the one spot where they would go to wait for Lily Mae to come.

Her old street. The street that she had lived on in the happiest days of her life. The place where a child would come, when it wanted to 'come home'.

The rise in sea levels had wreaked havoc with the shorelines of New York, and there were many places that had been abandoned, left to rot, too close to lapping waters that had never been there before, overrun by the wharf-side vermin seeking higher, safer ground. Lily Mae's old neighborhood was split between streets that looked as they had always had, as though nothing at all had changed, and streets which were empty, houses with broken windows staring empty-eyed into lots where other buildings had been permitted to disintegrate into collapsed piles. The building that housed Lily Mae's old apartment was only partially inhabited, and several more or less completely empty buildings marched further on down towards the old shoreline. Where those buildings ended, a number of more or less ruined ones covered the rest of the way, their foundations inundated by the water which lapped at the edges of some of the ruins.

What people there were on the streets above the waterline tried to ignore the four people who were obviously not part of the neighborhood; Stella, having led them here, took a step back and allowed Rob to take point. His eyes were darting around, from ruin to shadow to any scurrying human who might be the one he was seeking, but none of them were, not one of them was Lily Mae. He stumbled forward, one foot in front of the other, his eyes unfocused, almost blind, with Philip occasionally guiding him around obstacles in his path which he quite literally didn't even seem to know were there.

After almost an hour of this, with no success, Rob looked exhausted, defeated, lost. By this stage it was Joe who was beside him, one hand on his elbow to ostensibly guide him but sometimes literally supporting him. Stella was almost ready to call a halt, to say that they could try again later, when Rob suddenly stopped. His head went up. He shook Joe's hand off and turned unerringly, staring past a crumbling house a little way down the street. Everyone turned with him, four pairs of eyes scouring the area, which, for once, seemed empty of people.

It was Philip who reacted first.

"There," he said, pointing.

Sitting on the edge of a semi-ruined wall, with its gray-coated back to them and a hood of sorts drawn up over its head in a way that had disguised its silhouette, a hunched-over human figure resolved itself from the background. It appeared to be holding something in its right hand—a tire iron, a length of iron rebar, something long and metal and absolutely filthy—and it was hitting the wall upon which it sat with the length of the thing, in a gesture which spoke at once of a banked anger and a sense of bitter defeat. Stella peered at the figure, still far enough away not to have noticed them or responded to their presence, through narrowed eyes, frowning.

"Are you sure?" she said. "It looks like a child—"

"I hear a child," Joe said quietly. "I hear a child, crying. But what I hear... would be a much younger child than *that*."

"It's her," Rob said, and something in his voice made Stella turn quickly to look at him. His face was colorless, and his eyes were wide, focused on the grey figure.

She turned back to Lily Mae.

The object of their observation appeared to become abruptly aware of the four of them, its back stiffening as its head came up. And then, with the hand not holding the metal bar, she pushed the hood back, and turned her head to look straight at them.

There was a moment which Stella would later remember with crystal clarity, as though it had been caught in amber and preserved in every last detail—the quality of the light, the faint traces of blood on the pale palm and the inner wrist of the hand that had held the metal bar as the hand flexed and dropped the bar below the wall, the way the ill-fitting grey coat bunched up over Lily Mae's hips as she struggled gracelessly to get her feet under her and stand up. And then, finally, as she turned her body sideways towards them, the reason why everything was graceless and not fitting quite right—the curve of the pregnant belly that rounded into view.

The impossibly pregnant belly.

Stella dragged her eyes with what was almost slow motion back to Rob's face, in time to see him clench his jaw and close his eyes with a hopeless resignation.

"That's impossible," Stella said abruptly. "I saw her medical records, right up until the very end. Lily Mae Washington was not pregnant back at the habitat facility. And even if she had been—this—this... She's way *too* pregnant."

"Third trimester," Joe said, agreeing with her. "That is a pregnancy well advanced. In order to be this pregnant right now that woman would have had to be showing by the time you say she departed the place where your crew was held. That pregnancy would have had to have begun as far back as maybe April. She would have been pregnant on the *Parada*. She would have had to have come back to Earth pregnant. She would possibly have been showing when they took the crew off the ship."

"She wasn't," Rob said, very quietly. Everyone turned to him. "She could not have been. All of us were given... contraceptive treatments before we left on the *Parada*. They had no idea what was waiting out there, and we all got long-term contraceptive implants—there were drugs on board which could reverse that, but they were in the emergency kits, which could only be reached by breaking into a vault built into the wall of the ship. It was a life or death countermeasure. But it was obvious that they were sending a mixed crew, that the crew could not be expected to remain celibate forever, that physical relationships were not only expected but encouraged... and they happened. Han and Alaya were something of an exclusive item, but even they sometimes took other partners in the crew. I know Boz and Lily Mae were lovers for a brief while; I know Jerry was with her on a number of occasions; I was, once. But none of us could have got her pregnant—we were unable to, on a biological level. There were countermeasures, as I say, but I don't believe that they were administered even after we returned to Earth. They might have been, eventually, but I don't think that was anyone's first priority. No, none of us. And she hasn't been with any man who was not one of us, in the time frame that this pregnancy suggests."

"She may have been on the ship she took from Europe," Philip said, with careful choice of wording. "On the way here."

"That is true," Joe said, "but it does not change anything. Even if she had sex on board the ship that brought her here, any pregnancy resulting from that particular encounter would have been... less than a couple of weeks old. Not that. Not as she is presenting now."

"That," Rob said, and again, his voice was very low, "that is why she had to go. Why she had to get out of that place where they held us."

Stella rounded on him. "You *knew*?"

He hesitated, clearly casting about for a way to communicate things, and could not hold Stella's outraged gaze for long.

"Do you remember what I told you about Illogon, back in Istanbul?" he asked, speaking directly to Stella, ignoring the others as though they weren't even present. It was to Stella that he needed to make this case, now. He sounded as though he was actually asking for forgiveness, for sins of omission, for things he could have said to her, should have said; for being obliged to say them now.

"You said a lot of stuff," Stella snapped, not giving him the soft landing he had been hoping for.

"I couldn't tell you," Rob said, "I simply wasn't sure. None of us were. This may... or may not have actually happened, at least not in the way it appears to be happening right now. That... is a lot faster and more advanced than any of us realized. Including, particularly and specifically, Lily Mae. She must be bewildered. Terrified. But this— exactly this—it became an option the moment the Illogon crossed from Boz into Lily Mae, into Lily Mae's body, a body capable of doing this—of creating..." Rob pressed his lips together, an expression of pure frustration. "A shell," he said at last, helplessly. "Its own shell, a human body it could imprint without damaging or erasing any existing sentience, without effectively destroying any thinking feeling being with whom it is forced through circumstance to share a crowded existence..."

He paused as though trying to work it all out, then went on.

"Look what happened when it tried to deal with us. All of us, all of us except Boz. And that worked, for as long as it worked—and then—I can't be sure even now, because this was so deeply layered inside Boz himself and much of it remains buried within the Illogon mind. I think they might have tried a transfer, where Boz consented to... well... to die... to disappear... to offer up his body as the shell, in a sort of a legacy to the Illogon. But whatever went down there, it didn't work. Boz paid for it with his life. The Illogon fled the corpse into the closest living thing that it trusted, which was Lily Mae."

"Are you saying this creature is a parasite, now?" Stella asked. "It can only exist in a living entity? Doing what—feeding off that entity somehow? But that can't be true. The ship that held it in space wasn't a 'living entity', was it?"

"No, but while it was in the ship it was connected to such an entity," Philip said slowly. "With its own original body. Somehow. A link through the ship it was on. But it lost that when the ship was destroyed—and it was on its own—and was *that* when a living link became important?"

"I don't know," Rob said. "I really don't know."

"So why is Lily Mae important, in this context?" Stella asked. "Because... she is capable of bearing a child, because she has the gender and genetic set-up to produce... what... a special shell, just for the Illogon? Is *that* what this is all about? But you said it was in all of you. At some point. And then it settled into Boz. But it was within the women, too—Alaya and Lily Mae, both—we know, because they're both fragmented, because the symptoms of the alien's brief sojourn in their minds are present, and on the record. So if this was an option— why did it bounce out of the women at all? Why not find the thing it needed, and take it, back at the first encounter? Why go through all of you—one and then the next and then the next—and then settle for a *man* in the end, incapable of providing such a body on demand?"

"Stella," Philip said, "back when it first, as you so beautifully put it, 'bounced' out of the women... it was hardly sane itself—think about the circumstances..."

"Yes," Rob said. "It was frantic, back then. If I could describe a purely psychic presence in terms of a physical effect, you might describe that first encounter as a panicked cat loose inside a car that had just had a major crash and was falling ass over teakettle straight down a cliff, and the cat was being thrown around the passenger cabin like a rubber ball. The Illogon was using 'claws' to hang onto anything it could to gain a purchase, and the claws were what ripped us apart inside. It didn't set out to do damage, it was done in a moment of total terror, a severance of contact with its primary host mind, it was adrift, and alone and if you can think of it in terms of 'thinking' anything it was in no shape to think at all. It was looking for purchase, for a place to stand. It wasn't thinking in terms of making babies, I told you before that its racial memory of having 'known' about our species before... didn't even kick in until later."

"That still makes me... *when* did you say they did that?" Philip said, sounding uneasy without being able to put a finger as to exactly why.

Rob shrugged helplessly. "It would be really hard to pinpoint exactly, in our years," he said. "I got it from a creature whose calendars don't necessarily match up to ours. But at best guess—anything between two and three thousand years ago. It's been a while."

"And what did they learn, when they were here?"

"Whatever it was, it was incomplete—I told you, the exploration visit was terminated abruptly and without clear cause, fate of the rider who was here back then unknown to its people. They just 'remember' us as being part of their records. They have no way of knowing what happened after their own communications were severed. So far as I know, that was the only time they had been here—they didn't send a rescue mission, or one to continue observation, or anything like that. It was simply one of their probes, sent out to distant worlds. It crashed and burned, or the equivalent, and they abandoned further attempts at surveillance or contact. What they must have found here at the time—it might have just been too early, for us, to deal with, to handle, to understand—for all anyone knows they might have planned to come back, eventually. But that was strategic planning, and not part of our own entity's brief. The Illogon told us as much as it knew, later, when it had calmed from a state of fear and panic and come to terms with the circumstances of its exile, when it had accepted a place of safety deep inside Boz."

"But how did it know..." Stella began, obstinate, inexorable.

"Could it tell us more?" Philip asked. "Now?"

"How do you mean?" Rob said, blinking at him in momentary confusion.

"He means, is it at all possible to... communicate with this thing? I mean, for *us* to do so?" Stella interpreted, with a quick glance at Philip for confirmation. "Its communication with you—with the *Parada* crew—it would have been on an inside channel, as it were. There was no need for it to communicate with outsiders, it had you six. But now—with this—would it be able to communicate with someone like Philip, or me...?"

"It is an alien being," Joe said. "It would be hard to understand any of this within our own parameters. Its wants or requirements or needs or indeed ideas may not be anything that we can wrap our heads around."

"Well, we have to do *something*," Philip said. "We came all this way to find her. Lily Mae. There she is. We're standing here flapping our jaws at each other—and look at her. She's *waiting*."

"Yes," Stella said. "Let's go talk to her. To *them*. Come on, then."

She turned and led the way down to the edge of the tumbled wall, where Lily Mae had been sitting and where she now waited for them with one hand laid across her swollen belly in the age-old gesture of a pregnant woman protecting her child. Rob and Philip followed close behind, with Joe bringing up a slow and cautious rear.

A few steps from Lily Mae, Stella slowed, glancing sideways at Rob and waving him forward, past her. He murmured his thanks and sidestepped her, taking the lead, the first to reach Lily Mae. Stella put out a hand in a sharp gesture telling the other two to wait, watching Rob and Lily Mae stand for a long moment and stare into one another's faces, and then Rob reached out for her, carefully, and her own arms went around him tightly. The others could see her fingers bend at the joints from the force with which she held him. After clinging together for the space of a couple of breaths, they disengaged, and exchanged a few words of whispered conversation. And then Rob guided Lily Mae back to a different part of the wrecked wall, a flat portion which she could subside onto and sit with her sneakered feet flat on the ground before her.

"All right," Rob said, one hand protectively on Lily Mae's shoulder. "I don't know how this is going to work. But you want to talk to the Illogon, and she's willing to try."

"Try to do what? Be an interpreter?" Stella asked carefully. "Or is the Illogon able to come through, like... the rest of the personas do...?"

She came up to Lily Mae, crouching at her knee, reaching out to lay gentle fingers on the hands folded together in Lily Mae's lap. "Are you all right? Are you really all right? God... *God*... the last time I saw you, you were *dead*..." Her eyes filled with tears, in pure visceral reaction to the encounter.

"I want... I can't believe the risks you took—what you did—how you managed to—and then, on top of it, managing to make it all the way over here—I knew you were going to try, I knew it, but I wasn't completely sure that you could make it... I'm so glad to see you."

"It's good to see you too," Lily Mae said. Her eyes slid from Stella to Philip, back to Stella, up to Rob's face. "All of you."

"This is Joe," Stella said, indicating the quiet man waiting at the back of this emotional reunion. "Joseph White Elk. Of the *Juno*. He is one of the crew who brought you home."

"Dr. Washington," Joe said formally, inclining his head. "It is good to meet you, in person, at last."

"Lily Mae," Stella began, fumbling for words, "I want to talk to you...we all want to hear about everything that's happened to you since you left. But right now we really need to... is there any way to communicate with the...entity you carry within you...?"

She saw it happen, her eyes locked on Lily Mae's when the change came over them—she saw those dark eyes go full obsidian, flat, absolutely opaque.

"It is important to speak to me?" Lily Mae said, and her voice had dropped, into a gravelly alto, what some might have described as a 'whiskey voice' scoured by decades of heavy drinking. "I am here."

13.

Stella shot a quick glance to Rob, trying to find inspiration for the appropriate response, but she could find nothing helpful in his expression. *Was this Lily Mae talking through another personality? One that had manifested since the last time that she, Stella, had spoken with her? Or was it...?*

She took a deep breath. "Have we met?" she asked, very carefully.

"I know you," the gravelly voice said. "When I am born, my name will be Jerusha. You may call me that."

"Are you the Illogon?"

"Yes."

"You're not part of Lily Mae's fragments any more, are you. You're..."

"I am in the fetus that she is carrying. I am the child. I am Jerusha."

"You're too... too advanced to be..."

"I will be born human flesh and human bones, but the spirit inside me, the spirit that formed me, the spirit that makes me grow, I am Illogon. I made me, from the parts of this... human body... that exist for the purpose of progeniture."

"She's saying... there *was* no actual father?" Philip said slowly.

"Fascinating," Joe White Elk said, his scientific and medical instincts fully engaged. "If we are speaking to the entity within the fetus... accepted science has long had it that the fetus is *asleep* inside the womb. That is to say, that which we call consciousness does not even manifest until the sixth or even seventh month of pregnancy—before that the fetus is literally unconscious. After a certain synaptic bridge is crossed, the fetus... is conscious, but asleep. There are studies that say that it is asleep in what the adult human body knows as REM sleep, the kind during which we dream. Under the circumstances— because one cannot conceive of anything that an ordinary human fetus with no experience to put into a visual format could dream *about*— one does have to wonder what such a sleep might mean, inside that unformed mind. And right now I have to start wondering whether this particular fetus... is dreaming *us*..."

"I am not dreaming. I am awake," Jerusha said, turning unfathomable dark eyes on Joe.

"It explains the accelerated pregnancy," Joe said. "This fetus needed to develop fast to reach this level of consciousness. This woman could actually give birth to this child at any time. There is no knowing what actual physical stage this gestation is at. I posited six months, at least—I could move that forward. Maybe eight months. Maybe beyond. Maybe it is only a matter of days. Or even hours."

"How... did this happen?" Stella said, addressing the question to nobody in particular, but Jerusha answered, as though it had been aimed at her.

"I was lost," she said, and the oddly inflectionless voice that had been hers before dipped into an emotion—a difficult one to pinpoint, but there was sorrow there, and suffering, and fear. "I was the explorer. I was in the ship. I was in the stars. And then there was an ending—a break—a rupture—I was severed—there was no home, no sanctuary— but there was... there was... there were places to seek safety... but I did not understand, not then... I caused suffering. I caused harm. I cannot undo this. I am sorry."

"You sought shelter?"

"I was alone. I was alone." Jerusha's voice lowered again, almost into a whisper. "I was afraid. I did not recognize the entities who were there with me. I did not remember what I knew, that my kind had seen their kind before, not until it was too late."

"Did you communicate with us... before? That first time? Ever?" Stella said. "Were we aware of you? Afraid of you?"

"I am Illogon. We do not kill. We explore, we search, we learn. We do no harm. But I was alone. And then I was not."

Lily Mae turned the body's head, in a motion that was almost robotic, mechanical, as though the mind in control of the body did not quite know how it functioned. She looked up at Rob.

"This one was there. This one understands," Jerusha said. "I am sorry."

"Rob," Philip said, "can you shine a light here? I know what I think she is saying. But I don't understand..."

"Just as she said," Stella blurted out before Rob could answer. "I don't think any of this was deliberate. None of this was meant to happen. Everyone—the *Parada* and its crew, this creature—everyone was just in the wrong place in the wrong moment of time. The instant of first contact—the first time they 'met' us—Rob told me, before—that was something that just went bad, too. We don't seem to be very lucky with our encounters with the Illogon. That time, they came to us, and it could have ended a lot better than it did—but something went wrong, that explorer's ship blew up right up there in orbit around us, it must have been quite a sight, actually, I'm surprised that we never made a record of..."

"Wait," Philip said, and something in his voice made Stella look at him sharply. He sounded oddly strangled, as though he was trying to force words out of his throat with main force. "Wait. *When* did you say they were here before...? When that first—what was it—ship—when that blew up?"

"I said I couldn't be certain," Rob said. "Their years and ours aren't the same. I can't be exact. I believe it is anywhere between two and three thousand years ago, by our count."

"A babe without a father," Philip gasped. "A light in the sky. A star that led travelers to a child in a manger in Bethlehem..." His eyes were wide and black with pupils dilated with shock. "An angel who appeared to shepherds in the fields—and remember, remember, the way they drew the creature in those drawings the children did—the winged shape—and then the story, the story that it was the son of God."

A laugh that he could not stop from escaping, a laugh that had an edge of madness to it, broke on his words. "Can't you *see*? Look—look at us—" His arms rose, a gesture encompassing them all. "A woman, carrying a child who is incandescent, too wise too early, too... too *holy*... a child formed of her own body and of no human father. A woman whose very name means Star—and you led us here, Stella, you led us here like a shining light. And whom did you lead? Three men— three men who come to witness the birth..."

"Are you saying that the first lost alien was the being we all came to know as Jesus?" Joe said. "That Jesus Christ was... first alien contact?"

Philip rose and whirled away with a violence that startled Stella. "No!" he said, vehemently. "No, that can't be true. If that is true than *everything* has been a lie. My whole life is a lie. God had no son. There was no redemption of sins. Nothing is true—nothing—and we have never been the children of God, made in His image, created by his hand, with souls which can earn the right to enter Paradise and be in the light of that God. And I have... I have perpetuated that lie, passing it on, making others believe it and believe in it, giving others hope for salvation, if only they believed. If only they believed!"

"Jerusha," Joe said carefully, as though uncertain that the entity would even respond to him directly, "is this possible? Could this be what has happened?"

"I know the story," Jerusha said. "When I was part of them. The ones in the ship. The story was there. It was inside their minds. We have no way of knowing. The link was lost. That Illogon was lost."

"But you—here you are, finding shelter, a hope of existence, of survival, inside a human child. How did you arrive at this plan? Did you arrive at this idea... from the other story that you learned? Did you find that this was possible, from that?"

"I know the story. When there was an opportunity... it is possible I remembered."

Philip gasped, breath exploding from him as though someone had kicked him in the stomach.

"Philip," Stella said, seriously concerned at his reaction, getting to her feet and reaching out for him. "It was a story—a story of God—it was a path, not the ultimate truth—faith can—"

"You can't understand," Philip said. "You can't. You yourself said you didn't believe. For you, this is a step across a crack, maybe. For me... there is a chasm at my feet, Stella. And the place where I thought God was... is empty. It is who I am—who I thought I was. You can scoff at the idea, but I chose this place in the world because—because there was a call—because there was a true vocation. But what was it a call to? A call from? I listened, and I accepted, and I believed. and now I don't even know how to describe my own form in the void. If God made us in his image—and God did not send Jesus to help save our souls, in that image made—then what is left for me to put my faith in? That some part of me belongs to a creature that may or may not have been mistaken for an angel, once, by some ill-educated sheep-herder in Judea, and because of that... because of that..."

Stella reached out for him. "Philip..."

He turned to look at her, but his eyes were unfocused and blind, not seeing her at all. "Who am I?" he asked huskily. "If I am not a man of God, if I am not a priest from the ranks of the Society of Jesus..." He laughed again, the laugh as sharp as a blade. "The Society of Jesus! The very name of my order is a mockery! I thought I was safe, and saved for God, I thought I knew God, that if I knew nothing else in this world I would always know that God loved me. And now? Now there is no God. Just a lost alien being looking for its own salvation, not our Creator bringing ours. I feel as though I thought I was standing on a bridge across a void, and now the bridge is breaking, God is lost..."

"Seriously?" Stella said, suddenly furious. She was empathetic and understanding and she understood viscerally that Philip had just had a huge part of his self—of his *soul*—ripped from him... but there was something in his reaction that was on the edge of self-indulgence, almost of self-pity, and it suddenly made her angry.

"In the last couple of centuries... in the middle of the great extinctions, when we lost the last lion and the last polar bear that your God gave us to live in His wild places... when the Doomsday Vault failed, and the hoarded seeds were mostly lost, and the wheat harvest failed, and we had to go back to the humblest basest grains from which to make flour and when all the millions starved... when the bees crashed, and crops failed for lack of pollination... when the oceans began to die and the reefs bleached and we watched the lonely whales who were the last of their kind wandering the empty seas calling for mates who never came... when the winters went away and parts of the planet became an anvil upon which human bodies fried, when part of this God-given world became literally unlivable for His children... after the water wars and the food wars ... after all of that, you believe in a just and merciful God... but this—it's only one way of interpreting what we know about the situation, *your* way—*this* is what destroys your faith?"

She saw him flinch at that, but she found herself unrelenting in her sudden fury.

"There have been countless theories that historically the Jesus who was called the Christ might never have existed at all," she said, "or that he was just a perfectly ordinary creature whose higher identity was created for him in the aftermath of his life by 'prophets' like Paul or the Gospel writers. None of that ever mattered. But now—"

"Now," Philip said, his sense of loss transmuting into a fury of his own, "now I am looking at evidence. At evidence that might be shown as... yes, you are right. There have always been stories, and scoffs, and unbelief—but it didn't matter, Stella, because there was an underlying truth, an underlying mystery, something that connected with the idea of God and what He was and what He represented—but now, in the light of what I know, in the light of the facts... I feel as though I threw my support in for all of this, I did all that I did because of and in the name of God in whom I believed, because I thought that God could not be on the side of people who would lock away the *Parada* crew for no other sin than they had been sent out to the stars and were broken by them, because I did it in the name of Christ, and the greater glory of God as I saw it. And in the end... all I accomplished... seems to be that I killed the idea of that God."

"Did you ever consider that this might be your Second Coming?" Stella snapped.

Philip stared at her, his eyes wide with shock. "That's... heretical..." he said.

"But the facts would fit," Stella said, inexorably. "If the first encounter produced Christ... and there has *always* been the inherent promise of the Second Coming, Christ's return... why not this? Why not here? Why not now? I grant you, this time the mother is no graceful pale Madonna and we do lack a Joseph figure—but we have the rest. You said it yourself."

She gestured as she spoke, at herself, at the men surrounding her. "Your Star. Your Three Wise Men. Your Immaculate Conception, a child wide awake in the womb, with who knows what kind of potential when she is actually truly born into this world. Born as a human, like you, like your God said—born in his image. There could be a story of Jerusha, just like there was a story of Jesus."

"You can't understand," Philip said, looking shell shocked. "We are then... none of us saved. There is no Christian heaven. All the suffering and dying done in the name of the Christian faith—is that now—what—simply superseded? Are the saints still the saints? Is the Church still the Church? What is our catechism? Do we declare ourselves obsolete?"

He was looking directly at Lily Mae as he spoke, at the alien who lurked in her gaze, but Jerusha made no response to his impassioned question.

"Stella," Joe said, quietly but insistently, seizing the opportunity of this uncomfortable silence to reach out to the only one of them who had seemed to be focused on leading this particular expedition, "I know I asked you once if you had a plan for the aftermath of finding the woman you were searching for... and that you said you would know it when it came to you... but I think it is time you started thinking about it. We cannot stay here. She is too close to her time, sooner or later someone else will come to the same conclusion you did and come looking for her in this place and you could lose both the woman and the child she carries... whatever its eventual significance. And this conversation... is starting to attract attention." He gestured at the street on the far side of the rubble where the five of them stood, where a handful of curious residents had started to gather and to pay far more attention to the group than might have been safe. "We should go, at the very least back to the cabin we've been staying at, and away from there as soon as we can."

"I agree," Stella said. "Philip..."

"No," he said. "You go. You all go. I will... I will meet you there. I need... I need time."

"Philip—you can't just go off and—"

She flinched at what was in the gaze he bent on her. Anger, and disappointment, and fear, and pure desperation. "*Leave it*," he said, through gritted teeth. "I know where you are going to be. I'll find you. Leave me alone."

He turned and strode away, his steps a little unsteady, his shoulders hunched high by his ears and his head bowed, his eyes on nothing but the ground at his feet. It was as though his sudden and devastating loss of a higher plane had completely taken away his ability to look up—as though he had thrown himself from heaven, and had fallen hard, without wings, without faith to break the fall.

Stella's immediate instinct was to run after him, to say that she was sorry, that she understood, that she was grateful for everything that his faith had made him—but Rob reached out and gripped her by the elbow.

"He would not thank you." Rob said, "and Joe is right. We need to get Lily Mae out of here."

"Fine," Stella said, desperately, "fine. Come on, let's go. We'll wait for Philip at the cabin—we can load up the van to go, and as soon as he comes back..." She stopped, fighting tears. *When* he comes back. *If* he comes back. She was suddenly not sure of anything at all.

Rob helped Lily Mae to her feet, and Joe stepped up to assist. Stella, still staring at Philip's retreating back, saw with a sudden clarity that what she was feeling was in a way a weak echo of Philip's own loss. He had leaned on a pillar he had always believed had been there for him, and found that it gave beneath his hand, that it had never been more than smoke; the loss of foundation, the loss of support, was what he found so devastating. She, Stella, had never leaned on that pillar—but she had been leaning, heavily, on Philip. Philip, who had always been there for her, who had been an ally and a friend in desperate hours when she needed one. And now there was nothing where he had been except a narrow back, clad in a black cassock, only a man walking away from her, a man to whom she had said, perhaps, far too much for him to forgive.

As she looked back at Lily Mae, the pregnant woman's eyes flickered and faded, leaving, for a moment, a completely open and vulnerable person, only Lily Mae Washington, nothing more, nothing less. And then things *changed* again, in the way that Stella had learned to recognize back in the habitat, and a particular fragment, a particular soul, stepped forward to take charge of the situation.

"Oh boy," she said, her mouth twisted into a grimace, her face pure Diana, "you sure fucked up this city."

Lily Mae seemed untethered as they gathered around her and spirited her away from what was to have been a sanctuary of her memories of shelter and personal security, a childhood memory that was long vanished from the place where she sought it. She neither resisted nor fully acquiesced, and appeared to communicate with Rob, whom she accepted as the most trusted of her new companions, in a manner which would have in other circumstances riveted Stella's professional attention—they seemed to be in the process of evolving a fluid super-personality, one that could change without warning, with either one of them responding to whatever stimulus the other provided, with the Illogon persona, the one whom they had all heard name itself Jerusha, apparently participating in the meld as an independent entity.

When the four of them had arrived back at their lodgings—a somewhat down-at-heel hostelry consisting of a shabby central three-story motel building which had seen better days and several free-standing studio-type or two-roomed cabins on the far end of the narrow parking lot, one of which the four of them had commandeered when they had arrived. Stella had said that they should leave as soon as Philip returned; nobody had questioned that, or asked if she was sure that Philip *would* come back. She simply would not countenance the alternative, and that was written in every set line on her face. But then Joe, who had not stopped looking uneasy since they first encountered Lily Mae and her condition, had whisked Lily Mae away into the inner room to find out what he could about the situation, with the distinct implication that it would be his judgment on that matter that would determine the next stage of their journey. Lily Mae raised no objections to this examination, such as Joe could perform with little in terms of supplies or equipment; Rob remained with her, hovering nearby, never far from her side.

Stella, who could have simply withdrawn to the other room of the cabin while she waited for Joe to conclude his examination, found herself restless and almost claustrophobic within those four walls. If the small room had given her the space to do so, she would have paced restlessly—but between the two beds pushed into corners, and a small couch that took up most of the rest of the place with its back to the kitchenette beyond, there was barely enough clearance to sidle by with purpose, never mind prowl the place. Twice she jumped and turned to the door because she thought she heard someone approach it, or even knock lightly; twice she held her breath in vain as the door did not open and reveal Philip standing on the threshold.

Lily Mae was a problem, Rob was focused closely on Lily Mae, Joe was trying to figure out Lily Mae's status, and Philip was... gone.

Stella had never felt more alone.

She stepped outside the cabin and took the few steps down a short path that took her down to the parking lot where the mini-van that Philip had found for them was parked. A small wooden bench stood next to the path to the cabin's front door, and Stella subsided onto this, tense and unhappy, as the daylight began to wane and the lights began to wink on around her—no other cottages showed habitation, but the motel building became illuminated with outside lights, passageway lights, and the occasional sliver of escaping lamplight from a handful of occupied rooms. She was coatless, her arms wrapping around herself and clutching at her elbows, shivering slightly in the deepening October evening. The day had been cloudy, but dry; now she could smell rain on the way. She wondered, irrationally, if Philip would be caught in the downpour when he returned to the cabin. *When he returned to the cabin...*

She was staring into the shadows of the autumn twilight, completely focused on trying to rearrange them into a familiar figure in a black cassock coming towards her across the parking lot, and she literally flinched, startled, as she felt a jacket fall around her shoulders and looked up to see Joe standing beside the bench on which she was sitting. The jacket was his own, good leather, and she began to warm immediately, never having realized how cold she had been.

He gazed in the same direction as she had been looking for a moment, and then sighed and looked down at her.

"How long do we wait?" he asked quietly.

"As long as it takes," Stella said, and then bit down on the words, because they sounded almost petulant. She closed her eyes, drew a deep breath, and then opened them again. "None of this could have happened without him," she said. "None of it. If I am honest about it, he helped give me the strength I needed, all the way back to the beginning of it all, back when we first met. He always had my back. No matter what. I need... to give him... I need to have *his*, now. I just can't think about pulling out and leaving him here. Alone."

"It may be what he wants," Joe said.

"Well, we don't always get what we want," Stella retorted. And then sighed again. "I'm sorry. I sound like a virago. I don't pretend to understand what he is feeling, but clearly it cuts deep—and it may well be that someone like me cannot possibly help with it. But I can't just cut and run, Joe."

"You've lost Rob tonight, too," Joe said, "to Lily Mae, in there, and that is understandable. She is nothing less than the reason he is here, and he is a spar she is clinging to right now—they *are* connected, as you yourself knew from the beginning. But he is here for you, too, and that will penetrate their cocoon soon, and you will have him back. And I do realize that I have come into this late—but you have me to lean on, too, and you should. And in the light of that..." He frowned slightly, his gaze going unfocused, turning inward as he went over the result of his examination of Lily Mae in his mind.

"A doctor I may be but it has been a long time since I have practiced obstetrics. And even if I had been a specialist in the discipline—well, I can give you the long version if you like but the shorter version is this. I do not think this is in any way a normal pregnancy, and what that means is that I have no idea what exactly is going on inside Lily Mae right now. The entity—Jerusha—spoke of its kind in terms of 'we do not kill, we do not harm'—but it may not have a very clear idea of human gestation and what it means, and even if it did not mean to harm, it might be doing more harm than I know how to deal with. The pregnancy is advanced—so advanced that I would not like to make a bet on just how long Lily Mae has got. It may be, whether or not, or *if*, Philip returns, that Lily Mae should not be moved at all, anywhere, until she has had that child—which can literally happen at any moment, given the state she is in. But I have no way of knowing what that birth might entail, and I have to say that relying only on what we have—on me, and on you—I am concerned about the prospects of her surviving it."

"Should we try—should we take her to a hospital?" Stella gasped.

"I think it may be too late for that," Joe said gravely, "even if we could put together a coherent story which would explain anomalies which I am sure that medical personnel in that hospital would find with the pregnancy. And if we could not do so then you are exposing someone you have gone out of your way to conceal and protect to the prospect of mandatory reporting. They may not be looking for Lily Mae as she now is, Stella—if they are searching for her, they might not be paying attention to women this heavily pregnant, knowing that realistically Lily Mae could not be. But if she were exposed to closer scrutiny..." He made a small helpless gesture with his hands.

"Miracles are Philip's department," Stella said, marrying her twin concerns, "and I have never really believed in them... but now would be a good time for one. And I wish he was here to ask for it."

"I think miracles are part of the problem he is wrestling with tonight, already," Joe said. "Our problem remains a more earthly one. We have a pregnant woman who needs—or will need, very shortly— attention of the kind that you and I can only partly provide. And anyone who would be useful in providing the kind of assistance we need is also not to be trusted with the truth."

Stella laughed, the sound brittle in the shadowed parking lot. "We have the miracle of new life without the miracle of helping us usher it in with any degree of safety for mother or child," she said. "That *sounds* like God. He works in mysterious ways, as Philip himself would no doubt tell you."

Neither of them had heard footsteps, or anyone approaching, but a sudden diffident throat clearing from the back of the mini-van made them both snap to attention. A short, unprepossessing woman of indeterminate age, with an unflattering and old-fashioned haircut around a plain round face the focus of which was a pair of dark-rimmed spectacles, stepped forward with every appearance of reluctance.

"I'm so sorry," she said, "I didn't mean to eavesdrop—I was just in the next cottage, making sure it's ready, we have someone coming in tomorrow—I wasn't lurking out there to listen in, really—but I gather one of your party is expecting...? If it's going to help any, my niece— Nellie—is a midwife—if you wish, perhaps I can ask her to drop by tomorrow morning and have a quick look at your friend. You sound worried—perhaps she can help?"

Stella and Joe exchanged a glance, and he nodded, imperceptibly. Stella got to her feet and reached out a hand. "We would be grateful," she murmured.

The woman took the proffered hand, and shook it. "I'll call her right now," she said. "My name is Joanna Taylor, it was my husband who checked you in when you first arrived. You—uh—your pregnant friend—she wasn't with you...?"

"We came to the city to find her," Stella said, truthfully enough.

"I see," Joanna said. "Well, she is fortunate that you did. It sounds like you were just in time, too. I'll call Nellie at once, and hopefully she will be able to swing by and at least give you her advice. She's been doing this for a good few years, she's got the experience. It'll all be fine."

"Thank you," Stella said.

Joanna dropped her hand, murmured an apology again for "eavesdropping", and sidled away towards the main motel building.

"Well," Stella said, "there you are. It isn't the hospital, but..."

"She still may have mandatory reporting duties," Joe said, "and the problem of explaining that pregnancy remains—but I have to say that I will appreciate hearing what someone with a greater degree of experience than I do has to say on the matter. Although I do have to wonder just how much she overheard, and what she made of any of that. For now, though, you'd better come inside. I have the kettle on for tea. Stella, you cannot make him come back if you stand out here all night waiting for him."

Stella laughed hollowly, rising from the bench. "I might have wished him to be here. You spoke of wanting a miracle, and one got handed to you—a midwife, to look at Lily Mae and see to her needs. And Philip thinks this whole thing is a repudiation of his God. He would be the first to say that your speaking your heartfelt wish out loud, out where God might hear it, would constitute a prayer—where was he when he needed to see that prayers were still being answered?"

She searched Joe's eyes with her own, a little desperately. "I don't understand," she said. "I don't. It was he who connected the dots in the way that he did. It isn't as though he received an edict that he must stop believing in everything that mattered to him—he seemed to leap to that conclusion. And now he feels—what—lost, and alone, and abandoned—and in the context of what he said the thing that he has had ripped from him is the church, and we out here are the only thing that isn't the Church that he's got right now—and he runs away from us...?"

"He is a man of strong beliefs," Joe said. "Perhaps he does not wish to be reminded of the things he has already done flying in the face of his Church, in order to be there for the very person in whose body now lives something that threatens the faith in whose name he did those things. It is complicated. We are connected to the things we believe in. When they break—in our hands, in our hearts—the human spirit sometimes cracks under the grief of it. It is not enough to call something whole when the man who sees it broken is still feeling the pieces of it slipping through his fingers. Come inside."

"I won't sleep, tonight," Stella said, but turned to follow him back into the cottage.

"So you say, but I have heard that before and then people tell me in the morning that follows that they had strange dreams in the night," Joe said, smiling. And then paused, turning his head slightly as if he had heard something. Stella stopped too, seeing the gesture.

"What is it?"

"I thought I heard something," he said. "Go inside; I'll take a turn around the cabin."

"You think it might be Philip? Joe, if you think..." Stella began, unnerved, but he put both hands on her shoulders and firmly turned her towards the door of their cottage.

"There are no monsters," he said. "Not yet. I will be with you in a few moments."

She obeyed, but unwillingly, dragging her feet, turning twice to where he still stood a pace or two past the bench where she had been sitting. He had not moved by the time she slipped into the cottage and closed the door behind her.

Lily Mae was not in evidence, having been tucked into bed in the inner room, which she and Stella were now to share. Rob was in the kitchenette, pouring just-boiled water from the kettle into a mug. He looked up as she came inside.

"Tea?" he said. "Joe said he was going out to herd you inside. Any sign of..." He bit off the words, wincing. "I'm sorry. I am far too preoccupied with Lily Mae right now, I'm not thinking straight. Do you think Father Philip is all right?"

"I don't know," Stella said, "and I keep on thinking about what I said to him—I piled it on, rather than helping him deal with it— maybe I helped drive him off—"

"It's nothing you did," Rob said. "Lily Mae..."

"Can you explain that to me?" Stella said, a little desperately.

"Not much better than she did, than Jerusha did," Rob said.

"It could go badly," Stella murmured, accepting a mug of tea, not meeting his eyes.

"I know," he said bleakly.

The outside door opened, and then closed, very quietly. Joe raised a hand to forestall anything Rob or Stella might have said and spoke very quietly.

"I thought I heard something outside," Joe said. "Perhaps Father Philip. But even as I went to look... he texted me, on my phone. He does not want to have to face any of us, not tonight—he has found a church, and has asked the clergy to allow him to hold a vigil there. I told him about your miracle, Stella. He said he will return tomorrow, after the midwife has called. To hear what she had to say."

"Is he all right?" Stella said, surging forward a step. "Is he...?"

Joe stopped her, gently but inexorably.

"I will hear both your dreams and his, tomorrow," he said. "Until then... let him have this night, this silence. He needs it, and it is all he has asked for."

None of them, except Joe by the sound of his deep relaxed breathing, got much sleep that night. Lily Mae, insomniac and wide-eyed, had engaged Rob in something that was clearly between the two (possibly the three) of the *Parada* crew gathered there, and did not involve Stella. Although she had been told that Philip would not come back to the cabin that night, Stella could not help starting at every small noise she heard, waiting for the door to open, for Philip to return. She was in a bubbling soup of a crashing relief that Lily Mae had been found; confusion bordering on bewilderment at the state she had been found in; equal parts awed astonishment at that state, understanding how it had affected Philip, and resentment that he had allowed it to affect him that badly and that he could not hold it together for a little bit longer in a moment of crisis; a sudden and surprisingly devastating loss of everyone she had considered to be allies she could depend on and lean on.

Philip had retreated into the deep canyons of his unsteady faith; Rob, with whom she had gotten so close to during their short time alone together in Turkey, had turned away from her and was almost completely focused on Lily Mae. In the habitat, Stella might have been outnumbered when it came to doing the things she wanted done, but she had known her place, her position, and her adversaries. Now, out here, she was suddenly floundering, not sure whom she was opposing or why, and desperately wishing that somebody else would just take over, at least for a while.

Joe actually had been doing a yeoman job of that, for the time being—the only one of them all who seemed to be able to keep an emotional distance, a dispassionate observer's attitude. Stella honestly thought that if he had not been there, she would have gone to pieces already. She clung to him, his steadiness, his calm. But he was asleep. Philip was gone. Rob was busy with another woman. And Lily Mae, the other woman, was impossibly and improbably and hugely pregnant and apparently close to giving birth.

Stella was wide-eyed and awake, unable to turn off her mind and watching it run from problem to problem while gibbering with helpless inability to solve any of them, waited for the night to pass. Maybe a new day would begin to bring her the answers she needed.

She slept fitfully and in short dreamless catnaps which the smallest change in her environment would snap her out of. She finally gave up as a dirty grey light began to show through the crack in the drawn curtains, and slipped out of her bed. Lily Mae was finally asleep, and so was Rob, fully dressed and sprawled uncomfortably in a chair beside Lily Mae's bedside, his long legs stretched out before him. The room was starting to feel chilly, and Stella dragged the bedspread from her own bed and draped it over Rob, thinking that he was going to pay for this when he woke up and tried to rise from that chair. He did not stir as the bedspread settled around him. There were shadows under his eyes, and a slight frown had gathered on his forehead as he slept. He didn't look as though his dreams, if any, were pleasant.

Early as she was, Stella found that Joe was earlier. Neatly clad in tracksuit bottoms and sweatshirt, he was in the kitchenette, fussing with the kettle.

"I can still offer you a choice of tea or coffee," he said, without turning his head, even though Stella had made no noise at all yet aware of her presence there, "but there is a definite need for a supply run. There is also the baby. We are not prepared for its arrival in any way at all. If it comes this morning, all we have to wrap it in is a towel. We would have to put it into a dresser drawer, for want of a bed."

"Philip would tell you that it would be better than a manger," Stella said faintly.

"As for that, we do not even have straw," Joe said, but he looked around, and he was smiling. Stella managed to muster a wan smile in return. At the very least, that comment meant that air was getting to the parts of Stella that had been wounded. She had not even realized that she was capable of cracking at least a half-hearted joke on the matter.

But the ache was still there, the loss.

"Any word from him?" Stella asked, unable to help herself.

Joe shook his head, and handed her a cup of steaming coffee— instant and not great, but it was caffeine and it seemed to be necessary. "I would have said."

"Of course. Sorry." She took the coffee and retreated to the couch, subsiding onto it.

"I did, however, get a text from our midwife," Joe said, coming out of the kitchenette to join her in the room. "She said she would be by early this morning, to make a quick initial assessment."

"What are we going to tell her?" Stella asked, looking at once hopeful and trapped.

"As little as we need to," Joe said. "I am hoping she can help us deal with the physical situation. She cannot possibly be of any assistance with the backstory."

Less than an hour later, there was a knock on the door and Stella opened it to a short, dark-haired woman with steady eyes who stuck out one strong, capable hand, gloved in thin leather, in greeting.

"Nellie Trent," she said. "My aunt called. She said you had a *situation*."

The slight emphasis on a word that was at once all-encompassing and completely inadequate, lapped at the edge of a sense of humor which had almost completely been subsumed by the 'situation' in progress. Stella found she was capable of another smile. She stepped aside, releasing Nellie's hand as she did so.

"Come in. It was gracious of you to drop by. Our pregnant lady is in the other room."

Nellie entered, stripping off her gloves as she did so, revealing clean, close-clipped nails and no rings on her fingers. "Thank you," she said. "Show me."

"Let me just see if she's awake," Stella murmured, and slipped by into the second room. Rob and Lily Mae were both in there, both barely awake, and Stella dropped into a crouch beside Lily Mae's bed, at Rob's knee.

"There's a midwife who's come to take a look," she said. "Lily Mae... please... I need you to keep a tight grip. No Diana. No Jerusha. Don't scare her off. We need her. Rob, can you keep her steady?"

Rob glanced at Lily Mae, who looked up to meet his eyes, and gave the faintest of nods.

"I'll try," she said.

Stella reached out and squeezed her hand. "How are you feeling?"

"Pretty lousy," Lily Mae said with a watery grin. "My back is killing me."

Stella dropped her hand, stepped back to the door. "In here," she called.

Nellie stepped through into the room, a small reassuring smile on her face. "Hi," she said. "I'm a midwife. Call me Nellie. What's your name?"

There was a hesitation, a very brief one, and then a soft voice spoke. "Lily Mae," the voice said, and it was, it was the core persona. Behind Nellie's back, Stella briefly closed her eyes in relief.

Nellie was looking at Rob. "Are you the father?"

Rob shook his head. "No. A friend."

"The father... isn't in the picture," Stella said faintly.

Nellie glanced from Lily Mae to Rob, and to Stella, her eyebrow raised. "I take it none of you are family?"

"She has no living family," Stella said. She indicated Joe, who had come to stand in the doorway, with a toss of her head. "Joe is a doctor. So am I, of sorts, but I haven't dealt with childbirth in... well, ever. And Rob is a friend and a colleague. We're what Lily Mae has, right now."

"Ah," Nellie said. "Well, let's have a look at you, then, shall we."

She was kind, thorough, and efficient; but when she finally stepped away, permitting Lily Mae to be helped off the bed and assisted to the bathroom, she was frowning faintly and looking rather confused.

"I'm not sure I like her blood pressure," she said, to Joe and Stella, the self-avowed medical personnel in attendance. "And the rest of it... I can tell you that if I had to give you odds on that baby arriving within the next twenty four hours it would not be much of a risky bet. But although some of her is ripe for childbirth, some of her... feels like it's trying to catch up. She's giving me random symptoms from all stages of pregnancy. And it's a concern that her pelvic floor doesn't seem to be properly preparing for a childbirth—I don't want to frighten you but there may be... issues... there. If I didn't have the evidence before me I would say she was making the whole thing up from a set of notes she'd barely had a chance to study and has joyfully jumbled in her head."

"What are our options?" Joe asked quietly.

"Frankly, I would not move her," Nellie said. "You might end up delivering the child in a car by the side of a road somewhere, and at least here you will have a reasonable chance of keeping her as comfortable as possible under the circumstances. Your best bet— and my aunt won't thank me for it—would be to wait it out here. It really should not be long. I have another patient I need to rush to—the woman has been in early labor since oh-dark-hundred this morning, and I promised I would be there ASAP today—and then I have someone else I need to check in on—but I will try and swing by again tonight. In the meantime, forgive me, but you seem woefully unprepared for any of this."

"If you can give me a list I will go procure the immediate necessities right now," Joe said.

"I have a few things in the car I can let you have," Nellie said. "I think I have a couple of waterproof pads in there, for the bed, and I always carry emergency supplies of feminine products and such which she might be grateful for. But there are things..." She frowned a little deeper, pondering the conflicting results of her examination. "It may just be that there are issues which I haven't had time to go into—and

God knows not all mothers are able to breastfeed—but I think you should make plans to have formula on hand. And you need somewhere to put this child when it is born. Come with me, let me rummage around in the car, and we can see what else is necessary."

She swept out past Joe, who followed a step behind. Stella sat down rather hard on the edge of the other bed, and sighed deeply.

"How bad is it?" Rob asked quietly, from where he stood leaning on the doorjamb.

"We'll have to make do with what we have," Stella said, dropping her hand into her lap. "I am not certain that this Illogon creature thought this through at all."

There was a faint murmur of conversation just outside the cabin, and then the door opened and closed, and they could hear a car start outside. Joe, having deposited what he brought in, came to stand beside Rob.

"Right," he said. "I think I need to go pick up a few things—for Lily Mae, and for the rest of us. I take it you don't want to come, Stella?"

Stella whipped around. "No," she said, a little desperately, "I want to be here... if..."

Joe nodded. "Okay. I'll take the van. I hope I will not be too long, but I do have a number of errands to run. I will bring something at least halfway nutritious for dinner. We could all use a good hot meal."

He left, and Rob soon had his hands full again because Lily Mae had gone into the bathroom and someone else entirely came out of it, a personality Stella didn't quite recognize at all but which shaded into Diana at its fringes and whose presence spoke eloquently of Lily Mae's pain and frustration. Stella found herself hoping frantically that the baby didn't decide that it wanted to arrive right now, with even Joe away and only herself with any medical training at all in a situation which a trained midwife had sounded worried about. But Rob managed to get Lily Mae soothed and settled, and Stella herself sat, miserable and useless, by the window looking out into the grey day and watching the parking lot for any signs of Philip's return.

Even so, she almost missed it—she noticed a rangy black-clad figure approaching on foot from the direction of the main motel building and scrambled to her feet, peering through the window, trying to focus and see if it was indeed Philip. But if it had been, that time, the figure hesitated and then turned back, away from the cabin. Stella flung the door open and stood in the doorway, staring across the tarmac of the parking lot, but the figure had vanished, and she wasn't even sure that she had seen it and not just conjured it up out of her own need to see Philip come back.

But it had been Philip. The figure in black re-emerged, from the same place, after about an hour. It was Rob who noticed that time, at the window; he watched, saying nothing, as Philip approached the cabin through what had become a dreary, persistent drizzle, looking pale and haunted. The priest hesitated at the edge of the path to the cabin, then appeared to lose his nerve, and sat down heavily on the bench at the edge of the strip of lawn between the cabin's door and the tarmac. He glanced up at the window; he may or may not have noticed Rob standing there; and then he sighed deeply, and propped his elbows on his knees, burying his face in his hands.

"Stella," Rob murmured, with the patient air of repeating something already said, already discussed, already agreed upon. "No."

She turned to look at him, her eyes wide, haunted, and then inevitably back to look once again out of the window next to which she had been sitting. "He's been out there on his own for an hour. In the rain."

"I know. Don't go."

"Rob, he hasn't made a single move to come inside since he came back—and now he's been *out there*—all *alone*—in the *rain*—for at least an *hour*. Look at him. He's breaking my heart. He's a friend—mine, and yours—he's done all kinds of things that might have been against what he thought his God might want of him, or his Church, or his own soul. For my sake; for yours. If he had not come to our rescue we might never have made it out of Turkey, never mind all the way here; Lily Mae would have stayed lost; don't you think I owe him?"

"We all owe him," Rob said quietly. "But right now he's coming to terms with the real cost of it all and I don't think that you or I can ever be rich enough to pay that price. You *heard* him, before. This matters. The only thing we can do is let him find an inner peace with it, himself. If he can. It's a hefty burden to lay on anyone's back, especially someone who has believed all of his adult life that he has carried the light of God inside him—only to find out he's no more than only human, after all."

"I think he thinks that God is punishing him," Stella said.

"Yes, and he's allowing that. He's seeking that. Maybe he can figure everything out in the light of that small candle that he's still holding inside his heart. There are things which are broken and only he knows what they are, or how badly. You can't help him. You can't force him back here. There are things we are not meant to help anyone bear, no matter how much we care about them."

"That's the Poet speaking," Stella said, giving him a watery grin. "It's lovely language, and it's a powerful feeling, but..."

"No," Rob said. "I know when the Poet is out, and he isn't out now. This is me. This is *me* telling you. I don't know what else..."

There was a whimper from the narrow bed in the inner room, where Lily Mae lay stretched out, and Rob's head swiveled in that direction. Stella noticed, and indicated Lily Mae with a sharp toss of her head. "She's someone *you* have a responsibility for," she said. "You called her your sister, when Arslan asked you about her. You're all she has left. You, and that child. Who will not, I think, be a comfort. That baby is never going to be anything but a challenge—starting right now—and it is not nearly born yet..."

Rob rose to his feet and came to stand beside her for a moment, his hand heavy on her shoulder. Her own, after only a small hesitation, lifted almost instinctively and laid itself over his, but she did not look up at him, her gaze still locked on the man sitting outside in the rain with his head bowed and water dripping from his soaked hair onto the hands folded in the lap of his soaked cassock "I'll go see to her," Rob said, after a shared silence that spoke volumes even in the absence of a single word uttered out loud, that spoke about different kinds of love, and different kinds of need. "Joe's been away a good while—he should be back soon. Maybe... when Joe returns...I'm sure Philip will come back in then. Until then... Don't go. Don't barge in.

He won't thank you for it. You are too much a part of the thing that he is wrestling with."

He pulled his hand out from underneath hers, and Stella's own dropped in place, nerveless, with her arm draped across her breasts and the hand lying on her own shoulder like a wounded bird. She leaned over and laid her cheek on it, without once taking her eyes off Philip's forlorn figure. And then she got up, and padded softly over to the door of the cabin, ignoring Rob's swift urgent call at her back.

The rain that had started as a dreary drizzle had increased as the wind rose, and now it was falling steadily, in cold gray ropes of driving water, connecting the bruised sky full of low clouds which still had to release their loads to the miserable sodden ground below. None of them had thought of an umbrella as an essential item to bring along on this trip; they had one rain poncho between them, and Joe had taken that. Stella stepped out into the rain, bareheaded, wearing a wholly inadequate thin cotton sweater. Rain swept over her shoulders, her head, cold rivulets of it running through her hair; Philip's bench was less than ten steps from the door but by the time she came up beside him she was already soaked and shivering.

"Philip," she said helplessly. "Philip. Is there anything I can do? You should come inside. You are going to catch your death out here. I promise, I won't talk to you at all, nobody will, but come inside. It's at least warm, and you can change into something dry..."

He lifted his head up very slowly to look up at her and she nearly cried out at the bleak devastation in his eyes.

"I'm not ready," he said. "I can't... it isn't her fault. But she's in there."

"There are two rooms in that cabin," Stella said, "you can go into..."

"But it is under the same roof—and I am still faced with the fact that she is under it. They are. The mother and the child that is to come. I have spent this night on my knees and still I cannot quite accept what I think I have been told about... everything. But God isn't talking to me, or if He is I cannot hear him. And I know. It isn't rational. I certainly have no intention of blaming Lily Mae... or anyone else... for anything... but I haven't quite... I can't..."

Stella's breath caught on a sob she couldn't quite stop. "But it isn't like you're..."

"There are worse things than sitting out in the rain!" he said sharply, lashing out. "I'm trying to find out if I can..." He broke off. A short, hollow chuckle rose from somewhere and lodged in his throat like a bone. "I'm sorry. Thank you. Let me have another moment. I promise, I will try not to get sick on you. But it isn't as though I am not drenched already—it won't help if I—I just need to—I need to understand. I'm caught between what I *am* and everything that I thought I once was. I'm sorry. Joe texted me back last night, he said you were worried. I didn't mean to do that. I wasn't thinking. I needed to be alone. It isn't you, but there is *nothing you can do to help me.*" Stella flinched at the tightly leashed savagery in his voice, but then he glanced up at her and it softened again. "Go back in—before *you* catch pneumonia on us all."

"This isn't your fault," she said intensely, and with a gesture born of pure instinct leaned down to kiss him on the top of the head, in the middle of an elflock of hair dark with rain. "You can't be responsible for any of it. Not by yourself. *You did nothing wrong.*"

"Thank you," he said, and sounded sincerely grateful, as though she had offered up an absolution, even if it did seem to be for a sin he had not confessed.

"Rob said not to come out here," she said, starting to cry in earnest.

"Leave me, Stella," Philip murmured. "I need to think. Thank you for coming out. Thank you for caring. I know you do. I'll be fine. I hope. But leave me. If God lives in this world still then he is also in the rain. Let me look for Him there. If I don't find what I need... I am not going to be any use to you. To any of you. After all that happened. And there are enough problems to face right now. Without dragging around something that will only slow you down, if you need to run."

"What?" Stella said, rousing. "We're going nowhere without you— whatever you decide. There's a part of you that will always be with us."

"I know," he said, and this time his smile was genuine, if a little wan. "Stella. Go back inside. Listen to Rob. Take care of Lily Mae." He looked around, as though he was groping for something, and then grasped it. "You're here. I assume Lily Mae went nowhere and you said

Rob is in there. But the van's gone. Where did Joe go?"

"He left to get us something to eat," Stella said. "And to get things we might need..." That was skating too close back to Lily Mae again. Stella bit back the rest of the things she might have said. "It's been nearly three hours," she said. "I hope *he's* okay."

"Why wouldn't he be?" Philip asked, looking away from her again, his eyes unfocused and staring off into the middle distance, through the curtains of rain. "Go back in. Stay warm."

She started to say something, reconsidered, thought about something else, shelved that too, and finally clutched her arms around herself, shivering, her hands folded around her elbows. Water dripped from her fingers.

"You're probably the best friend I've ever had," she said, her voice soft but stubborn. "I love you. I am afraid for you. I want to help you. Tell me how. I'll leave you alone if that's what it takes, for now, but please don't forget that I am never going to abandon you or leave you or blame you for anything at all. No matter what you think you're out here trying to atone for." She sniffed, releasing one elbow to drag the back of her hand across her nose in a gesture so childlike that Philip, who had glanced back at her as she spoke, had to smile. "There's cocoa," Stella said. "I'm keeping it for you. No matter who else wants it or lays claim. I'll keep it warm." She hesitated, for the last time, and then dropped her arms to her sides in a gesture of resignation. "Just remember. You are not alone."

She walked back to the cabin, her wet hair hanging in strings across her face.

Behind her, Philip buried his own face back into his hands.

Joe White Elk returned maybe half an hour later. They heard a light kick at the door and Rob opened it to reveal Joe standing there with both arms around somewhat soggy grocery bags.

"There's stuff in the van I could use a hand with," he said, passing the bags into Rob's arms. "I guess I will go press Father Philip into service." He glanced at Stella's red eyes and her own wet hair, hanging around her face in pathetic damp strands. "There would seem to be an argument to be made against anyone *else* getting soaked. Make some hot tea. We will all need it."

He didn't ask if she was all right, or if Philip was, and she was grateful for not having to answer either question. She followed Rob into the kitchenette, helping him put away the food from the grocery bags in silence, her back to the door but with all of her attention focused on the sound of it as it opened and closed, and the sound of footsteps coming inside. Two pairs of footsteps.

Rob saw her tense shoulders relax, and he poured hot water from the kettle into a mug with a tea bag in it.

"Here," he said, "per Joe's instructions. Go sit in front of the heater or something. You're still soggy. I'll put the rest of this away."

Stella turned in time to see a soaked Philip trying to wrestle a medium-sized padded cat bed, lined with pristine faux sheepskin, into the room while both keeping it out of the rain and attempting not to drip too copiously into it himself.

"Are we getting a *cat*?" she blurted, unexpectedly smitten with a stab of yearning for her own lost companion.

Joe, following Philip with his last load of bags, shrugged. "It is clean, it is soft, it is warm, a baby could do worse for a bed in an emergency."

Stella backed up towards the heater, and more or less collapsed onto the floor beside it, feeling unexpected tears prick at the back of her eyes. Rob, having disposed of the things in Joe's grocery bags, came over with his own cup of tea to sit down on the chair behind her.

"What?" he said quietly. "You suddenly look like you've seen a ghost."

"I have, sort of," Stella said. "I have... maybe it's more accurate to say I used to have... a cat. Smokey. I thought I was only leaving him for a little while, when I came to the facility where you guys were. I haven't seen him since, probably won't ever see him again, they said he would be 'cared for' but it isn't me—and he's got a cat bed, not too different from that one—and all of a sudden it just hit me—"

She leaned into his knee, her face down in the mug whose warmth she was inhaling.

Rob sighed, letting a hand come to rest in a comforting gesture on her back, just below the nape of her neck.

"Saying I'm sorry sounds so ridiculous," he said. "But I'm sorry."

She glanced up at him, her mind wheeling back to the current problem. "How's Lily Mae doing?"

"She's sleeping," Rob said. "She was up most of the night but she's sleeping now. Which means she'll probably be awake all night again." He sighed. "She'll—they will both be fine."

Somehow the day had got away from them all—the light outside was already beginning to fade, the greyness sliding into night without the blessing of a setting sun. Joe had turned on a couple of the lamps as he had come in, and now they cast small comforting pools of yellow light around them. There was no analogue clock in the room but Stella could hear the steady ticking of time passing by, coming from somewhere deep inside her, as though she was sitting right next to a tall antique grandfather clock with a swinging pendulum. One by one the seconds passed, and then the minutes, and finally both Stella and Rob looked up as Joe came out of the other bedroom where he had stealthily stowed all of the materials he had gathered for Lily Mae, Philip emerged at the same moment out of the bathroom where he had gone to at least try and mop himself up. Apparently Joe had handed the priest one of Rob's dry sweatshirts, and Philip looked very young and vulnerable all of a sudden, out of his stern black cassock, his wet hair standing on end from a vigorous toweling.

"I think there is still much to think on, and talk about," Joe said calmly, "but I did manage to convince him that drowning himself was not a requirement for any of it. I know it is not much, but I brought macaroni and cheese—it just needs re-heating—and I think we could all do with something hot to eat. Somebody go wake our girl up. She needs her sleep but right now perhaps she needs something solid inside her far more than that. Make room beside the heater, Stella, so Philip can get some warmth back into those bones, and I will fix dinner."

It was still raining outside by the time they finished their mac and cheese. Lily Mae insisted on helping clean up (which mostly consisted of filling up the room's small trash bin with the packaging the fast-food meals had arrived in, and rinsing out the mugs they all had various beverages in). She archly told Philip and Stella, both still damp around the edges, to stay by the heater and to try and not throw a spanner in the works by coming down with something that would—at least in the short term—be far more physically draining and incapacitating than— as she put it—merely waiting to carry a child to term. Joe, behind her, rolled his eyes at that but said nothing. Stella might have argued; Philip made no attempt to do so. He had in fact been completely silent the entire evening. Just being in this room, in the same space with Lily Mae, was a major victory for him. He was not yet ready to break his walls down. Joe, aware of the silence and taking matters into his own hands, came to stand in front of Philip and caught his eye, then gestured with a toss of his head in the direction of the second room.

"Philip," he said, "we need to talk. I am sorry to commandeer your space, Lily Mae, but that room is the only bit of privacy to be had in here. I would take him outside but he just got dry enough to be fully human again and I would hate to undo all that good work. I will try not to keep you from your bed for too long."

"Make yourself at home," Lily Mae said with a wry grin.

Joe maneuvered Philip into the room, and closed the door behind them.

"I'm bored and my ankles are the size of elephant feet and my back hurts," Lily Mae said. "Distract me. Didn't someone say there was a pack of cards out here? And damned if I don't need to go to the bathroom again. I swear, if nothing else, I will be grateful when this is all over so I can manage to string together an hour in which I don't need to go pee three times. I'd love another cup of tea if anyone's making any— something warm inside of me, on this night—but if I do I will never get any sleep tonight. Or I might as well sleep in the bathtub."

She waddled heavily into the bathroom and snicked the door closed behind her.

Rob caught Stella's gaze wandering to the closed door, apparently unable to stop worrying about what was happening in the other room, and finally said,

"He is in good hands. He needs somebody to talk to about all of this,"

"But I..."

"I know. You already told him. He knows too. Now let him find a solid place to stand before you insist on holding his hand. And speaking of sleeping, which Lily Mae mentioned, I shouldn't think that those two are going to be out of there any time soon. I'll nap out here with you ladies tonight. I can take the couch."

"Don't be silly," Stella said, "I'm a foot shorter than you are and even my feet would hang off that couch from halfway up my calves if I tried to stretch out there. Lily Mae can have that one bed, you take the other, I'll curl up on the couch if need be." She glanced back at the door again. "Whatever helps."

"But you're..."

"I'll be fine. I'll be *fine.* Is she really set on *cards* tonight? I mean, we might as well try and grab some shut-eye. We may have a long way to go, tomorrow."

"I thought the midwife said to stay put, for now," Rob asked quietly. "Where were you planning to head to?"

Stella gave him a look, full of desperate uncertainty. "Pick a direction. All right, maybe not bright and early tomorrow, but we can't stay here, not forever, not even for long. We need to find a place to go to ground. A safe place—for *her.* For Philip. For all of us." She made a small frustrated gesture. "We can discuss it in the morning."

Lily Mae came back from the bathroom, padding over to one of the beds in bare feet, ignoring the probable state of cleanliness on the threadbare carpets. She yawned, but her eyes were bright, wakeful. "Did you find those cards?"

"Stella thinks we should probably try and get some rest," Rob said. "I mean, we don't know how much time we have—before you—"

"All right, no cards. But then someone tell me a story," Lily Mae said. "I'm going to need to know some bedtime stories, soon."

"Lil," Rob said, "that child is going to be telling *you* stories."

Lily Mae grinned, her white teeth a flash against her dark skin. "There's a part of me that is looking forward to that," she said. "And a part of me that is frankly terrified of the idea."

Rob got up from his seat beside the heater and fussed with the bed that Lily Mae was about to climb into, putting one of Nellie's waterproof pads on it before Lily Mae climbed in—just in case, he said—before reaching over to pull the thin blanket and the bedspread atop it over her, tucking it up against her back. Stella heard his voice drop into the Poet's tones, and closed her eyes, leaning her head back against the chair, listening as the words drew her in and wrapped her in beauty. It took her a moment to drift back into full awareness, when she realized that he had stopped talking and the lamp beside Lily Mae's bed clicked off. In the deeper shadows, cast by the single remaining lamp, she saw Rob come back towards her, and lifted her head.

"I thought you were asleep," he said, and the voice was still not Rob's.

"No. But I may have been dreaming," she said.

"The couch is still..."

"Go to *bed*," she said, decisively enough, rising to her feet and gathering up the blanket she still had wrapped around her. "I mean it."

He looked as though he wanted to insist—and if he had been fully Rob he might have—but his eyes were still the Poet's, huge and shining, and he said nothing more. He inclined his head at her, in silence, and stepped across to where the other bed in the room was tucked up against the window. He waited until she had taken the few steps across to the couch, and switched off the second lamp. The room plunged into shadows, lit only dimly by the nightlight whose wan illumination came past the half-open door to the bathroom.

Stella did curl up on the couch, trying to make one of the stiff, board-hard cushions serve as a makeshift pillow, but she was wide awake, and it wasn't just the comfortless couch that was to blame for that. She found herself listening, straining with every fiber in her, to the soft murmur of conversation that she could still hear in the second bedroom. Behind her, in the two beds, Lily Mae's breathing soon deepened into sleep, and she thought she heard Rob's change, too—but even lying there as still as she could with her eyes closed Stella could not seem to make her body release the tension in her shoulders and her back. Her hair was still damp at the roots, and felt cold against the back of her head where she lay against the unyielding cushion; her feet kept sticking out from under the edge of the blanket, cold even despite the socks she had kept on. Finally, feeling guilty for even thinking about it, she swung her legs down off the couch, wrapped the blanket around her like a poncho, and padded carefully to where she could curl up on the floor in front of the door to the second bedroom, leaning the side of her head against it, straining to listen.

The door was not built to be soundproof. The conversation in the other room was low, and from the couch it had been just a murmur—but with her ear against the door it was easy to make out the words. Silently, carefully, guiltily, holding her breath, she listened.

"But what is it that you have lost?" Joe asked quietly. "Merely the frame. God is greater than the story in which you try to put him in order to understand an existence of such a being. It only makes that god smaller—and, instead, you have blown away that confining frame and expanded the story instead..."

"I know that," Philip said, sounding so bleak that Stella's breath caught in her throat. "I understand—but that frame, that story, that is the foundation my life had been built on. It was not just God it was necessary to believe in. It was Christ, and what he stood for, and what was supposed to have been said and done in His name."

"Christ is not lessened by what you now know."

"How can that possibly be true? If all of it isn't true—if Jesus, as we know him, was not the son of God but instead carried the soul of some marooned star traveler who had nowhere else to go..."

"It made him human," Joe said. "And that was part of what you believed, part of what made the story true for you. It is difficult to make the case that anyone—not even a priest of your clear deeply held faith—can possibly believe that every single word of the holy books is literally true. I have not made half the study of those that you must have done in your day, but I know that when Jesus was supposed to have walked the Earth—in those very days—he himself might not have been what the religion created in his name eventually made him become. *Others* made him into a deity. In the beginning—in his mother's womb, as a baby, as a toddler, as a small child—he was no more than what he seemed. No more than Lily Mae's child will be. In that way, they are the same—even if you see one as a young boy born of Middle Eastern parentage, and the other, a small girl-child who will come of a young black woman and of no known father. But when they were born, they were just that—small squalling babies. It is what Jesus did as a man—the miracles they attributed to his hand as a man—that made him different, rendered him holy. We have no idea what lies waiting for Lily Mae's child."

"Just her existence—" Philip choked. "It means none of it was ever true. No, not even in the metaphorical sense. And I—who was called to the faith, who built my life on it, who offered up my soul freely when it was asked for—what does that make of me—who am I now, if I am no longer a priest, a Jesuit, a Christian...?"

"It may mean that your ministry has become bigger than you bargained for," Joe said. "That the God who called you is not confined to a single world, a single sun, a single system. It may be that we are all made in the image of God but that the image we perceive of Him may not be the same for all of his children—and that He is a greater thing, a greater thing by far, than you may have even begun to believe. My own people believe in a spirit that is inside all things—there are scientists who will tell you that we are all made up of star stuff, the same elements born in the hearts of living stars—so how is a blade of grass or a rabbit or buffalo or a sequoia tree not made in the image of God, then? How is that not true of every star that ever burned? What if God isn't just a tiny shard of all of his creation—not just human, not just us in all of our hubris—but what if He is also what made the Illogon, the creatures whom he then may have sent to change the worldview of you, a different part of his creation? What if all of this only means..."

A hand on Stella's shoulder made her jump, and she lifted her head from the door, turning to meet Rob's eyes where he was crouching beside her.

"Stop," he said quietly. "Come to bed. Don't do this to him, or to yourself."

"But he..." Stella whispered, in protest.

Rob shook his head, and tightened his grip, helping her struggle to her feet. "Come. Leave it. This is something that is not your task to tackle."

He guided her back to the bed, not the couch, and helped her climb under the covers, but when he would have turned away to seek the couch she had abandoned she reached out for his hand and gripped it hard. Rob stopped, half turning, the line of his body a silent question.

"No," Stella said, suddenly shivering. "Here. Come here. Hold me."

14.

He hesitated, but only for a moment, and then nodded, turning back towards the bed. He did not release her hand until they were both fully under the covers, sliding his arm around her and holding her close as she laid her head on his chest and listened for a couple of breaths of silence as his heart beat steadily beneath her ear, another message she was overhearing and eavesdropping on but this time one meant for her to hear and understand. Rob said nothing at all, lying stretched out beside her, his chin on the top of her head, the sound of the rain still pattering against the windowpane behind its thin brown curtains.

After a moment, Stella sighed, and something inside of her gave—she finally relaxed against him, only then aware of how tense and tight and rigid she had been. A shift in his jaw on her head told her that he smiled.

"I can't have this," she said against his chest. "I can't, you know. It is entirely wrong for a doctor to have a patient as a..."

"Even if you ever were," he said, "I don't think that applies. Not really. Not anymore. If that's all that you can hold against it."

"So what do *you* want?" she asked, pushing into him, lifting her head to look at him, searching his eyes with her own in the deep shadows of the bed.

"Me?" Rob asked, his tone reflective. "Mine are much smaller questions than Philip's or even Lily Mae's. I don't have to question my position in this world—I know I gave that up a long time ago, when I first left it, and I can never go back to that place. So I am a leaf in the wind, as it were. I might remember what I once had—a family that was once mine, a brother who will always be a part of me but whom I very probably will not see again in this life unless something big changes—and I might consider what I brought back with me from a journey which I may or may not have believed that I would ever really return from—or what I found here, unexpectedly and with an unlooked-for quiet joy, if I were permitted to claim it—"

She lifted a hand and put it across his lips, preventing him from talking.

He obligingly stayed silent, for a moment, waiting for her to say something, but as the silence lengthened he reached up and closed his hand over hers, pulling them both down to rest on his chest over his heart.

"I mean," he said, "I know that I am two hundred years older than you are..."

"The person who existed those two hundred years ago is long gone," Stella whispered. "If anything, you're only a few weeks old, maybe a month or two, depending on when you start counting from, when the *Juno* picked you up or when they hauled the *Parada* crew back to Earth—I'd be *cradle snatching* if I were to marry you—"

"So you are going to marry me, then?" he asked, laughter bubbling in his voice.

She blushed furiously, thankful he couldn't see in the dark, tucking in her chin so that her face was hidden against him again.

"Well," he said, and she could still hear the echo of a smile in his voice, "I guess I can call it some sort of a residue of that time dilation thing. More happened to me out there than I knew, mayhap—because I am getting an answer to a question I haven't asked yet, not properly—but for what it's worth, Stella, I was going to come to you anyway. Don't ask me when. Sometime. Soon. And tell you that I know I bring absolutely nothing I can usefully offer you in return but if you were willing to..." He paused, slipping one hand down the curve of her jaw to gently lift her head back up. "Are you laughing or are you crying?"

"Neither," she hiccoughed. "Both. Lord, if I had ever really pictured a moment like this it would not have been a place like this, it would not have been at a moment like this, it would probably never in a million years be anybody like you, but still, I..."

"You what?" he asked "I am not just doing this to distract you from what is going on right now on the other side of that door. I mean it—I was going to circle around to asking anyway. If I hadn't thus far that's because I—maybe because I couldn't think about what would happen if—"

She hushed him again, her fingers against his mouth, but this time he kissed them, and felt her hand tremble at the touch of his lips.

"Stella," he said, and she could hear the first cadences of the Poet come into his voice, but he didn't allow that fragment to manifest, not fully—this was only that part of him that fragmented to give birth to the full persona of the Poet, not the entity itself, he was still holding on to the core of himself, speaking as Rob. "Do you remember what I told you, about the way the Illogon travel the stars?"

"About sending out their mind—their spirit—whatever you want to call it—in the shell of the ship, out to the stars, you mean?"

"And why?"

She hesitated. "You said... something... about it holding them together... about how without the shell they would dissipate into the fabric of the universe, stop existing..."

He nodded against her hair. "That, yeah. In an incoherent nutshell. But here is what I am telling you, now, tonight, and here is what I want you to know, and to believe. If I am no more than a soul adrift on the wild winds of the cosmos, trying to make my way through the galaxies and the constellations tumbling and burning in my path—there is one thing I have come to know about that soul and its journey. It needs its shelter, its shell, its vessel, something that will help it hold together, that will keep this already fractured spirit that you have come to know all too well from spilling out into the empty universe and losing all shape and form and memory of who I was, and who I am, and who I am supposed to be. And for me... that shell, that sanctuary, that peace that is my armor... that's you."

Stella sighed, softly, and lifted her head to his, brushing his lips with hers.

"I know," she said. "I think I've known... There were times I might have thought, or even said, that I couldn't tell you and Jerry apart. But I could. It didn't take me long. And I have always tried to be..."

There was a noise from the other room, a soft thud, a shuffle, and Rob felt her head move instantly as she listened.

"But a part of you is still listening at that door," he said. "Isn't it?"

She turned back to him, sharply. "What did you think—that Philip—"

"I watched the two of you, back at the habitat," Rob said. "You worked well as a team. But he is what he is, and I didn't think that he would have..."

"But now," Stella said. "After... after everything. In the throes of his doubts. When he doesn't think that he can be that thing which he was, not any more. Did you think...?"

"He is good, and brave, and gentle, and kind," Rob said. "There are worse men, worse reasons to care for any man."

"We were thrown together, he and I, back at the habitat—and it was easy to count him as a colleague, as an ally, as a friend," Stella said. "He will *always* be my friend. I love that man, and everything that he is—he gives without asking the cost, if he thinks it right. That is why I grieve so much for the hurt that I can feel in him—because he has nothing left to give, Rob, not even to himself. Unless he can find a way back to the deepest parts of his soul and come to terms with what all this might mean, for him, I don't know, I am frightened about what might be left for him. He has given everything else away except that, and now that has been taken from him—and I don't know if he can come back from that, and still be himself, and still consider himself as consecrated of God..."

She lifted her head, abruptly distracted by something new. "Listen. Did you hear that? Is Lily Mae..."

Rob shifted, throwing a glance over his shoulder at the other bed— and he was just in time to see Lily Mae, improbably, sit up in bed. Her dark skin made her face part of the shadows across the room, but he glimpsed the sudden flash of the whites of her eyes as she turned her head to face him.

"I am coming," a voice said from that other bed. Not Lily Mae's voice. The voice of the entity who had identified itself as Jerusha. The Illogon. The alien. The *baby*.

Rob and Stella released one another, all but fell out of the bed they had been sharing, and then Rob crossed the room in two long strides to crouch by Lily Mae's bedside while Stella crossed to the door into the other bedroom and pounded on it with her fist.

"Joe! *Joe!* We're out of time! The baby..."

Both the men in the second bedroom were still fully dressed, Joe in an open-necked shirt and casual corduroy trousers, Philip still wearing the borrowed clothes he had put on when he shed his wet cassock. Joe, who had opened the door to Stella's knock, looked focused, intense, even a little grim; behind him, Stella glimpsed Philip standing with his hands curled into loose fists by his sides, his face drained of color.

"What happened?" Joe asked.

"Rob's over there—all we know is—we heard her say—we heard *Jerusha* say—'I am coming'," Stella said.

"Has Lily Mae complained of pains?"

"Not to either of us."

"Let me speak to her," Joe said, and Stella stepped aside to let him pass.

Rob had switched on the bedside lamp beside Lily Mae's bed and Stella could see the other woman's face, laid back once more on a pillow. Joe approached, murmuring something Stella could not quite make out, but she clearly heard Lily Mae's response—the same voice she and Rob had heard, the same words. *I am coming.*

Joe lifted off Lily Mae's covers, laid gentle hands on her stomach, held them there for a moment; as though triggered by the touch, a low moan escaped Lily Mae's throat.

Joe straightened. "She is in labor. I would say it is an early stage but where this pregnancy is concerned everything I think I know does not apply. Still, we will try and deal with things as they come. Stella, get spare bed linens, we may need them—get them off any of the other beds—help get the bed ready for her. Rob, help me get her up. Her water has not yet broken—and sometimes it helps if the woman is on her feet, if we can get her walking, at least until the process is advanced enough to..." He paused, glanced back at Philip. "My phone is on the bedside table," he said. "I know it is an ungodly hour, but call Nellie Trent, or text her, her number is in my contacts. Leave a message that if she is still willing and able to assist, we need her. In the meantime... Stella, I have not properly unpacked any of the supplies I brought in. Bring the bag."

"Should I be boiling water?" Stella asked, with a ghost of a smile.

"Only if you want to make tea," Joe said. "But that can wait."

The Illogon—Jerusha—seemed to have withdrawn, after making an announcement of its imminent arrival; so did every other personality that had crowded Lily Mae's mind. All that was left at this moment, it seemed, was the woman herself—but it was a woman whose body and mind were currently a battlefield. She might have retreated into her primary core persona, but Stella had no idea how something which was as much of a loss of control as childbirth had to be would affect Lily Mae's other personalities, or if her well-meaning but possibly woefully inadequate support team would be left trying to talk someone like the passionate, quick-tempered Diana or, worse, the impassive Alabastra down from some impossible ledge at the worst possible moment. She and Joe hadn't even had time to discuss that, not properly, but Stella knew that if anything like that did slip sideways it would be Stella herself and possibly Rob who would have to deal with that situation while leaving Joe to handle the actual physical aspects of the process by himself. And as far as that went—it wasn't as though Lily Mae was some narrow-hipped, sickly child unprepared for the process of giving birth. Nor was she, at the chronological physical age of thirty three, potentially catastrophically too old for having her child. But the vessel of her body had been usurped and ill-used by the alien entity which had created the child into which it had poured itself, and none of the people in the room knew what long-term consequences that would have—or even how such changes would affect the process of childbirth.

"When was the last time you delivered a child?" Stella asked Joe quietly, as he and Rob, supporting Lily Mae between them paced the pregnant woman alongside the bed which Stella was quickly remaking with the addition of a layer of protective plastic-backed pads which Nellie had left them.

"Too long ago," Joe said. "I think she should be more dilated with the birth this imminent. I have no idea what I am doing except that I am following her body's instructions. I just have to be ready for what comes, whenever it comes."

Lily Mae's back arched, and she lifted her head, a low moan escaping her lips, her eyes closed. Her bare feet tangled beneath her and for a moment she hung between the supporting arms of Rob and Joe which held her upright from both sides.

"They are coming closer now," Joe said. "Maybe it is time to get her back into the bed..."

Lily Mae managed to shake her head, her eyes still closed. "No," she whispered, "no, I can't be lying down... no... I need to..."

She began to subside beside the bed, even as an unexpected liquid splash washed down the insides of her thighs and puddled around her knees even as she sank down into it. Rob flashed a question with his eyes; Joe nodded.

"Do what makes her comfortable," Joe said. "Gently. Philip, did you find...?"

"Called. No reply, left a message. Texted another." Philip consulted the phone he had laid on the kitchenette counter. "No response," he said.

Stella wanted to cry at the sight of his face. This was not his world, had never been part of his life, and it was not something he had ever expected to encounter at these visceral close quarters—but over and above that, there were the circumstances, the context of this child, all that it still might mean to him. He was still very white, his shoulders hunched and rigid, his eyes fixed and dilated with shock, looking like he was frozen in between an instinct to help—an instinct he would always have—and a passionate desire to be somewhere else, anywhere else, anywhere other than in this room, with this woman, in these circumstances. He could not run—he could not do that, and live with himself—but it took pure concentrated willpower to stay.

"Well, it will be a while, yet," Joe said. "Or it would be, if this had been anything like a regular pregnancy. I cannot really plan for anything."

Lily Mae clutched at his hand, abruptly, her eyes round with pain and with fear. Joe gave her fingers a reassuring squeeze. "Do not try and push yet. It is not yet time. Trust me."

Lily Mae's contractions began to increase in frequency and intensity at a frighteningly fast rate; and Joe's face was grave and focused as he talked to her constantly, in a low and gentle voice, taking care of her physical condition while Rob and Stella stayed close by her side to support her and keep her in a stable psychological frame. Twice she nearly escaped, into different personas, anxious to be anyone—to be anywhere—other than the person or the place that she was. But Rob would be there, holding her hand, calling her back, or Stella would murmur encouragement, and Lily Mae stayed. She gasped and moaned as the contractions began to come closer and closer together, for an hour, another hour, and another.

Joe, taking stock of the situation, glanced back at Philip, who shook his head. No word from the midwife. Taking a deep breath, Joe turned back to Lily Mae.

"I think it is time," he said. "Push, now. It may not be long before your baby is here."

"Tired... tired..." Lily Mae murmured. And then caught her breath again and screamed as another contraction took her.

"Courage," Joe murmured. "Only a little while longer."

It was in fact only some half an hour after that Joe straightened from an inspection and said, "I believe the baby may be crowning."

Lily Mae suddenly went still, silent, so completely frozen that the three who were clustered around her actually thought that something terrible was wrong—but she had only allowed, one last time before the physical severance of her own body from that of the child she was about to bear, the Illogon to take control over her body, her mind, her voice.

"It is important," Jerusha said, very softly, almost too softly for anyone to hear. But Stella, her head close to Lily Mae's, trying to prevent a catastrophic abdication of the physical body to a new persona, heard the words clearly, and stared at Lily Mae as she spoke them. "The priest. He needs to know. He needs to see. He needs to hold the child. It will be a long time before that body will be ready to speak to him—but he needs to understand—I am sorry I have hurt him. I am sorry this body is in pain. I am sorry for being... for hurting... for causing harm. I never meant to hurt. I was... it was... to survive. But he needs to know. He needs to know. He needs to..."

Rob and Stella exchanged a frightened glance above Lily Mae's head, and then Stella glanced back to where Philip stood frozen and ashen-faced, too near not to have overheard those words. If any moment existed when he needed Stella's support, it was right then—but she had her hands full with the woman whose body writhed under her hand. She bent down again, whispering into Lily Mae's ear. "All right. We will do what we can. Lily Mae, come back. Come back, or we can lose you both. Lily Mae. Lily..."

There was a gasp, and a moan, and Lily Mae was back. Stella caught Rob's eye, and then glanced back at Joe.

"How soon?"

"Any moment," he said.

"We need scissors," Stella said. "For the cord. Philip... we need all hands." She gave him a look that was full of love, full of pity, but without a release. "I'm sorry, we need you. Rob needs to hold onto her mind, Joe is holding her body together, that baby is coming *now*. I'm sorry, we need you, *we need you*."

As though in a daze, Philip took a few steps forward, and knelt beside Lily Mae.

"Hold on to her," Stella said. Her hand lifted from Lily Mae's arm, fluttered helplessly and sympathetically down on Philip's shoulder for a moment, and then she stepped away from the bed. "I'll be right back."

It was thus that she saw it all, on her way back to the bed holding the surgical scissors that Joe had acquired for the birth. She saw Rob holding both Lily Mae's hands in his own, close beside her, supporting her mind with every ounce of that shared link that was the legacy of the *Parada* and of that entity which even now was being born into its own life and existence outside them all. She saw Joe, focused and intent, his medical focus on the body that was in the process of giving birth to this child. And she clearly saw the child itself, the newborn babe, suddenly slide, slick and perfect, into Father Philip Carter's hands.

She saw him holding the little girl with one hand carefully cupped behind her head, the other slipping down to support the baby's back, and she saw the baby, preternaturally still for a moment, lying completely helpless in the priest's consecrated hands, her eyes wide open, holding Philip's own.

Lily Mae folded over with a deep moan.

"She is here," Joe said. "Your little girl is here. It is over."

"Her eyes," Philip whispered. "Her eyes..."

"Is she *breathing*?" Joe demanded, coming round to take over. He plucked the baby gently from Philip's hands and as he turned it expertly it let out a lusty wail, exercising a healthy pair of lungs.

"Let me see her," Lily Mae whispered, lifting her head. "Let me see her..."

Stella hurried forward with the scissors. Everything else was confusion, smiles, exhaustion, dealing with the expulsion of the afterbirth, helping Lily Mae clean up, getting her back into her bed, laying the baby wrapped in a clean pink towel in the crook of her arm. It was nearly a full half hour later that Stella realized that Philip was gone.

Stella glanced into the second room in the cabin to confirm that Philip had not retired there, and found it empty; the bathroom door was open and showed it to be likewise. She had not heard the outside door open or close but he had to have gone outside, and Stella, after catching Rob's eye with an unspoken question and receiving a faint nod of reply affirming that he would remain beside Lily Mae in the immediate aftermath, made her way towards the door. When she opened it, though, she was startled to almost plough into a body standing on the threshold, arm raised to knock even as Stella flung the door open. Both stepped back, away from each other, and that instant was all it took for Stella to recognize the new arrival—the midwife, Nellie Trent, her hair scraped back in an untidy hit-or-miss ponytail, her eyes tired.

"I got your message," Nellie said. "I came as soon as I could."

"She had the baby," Stella said, stepping aside. "It wasn't a long labor, as far as I know, particularly for a first child—but she's wiped out, and we still don't know if there was any... real damage done. Thanks for coming." She glanced back, to where Joe had become aware of the presence at the door and had turned to look. "Speak to Joe. He did all the necessary. He's the hero."

"Excuse me," Nellie said, sidestepping past Stella into the room. "I'll just take a look at things. Where's the baby?"

"Joe bought an emergency crib for her—it's a cat bed, but eh. Until other arrangements can be made..." Nellie couldn't help a grin at that, and Stella gave her a tired smile in return. She hadn't had the baby but she was almost as exhausted as Lily Mae, her thoughts slow and barely stirring. "She's got the baby with her in bed right now—we wrapped her in a towel like a burrito."

Nellie reached out with one hand to give Stella's arm a quick squeeze. "It looks like you all pitched in," the midwife said. "I'm just here to mop up. Well done. Now let me take a look at the both of them."

They slipped past one another, Nellie into the room and Stella outside. She paused as she closed the door behind her, raking the parking lot with her eyes, but could not see Philip anywhere. Stepping away from the cabin onto the path, she strode to the edge of the tarmac and along the length of their van.

Philip stepped out from the other side of the van unexpectedly, into the path of the light spilling from a parking lot lamp-post, and even though she had been looking for him, hoping to see him, expecting to find him nearby, Stella still jumped as he came to stand beside her, his hands stuffed into the pockets of his sweatpants.

"Are you all right?" she asked, after a moment of silence, only lifting her eyes to his face as she spoke.

She was surprised to find him smiling—just the faintest shadow of a smile, to be sure, but the corners of his mouth were curved upwards, and his eyes looked serene in the shaft of light that fell across his face.

"Yes," he said. "I think I am. I really think I am going to be all right."

"So you and God are on speaking terms again?" Stella asked, and regretted the levity as soon as the words left her mouth. She flushed, dropping her eyes, and then lifting her gaze again in surprise as she heard him chuckle.

"You don't believe in God," he reminded her.

"I believe in *you*," Stella said. "And it hurt to watch you hurt."

"I know. I'm sorry. But if you 'believe in me'... then you have to believe in God, too, Stella, even just a little, because God is the reason for me. And it's okay. Really. God may have put me on hold for a while because I had too many questions—at least until I could sort it all out in my head and distil down just what I wanted to ask into something that could be answered—but I think we're talking again."

"You... you're so *serious* about it all," Stella said. "And yet you can poke fun at it too."

"I don't poke fun at it but if you don't have a sense of humor about the business of living you might as well close up shop completely. And God is far from not being able to laugh, no matter what some people will tell you." His lips stayed curved into the smile, but his eyes sharpened into an edge of solemnity again. "And trust me. I had to go through the thorn thickets in the vale of sorrows before I could come scrambling out on this side. But that child..."

"She asked. She wanted you to see. She wanted you to be there. The child. The... Illogon. *Jerusha*. She told me to call you—to make sure—"

"I heard," Philip said softly. "And I nearly... so nearly... turned and ran. And then I held her, naked and newborn, and I looked into those eyes. And I understood."

"Tell me," Stella said.

"I don't know if I can," Philip said. "But let me just say—what stabbed me to the heart of my faith was the sudden mapping of what was happening to us—to all of us right now—to the holy mysteries of the birth of the man my deepest beliefs hold to be Christ, the Son of God, the Savior. And if I could suddenly dismember that story—if all it ever was, in scripture, in literature, in faith—if all that story meant was no more than an accident, a desperate act of survival by an entity from beyond this world, a creature not human but never divine—if I could not believe in the crux of my belief—I did not know what that made me, any more. But then I looked into that child's eyes, in there, and somehow... God was in there. God was still in there. This child doesn't have to mean that everything before it is erased. It may mean confirmation. It may mean an enrichment. I am still a long way from processing all of it, but then, the baby has been born into human form and I have a few years before I need to face any real questions about her identity."

"Even Jesus was thirty when he was supposed to have performed his first miracle," Stella said, "wasn't he? If miracles are in Jerusha's future you're going to be an old man by that time..."

"Well, Jesus called his Father by name long before that," Philip said equably, "being only twelve when He got lost in the Temple and expressed his confusion about why anyone would be surprised to find him in His Father's house. But I actually found myself remembering a quite different part of the Scriptures, when I looked into Jerusha's eyes. Old Testament, not New. Leviticus, nineteen, thirty three to thirty five. 'When an alien resides with you in your land, you shall not oppress the alien. The alien shall be to you as the citizen among you; you shall love the alien as yourself, for you were aliens in the land of Egypt'. And oh boy, is this an alien. A real, true, honest-to-God, if I may be permitted the expression, alien. And Stella... if she *never* does a miracle, that's all right. She is mine to hold and to care for and to protect. That much, I took on as soon as I stood with you for them, for the *Parada* crew, as soon as I began to work towards understanding them and all the pain they brought back from those stars. This moment is the culmination of all that. Whether or not this can be described as a Second Coming, in any way whatever, my first priority as a man of God, a man who serves that God in whom I still completely believe, is to protect and shelter and, well, love this alien amongst us. Because few would, or could, or would dare, if they knew the truth."

"We need to find a safe place," Stella said. "A sanctuary. A place where we can keep her out of sight, and out of mind, and away from scrutiny and attention. Because, Philip, if you and I ever agreed on what would be done to the *Parada* people if anyone learned the truth... that goes for Jerusha, an order of magnitude greater. If they got their hands on that child..."

"I have to tell them, Stella," Philip said, inexorably.

She flinched, as though he'd poured cold water on her. "Tell whom? *Why*?"

"I need to tell the Church," Philip said.

She roused. "You can't," she said. "You *can't*. Do you remember what you told me, back at the habitat? You were eloquent on the matter, I remember your face when you thought I might tell Martin about the presence of the alien, and now, now you want to..."

"That was when it was just a matter of announcing the presence of an alien entity. And all of that still stands. But we're beyond that, now. It isn't *just* a matter of the existence of an alien amongst us. It's what that alien has become, what it could possibly mean..." He lifted his hands in a helpless gesture.

"Stella, Stella, look at the way it hit me. I have to warn them. It may come the same way to others, in time, and I can't let this come completely unawares, I cannot let it shatter everything that I have ever believed or worked for or stood for. I am a priest, and more than that, I am a Jesuit, whose guiding light has always been a pursuit of knowledge. This cuts across both, knowledge and faith, and I don't know if I may continue to call myself a member of the Society of Jesus if my central message concerns casting doubt on the very Gospels that give us His life and story, but I will *always* be a priest. That was a calling. It never went away. The voice of God still speaks to my soul. But the Church... the Church has to know about her existence."

"But you said we should not tell *anyone* about the Illogon," Stella reiterated. "You said—you *agreed*—"

"I will tell them nothing specific," Philip said. "Not who she is, where she is, what name she goes by—not yet, anyway. But I will tell them that a woman whose name means Star guided me to another woman whose belly was full with child not born of human seed, and how three men—whom you may or may not call completely wise— were there to witness the birth of that child. It is all too close, too much, and the Church has to know of it. I can tell you now what the response will be, though."

"What?" Stella said. "Philip, they have just as much power as Martin and his crew—to find her, to destroy her before she can live to destroy them. It's so dangerous..."

"I will write the letters," Philip said. "To the Holy Father, and to my own Father General. I will be regretfully asking to be absolved of my vows to the Society of Jesus. They may or may not take action concerning my status as a priest. Because I won't tell them everything, and I will not make myself available to be questioned more closely—I am sounding a warning, that is all. Giving them a heads-up that things may be coming with which they might need to find ways to cope, in the fullness of time. But my work... is with her now. I will stay by her, watch her, guide her. Educate her about our world, and educate our world about her, if that becomes necessary."

"The Gospel according to St Philip?" Stella queried.

"They'll hardly offer me sainthood," Philip said, grinning. "I might as well tell you that I don't expect them to do anything. The moment they try to, they make the whole thing play out in the public eye. And there are certain sacred mysteries that the Church has always preferred to keep to itself. Once the ponderous wheels have been set into motion, it is going to take a great deal of power to grind it all to a halt—and that is why I suspect that the response to my letters will only be a grim silence. A hoping that it will all go away. That is not to say that—quietly, without fuss—they might not send people to seek me, and through me, her. Those people may or may not have their... orders... to solve the problem in ways that might make things easier for the Church to handle, but that is something that I will have to deal with if and when I meet it. In the meantime, I think... I am at a true crossroads of faith, here. I know one road leads into darkness, and I have already turned from that. Another would take me back to where I have come from, but I can't ever go home again, not in that way. That leaves... a strange road to follow. One that leads into a different country, under the light of a different sun. It will be a test of my faith to travel that road, but I think, at the end, that the faith I carry is big enough to take it. And in the name of that God I swear that I believe in... it is as I have said. My place is beside her now. Whatever comes."

"I suspect mine is too," Stella said. "It isn't as though I have a life or a career to go back to. I burned a lot of bridges behind me. And Rob..." She roused, suddenly, her eyes flying back to search his. "Do you still consider yourself priest enough to perform holy sacraments?"

"Yes," Philip said, taken aback at the sudden intensity of her voice. "I mean, I could baptize that child, but in whose name..." He stopped, tilted his head at her. "Oh," he said. "I see. Well... that could be arranged. When, my child, would you like the wedding?"

She lowered her head to hide her sudden blush, and gave him a small, fake-outraged smack on his shoulder. "He only just *asked* me," she said, with an edge of asperity. "And yes—there's the link—he isn't going to leave Lily Mae, not now. And Rob and I... make a good team."

"Yes," Philip agreed equably. "You do. Which just leaves Joe. Our third Wise Man. What do you think he is going to do now?"

"Well..." Stella's eyes slid back up the path, back towards the door of the cabin. "Why don't we go back in, and find out?"

Philip held the door open for Stella as she slipped back into the cabin. Nellie, standing with Rob in the middle of the room just in front of the sofa, glanced around and smiled at them.

"There is some damage," she told Stella, "but on the whole your friend is doing better than, frankly, I would have predicted that she would. The baby is beautiful. I have seen those amber eyes in a newborn so very rarely, it's a very unusual thing, but they are heart-stopping, aren't they?"

"Indeed," Philip agreed.

"I have suggested another day's bed rest," Nellie said "Your other friend, the doctor, he just slipped out to the office to make sure that the reservation is extended for another night—it shouldn't be a problem, it isn't exactly high season, and I'll stop by on my way out and give my aunt a good report on you all." She looked over at the bed where Lily Mae's head was bent over the swaddled baby in the crook of her arm. "I've given her a little something to help her sleep—your friend put the kettle on just as he left, so give her a nice warm cup of tea and that and a good night's rest will probably do wonders. I stayed to help you put together some formula for the baby for later."

"Thank you," Stella said. "You're very kind."

"Not at all," Nellie said affably.

Stella busied herself in the kitchenette until Joe returned, only a few minutes later, announcing that there was room at the inn for one more night. Nellie looked up, rather startled at the amount of mirth that that innocuous statement seemed to generate in the room, but didn't comment on it. She stayed for another half hour or so, dispensing assistance and advice with various imminently impending tasks with the newborn, and then took her leave. Joe made the tea— "So someone did boil the water," Stella said, feeling quite giddy all of a sudden, as though the air she breathed was champagne—and they all sat down wherever they happened to receive their mug, on whatever surface was closest.

"Well," Joe said, his hands wrapped around his own teacup, "we do not have to do it all right now, but we need to figure out our next move. We have tomorrow, here, but after that... we are going. Somewhere. You did not scour the planet for that one, Stella, to leave things to chance now."

"No," Stella agreed.

"I want to make an offer," Joe said. "Do you remember what I told you of my childhood and upbringing?"

"Some," Stella said. "What are you thinking of?"

"My maternal grandparents more or less disowned me, at a certain point, and we did not speak for a number of years. But apparently their wills were made long before that and they never changed them. When they both died—my grandfather only about three years ago now—I was informed that somehow I had inherited their residence. You might have thought, given the relationship—or more accurately the non-relationship—we had, that I would have immediately taken steps to sell the place and thereby rid myself of any lingering links to those people who had never really given me any indication that they had cared what became of me after I repudiated their vision of

my life. But I did not do so, and since the house has been in my name
it has been rented out—and that rent has gone straight into a fund
which I had established as a charitable foundation to provide financial
assistance to my own people. That now changes. I have a roof that
is mine to offer, and while my tenant has a current lease that has a
ninety-day termination clause, I would like to propose that I invoke
this, and when the house becomes available it is a place where Lily
Mae and the child can reside in safety and some comfort. Until this
becomes the case, we can find them a temporary place of refuge—for
a little while they can stay with Amelia, in Chicago, I know she would
welcome them, and after that, until the house is free and available, I
will make room in my own house."

"That is... generous, Joe," Stella said, taken aback.

"Gold, frankincense and myrrh," Philip said quietly.

"What was that?" Joe said, turning.

Philip looked up. "It all just plays to script," he said, "or scripture,
if you will. We had that baby, the baby that was a miracle, and then we
have us—the three men—the three wise men. And now one of them
comes bearing gifts."

"All right," Joe said, with a sudden smile, "so let us do this properly."
He stood up and retrieved his keychain, which had a number of
jangling keys on it, and finally teased out one and took it out of the
key ring. He brought it back to where everyone was sitting, watching
him curiously, and laid the key on the table in the middle of the room.
"Call it gold, if you like," he said. "I lay it down, as my gift. If you do
not want to speak of what we bring, then let us speak of what we come
to take away. I come with a promise to take away need. I offer food
and a roof over the baby's head, for as long as required, for as long as
I am able. The mother and the child shall not go hungry or go cold."

Rob got up and fumbled in his pocket, coming up with a small
folding multi-purpose tool pack. He tweaked out a small pocket knife
and laid it down beside the key.

"My turn," he said. "Lord, this looks terribly bloodthirsty, pulling
a knife, such as it is, but let's just call it symbolic, if you like. I will
pledge to take away fear—I will protect that woman and that child

with all I have got, even if it is just that little knife there. I offer safety and a shield against harm to the best of my ability, yes, even in this strange new world in which I have yet to find a place where I truly belong. God knows that Lily Mae and I are the closest thing to family that either of us has out here right now, and it is as family that I will stand with her and with her child, and for them. I was, after all, brought forth to help find them, when they were lost, and it is not something easily done by anyone else. And more than that... I know I can't *offer* this—she isn't mine to offer up—but I can hope that she will stand with me here. Stella, Lily Mae and that baby are my family, but you are my heart—and you have been our guardian angel ever since you met us, anyway. Will you stay with me—with us all?"

Stella slipped her hand into his, and smiled.

"Well," Joe said complacently, "not before time."

"Stella told me, just now, outside," Philip said, smiling. "I suppose congratulations are in order About that—we need to talk—but first— my turn." He looked around for something to serve as a symbol for his own offering, and finally reached up and took the small polished obsidian cross that he always wore from around his neck, bringing it down on the table next to the other objects.

"All right," he said. "In the name of that faith which I hold, which I have always held, and in the name of knowledge, I pledge to take away ignorance. I will stay with that child for as long as she needs me, I will teach her about the world, and in time I may be the one who is able to teach the world about her. I bring light, and enlightenment. I will do my best to..."

"Hey," said an unexpected voice, from the corner bed where Lily Mae and the baby were lying. It was Lily Mae's voice, but it had an edge to it that was pure Diana. " 'S *my* damn baby."

"It's your baby, but I suspect she will turn out to be the world's child," Philip said. "But indeed. She is yours to claim, and to love, and to cherish. We—all of us—all we can do is offer to help you. When you've been to the stars and back, in our name, the least we can do is make sure that you don't stand alone when you come home. And we have more than enough room to make an alien welcome among us.

There is even scripture to support it, but there's time enough to quote that at you when you want to hear it."

"Philip," Stella said, "do it now."

"Do what now?" Philip said, mystified, turning to her.

"In a day or two or six you are going to start sniffing around the edges of what you officially still are—but for tonight, for right now, you're still a priest who is ordained to perform a marriage, aren't you? Joe—Lily Mae—you can be our witnesses. And Rob did just kind of ask me in public, in front of everyone—well—I accept. I am not wise or a man but I'll add myself to that pile on the table. Can you marry us, Philip? Now?"

"We have no props," Rob said, laughing. "I don't even have a ring to put on your finger."

Joe slipped a silver and turquoise ring from his little finger and held it out. "It may be the wrong size and altogether the wrong ring, but on a night where everything else is a symbol this may serve as another, if you wish to accept it in that context."

Rob held Joe's eyes for a long moment, and then reached out and took the ring, with a small nod of respect and appreciation.

"Well, get on with it," Lily Mae said. "I don't know about the rest of you but I just had a *baby*. I'd like to get a bit of shut-eye if I can. So I'll stay awake long enough to witness Rob and the good doctor get hitched but then I want some peace and quiet. Jerusha and I... have had quite a day."

"Well," Philip said, "it *will* be a new world in the morning. All right. Gather round... does this place at least have a *candle*?"

Incongruously, it did—a plain white candle tucked away in the back of a kitchen drawer. Lit, it gave the plain little cabin a quiet glow— or maybe it was just the way that Stella suddenly saw it through eyes that she could not quite keep clear, blurring constantly with a well of tears. She stood for an unlooked-for wedding to a man she had known of as a legend all of her life but had barely had a chance to really get to know as a living breathing human being and she knew that some part of her should have been seriously alarmed at the proceedings but she could not bring herself to take that part of her seriously. This all seemed to have been arranged for her a very long time ago and she had just taken her time to arrive at a time and place when it was turning into a reality. Even Joe's ring, somehow, fit when Rob slipped it on her ring finger. It was all quite, quite preposterous; if she were to tell the story of the last couple of months of her life, she would have been hard pressed herself to believe all that had come to pass. And yet.

Here she stood, with two people from her history and her past, and a child who was a twist of the unknown taking them all into an only barely-glimpsed future, and not one but two deeply spiritual men who stood as bridges between history, dream, and the mysteries of the human soul. It was something that even Rob's Poet persona would have been hard pressed to wrap in words, and it kept escaping Stella, like bits of bright light that would dart off if she tried to look at them too closely. She could not begin to understand how or even why she felt happy, but she did—and the feeling stayed, long after the candle guttered, and Lily Mae and the baby named Jerusha fell asleep (the woman in the bed, and the baby in the cat's-cradle makeshift baby bed beside her), and Philip and Joe retired to the second bedroom, and Stella herself lay, wide awake and banked like a live ember, wrapped in Rob's arms in the narrow little bed by the window.

"You know," Rob said suddenly, apropos of nothing, as though he were picking up a conversation they had left off in the middle at some point in the recent past, "there are times that you are disconcertingly aware of what is inside my head at any given moment. Even when I am someone else than myself entirely. But it is very difficult to figure out what you are thinking. You use silence as a shadow and a shield."

"You mean right now?" Stella whispered, with a small smile. "I'm sorry, if you think the drawbridges are up. I didn't mean to raise them."

"I know. But what *are* you thinking?"

"About what you have lost."

He roused. "About what I have *lost*?"

"It doesn't seem likely that we will set our eyes again on the last three of your crew that they still hold in the habitat," Stella said. "And once you were willing to give up the stars themselves if you did not have your brother beside you amongst them. And now..."

"I carry him," Rob said, and tapped himself on the chest, and on the temple. "Here, and here. We both knew what the possible price would be when I came out with you, after Lily Mae. We both agreed to it. We said the *au revoirs* there in the habitat."

"More of an *adieu*," Stella said. "The other sounds like you planned to..."

She could have kicked herself. This was hardly the moment to point out the permanence of what Rob had done.

He didn't respond, not directly, but a small sigh did escape him at her words. "I won't say that it didn't—or even that it doesn't—hurt to feel that separation," he said. "But neither of us is alone right now. He has those companions with whom he has endured so much, with whom he shares so much that can never be told to anyone outside that circle. And I... look at what I have."

"Me," Stella said. "Only me. It doesn't seem like an equivalent..."

He laughed, softly, in the dark. "Dear heart," he said, "you could never be an *equivalent* to anything. But you are a treasure in yourself. And Lily Mae is here, for me to be able to fulfil all the things that I need to be for her, as part of that crew. And then there are the friends in the other room, unlooked for, people I am still not entirely certain I deserve. I am a starship navigator by trade, Stella, and Philip called you our guiding star—the second star, maybe, for him, for his own purposes and his own story. But I am quite happy with the journey on which your particular star has led me, and while we may never again have a quite completely safe berth in a quite completely safe harbor, or any specific or closely planned-for destination, I am content with the voyage of the ship I have been given to guide. Are you?"

"He said he was going to tell the Church about it," Stella said, a complete non sequitur that took Rob by surprise.

"The Church? About what?"

"About Jerusha. About his wrestling with what she means. He says the Church needs to know."

"Maybe they do," Rob said after a beat. "He knows them better than..."

"We made a deal," Stella said, "not to tell anyone about you. About

Illogon. Never mind about Jerusha and what it all came to be. We still can't—I think we still can't—if anyone on Martin Peck's crew knew the truth. If Philip is going to write to the Church and tell them everything, I should write to Martin and tell him nothing. Just tell him that we found Lily Mae. That we are all out here. That none of us is coming back."

"He knows," Rob said. "But write, if that will give you the kind of closure you need to have. As for Father Philip and the Church—that's complicated. But I think you know that he would never put that child in danger. If he wrote to someone in the hierarchy about all of this... it will be to build a wall around her, until she is ready."

"Ready for what?"

"Maybe nothing," Rob said, smoothing her hair away from her forehead. "Maybe things none of us are prepared for on this night. Stella, I ask you if you are happy and you start talking about conspiracies and the big picture. You aren't there, not yet. You're here, now, tonight. Are you..."

She curled up against him, closing her eyes.

"Best kind of voyage," she murmured against his chest. "The night behind, and only dawn and a horizon ahead. And I trust the navigator."

"Then," Rob said, "the stars are waiting."

~*~

To His Holiness, Pope Constantine II
Most Holy Father,

I write to you from a place both difficult and exalted, and I barely know where to begin—this is, of course, a very personal account on behalf of a single soul of which you have the titular care but I believe, should this story become more widely known as there is every possibility that it may do in time, many more people who share my faith will be in a position to wrestle with the same questions which have troubled my own thoughts and prayers.

If I begin by reminding you of the basic premise of our doctrine and our faith, please forgive me for expounding on the obvious—but the Christian faith began with the birth of the Christ Child, fathered by God upon a virgin unspoiled maid whom no mortal man's hand had touched. A birth prophesied before it came to pass, a birth to which a star shining above Bethlehem's manger led the worshipping shepherds, and the three wise men of legend. The divine Child then grew to manhood and was given the power, by His Father, to perform the miracles that proclaimed Him as who he was, the Son of God, come to Earth to speak for the sinners who dwelled upon it and to save their souls for God.

Recent circumstances to which I have been personal witness have shaken my complete unsullied faith in that story, as it has been always told, to its foundations. Because I am here to tell you this: that three men (of whom I am one), who may or may not be reckoned 'wise' in the manner of those Kings of old, were nevertheless led—by a dedicated and passionate woman whose given name literally means "star"—to a young woman carrying a child through no mortal agency, a child that carries a spirit that is known to me to not originate on this world. You may dismiss all of this as complete coincidence but I will also say that the spirit in the child of whom I speak of here has communicated that this is not the first time that one of its kind has visited the Earth, and that the first visit ended in a particular kind of catastrophe which caused that original visitor to snatch at survival in the only way open to it at the time—that of entering a newborn child. When I heard that the first visit occurred almost exactly at the time when the story of the Christ Child is said to have taken place, the coincidences became too much to be accidental.

Most Holy Father, if the Church gives credence to prophecies concerning the Christ's birth, there are also the prophecies invoking his Second Coming, to finally deliver this world from its iniquities. It might be possible to account for these new circumstances of which I speak by invoking those prophecies—if the babe, who is now four weeks old—lives to the age at which Jesus of Nazareth began the ministry on which our faith is built, and finds itself possessed of similar gifts. If so, then maybe it might behoove the Church to prepare for such an eventuality. If the babe does not do so, or if the Church chooses to dismiss everything as no more than the coincidence that it might wish things to be, then of course nothing changes—but I believe, fully and completely, knowing all the circumstances that underlie this birth, that this child might shake the ground that the Church stands on, the ground that has been firm and steady for thousands of years. I believe in this so strongly that I will be writing to the Superior General of my order, the Society of Jesus, to request dispensation from my vows—I intend to renounce all that stands in the way of what I now perceive to be my duty, and that is to remain close to this child, to shelter and protect it until it reaches the age and maturity to take over that responsibility, and thereafter to provide such aid and advice as I am able in the light of the role which I believe this child may be called upon to play in the fullness of time.

I fully realize that I am not giving you all the details necessary to corroborate my report—but you already know all about the Parada and her crew, and you can build from that. With respect, I will not be doing anything to make identifying particular actors in this drama any easier, or helping to locate them. The new identity of the mother and child I will keep hidden— because while my faith has been the guiding light of my life and my allegiance to my Church has been absolute I am also not completely unaware of the times that the Church has taken the necessary steps to remove that which it perceived as a threat to its existence—and this child might prove to be a threat to the existence of the Church as we know it today. It may be that the Church will need to adapt and change because of this event. But I will not sully my own soul nor throw temptation into the path of the Church's own great power and pride by offering up this innocent as a sacrificial lamb, at least not unless or until more coincidences start playing out and the child, when grown, is subjected to the same judgment as that which our Christ once faced. But I will not hand the babe unto Herod, or unto the Pharisees; I have no doubt that the Church, if it cares to delve that deeply and that hard, might well discover this information for themselves, but my allegiance in this case would lie with the child and I would rise to stand against the Church I have loved and obeyed all my life in order to protect that child.

My life, my faith, and my immortal soul are laid down upon this altar.

I know that I cannot let the Church continue to exist in ignorance of what has happened, and what I believe it signifies, and I have done my part in dispelling that ignorance by means of this letter. I write to you in fulfillment of duty, and from a place in which I continue to believe I stand in the light and the glory of God. Whether you choose to disregard this missive completely and chalk it up to folly or error of a broken faith, or take it seriously enough to give it doctrinal consideration, that remains your own prerogative.

I remain, although I may be signing myself thus for perhaps the last time in an official capacity, faithfully yours,

Father Philip Carter, S.J., PhD.

(CC Father Lorenzo Garibaldi, S.J, Superior General of the Society of Jesus)

~*~

To: Father Lorenzo Garibaldi, S.J., Superior General of the Society of Jesus
Dear Father General,

I am enclosing a copy of the letter I have written to His Holiness Pope Constantine II in regard to the matter about which I write to you now.

Father Garibaldi, I am the fourth generation of my family who has embraced a vocation and a call of faith and has joined the clergy. In my great grandfather's generation one of the family's male progeny became a priest; in my grandfather's, a younger son of the family chose to join the Society of Jesus; in the generations that followed, including myself, that became the order to which those of us in our family who entered the service of the Church all chose to give our allegiance. The Society of Jesus has had a hand in my upbringing from a very early age—from the family connections to the order, through my education right until my postgraduate degrees which were entered upon in consultation with the order, and it has been a pillar of my existence, part of the altar upon which my faith has been laid, for as long as I remember. I have been proud to serve my order in any way in which it called upon me to do so, up to and including serving as one of your own under-secretaries for just under two years—at which time I was seconded to a Government project involving a top-secret clearance, as the priest sent at their request to be a part of the team to deal with the return of the starships sent out by this planet. I was uniquely qualified to take this position, as a Jesuit, as a man of faith and of science, possessed of a strong faith in my God and my Order and my Church and also of a solid secular education with my doctorate in psychology. I went where my superiors sent me, to serve where they believed my gifts to be best placed and most valuable in that service.

What I found in the place where I was sent began right from the outset to test the limits of both my own personal values and beliefs and those of the authorities I went there to serve and represent. I used my personal connections to remove myself from a place where I perceived myself to be in a position precarious to both my own physical self and the position of the Church—and then I found myself in a position that was even worse, because I had to choose between my absolute obedience to everything I had vowed to respect and obey, and a possible catastrophe which I could not bear to consider myself (or the Church I stood for) responsible for.

So I confess, here, that I used what power I had in the Church and in my Order to make certain the safety and indeed survival of individuals I believed to be in danger—perhaps in danger of their lives. I lay that at your feet, in penance. Some of this I have already laid at the feet of a confessor—but much of it was the product of wrestling with both my own fears, doubts and inadequacies, and with my strong convictions that I did what I did as the only thing I could have done in the name of that Christ and that God whom I came to lay my life at the feet of, and whose guidance I have always striven to follow in that life.

It has now become clear to me—for reasons which will become clear to you when you read the letter I have written to His Holiness the Pope—that my path diverges from the Society of Jesus at this point in my life, and I will be seeking formal dispensation from my vows. But that remains a formality, because as you will glean from the letter to His Holiness I fully intend to pursue a course of action which will not be subject to any further orders, requests, or suggestions from any source considered to be doctrinally 'official' in the hierarchy of the Church. I have come to a moment where the only thing I feel I am able to listen to, and follow the guidance of, is the conversation that is taking place between my own immortal soul and my God...

Philip stopped writing, his pen poised above the paper mid-thought, his eyes suddenly and inexplicably full of tears. He stared at the letter he was in the middle of writing as though he had never seen it before. He recognized the words. He recognized the thoughts. He would not have taken a word of it back. And yet...

He put the pen down and pushed his chair back, just far enough from the desk to lift his hands away and lay them palm-down on his thighs. He still wore a cassock—out of habit and out of comfort—although the letters he was in the process of writing were more or less his letters of resignation after which he would probably no longer feel completely entitled to do so. But right now, his right hand still remembering that the last thing it had done was to write down the word 'God', it felt as though touching the cloth of the cassock was an answer to a prayer he had not been aware he had even been thinking about making.

He stared at the letter which he had just been writing, and found his mind curiously blank. He remembered having talked about doing this with Stella, back in the Fall, in the dark empty parking lot sheened with October damp, in the immediate aftermath of Jerusha's birth; it was early March now, and it had taken him this long to bend his will to the task. Stella had not pressed him about it in the interim, but she had made no secret about being against the idea right from the outset. Philip understood that, and yet he had felt driven to write the letters anyway; but now, finally in the process of obeying that urge, he found himself unable to pin down exactly the instinct that had made him do it. It wasn't that he had changed his mind and had come to agree with Stella—it wasn't as coherent as that. It was just an edge of something that he could not quite identify, and he hesitated. The world was still not completely firm under his feet. This had seemed like the right thing to do. How was he to know? How was he to trust any instinct at all?

His hands spasmed into fists against his legs, and then he relaxed them again with a deep sigh, bowing his head, closing his eyes, as though in prayer. When he looked up again, it was to meet Joseph White Elk's understanding dark eyes.

"Are those the letters for your superiors?" Joe asked.

Philip's head jerked up sharply. "Stella told you?"

"Just that you thought you needed to do this. Not why. Although I can probably fill in the blanks." He paused. "This thing of which you wish to speak to the people you are writing to... what is it that you think it is going to make them believe, or do? If you tell them too little... they may itch to find out more. If you tell them too much... it will be very easy for them to find you, then. And through you, *her*. The child. And I do not think that you wish them to do that."

Philip grimaced. "I have thought about it. It's just that I think God should know—that I feel compelled to make sure that those who speak for Him here on this world..."

"Nobody speaks for God but you," Joe said calmly. "You and I, my friend, I think we are fundamentally alike in one important aspect. We both believe in that Something that is greater than ourselves. Where we diverge is that you put human intermediaries between you and the holy thing that you carry, and you somehow see them as being closer to your God than you are. But how can that be? God— or that great Spirit in whom I believe, who holds the world in his hand—that being, that mind, that soul, he already knows all that can be known. And you have used a word that speaks to me of how you are seeing this. You say you were *compelled*. What compels you?"

"I swore a vow, once," Philip said. "Amongst other things, a vow of obedience."

"The vow that made you a priest."

"Yes."

"But," Joe asked, his eyes soft despite the weight of his words, "are you still that priest?"

"*Sacerdos in aeternum*," Philip said. "A priest forever. One does not shrug that off."

"In a bigger sense," Joe said, "yes. But in the specifics—a Jesuit? A Catholic? Do you still hold the beliefs that took you to those particular altars?"

Philip knotted his fingers together. "I don't know how to answer that," he said.

"I see us both as men of faith," Joe said, after a pause. "With me, the faith is the deep pool—the water itself is a holy thing, and there are other things, even holier, that lie hidden underneath, things that the water protects and conceals. And all the while the surface acts as mirror and reflects away anything that would be a danger, while at the same time showing nothing but the truth to any who gaze upon it seeking answers. You carry your own faith inside you, here, and here..." Joe touched his heart, and his temple. Then he crossed his arms across his chest, his gaze steady upon Philip. "If my faith is water, yours is fire. The fire that purifies. But fire is a bad enemy, if it is allowed to scour away everything in its path. And it is my fear that a letter like the ones you have written... landing before the wrong man, at the wrong moment... might unleash that fire. Against yourself, and against the things you have, I think, made another vow to yourself about—a vow to protect, and defend, and love. And if you do unleash it, then you will have to answer—if to nobody else but your own soul—for the ashes that will be all that remains."

"You make the Church sound like the wrath of God," Philip said.

"For some," Joe said, "that's exactly what it ever was. Or the only thing that it ever could be. Your Church was ever jealous of her privilege, and her place, and her pride. It has not flinched from sweeping aside things that stood in her way. And..."

"And what?" Philip asked. "You think they would come and get her? Jerusha? That they would sweep her aside?"

"I saw what knowledge of this matter did to you," Joe said. "I can imagine what it would do to people like you—but with greater power. People who might react in fear or in anger."

"These were the people who sent me in, Joe. Without their word I would never have known the *Parada* existed."

"Yes, and then you learned about it," Joe said. "And now you understand far more about it than they ever could."

"Then it is my duty to tell them..."

Joe looked at him in silence, with deep sympathy, for a moment, and then shook his head slightly.

"I cannot tell you what is right for you to do," he said, "that is a decision that only you can make. But let me just say this. You were compelled, you say. Well, you have obeyed. The letters are written. Honor, and duty, and obedience, and that part of your faith which is rooted in our own mortal world, all are satisfied. What you do with those letters now, that is a different thing altogether."

Philip dropped his eyes onto the two letters on the desk, and finally nodded after a long moment.

"Yes. Thank you. I believe I understand now."

Joe reached out and briefly laid a hand on Philip's shoulder. "Walk in peace," he said, "my brother."

Alone again, Philip stared at the letter he had been writing when Joe had come in. He re-read the last paragraph he had set down, and then, slowly, picked up the pen again and continued to write.

Father Garibaldi, I have spoken to you many times both as a superior and as, I hold, my friend. I know that what I speak of is difficult to hear, as it is difficult for me to say. All I can say is that I strongly believe that I am in a place where no man has stood since possibly the first disciples that flocked to the feet of our Lord. It may be that I am wrong, and that nothing at all will come of any of this. It may be that I will be in a position to shine a light on a brand new chapter of our faith. This may mean a number of hard choices and sacrifices the value of which I cannot begin to tell you about. But to do otherwise, at this moment, is impossible to contemplate. There is enough uncertainty in all of this for me to be able to tell you with complete honesty that I have no idea if at some point in the future I won't look back on this time with a sense of the most profound regret—that may still happen. I accept that as a possible consequence of my decision. Life is often built, or broken, on such regrets. But right now, it is impossible for me to do other than as I do. Believe me, I have thought on this long and hard, and I have prayed on it, and I am doing what I have no choice but to believe that I hear God asking me to do. I hope, at some future time, to be in touch again with you or with the one who may be in your place at such a moment—with further news, with a piece of certainty, with a sense of vindication (or perhaps even with that regret). I will certainly be keeping such notes on it as I have been taught by my order to do—even while requesting dispensation from my allegiance to the Society of Jesus, I remain trained by Jesuit rules and Jesuit minds and I cleave to the rigidity of scientific inquiry that has been so much a part of that legacy.

I wish both you and my order well as I embark on this daunting new path, alone.

But it is alone that I must continue. At least for now.

As with the Holy Father, I sign myself—perhaps for the last time in an official capacity,
   Father Philip Carter, S.J, PhD

Philip put down the pen, and rubbed his chin in a thoughtful gesture.

The two letters he had written lay on the desk, two innocent sheets of paper bearing his signature and the weight of the world.

He swept the two pages off the table and crossed over to the half-open window, the letters held loosely in his left hand; he gazed outside, barely registering the things he saw—until movement made him focus his attention on the path leading from the front door. Stella, seeing him at the window, lifted a hand which held her car keys.

"Just popping down to grab a couple of things—we're out of milk—do you need anything?" she called out.

Philip hesitated, for the longest time, and then the hand which held the letters folded the papers in half, below the windowsill, out of sight of anyone watching from outside. He shook his head at Stella, smiling a little.

"No," he called back. "I'm good."

He watched Stella walk out to the car, no longer looking in his direction, and he glanced down at his hand and what it still held. In a movement that was slow, thoughtful, decisive, he finished folding the letters in half and then in half again and tucked them away into his pocket. From somewhere in the house came the sound of a child laughing, and Philip turned away from the window, seeking the source. Everything might change, in the pale light of ancient stars, but faith remained. There would be something to believe in. And that was enough.

Dear Martin,

I feel like I pulled a fairly crappy double-cross on you. In fact, I know I did. But let me recap just a bit.

You (the rhetorical you, your superiors) let the Juno people go. That was good. It was necessary. It was the right thing to do. There were no reasons whatsoever to hold them. I stood for that long before I knew the full story, which was that...

...there were very real differences between the two crews. I wish I could tell you everything, all that I learned, but I can't, Martin, I can't. If you knew all that I know it would be obvious to you why I did the things I did. As it stands, I can only say that there was one thing—one big, huge, enormous thing—that hit the Parada crew while they were out there which never happened to the Juno three. That alone means that releasing the Juno crew was the only thing that could have been done. It also means that the Parada people remain—will always remain—afflicted with this. Now I'm going to go all professional on you.

But before I do that, let me just say one thing. I am safe. Rob Hillerman is safe. We have found Lily Mae Washington, and she is safe, for certain values of that word. I'm sorry, that's all I can give you. But about those two.

Yes, they were full participants in the Parada syndrome and when they left your enclosure they took ALL their other selves with them. But in my travels with Rob, and in some extremely trying circumstances with Lily Mae, my considered professional opinion is this.

They will ALWAYS carry those other 'souls' within them. They will always have them, be bothered by them, may be taken over by them in specific circumstances. But with the empirical data I now have in hand, with the two of them out here in the 'real' world, as it were, I can tell you this much. This can be handled. Rob in particular has been practically stable as Rob Hillerman, the original Rob Hillerman, for a while now. Yes, I still see his other bits and pieces as they manifest themselves now and then—but the point is that he is able to control them. Lily Mae was in fact able to do so in a situation where even a perfectly normal single-personality mind might have lost it completely. But she didn't. She did not. What I am trying to tell you is this—you (rhetorical you) would never have considered releasing these people into the world from your locked-away little habitat because you consider them loose cannons, because you are afraid of what they can, what they still might, do. Well, you were wrong. They can exist out here. They are contained. They are, in both senses of that word, safe—they are safe from you, now, and they are demonstrably safe (i.e. not a threat) to other people.

So can you try and let them live? As for the rest of them—

—you still have three of them in your custody. Again, considered professional opinion (and in at least one case bolstered by privileged information, particularly from Rob on his brother) but they may NOT be as 'safe' as the others are. Jerry is simply a selfish personality, and will use what he has to obtain what he wants and if in an outside environment that involved resorting to a different 'personality' in order to shrug off responsibility he might be tempted to do exactly that. Rob loves him and misses him fiercely sometimes, but even he feels as though it might be a long road back into society for Jerry. Han is too unstable, from what I saw while I was working with the crew. It might be surprising for a man who was once in sufficient control to be considered qualified for a command position, but he has somehow lost control of his internal crew. From what I observed of him, he simply doesn't seem able to hold on to a coherent personality for long enough for it to be impactful—or, possibly, he holds onto it longer than he needs to, with disastrous consequences. Alaya is too vulnerable—there are one or two of her personalities whom I might trust, if they took over as primaries, to support her through the tough thickets of an ordinary everyday existence, but they are NOT her primaries and what IS her primary personality seems to be too shattered to hold it all together permanently. So even though it kills me to say that you might be right—there may be a case for those three to be kept sequestered somehow. But Martin—this is important—unless you want to lose them all to permanent insanity, do not lock them away by themselves in solitary. That group—especially now, diminished as they are—is something of a new thing—they're more of a symbiont entity now. They all help support each other's existence. I think separating them from one another would lead to a deepening and much more irreversible mental dysfunction. They may be alone, but they are alone together.

I know you must be angry at me. But I could not stay. And I could not leave on any terms that you needed to dictate. Believe it or not, though, when I first set out to seek Lily Mae—with Rob in tow—I really did only have it in my mind to find her first, to get to her before some of your more trigger happy lunatics (sorry, but some of them are) decided that she might be more of a danger on the loose than was outweighed by the benefits of her continued existence. One very easy way of solving the thorny problem that she left for you by escaping was simply to give orders to shoot on sight. I knew things about her that I cannot possibly tell you. All that I CAN tell you is that it would have been terrible and terrifying if that scenario I posit above had been allowed to come to pass. I might have considered—considered, I say, I don't intimate that I would have gone and done so—bringing her back, if I had found her and ensured her safety—but then you quartered those two guards on me and Rob when we left to look for her and—well—sorry, but once I ditched them, and I had to ditch them, it all became a different ball game. And then things got complicated. And then I got help. And here I am now, writing to you just to tell you. I'm safe. And in some respects, I really am sorry. Because I know I must have loused up your own situation possibly permanently by my actions. I never meant to do so. You have to believe that. I think that we both knew—there was a moment—we could have possibly had something, you and I. We could have. But we met in the wrong place, at the wrong time, and in all the wrong circumstances, and you were right, I never was one to do what I was told. I don't necessarily believe in the chain of command. I made Father Philip Carter despair of that because I went so far as to tell him I didn't believe in his God, which is in a way a repudiation of the ultimate chain of command. But I have free will. And so, Martin, do these people who had the misfortune to go out on the Parada, to fall foul of what befell them out there, and to return in pieces to be laid at your feet. At least the two out here will have a chance to make their own choices, exercise their own free will. I fully intend to spend the rest of my life making sure that this remains so.

About that. I realize that I have burned a lot of bridges and that you (rhetorical you) are in a position to make the rest of that life very difficult. For instance, there was no way I could access any part of my former existence for the last little while, because I have a horrible feeling that you guys had little green imps lurking in every shadow where you thought I might have jumped. But now that we have established some ground rules—are you guys going to make it your ongoing mission to destroy me? Over what? You can't make a case. You can't because you can't mention the Parada and its circumstances. The moment you do you have uncomfortable questions to answer. So your choices are to arrange to discreetly assassinate me, or else to let me at least pick up sufficient flotsam and jetsam from the shipwreck of my life in order to continue living it in some other guise. To that end, I have a request. May I please have an assurance that I can access my bank accounts—for at least long enough to clear and then close them—without being afraid that there will be an armed patrol standing with a gun pointed at my head before I am done? I am NOT giving you an address where you can reach me to tell me so—but I'll be watching the social forums on the official website of the governing body of my (former) profession, and you can leave me a message there. If it has to be in code, just post a note about how you know the best place to get pomegranate sherbet. I will understand. Also, I would very much like, once I establish a home base again, to go and pick up my long-suffering cat. Believe it or not, I've MISSED that animal. I like to think that the beastie has missed me even just a little. And I don't think you should punish a dumb animal for the sins of its owner. So if I give you the three remaining Parada people as perennial hostages—can I have my cat in exchange? Please? It would be a kindness. I know you probably hate me, but you liked me once. Can you like me enough to let a cat back into my life?

I'm sorry. I really am. But I really can't tell you any more.

I can't even tell you if I am going to be staying together with any of the people who are on THIS side of the barricades, because I won't risk the possibility of you looking for a couple (in any iteration—the two of them, or either of the two of them and me) or a trio or just any one of us in a singleton guise. We ARE in touch, the three of us. Not in a way you can easily track. That's all I can say. Don't look for us, Martin. Nothing good will come of finding us. We'll find our own way. You—or someone who comes after you— just take care of the ones who are left behind because they need you, they need someone to help them to survive. Those of us out here, we'll take our chances. Can we call it even and leave it at that?

If you and I are still alive twenty years from now, maybe we can meet in Istanbul—in a place a little like the one you took me to on that one day of freedom that I had while we were both locked up in the Parada dungeons. Perhaps by then everything will have shaken out the way it will shake out, and I may be able to tell you more, more about what I cannot speak about right now. Don't call me, I'll call you. I promise. You will be that much easier to find. But until then, this is goodbye. And I wish you well. And there have been moments when I have wished that things might have been different. For both of us.

I wish that you had never chosen me for this project.

I am grateful beyond words that you did.

Give my love to everyone who remains in the habitat who might have known me, or might care to have that parting word. Take care of Jerry and Han and Alaya, Martin. And if at all possible... take them out into the garden sometimes, and let them lift their eyes to the stars which were once their playground.

Tell those who need to hear it that it's safe to send other people out there. Let the Parada become a talisman, a mystery, a legend, an inspiration for the continuance of a dream. Don't let it end here. None of us deserve that.

Thank you. I'm sorry. Good bye. Good luck.

Stella Froud

About the Author

ALMA ALEXANDER's life so far has prepared her very well for her chosen career. She was born in a country which no longer exists on the maps, has lived and worked in seven countries on four continents (and in cyberspace!), has climbed mountains, dived in coral reefs, flown small planes, swum with dolphins, touched two-thousand-year-old tiles in a gate out of Babylon. She is a novelist, anthologist and short story writer who currently shares her life between the Pacific Northwest of the USA (where she lives with her husband and two cats) and the wonderful fantasy worlds of her own imagination. You can find out more about Alma on her website (www.AlmaAlexander.org), her Facebook page (https://www.facebook.com/AuthorAlmaAlexander/) or on Twitter (https://twitter.com/AlmaAlexander). You can also support her on Patreon (https://www.patreon.com/AlmaAlexander)

Curious about other Crossroad Press books?
Stop by our site:
http://store.crossroadpress.com
We offer quality writing
in digital, audio, and print formats.

CPSIA information can be obtained
at www.ICGtesting.com
Printed in the USA
FSHW011343290720
71955FS

Printed in the United States
148759LV00001B/61/A

9 781585 869329